SULTANZ :

THE PHANTOM

ROBERT FELTON

• Published in 2012 by FeedARead Publishing

British Library C.I.P.

A CIP catalogue record for this title is available from the British Library.

For Martine, family, and friends who thought I could do it.
And said so.
And let's not forget all the authors of all the books who taught me to fall through the page.

PROLOGUE

Sunday 16th December 2001
04.02AM

It was the eve of the eve of the eve of the eve of Midwinter's Eve, and the sky had opted for a minimalist look…

…Bare as the face of a liar, cold as a killer's handshake…

…The landscape as welcome as a dentist's chair…

…Lifeless as a Monday afternoon in Morecambe…

…Except…

On this frosty twinkly-starred night, two figures shambled their way through Tepid Ashton cemetery.

'Here we are.' The older man tapped a gloved hand upon a new headstone. Marble, it was. Quality.

They laid down the tools of their trade.

'Right then.' he said. 'Get stuck in.'

Spoken with indecent heartiness, given the hour and their business.

The old man, cheeks webbed with crimson broken capillaries, wrapped in a donkey jacket and Bath City FC scarf, sat down, perched on the edge of a slab that wished Mum and Dad a nice *undisturbed* sleep. Most of the memorials around them bore the same sentiment. On this particular night, they were badly mistaken.

'It's too bloody cold for this shit,' said the second man. He was younger than his colleague, similarly dressed and with nerves – as his mum had always told anyone (interested or not) – that were "delicate". His voice had a tremble to it and he shivered, not entirely due to the cold. His army surplus great coat was too cumbersome for work like this, and his knitted paisley cravat was itching like buggery. 'Can't you help for once?'

The older man, Dougal by title and father by accident, took a shot of something illegal from a hip flask. It was no wonder the old bastard was going blind.

'I hate this job,' muttered he of the delicate disposition, Joel by name and son by relationship. He did not take too much care in the tone of his muttering. His old man always left the hard digging to Joel and tonight the soil was as hard as a copper's stare – which, like physical exercise and dentists, was something Joel tried to avoid.

'Aye. I expect you had better things planned. I've told you– them magazines will give you blisters.' Dougal, the eldest of the pair, slurped from his hip flask and shook his head. Scalp flakes dusted his shoulders.

The digging began. Joel used a pick to loosen the top layer.

'Watch your down-stroke,' said his Dad, casting a critical eye on his progeny's handiwork. 'You'll take your foot off one of these days.'

In fact, the pick wasn't needed. The grave was only a few days old. Joel selected his shovel and began to shift the heavy frozen soil.

Dad rolled another fag, lit it, and looked around the bone yard. Off to his right, the yellow-orange of the street lamps fizzed in the distance. From here, he couldn't see any lights in the few houses close enough to overlook the cemetery. The little chapel, near the centre, was locked and unused. No one with any sense came out in weather like this, and he wasn't worried about any late night mourners traipsing about. It was, as he often quipped, dead quiet.

After three hours of solid digging, interspersed with curses and grumblings below, the final spade full of dirt flew skyward. A pair of mittened hands appeared at the edge of the grave closest to the old man. 'Give us a hand, Dad.'

The old man gave him a heavily gloved round of applause.

'Oh chortle chortle. There I was, freezing my nuts off, and your rapier wit has brought cheer to my heart.'

Dougal, or just plain "Dad" to most (including his mates) stood up, rubbed his backside where the edge of the stone had left a crease, then stooped to retrieve another piece of equipment from the rucksack. He hefted it, stepped closer to the edge of the grave, and dropped it in.

'Ow!'

'Sorry, son. Thought you were paying attention. We've got to get the lid off, see. Then we can get started on filling this lot in.'

We? Joel muttered something unhealthy, rubbed his balaclava'd head, and stooped to pick the jemmy up. Like the rest of the tools they – *he* – used, it was heavy, robust, and had seen a lot of action. Joel carefully stepped around the coffin, keeping his weight on the edges. With the timber they used for caskets these days, you could go straight through. This one, if he was any judge, was made of MDF. A sign of the times.

He knelt down, manoeuvred the tip of the crowbar into the join between lid and casket, and began to lever it up and down the best he could, given the limited space. He didn't have to work at it for too long before he was rewarded with the sound of cracking panel.

'You ain't broken the lid, have you?'

Joel rolled his eyes. Always ready to help, his Dad. Usually with unwanted advice and a generous statement of the obvious.

'No, Dad. It's MDF. It bends.' Joel heard his Dad tut-tutting. He knew what was coming. He mouthed the words in perfect synchronisation.

'They don't make coffins like they did in my day, ' said his Dad. 'It'd take two of us to get a lid off, one at each end. And they used screws, then. Proper brass ones. Deep. When they buried you, when I was a lad, you stayed buried.'

'That would be in the good old days of premature burial, would it?' Joel had already made such plans for his father's box when he carked* it - which, given his fondness for old shag and these ferkin† cold nights, shouldn't be too far in the future. Joel spat. It was something his Dad hated, especially when he was on the job. Mind, his girlfriend did too. He chuckled to himself‡, as he often did at his own double entendres.

'Have some respect, boy, ' snapped the old man.

Joel swore. 'We're robbing graves, Dad. Strippin' the recently dead of their personals.' He shook his head. Respect?

'We're just relieving them of what they ain't got no use for.'

'It ain't right' muttered Joel.

'What's that, boy? '

It was an old argument. Joel waited for the response, and here it was, right on cue. 'I *said*, ' repeated Joel, testy of tone, 'it ain't *right*.'

'It's all a matter of perspective, ' his Dad began, and once again, Joel mimed the words perfectly. He looked up at his Dad, who was in his usual pose: one foot leaning on the business end of a spade, his elbow leaning heavily on the handle, which is all he used the bloody thing for these days.

'If we wuz to leave this 'ere corpse for a couple of hundred years, they'd call us archaefolomists…'

Joel tittered. 'Archaeologists, Dad. And no, they wouldn't. Archaeologists have *degrees*. They study for years; write lengthy erry-oo-dite books about the tombs they've opened, and stuff. That's what an *archaeologist* is.'

---

*Carked: died. Derived from something or other. Don't ask, because I don't know.

† Ferkin': Ah, I know *this* one. Derived from a quaint old Anglo-Saxon word, meaning to fu-

‡ Being the kind of wit only he appreciated.

'Bloody foolish,' said his Dad. 'And what d'they do with all the stuff they nick? They clean it up and stick it behind glass cases in moozeums. Where's the profit in that? '

Profit, thought Joel, when his Dad had finished. *Now, there's a thought.* 'Dad? '

'Son? '

'When do I get paid? '

There was a silence. That is, a silence deeper than the healthy quiet of a frozen night. A field vole paused in its manic search for nourishment and twitched its ears, as if it anticipated the punchline to a joke. It wasn't far wrong.

'That's all you ever think of, you kids. Where's the pride in your work, boy? '

'We're grave robbers, Dad!' said Joel; his voice had a hard edge to it and louder than was advisable, given the time and place.

'Just get the bloody lid off, you cheeky shite.'

The vole twitched its whiskers, shook its head, then bounded off.

Joel rammed the jemmy home again, pulled viciously at it. The lid split in two to reveal the head, shoulders and chest of a young woman. Joel stepped back from the gap. The smell. That was the worst part. Still, it could have been worse. At minus ten centigrade, as it had been for most of the week, a corpse would keep pretty well.

Joel sniffed, puzzled.

'What's the matter, boy? You've smelled worse than that. Remember last summer? Bugger, that was a job. Especially when you took a hold of that arm and the skin came away.'

Joel wasn't listening. 'That don't smell like…it ain't…' He leaned down, took his torch out of his coat pocket, and focused the beam. 'Dad…look at this.'

The old man groaned and made a good show of getting down to his hands and knees. 'Bloody arthritis is killing me tonight.' He peered myopically over the side of the grave.

The corpse was in the usual pose, arms crossed at the chest, hands resting one atop the other.

'How long did you say she'd been 'ere? ' Joel said. There was something odd about that smile. Sure, you had your corpse grins. Rictus, they called it. Skin around the mouth tightened up, teeth pearly white; but not this one.

'Lessee…' The old man's face took on that expression of ear-haemorrhaging concentration common to those who have to rely on a full set of fingers, toes, and thumbs in order to count backwards from twenty. '…Thursday, Friday, Saturday, Sunday…five days, near as makes any difference,' concluded the Dad. 'Why?'

'Look.'

The corpse was – well, it didn't look like a corpse *should*. For a start, it was a healthy pink.

'Ar. One of them carbon monoxide suicides. They always comes out pink.'

'It's been almost a week, Dad. Since she died. At least a week.'

'You wanner stay down there all night? Or you gonner do what you come here to do? We got two more to do other side of Bath, before we go home.'

Joel shook his head.

Something isn't right.

He looked up at his Dad. 'Are you going to help, or what?'

'Wasted enough time already. Get on with it, boy.'

Joel looked back at the girl's face. She couldn't have been twenty-five.

Nice looking. Nice gazonkas. Nice…

Joel swallowed hard. That was another thing he hated about this job. It made him think about things…things he shouldn't. Sometimes he wondered if he was turning into a pervert.

Maybe it was too late. Maybe it was too late to wonder if you were on the turn when the thoughts were already there.

What would it take, to actually…

Joel shook his head hard. Nah. Even if his Dad wasn't there, he doubted if he could actually get a boner.

But she's got a good figure. Firm . Well, as firm as a week old corpse could be. I used to be a necrophiliac until a rotten cu-

Fuck.

She smiled.

Joel dropped the jemmy, stumbled back against the side of the grave. A shower of loose, frozen soil dropped down his neck like a handful of chilled rice. Or like a handful of beetles, or any number of little crunchy buggers that attended those who slept the Big Sleep.

Recalling those words, the ones he'd read in an old copy of Raymond Chandler's classic, Joel derailed his morbid train of thought.

It's just a corpse. Like Dad said, one of those suicides they find in cars down country lanes sometimes, a hose pipe feeding exhaust into the driver's side, skin the colour of an Englishman on a Spanish holiday.

Joel got to work. Underneath his mittens, he wore a pair of latex gloves. It was worth the odd looks that the girl at the checkout gave him when he took them to the till at the chemist. What did she think he did with them, anyway? It wasn't as if he stuck his fingers anywhere anti-social. He was just glad of the protection. Not because the corpse was a soft one, because it wasn't; the fingers were supple and the rings came off easily. It was better than breaking the bone, which he sometimes had to do. He refused to snip them off at the knuckle, like his Dad told him. Barbaric, that's what it was.

No. He wore them because you could never be sure what was living on the skin. Very toxic, your average corpse. You could get into a lot of trouble mauling stiffies. Stiffs! *Stiffs,* he meant.

Joel forgot about his earlier misgivings about the remarkable health of this particular…well, *corpse* didn't really describe her, the way she was lying there like that, all pink, her shroud tight against her body because someone at the funeral parlour hadn't bothered to loosen the thin plastic, hadn't taken any *care* when they laid her in the casket. Her hair was pretty good, but here and there, a curl had come loose.

Pretty face.

He removed the bracelet from her left wrist. He took the amber from her ears. Good pieces, little globes the size of boiled sweets set in simple cages of finely wrought gold and silver wire. There were bits of insect in the amber, just like the one in Jurassic Park. Joel stuffed all the items in a waterproof pouch.

Was that it? Surely they'd have buried her with something…well, something a bit more *flash.* His Dad had been scouring the obituaries for a fortnight, looking for the families with the right connections. The right *pedigree,* he'd said. As if they were digging up dogs, for fuck's sake. "Tisn't worth the bother", he'd said, "unless you have a good chance of a couple of hundred quid's worth at the very least."

So where was it?

Joel looked at her speculatively. Considering her *pedigree,* and the jewellery she wore, the shroud was cheap and nasty. Odd.

Was she the sort to wear anklets? He'd heard that only prozzies wore those. It was supposed to mean they were high-class whores, the sort who only took bookings through an agent and expected a good dinner and a night at the opera before you even got your fingers in their…

There he went again. Despite the cold, his trousers were suddenly too tight.

Pervert.

All the same…great gazonkas.

He looked over his shoulder, checking to see if the old man was watching. A loud slurp told him that his flask was having a good seeing to.

Oh dear. Now he was *thinking* double entendres without trying. And he was getting hot…

Lovely gazonkas.

…His trembling hand, already sweating beneath the tight rubber, reaching for those tight starchy –

'Oi! What you doin', eh?'

Joel squawked. 'Nuff. Nuffin'! I was just –'

'Aye. I know what you wuz doin all right. Get the rest of that lid off, boy. We'll have a word, you and me. Later.' The old man disappeared again.

Old bastard.

Joel was trembling all over now. He couldn't wait to get the lid off, in fact.

He was too eager. The MDF split again, bringing his Dad scuttling to the side of the grave once more.

'Why don't you just get 'ammer and be done with it?' snapped the Dad. 'Look, I'm gonner start packing everything. If you ain't done in five minutes, I'm off.'

Stupid old bastard.

Joel pulled the remainder of the lid free, laid the pieces against the side of the grave.

Great thighs. Long. Not muscular, but shapely.

He laid a hand on her right leg, ran it downwards to the calf.

Long.

His Dad was slinging stuff into the sack.

He would, too; just bugger off and leave me to fill this lot in myself.

Joel checked the bare ankles. Nothing.

What a waste of time. A pair of earrings and a bracelet; maybe those gems aren't paste, but I bet that no one buries that much gold, with diamonds and sapphires that big...

…Even for a "Beloved Daughter," as the marble header said. He made one last check beneath the high collar of the plastic shroud.

Bingo.

Joel gripped the torch between his teeth and tried to keep the beam steady as he used both hands to lift the head. The heavy necklace was fiddly and he couldn't keep his balance as he struggled with the bloody thing. It wasn't a regular hook. Double clasp, probably. Wouldn't want to lose that much gold, with emeralds you could probably play snooker with.

This means pay day. At last.

He slipped, fell onto the corpse, his knees making contact with her thighs. Perhaps if he lay down on top of her, he could do it much faster that way.

Oh dear. This is worse than a British sex comedy.

Slowly, trembling, he eased himself down, lay with obscene intimacy on top of the still-pink body of the woman, and continued his combat with the necklace clasp.

…Definitely a woman, not one of those skinny teenage girls, all ribs and fried egg chests.

The necklace came free. As easy as that. Just when he was getting comfortable.

'Joel, you get out of there this minute. This *minute,* you hear me?'

Joel glanced over his shoulder. If his Dad caught him in this position, he'd go spare. 'Just coming, Dad.'

Oh dear. It was almost funny. Except that he couldn't seem to…

'Dad!'

'What?'

'I…Dad! DAD!'

Something in the tone, the high pitch, of his son's voice made the old man's scrotum shrivel even more than it had already. He dropped the rucksack.

'Joel?' He took a step forward. He could hear the little shite struggling down there. Probably got his foot stuck between the coffin and the side of the hole. Silly little –

'DAD!'

Joel's father had never heard his son whimper before. Well, not since he'd caught him in their bedroom, trying on his wife's clothes.

'Oh, oh, shii—'

The words were cut off.

'Joel?' What're you doin, I said?' The old man didn't want to look, but he couldn't go home to his missus, leaving her pride and joy in a grave. His wife thought Joel was on a college course, jewellery smithing. It accounted for nights like these when, with any luck, they came home with an assortment of trinkets – some good, some bad. Amazing what people would believe. He loved his wife, but he had to admit, she wasn't the sharpest tool in the box.

At the edge of the grave now. And there he was, the dirty little shite. He'd even arranged the poor lass's arm so that it looked as if she was embracing him. He'd have more than a word or two with the lad, that was as certain as the skid marks on his Y-fronts. Given him a right fright, the little…

'Joel?' His son wasn't moving. His face was turned away.

My god…he's giving her a hickey.

'Joel!' repeated the Dad. He coughed, a good lung wrencher. It was meant to be a command, but he hadn't the breath in him. Or the courage. His breathing came in short pants. *Likely as not Joel would have a smutty little snigger over that double intender,* thought the Dad. He wasn't in the mood for this nonsense. His chest hurt bad, and something was all wrong about this. *Bad.* Like the hitch he felt in his ticker when he noticed the shudder that ran along Joel's body. Like he was struggling.

His stomach knotted. He felt his anal ring start to stutter, threatening disgrace.

The light down there was barely sufficient. Joel's torch had dropped underneath him, a few stray beams uplighting the girl's features. He took his own torch out, an old army issue angle-head, and he pushed the button.

Her head was turned away – or perhaps her hair had come loose from the band that had kept her hair pulled back, had slipped and covered her face where it lay in profile. That was it. It looked as if the two of them were necking, giving each other love bites. Something.

There was no choice. He had to get into the bloody hole.

He'd have more than something to *say* about all this and he wouldn't mind bruised knuckles. It would be worth the screaming hot pain in his joints after. The boy had to learn.

He sat at the edge of the oblong hole, not sure he wanted to do this; he *knew* he didn't, but that was his son, the dirty little git, and he obviously needed a good kick to get him back to whatever passed for his senses. He took a deep breath, ready to drop, bracing himself for the pain when his knees took the shock of the fall.

The shite. The snot-eating, todger*-pulling little shite.

He'd pay for this. Oh yes.

He took one last look at the two of them.

The scream locked in his throat.

In repose, she'd been beautiful. Awake, with that long blood-soaked thing whipping about in her mouth, licking his son's blood from that great hole in his neck…

She winked at him, pushed Joel aside as if he were no more than a take-away she didn't feel like eating any more…

…And came *for him…*

Oh dear.

---

* Todger: Sounds much less rude than the correct term, penis. Strange, that.

CHAPTER ONE

Monday 17th 2001, 02.00.

Bath city centre. What a rockin place to be.

Such was the merry turn of thought of Wesil, five feet nine and the owner of a face only a forensic pathologist could appreciate. Currently, he was practising the art of The Lurk behind the rubbish skip at the rear of the Disney shop. It was late, and so far past being a late Sunday night that it was now early Monday morning. It was as frosty as a banker's smile in this part of the country, and for most of the locals nothing would rock until Friday night…

…But Wesil did not intend to boogie. Well, you don't when you're clad in black Para-military gear, with a woolly hat that pulls all the way over your face.* Wesil had a lot of anti-social habits. Many of them could be described as dirty, but that would be like calling the Borgias just another dysfunctional family.

Wesil liked to follow lone women home.

He liked to walk up close behind, thinking of all the things he could do. It made them nervous, that did: the sound of heavy footsteps matching theirs, his heavy breathing almost at their necks; and when they cracked and started to run, he would chase right along, just to hear them squeal.

But never more than that.

It was enough to get his jollies without the risk of DNA tests and a long sojourn at Her Majesty's pleasure, sharing a cell with a bloke called Mutha. Wesil often wondered if Her Majesty ever knew who resided at her secure hotels. Did she go through the lists, when she had a spare few minutes, and chortle to herself? Did she think, "Right, I don't like the sound of this geezer. I think I'll send a little note on the old Buck Pal. headed stationery to the Prison Governor and make sure he does the full sentence."

But then Wesil was a sad man. In fact, he'd already done a stretch at one of the Old Gal's resorts. Borstal. That must have amused Her Maj. no end. His roomie had been a bloke called Gerbil, who had an ongoing not least torrid affair with a rabbit called Hector. You met the oddest people in places

---

*Not unless you're invited to a certain kind of party.

where they were supposed to rehabilitate you. He had no enduring wish to meet lads of Gerbil's ilk ever again.

Tonight was different. Tonight was special. Tonight, miserable as it was, meant fewer girlies out in their tease gear - hence, fewer plods out looking for the likes of Wesil. It seemed reasonable to suppose that his would reduce the risk of being collared. For what he had planned was this:

He would wait in this doorway, behind this wheelie-bin*.

He would spring out when some tease happened by, expose himself, and then take a photo of said tease's horrified face.

Then off, back to his grimy little bed sit, get the Polaroid on his bedside table and make with the hand cream and box of tissues.

He was so excited that he hadn't considered the odds against any female "happening by" *any* dark alley, especially given the nadger†-biting cold.

By half past three of the early morning hour Wesil was shivering so hard he had no small difficulty in stopping his teeth clacking together like novelty clockwork dentures. The doorway offered little in the way of shelter. He was suffering the effects of wind chill, too, and this combination should have cooled his ardour somewhat. And so it did. When the Abbey tower tolled four o'clock, Wesil decided to call it a night. In fact, he called it quite a few nasty names. He took off his gloves, blew into his hands, and risked a quick shufti up and down the service alley.

Wesil sighed a good 'un, removed his terrorist style face gear, which was in fact a balaclava turned the wrong way around, and thanked the night, once more, for a bastard waste of time. Which is when he saw her.

She didn't appear particularly stupid. That is, she wasn't rolling around the street with alcohol-induced screaming giggles. She wasn't conventionally dressed for late night revelry, either. Her dress was mid thigh, true; her legs were long, firm and brown from much exposure to the sun, and that qualified as dressing to tease and therefore "asking for it;" but she didn't enter the alley timidly, looking at shadows, glancing over her shoulder. She walked boldly up the centre of the narrow street, her head erect and high. A real ball-breaking bitch, according to Wesil, who slipped back into the doorway and dragged the mask over his face once more. He pulled the Polaroid camera out of his duffel bag, set it for flash and made ready.

---

*Where someone had recently vomited. Copiously.

† Nadger or Bollock, either/or: Another euphemism for a male sexual organ, but why anyone should bother s mystifying. So testicles to you.

As he watched he felt his cock grow; he loosened his zipper and his oldest (and only) friend popped out to greet him.

'Hello, Plasticine Man,' whispered its owner. It was the biggest damn erection he'd ever enjoyed, including the time he'd seen Sophie Dahl lying spread-eagled and all come-hither. Mind, that was on a poster, but the Plasticine Man wasn't proud.

Now, though, he certainly was - all of five inches. A monster. The Man steamed gently in the bitter cold. Wesil would have to act soon, before nature did something embarrassing to his todger. Like shrink.

The bitch was close now. His camera was ready, his finger on the shutter button. Footsteps drew alongside the skip. He jumped out.

The girl wasn't in the least startled. She just stared at him as if he were some bloke who'd arrived at a hen night to strip and sing some stupid friggin' song. A bloke who'd turned up at the wrong house, wrong time, wrong day.

Wesil jiggled his hips, the better to make his beloved bounce. That'd frighten her. Well, it ought to. Any girl faced with a man-beast such as he, should.

He really needed that photo but she didn't look even mildly surprised. Like the aforementioned girl at the non-existent hen party, she just smiled in a bemused sort of way; she paid no more than a cursory glance at the Plasticine Man and that, more than the cold, did for him. The Man shrank back into the warmth of his nest. Wesil watched him retreat.

Traitor.

He would get a right old smacking for that, later. Maybe he would hold him under hot water for a bit, show the little bastard who was boss. But for now, Wesil had to deal with the hideous anti-climax of his present situation.

'Are you going to rape me?' she said, calm as you like. 'Only, there are two tall men in blue uniforms about ten yards behind me, so you'd best make your mind up.'

So. She was making jokes. Mockery. The icing on the shit cake.

Maybe he should do as she suggested.

Maybe she was bluffing.

She walked toward him.

This wasn't how it was supposed to go. Panic rose faster than his erections did, these days, and in his distress he not only pushed the button marked Panic, but also the shutter release on his camera. He staggered back as his vision turned brighter than a good A level result, then blacker than his actual future prospects. A Polaroid snap of his left ear slipped out and onto the ground.

It was about then that he felt her knee – that shapely, brown leg – driven up hard into his crotch. Pain sang high and nausea warbled its own harmony.

So much pain. So many chunky bits.

When he was done tossing said chunks in a yellow spatter, she pushed him back into the doorway. She pressed her hands either side of his head, forced him to look into her eyes.

He felt himself slipping, falling away, and not caring very much.

He was vaguely aware that a car was driving slowly past the mouth of the alley, but only in the sense that he might be aware of his TV blabbering in the background while engrossed in a picture of Sophie Dahl.

She pressed her body against him. She was firm, almost hard, like she worked out with weights or something. His thoughts grew more sluggish, found it hard to hold onto them. Even the Plasticine Man paid no interest, the little bastard. This was the first real contact with a member of the opposite sex who actually seemed to want him to Do It, and she was making all the moves (as was right and proper, he believed).

She was nuzzling into his neck, sniffing, like a dog inspecting the arse of a bitch. He felt her teeth - sharp – pricking his skin. Then she drew back and he got one last hard look at her. Her eyes looked like a dog's – a *wolf's* – and her canines dripped saliva…

..And they were growing…

…Which was all he needed, all the encouragement necessary to fill his pants.

He dropped the camera.

She lunged.

He squealed.

The flash went off again.

She squealed.

It was the first time she'd shown any sign of fear.

The car he'd heard seconds before now reversed. The beam of a powerful torch hit his face. A voice, West Country and pissed off with it, too:

'Oi! *You!*'

They must teach plods to say things like that at plod school, Wesil thought as he pounded up the alley. His bowels had not finished their dastardly business, however, and he left a trail even a bat could follow.

Great, thought Wesil. *Fleeing for my freedom and I've got hot and cold running diarrhoea spraying from my kecks.*

He risked a glance over his shoulder. The plods were out of the car. One was heading for the girl. Served him right.

The other, however, was younger than his colleague; he was galloping after the guy with the mask, clad in black.

And this particular plod was a track star. He was gaining. He had a predator grin that said You're Mine. Wesil scanned the alley ahead, looking for an escape route, any open doorway. Anything. He turned left, through a gap in a chain link fence, a little car park looming up. He barely avoided ploughing straight into the side of a bloody great Shogun, a black one, inconsiderately parked.

It was all that the track star needed. A second's hesitation was all it took, and Wesil was down. His hands were trussed up behind him faster than a session with Miss Discipline*.

In any case, the plod did not beat about the bush, unlike Miss Discipline, but he did beat Wesil about the head a bit. He did not read Wesil his Rights. He said: 'Look at my feckin' uniform, yer bastard. You're dead, you are.'

Shortly after that, Wesil felt the long arm of the law. It was prodding him along, none too gently. They passed the other, older plod.

He was perplexed.

'Where'd she go?' said the perplexed.

'You lost her?' said the other, incredulous.

'No. I mean, yes. Er. She just… went,' he said; 'Whoosh,' he added, miming something that went whoosh. Then, evidently feeling silly, he hit Wesil.

They reached the patrol car.

Wesil stood in a growing puddle of brown knacky† stuff.

'He's not getting in here,' said Older Plod, tapping the roof of his jam sarnie. Police vehicle, that is.

'What?'

'He ain't getting into *my* car, pal.' Barry, the elder of the two, threw Wesil's camera and the Polaroids he'd found into the glove box.

'So, what d'you want to do – call in for a van?' said Clive the track star.

'Can if you want,' said Barry

---

*Which is supposedly very fast indeed, so we'll leave it at that.

† Kacky: shitty. A flexible adjective, much like "Bollocks".

'But they won't give us a lift either, will they?'

'Would you?'

Clive looked Wesil up and down. 'It's because I'm a probationer, innit? That's why everyone picks on me.'

'Welcome to the exciting world of city policing, old son. Try not to step in anything nasty.'

*

Which is how Wesil came to end up in the local Infirmary, handcuffed to a plastic chair bolted to the floor, waiting for stitches and an X-Ray. This turn of events has much to do with certain other events, which may never have happened if Wesil had not shat on the arresting officer, which led to said officer making free with his truncheon. Then, having vented his feelings, Clive reconsidered the situation and decided he'd best get his prisoner cleaned up before the scumbag's Brief* arrived…and the best place for bruises, grazes, and to get shit cleaned off is a hospital.

Thusly did he reason, and therefore it came to pass…

*

…And it also came to pass that Wesil had a little chat with a psychiatrist, who understood Wesil's wild babbling about the wolf, the girl, and a Polaroid camera flash that made him think of A levels†…

…Which led to a visit from two Section 12 psychiatrists, an Approved Social Worker and a longhaired poof who said that he was a mental nurse, which went without saying (Wesil thought) because all nurses were mental.

*

The short version is that the four of them got together in a huddle, in a corner of the room in which Wesil sat, and unanimously agreed to forcibly remove him to a secure wing of the local nuthatch.

Which is where life will show Wesil what a rockin' good place Bath is.

---

* Brief: A Lawyer who only sees you for five minutes before you go to court (hence the name, probably). Tend to nod and smile a lot.

† A levels: Kids are encouraged to study at advanced level to "improve their prospects", when all they want to do is get laid. Apparently it's impossible to be overqualified for anything (including getting laid), which is oddly reassuring. Or not.

Or not.

CHAPTER TWO

Monday 04.00
Peat lands, Somerset.

So, thought Jan. *This is fieldwork.*

The last of the matches had disintegrated when she struck it (Jason had left them out again). She searched for her lighter.

Gone.

No smokes, no coffee. Life was wonderful.

Still groggy from a lousy night's rest, she pulled a blanket around her shoulders and then unzipped the flap to her tent.

Outside, a light drizzle looked to be set in for the day. Glastonbury Tor* rose out of the flat landscape, poking its phallus above the tree line. Footprints led from her shelter to the excavation site, out there amongst the soggy trenches they'd dug the day before. The peat absorbed the steady fall of light rain, making the work unpleasant and more of a chore than she'd expected. She stamped her way over to the dig, ready to wrap her frozen fingers around Jason's throat. Within a minute her fair hair was plastered flat to her head.

Jason looked up as she loomed before him. Her countenance was terrible to behold.

'Shat the bed?'

'You bastard.'

'Ah. Now you have me. Mea culpa.' He spat the butt of his stolen cigarette, where it met a watery grave at the bottom of the ditch in which he stood. 'Are you going to do any work today, or are you going to glower menacingly before…'

'Before I wring the life from your body?' said Jan., her teeth rattling together. She stamped her feet in the spongy, moss-rich earth, sending gobbets of dirty water in all directions. The edge of the dig gave way.

'…you fall arse over tit, I was going to say.' Jason held out his hand, offered it to his colleague.

Popular landmark in Somerset where you can believe in just about anything without being forced to take antipsychotics.

She stared at him, unable to decide whether to scream abuse at him, or possibly to scream on general principles. This particular dig wasn't what she had expected. Jan was sure that the site was a protected area for wildlife. There were other peculiarities, too; far too many. Like the contract that forbade them from discussing any artifacts that may be found.

'Archaeology should never be like this,' she said.

'This much is self evident,' said Jason. He grabbed her hand, hauled her upright and then slapped a trowel into it. 'Come on. Get busy. You'll feel much nobler if you ignore the physical torment.'

'Give me a cigarette.'

'It's my last one.'

She wiggled her fingers in the accepted "Gimme" fashion. Jason lit it, took a deep drag for himself and then grudgingly[*] handed it over. She had smoked half of it before she paid any attention to what her associate was doing. He was gently[†] scraping soft peat away from what appeared to be a nub of old tree root.

'What's that?'

'Dunno. Pass me that mug of ditch water.' Jason took the plastic beaker (which, he was sure she noticed, he had stolen from her flask) and washed off the dirt and other detritus from the exposed root.

'Is that fibre or hair?' said Jan.

The nub of wood, now exposed and washed, looked promising. Perhaps it was the hilt of an ancient dagger, the hoof forming the pommel of the weapon. Maybe they'd found a sacrificial site, somewhere nearby a preserved corpse.

Jason tore a large lump of sodden peat from the side of the ditch. The dagger hilt, to the evident distress of his partner, turned out to be attached to a haunch of venison. Old, leathery, and by now very gamey.

'Great,' said Jan. 'Two days wallowing like a bloody hippopotamus and this is what we get. Road kill.'

'I beg to differ,' said Jason. 'Take a look at this.' He removed more earth around the find, gently scraping with a spatula, until he exposed another leg. He sluiced it off with more rainwater. 'There,' he said, indicating the holes along the meat of the leg.

It was still dark, the sun barely breaking through the heavy sky. It wasn't usual practice to work at night, and the dig supervisor hadn't

---

[*] I feel obliged to apologise for use of an adverb; much like farting in a lift, for a writer.

[†] Shit, there's another bugger. Sorry, sorry.

explained. Everyone was tired and getting a little jacked off with the way the excavation was being conducted. Jason cupped his hands, lit his stolen lighter and ignited the wick of a storm lantern that hung from a peg in the opposite wall of the ditch. There was enough light for a cursory examination.

'Arrow wounds?' said Jan.

'Unlikely,' said Jason. 'Not in pairs. See?'

The holes indeed seemed to be grouped in sets of two. When they'd cleared enough peat to expose a section of the belly they could see punctures everywhere.

'Redneck bastards,' was all Jan had to say. 'Fox-fucking, badger-baiting wankers!'

'That's not a fair description of the local populace, now, is it?'

'*Look* at it. What possible excuse can there be for cornering a stag, then poking it with sharp sticks? We should report it.'

Jason shook his head. 'You really don't think straight without a coffee inside you. Come. Allow me to spoon-feed you with the blatantly obvious.' He pinched a piece of skin and hair and tugged gently. 'The epidermis is intact and, by all appearances, tough. This indicates a degree of preservation by the acidic chemistry active in the peat.'

'I'm not stupid,' said Jan, although this belied how she felt. Well, it *was* obvious.

'And the cadaver is below the level we'd expect of a recently discarded corpse. I mean, the ground above is undisturbed, no sign of burial. No, compadre. This is at least two thousand years old.'

*

Professor Leonard Pitt, learned and fearsome, cut a handsome figure in his fleecy Happy Hippo* pyjamas. As Doctor Emmerson, his chief assistant on these digs, remarked,

'Especially with your finger buried up to the knuckle in your left nostril,' said the Doctor. Wrapped in her sleeping bag, she smirked at the scowl the Professor gave her.

'Must you be so infantile?' said Pitt, flicking a dry crust from the finger and then pushing the luxuriant nasal hair back in place.

---

* Popular amongst academics, but they'll never admit it. I can prove it. Ask one.

'No need to snap,' said Emmerson. She turned away from him in her bed roll. She knew better than to test his patience further. Banter was not a Pitt skill. *Social skills, period, actually,* she thought.

She also knew that the Professor was especially irritable this morning due to the lack of success over the past week. Ten trenches had yielded nothing but wet peat, disappointment, several cases of an especially offensive fungal foot infection and the occasional remains of wildlife. They had to return to the University later that day.

'Are you getting up any time soon?' said Pitt to Emmerson.

Emmerson didn't respond.

'Must I do *everything*? What is wrong with you lately, hmm?' Pitt hopped about, trying to put a sock over a damp and inflamed foot, almost bringing down one of the tent supports.

It's like living with a superannuated adolescent, thought Emmerson.

'Exactly what do you require assistance *with*?' said she, scratching her breasts as she rolled onto her back. 'Finding your arse without a map? Or explaining why we just spent seven buggering days – and *nights* – digging through this muck?'

'You know why,' said the Professor. He had no patience with her this morning. Well, that wasn't true. He had no patience with her at *any* time of the day. This morning, he just had a better excuse to be snotty. He had spent six months planning this dig and he couldn't accept that there was nothing to be found here. Perhaps he should have spent more money on professional archaeologists, but full-timers were worse gossips than churchmen and politicians. If anything was found, Pitt wanted it kept within the circle of diggers. It was easier to frighten undergraduates into discretion – especially when you marked their papers.

He was attempting to force a swollen and fungous foot into an ancient Wellington boot* when he suddenly stiffened. There was movement out there among the trenches, but that was not unusual on his private digs. He insisted on round-the-clock activity. It was no fun being an irascible, psychotic old git if you couldn't do it twenty-four hours a day and he liked to have someone around to enjoy it. Besides, he felt that it was his job to test the fortitude of his students. It built moral strength and a capacity to endure mindless cruelty. It was amazing what the prospect of an A plus mark would do.

He had sensed something else. Excitement?

---

*The font of many an offensive fungal infection. And bowling shoes, of course.

He closed his eyes and reached out, seeking the source.

Emmerson snorted and laughed aloud when the Professor forgot that his foot was still in the process of being shod and fell sideways, snapping a tent rod.

'Vebbun mwerbulla*,' said Pitt through a mouthful of tent canvas.

*

'A real find?' Jan, for the first time since her arrival at the dig, forgot her discomfort. This could change everything. Even Professor Pitt, the dig supervisor and sponsor, would have to share kudos with his junior crew. The Pitt, as he was known, did not like to acknowledge undergraduates with anything more than a grunt unless he was dictating his wants or berating his lackeys for sloppy work. Now – oh my god – he would have to *talk* to them.

'I'll go find the boss man,' said Jan.

'No!'

Jan had to double take. It was unlike Jason to snap.

'Sorry,' he said. 'But you know what'll happen. He'll order us out of our ditch and finish the excavation himself. You want to be laterally promoted to digging more trenches?'

Jan considered this. She shook her head. There had been more than enough donkey work on this project, but didn't feel she'd learned anything but how to avoid hypothermia and the best way to throw a trowel at Jason.

'This,' said Jason, patting the belly of the stag, 'is *ours* - at least for now. Let's get some photos of its position, before the whole thing falls out. This peat is saturated.' As he said this, the body encased in the earth slipped. They hadn't removed much of the surrounding peat but the rain had made the site a risky place to dig.

Jan needed no prompting. This wasn't a routine excavation, but Pitt could ban them from future digs. She cleared the ditch with one boost, scrabbling for purchase on the waterlogged surface. She paddled back to her tent to retrieve the camera.

Meanwhile, Jason leaned against his find and lit another stolen cigarette. He could feel the thing shift behind him again; as careful as they'd been, the peat was near saturation point and Pitt would go bug-eyed if they didn't get reference shots before the whole side of the ditch fell inward.

---

*Fucking marvellous.

Jan jumped back into the excavation, missed her footing, and went down once more into the freezing run-off. She said nothing, and her glare did not invite comment. She stood with difficulty, dripping now from head to feet, and began to take pictures from every angle using flash.

'That should do it.' Jan finished the roll, packed the camera away. 'Pass me a trowel.'

The two worked hard, carefully sifting through the peat and moss they'd removed. They could not afford to miss any artifacts, any evidence that would give meaning to their find, but all they found was dirty water and more filth.

'What are you doing?' Six feet tall in his socks, eyes that could scratch diamond, to his students Professor Pitt defined scary. His nose twitched, and his eyes widened, as he took in the scene below him. He looked like a rabbit that had caught a whiff of a close relative being turned into stew.

'We were just going to fetch you,' lied Jason.

'Indeed.' Pitt slipped into the trench. Down he came, a glorious splash of chunky sweater and corduroys*. A runnel of dirty water dripped off his nose and he sneezed, spraying both of his undergraduates. 'I made it clear that upon discovering an artifact I was to be informed immediately.'

Jason nodded vigorously.

Creep thought Jan.

The Professor's eyes narrowed. 'Hand me that lantern.'

Jason stood next to the supervisor, handed over the lamp. 'He's beautiful.'

Pitt glanced at him. 'And what can you tell me about it, hmm? What clues do we have, now that you've been hacking at the bloody thing in my absence? Did you make any drawings?' He leaned closer to the find and prodded it with his finger.

'Ah, no, not as such.'

'Amateurs,' muttered the Professor. 'Lord save me from amateurs.'

Jason looked askance at Jan. Jan made a face. *Told you,* she was saying. *You had to do it your way.*

'This is a rare opportunity,' The Pitt was saying. His eyes were feverish, glinting in the lantern light. 'This is a true native. Wild as they come. You might find one specimen in a thousand like this. Brought down by dogs, shouldn't wonder.'

'Not tortured with sharp sticks, then,' muttered Jason.

'What was that?' said Pitt.

---

* Over an inner shell of fleecy Happy Hippo pyjamas. They'll deny it, of course.

'I was just saying that we should have alerted you earlier,' said Jason.

Creep! mouthed Jan. Again.

'All right,' said Pitt. He straightened up, having subjected the corpse and the puncture wounds to a preliminary analysis. He wore a magnifying glass on a cord around his neck and used it to examine the punctures. 'All *right*,' he repeated. Pitt turned to the two junior dig members, aware that they were staring at him. He sniffed, licked the peat water from his mouth, then smacked his lips. 'Well done, I suppose. A little more finesse would have been appropriate, but nevertheless…'

'Would you like me to –' Jason began.

'No. No, what I would like you to do is go to my tent and inform Doctor Emmerson. Tell her to meet me here, and then the two of you may employ your admirable skills at dislodging large lumps of peat. Over there. I want this ditch extended by at least twenty feet.'

Jason made a face at Jan. *Told you so*, the face said. *Lateral promotion.*

'Do you have a problem with that?'

'No. Sir.' Jason clambered from the trench and headed for Pitt's tent. Jan watched him go.

'You,' said Pitt.

'Huh?'

'Do something useful. Go and rouse the team. Tell them to bring the hoist and the lifting equipment. *Quickly*, girl; the longer this meat lies around exposed to the weather, the less we'll have to work with.'

'Of course. Yes.' Jan dropped her trowel, climbed without grace out of the excavation then trudged off to complete her errand. *This* was archaeology: shovelling shit and running messages to her betters.

*

When they'd gone, Pitt hunkered down to re-examine the punctures in the leathery hide of the corpse. 'Finally,' he said. He took an old notebook from a pocket and began to make notes. His hand shook as he wrote. Putting the notebook away, he selected a trowel from the tools on his belt and began to pull large sections of peat away, oblivious to scientific method.

Emmerson arrived. She hesitated by the edge of the excavation. Pitt beckoned her, impatient. With evident reluctance, she joined him.

'My god,' she said. 'It's a haunch of venison. I can hardly contain myself.' She screwed her eyes tight and held up her hand, palm out. 'Actually, I don't think I can. Whoopee-do.'

'Perfect,' said Pitt, ignoring the hyperbole. His voice wavered, betraying his excitement. 'Absolutely perfect. An Elk stag. Ee gods.'

'Who found it?' said Emmerson, without real interest.

'This is *my* dig.'

'No one else would finance it.' Emmerson laughed, but there was no humour in it.

'Exactly. The finds on these digs are *mine.*'

'Have it your way,' she shrugged. 'I don't see that it matters.'

Pitt's hand moved so fast she hadn't time to react. His long, slender fingers found the collar of her coat and closed around it. He moved closer, his face barely an inch from hers. 'It *matters.*'

Emmerson wrinkled her nose. 'You could at least brush the lamb chop from your teeth when you're trying to intimidate me.'

'Fetch my camera,' said Pitt. His hand dropped away. He stared at it for a second or two, and then seemed to jerk back to reality.

Emmerson turned away from him, made a passable attempt at climbing the yielding wall of the ditch but fell back in. A wave of ditch water rose up, washed away the peat at the base of the stag and the entire corpse fell out. Pitt growled, stomped over to her, picked her up and all but threw her over the top. He glared at her as she tried to regain her feet. She was covered in mud, bits of twig and leaf; he sneered at her, shook his head. 'Get out of my sight.'

Emmerson returned the eye contact and there was more than a hint of challenge to it. 'You know, I don't think I'm interested anymore,' she said. 'This is my last dig with you.'

'I don't have any time for tantrums,' said Pitt.

'You don't have time for anything but this obsession of yours.' She turned to go, muttering something about sad bastards.

'Adolescent,' Pitt said, and then spat.

'Er. Will that be all, Professor?'

Pitt spun around. His face registered a moment's confusion, a suggestion of anxiety there. But only for a second. 'I thought I told you–'

'Doctor Emmerson. Yes. I just wondered if you wanted anything else.'

'No.' Pitt picked up a spade, threw it with more force than was necessary at Jason. 'Just dig.'

Jason sidestepped the blade of the tool, narrowly avoiding the traumatic removal of a kneecap. 'Fine,' he said.

*

Later, Jan caught up with him as he walked back to the tent. 'Makes it all seem worthwhile, doesn't it?' she said, taunting.

Jason said nothing. He pulled back his tent flap, flung himself on top of the pile of blankets and clothes that served as his bed. He lay there, motionless, scrutinizing the water droplets that had gathered around a new tear in the roof. At length he spoke.

'Jan?'

'That's me.'

'Listen up; take some advice. Stay away from Pitt.'

'That's going be difficult' said Jan, bewildered.

Jason sat up. He grabbed her arm. 'No. Look, I mean it. The man is deranged.'

'The entire faculty knows that,' said Jan, with no small helping of scorn.

A figure appeared on hands and knees. Tim, one of the first year undergrads, freckles indistinguishable from the mud spatters he wore, pushed his way into the tent. He was breathless.

'Come on, you two. Get your knickers on. You'll never guess.'

'What?' said the supposedly knickerless, in unison.

'The Pitt. He's found something. Something big.' Tim grinned. 'Chop chop, children. Come join the fun.' He left the tent, reverse fashion.

'Pitt? *Pitt* found…?'

'Forget it, Jan. Leave it. Let him take the cred. Believe me, you don't want to cross the old tosser today.'

'Well, bollocks to him.' Jan stripped off her sodden clothes and plucked some of Jason's dry stuff from the pile. 'I'm going to dig. If we found one body…'

'We?'

'Okay. But I'm going to get something out of this trip apart from Athlete's Foot and bad breath.' She finished dressing.

'That's my bed you're wearing,' was all he had to say before she left Jason to his thoughts. Which, at 09.00 on a wet Monday, had become dark indeed.

There was something amiss on this dig, and it wasn't the lack of toilet facilities. There was a hidden agenda, and Jason decided that he wanted answers.

CHAPTER THREE

The early hours of Monday became the grey-silver light of dawn*. The frosty streets of the city centre had turned damp, a slow thaw giving them a washed-out look. It was unusually quiet, only the gulls calling overhead, ready to swoop and crap on the unwary. In the mundane, gullish round of day-to-day living, it had become the scavenger's favourite sport. Well, that and tearing bin-bags apart. As they were doing now.

The gulls circled the bin men, angry at this disturbance to breakfast. George, who thought of himself as an Environmental Health Operative, swung a fist at one. 'Nearly had my ferkin' eye out, that did,' he said.

'I quite like 'em,' said his colleague, new to the job, whose name escaped George.

'Ever been shat on by a gull?' said George, wrinkling his nose.

'No. I find people manage that, though.'

'I am sorry to hear that, Reg.'

''Tis the way of things. And it's Ted, George.'

'Yes. I myself have had such life experience of the shat-on variety, Ted-George. Is there a hyphen in that, by the way?'

Ted shrugged. 'If you insist,' he said, giving his workmate a bit of a look.

They finished throwing the black bags into the rear of their truck, which chewed them up in short order.

'And now the skips,' said George. He shivered, wrinkling his nose once more and turning the corners of his wide mouth down.

'Is this cause for alarm?' said Ted, just Ted, with no hyphen of any kind. He adjusted his square, dark framed glasses . They had a tendency to slip off his nose without provocation.

'Depends. You never know what's in 'em, see. End of the weekend, people getting caught short on the way home from the clubs…anti-social, it is.' He approached the slate grey refuse container, tentative, wary.

One would be forgiven for surmising that had he been in possession of a ten-foot barge pole, he would have employed it to lift the lid. He was not so equipped on this occasion, but he had gloves…which is what saved him from the flash of dazzling white teeth that snapped upon his fingertips.

George yelped, staggered back.

---

* Mandatory for a Monday morning. It's the law, in England. Especially so in Morecambe. Allegedly.

' Ay, do they include danger money in this job?' said Ted. He, too, backed up a few paces.

'See what I mean?' said George, pulling off his glove and examining his fingers. Fortunately, they were undamaged. The tips of his gloves, however, had holes in them. He combed back his thick, greying hair with his intact digits. 'Shag this for a game of Trivial Pursuit,' said he. 'Get the dog warden.'

Ted looked this way, that way, and t'other. 'Lives local, does he?'

'He works under contract for the council. Ring 'im.' George tossed his mobile to his slow-witted associate. He repeated the number aloud as he moved cautiously toward the skip. He looked about for anything that might serve to insert under the lip of the skip lid, the better to save his tender flesh. The possibility of rabies crept out from the corner of his imagination.

He found an empty alco-pop bottle, inserted it beneath the lid of the bin and then flipped it open. He jumped back, well out of reach of the fangs that dwelt therein, but there appeared to be no immediate danger. No canine assault presented itself.

However…

'What's that noise?' said Ted. He'd called the warden. The warden, having a gap in his diary, said he'd mosey along presently – which meant anytime in the next twenty-four hours.

A low growl, menacing in its own right, became a whimper. The whimper rapidly became a howl. George, being of tender heart as well as of flesh, recognised distress when he heard it. Some bastard had dumped an injured dog in there. A bit premature for the usual post-Christmas rush to abandon puppies, he thought, but that was folk for you.

He set his jaw, hero-like, and did likewise with his shoulders. If there was one thing he could not abide it was cruelty to animals - apart from gulls, which he thought must have been created by God on an off day.

As he moved closer to the skip, an arm streaked out of the dark recesses. The lid was slammed down with impossible speed.

His heart danced a jig for a moment or two. He shook his head, as if denying what he had just seen.

Which he was.

'Did you see that?' said Ted, oblivious to the stupidity of the remark.

'I did,' said George, and his voice trembled. 'And I wish I hadn't.'

All thought of work had gone. In another hour or two, shops would open. Shoppers would begin to tread the streets. Complaints would be made to the relevant department. It is not the done thing for bags of rotting, malodorous refuse to spoil the day of those with money to spend, nor mar the pleasant Georgian byways as they did so. But, at that particular minute, neither Environmental Hygienist gave a toss. Something terrible lurked within the skip. Something far worse, and far more lethal, than an injured puppy left for dead.

The two of them shared shag as they waited for something else to happen. The dog warden arrived within the hour, against all probability, which told George and his new mate Ted that this was going to be that sort of day.

'Where's the perp?' said the warden. His ID badge, against all the odds, proclaimed him to be Kevin Costner.

George didn't know what a Frenchman should look like. This one did not wear a stripy tee shirt, a beret, ride a bicycle or carry a string of onions*. He wore a uniform composed mainly of black, which obviously never goes out of style for paramilitary chic, with many pouches and gizmos hanging from his belt, none of it council-issued kit. But his accent fitted all right.

'The *pup* is in there,' said George, 'but I don't think-'

The warden waved him aside. 'Perp. *Perpetrator*. Technical jargon, mate.' His smile was unreasonably condescending and his teeth flashed, even in dull weather. He pulled a rod with a noose attached from the rear of his white van. It was a smart white van, clean, reassuringly professional. Like the warden himself, even if George felt his fists itch. The man had an officious manner that grated on George's raw nerves, but he was content to stay his tongue and his knuckles and watch.

'You reckon you can get close enough to get that thing over its head?' said Ted. He didn't sound hopeful, although he tried not to be negative. No point in being negative. He let others do that.

'It's in a skip,' said Kevin the warden. 'How difficult can it be?' His nostrils flared.

'Right you are. In your own time, then.' Ted found a scrap of loose tobacco in his overall and wasted no time in rolling it.

The warden sneered at the timidity of the general public. He was a professional. He had faced down Jack Russells in his time. He lifted the lid. A smoke-like vapour billowed out. He turned to Ted, who had lit up. 'Did you throw a butt in there?'

'Not me, sir.'

The warden glared at George. George shrugged.

---

* A scandalous stereotype of your average Frenchman. But as anyone will tell you, who cares?

'Right. Best get the bugger out, then.' Kevin stepped closer. Something whimpered.

'No need for alarm,' said he.

'Wasn't me,' said George.

'Nor I,' said Ted.

The whimper became a pitiful howl, drawing the attention of those passers-by who would ordinarily be hurrying to work. A modest crowd began to gather. If there was one thing this professional appreciated, it was an audience.

'Stand back' he said, without necessity. He looked into the skip.

It was still dark enough to make it difficult to locate the source of the noise. And noise it was, rising to an ululating shriek.

The crowd had grown, and it *oohed* and *aahed* right on cue.

The warden waved his hand, trying to clear the vapour that rose in a thick, noxious cloud.

'Ay, I know that smell,' said Ted. His nostrils twitched some more. 'I worked in a hospital, once. I remember one wing was just like that.'

'Mortuary?' said George.

'No. Burns unit. The smell doesn't go away, see. Hangs in the air.'

'Well, thanks for sharing,' said the warden. The crowd looked on expectantly. He was under pressure to save the poor pooch from incineration. He decided to go for broke. He did something rather foolish.

'Oi, mate,' said George. 'That's not a good ide –'

But the warden heeded him not. He leaned right into the skip. 'Do not fear,' he said, 'for I know my Craft.' There was a muffled yelp, which could have been the poor pup or the warden, but one thing was obvious: there was a bit of a struggle going on. The skip rocked from side to side, back and fore, and there was much in the way of squealing. And then it stopped. The warden emerged, red of face and bulgy of eye. He strode back to his van, pulled a tarpaulin from the rear of it and returned to the skip. He blew air from puffed cheeks, then went in.

'Brave bloke,' said Ted.

'Ferkin' raving, if you ask me, ' said George.

There was more skip rocking. The tarpaulin was dragged in. The crowd grabbed a breath, having forgotten to do so for a bit, and then vented a collective *ooh*.

There was a sudden thrashing of legs. Kevin evidently had his hands full. The skip rocked, and rocked some more.

'She's gonner go, ' said George.

'Could be,' said Ted.

Then down it came.

And the crowd went *eek.*

The warden screamed.

Aaaargh, went the crowd.

'Oh my gods,' said Ted.

'Someone get an ambulance.' George grabbed a thrashing ankle, tugged hard, but something had a firm grip on the other end.

'Give us a hand,' said George.

Ted grabbed the other ankle.

The crowd applauded.

The warden slid out. He was holding onto a tarpaulin-wrapped bundle, much larger than your average discarded puppy. It smoked.

'Get it into the van!' Kevin was shrieking, holding tight to the struggling form beneath the tarp. Between the three of them they bundled their burden to the cage in the warden's vehicle, slammed the doors shut. There were no windows, so they couldn't see what it was that hammered and screamed and howled obscenities.

'Oh Jesus,' said Ted. 'Listen to it.'

'It's pissed off, That's for sure,' said George.

'Are those obscenities I hear?' said Kevin.

They fell silent, listening. The crowd backed up.

'Yep,' said Ted. 'Them's swear words all right.'

'But I thought you said it was a shaggin' *dog*,' said the warden. He was sweating. It was pouring from his face, his neck. He wiped it off, his eyes stinging as it ran. 'That was no dog. That was a wol-'

'Oh my gods,' said Ted again.

Yuk, said the crowd.

'What?' The warden became suddenly aware that he was the focus of everyone's attention. *The faces of morbid fascination*, he thought.

'You'd better sit down,' said George.

'I'll get that ambulance,' said Ted.

Kevin looked at his hands. It was not sweat that he saw there, congealing in mucousy clots. He felt at his neck. A jet of something pungent and sticky and bright scarlet spattered the crowd.

Gross! went the crowd, which then buggered off in many directions. Some buggered to their homes to clean up, while others who had the sense and the reactions to duck behind their fellow spectators stepped out of range and continued to rubber-neck.

George pulled a soiled handkerchief from his pocket, wadded it then pushed it firmly onto the wound in the warden's neck.

'What the fuck is going on?' said Kevin, as the van rocked on its suspension and the side panels at the rear began to bulge outward. Something insanely angry was trying very hard to escape the dog pound. The warden's eyes rolled up into his skull. He passed out.

'Them's big beef marks,' said Ted. He had applied a similarly soiled hanky of his own to the deep lacerations in the man's scalp and forehead. There wasn't much he could do about the missing ears, or the bit that had once been the end of his nose.

'At least he still has eyebrows,' said Ted.

George wiped at them. 'Oops,' he said, as they came off in his hand.

Ted leaned over to have a look. 'That's dog hair, that is.'

'Whatever,' said George. He hadn't seen so much blood coming out of one person before. In fact, he'd never seen that much blood before at all[*]. He demonstrated this by throwing up all over the warden's once pristine uniform.

An ambulance arrived, followed closely by a squad car.

The crowd[†] booed as the police told them, despite all the evidence, that there was nothing to see here and so disperse. They took to dodging the officers, or pogo-ing up and down to see what happened next.

The final act had been played, though, and the curtain was coming down; alas, there would be no encore.

The warden's van was driven off by a young Constable who was correct in thinking that being in the same vehicle as the thing in the back was an extremely silly venture.

The Constable did not mess about and drove as fast as the engine would take him. He drove around cars that weren't quick enough to pull over; he swerved around bewildered pedestrians, of which there were now quite a few. Finally, hitting a solid line of traffic leading all the way to the train station, he dodged around a man in a wheelchair, a lamp post, three born-again Zoroastrians and an unemployed Hansom cab lamp fitter, hurtling along the pavement until he reached the cop shop. Here he negotiated the tangle of

---

[*] Apart from a Wes Craven film he'd once seen. Most people assume it's fake. You can never be sure.

[†] This being a different crowd, for those who think they're awfully clever to spot a continuity error. Crowds, like hot dog stands, spontaneously exist wherever there's something remotely interesting going on. Except crowds don't normally give you a dose of diarrhoea and vomiting.. Unless you're especially sensitive or nervous. Which is probably more information than you need, but at least you're getting you're money's worth.

police vehicles with varying degrees of success, finally applying the brakes at the rear of the building. The Constable jumped out.

'Picking up or dropping off?' said the Duty Sergeant, who had been forewarned of the van's arrival.

'Don't be funny, Sarge.' The young officer was pale, his lower lip trembling.

The doors at the rear of the van exploded outward. Something leapt from the cage, wrapped in a tarpaulin; it hesitated, turned, ran straight for the Sergeant. The Constable rugby tackled him, pushing him out of the way. The tarpaulin jumped over them, trailing smoke behind it.

The two officers got to their feet.

'Don't often see 'em that eager to get *in*,' said the Sarge.

'Nice legs, though,' said the Constable.

*

The crowd dispersed, the warden dispatched, the two Environmental Hygienists resumed their work. They emptied the skip when they were sure that nothing else lurked within, loaded the blood soaked contents into the rear of their truck, and then they took to leaning against the side of it.

'I could use a smoke,' said George. His legs felt wobbly.

'I'm going home,' said Ted. He had not been given fair warning that the job would be this dangerous.

'That sounds right and fitting,' said George.

They looked down at their boots, unable to discuss the incident further. Thus, they did not notice the approach of a large (but short) leather-clad man. He took up position between the two. He lit a roll-up, sucked hard and long, and blew yellow-brown smoke. It wafted across the nostrils of the exhausted pair.

George looked up. He did not remark upon the sudden appearance of the biker – five feet four, bewhiskered and sweat stained, heavy on the black cowhide - but he glanced at the cigarette he held, as smokers do when they need one and haven't got any. The biker passed it to him without a word. George nodded his thanks, took a few drags from it then nudged Ted.

'May you be blessed with many children,' said Ted.

'Already got those,' said George, and Ted did not comment on the sadness in his tone. Instead he smoked the acrid smelling cigarette, passed it back to George.

The newcomer intercepted it. 'You lads look like you could use a strong drink,' he said.

George glanced at his watch. It was filmed over with blood. He wiped it off. 'A bit early in the day,' he said. '*Excellent* idea.'

'But where?' said Ted.

The biker finished the cigarette, climbed up into the cab of the disposal truck and beckoned them.

'Trust me,' he said. 'For I am Dai.'

Which, despite the trauma of their experience, or possibly because of it, they did.

CHAPTER FOUR

Monday 08.37. Box Woods.

Dr Carl Berkoff had been enjoying his morning constitutional when he saw the headline on the front page of the Chronicle. With the newspaper spread across his lap, he read the article as his bowels welcomed the day. With each paragraph, his hopes for an early spring opening for the wildlife centre became as cold as the toilet seat and damp as the roll of tissue at his feet.

The *Phantom* had been active again. This time it had been a young girl. The body had been discovered on Tuesday morning, a week before. Same modus operandi – throat torn out, no detectable tracks leading up to or away from the corpse, apart from those footprints belonging to the victim. The site of the latest murder was just a short stroll from where he sat.

If they didn't catch the bastard responsible before March, the scheduled opening of the centre would have to be postponed indefinitely. The Wood had already been closed to the public but hadn't stopped anyone. It had only been Friday last that he'd caught a couple, engrossed in coitus, near the site of the previous murder. He farted and then sighed.[*] Berkoff knew that some people liked to get their rocks off in the back seat of cars recently involved in fatal accidents, sometimes with the blood and other grue still sticky beneath them. This was something to do with the genetic imperative to procreate; heightened by the close proximity of death, the body cried out, "make babies!"

Berkoff had no time for such excuses. Humans were supposed to have higher consciousness, overriding such basic impulses (thought he, farting again and giggling[†] at the echo in the little cubicle). The fornicating pair acknowledged Berkoff's presence by telling him to go forth and multiply, and then continued their noisy business until they achieved mutual satisfaction.

Berkoff shook his head as he recalled the incident. He had nothing against locals using the site for such purposes, if they were discreet. Indeed, when planning permission had been sought to establish the centre, he had been sensitive to local opinion. As long as dogs could still be walked, BMX bikes could be ridden and lovers demonstrate a total disregard for public

---

[*] Not at the time, you understand. *That* would have been gratuitous and unnecessary.

[†] As folk do. No matter what they say, farts *are* funny. And yes, *that* one was gratuitous.

decency, the centre was okay. Box Wood was the local's playground, and long may it remain thus; but you had to draw the line.

There was no way to secure the area short of building robust fences, and that was obviously not an option. Berkoff folded the newspaper, dropped it on the floor of the cubicle and sighed again. He sympathised with the victims of the so-called *Phantom*, their families, but he had invested too much time and sacrificed other activities at the University to be anything but devastated.

And then there was Pitt to deal with. Pitt had invested no small sum in the centre. The trade-off for dealing with the man had been open access to the site for his "team" (whoever they were). Berkoff had already researched the area on behalf of the Faculty of Biological Sciences and found nothing in the history of the site that would merit the interest of the archaeologist. Quite why Pitt would use his own money to finance the venture was a mystery. He was no philanthropist.

As much as Berkoff disapproved of vulgarity, he had to admit that the man was one of life's born wankers. Supercilious, even toward his peers, he was the scourge of the undergraduate and senior lecturers alike, and the reason for the appalling fall-out rate amongst the students. If it hadn't been true that those who survived the course went on to enjoy outstanding careers, bringing the prestige so desired by the University, Pitt would not have retained his Chair in Archaeology.

Berkoff despised him. He avoided him wherever possible.

Now he would have to tell him that the centre was unlikely to meet the contracted date for the grand opening.

Berkoff considered his options as he made liberal use of toilet paper, adjusted his clothing, flushed and then left the cubicle. His Land Rover was parked outside, near the aerial mast a few yards away. He considered driving on up to the *Quarryman's Arms* but it was too early, even for Pete, the pub's landlord and only barman. Berkoff turned away, mildly irritated with himself. He was not a morning drinker, but today…

…He walked deeper into the wood, despite his need for a tranquilliser…

…And came eventually to the location of the latest homicide. The yellow tape, an inadequate "secure" area for forensic investigation, was still in place; Berkoff wondered if there had been any clues at all. He knew that police teams had been exploring the caves and tunnels beneath the old stone quarry, but the authorities were silent about any discoveries that may have been made.

Berkoff stamped his foot on an exposed slab of rock; hard to believe that beneath him caverns and fissures led deep beneath the hill. He had been tempted by an invitation to join a local potholing club; they offered to conduct him on a tour of the more accessible subterranean caves, but Berkoff hated enclosed spaces. He was not claustrophobic, as such, but the thought of being beneath so many millions of tons of solid stone brought him out in a cold sweat and turned his intestines to water. People *died*, potholing; stuck in tunnels as floodwater poured down, they sometimes remained wedged until the water receded[*].

Nevertheless, these entrances to the caves held a fascination for him. He wondered what it would be like to put caution and good sense aside, slip down there unequipped, except for a torch. Just to see…

…Only to have a glimpse of that alien world beneath his feet. It would be so easy…

Duck beneath this tape. Stroll over to the cave entrance. Nothing to fear here. Nothing to fear. One foot in front of the other. One step at a time. Just to see…

Berkoff blinked. He had no idea he had been putting thoughts into action. He found himself crouching beside the gap in the bedrock, peering down into this black eye socket in the earth. His shirt clung to his skin, already sour with sweat[†]; the cold no longer bothered him. He felt strangely excited. He had a torch in his pocket. It would be so easy to –

'Good morning, doctor.'

Startled, Berkoff turned. Wainwright, the Anglican priest for the parish, stood a few yards away beyond the police tape. He was sucking on a cigarette, grinning as if he'd caught Berkoff doing something anti-social.

Berkoff raised a hand in greeting. He stood, wiped sweat from his face. As he walked over to the priest, his legs trembled.

'Are you looking for evidence?' said Wainwright, altogether too jolly. Berkoff approached, attempted a smile but found he couldn't manage it. The urge to drop down into that hole had been nauseating in its intensity. He was left bewildered, deeply disturbed. His trousers were damp at the crotch[‡].

---

[*] Never to be discovered, usually. Well, until the next potholer gets wedged, anyway.

[†] They used to make nylon shirts for this purpose. The smell of a real man is rancid sweat.

[‡] Reason: unknown. Just threw that one in. Gratuitous, that's what I call it.

'Are you all right?' Wainwright grabbed Berkoff's elbow as his legs suddenly gave way.

'Okay. I'm okay. Just…'

Wainwright raised an eyebrow, no longer jovial. 'Do you need a doctor?'

'No…really.' Berkoff just wanted to be alone. It was too subjective, too disturbing to discuss the experience with someone he didn't know that well, even if he'd been able to explain it.

'I think I'll go and have a coffee at the centre. Probably just over indulged last night.'

It sounded lame. Wainwright did that thing with his eyebrow again. Bullshit, he was thinking, and Berkoff had no illusions that Wainwright was the sort who'd use that very word, clerical collar or not.

'Well…if you're sure.' Wainwright patted Berkoff on the shoulder. 'You should look after yourself, lad. Go somewhere warm.'

'The heating should be on at the centre.'

'I meant geographically. A holiday, doctor. *Get away from this God-awful British winter for a couple of weeks*. You look washed out.'

And with those words and strange emphasis, Rev. Wainwright strolled on. He whistled for his dog.

Berkoff watch him go. *Did he say God-awful*? He shook his head. It was no wonder the Church was on a steep decline. He liked Wainwright, but Berkoff had an old fashioned view of how a Rector should conduct himself… and had that been a whiff of whisky he'd smelled when Wainwright had leaned in close?

His thoughts were shattered as he heard, too late, the gallop of paws pounding up behind. Wainwright's dog, a golden Saluki bitch, decided to go through Berkoff's legs, barely slowing its pace as it followed its master's calls. Stupid name for such an elegant creature, "Scubbers", but that was modern clergy for you.

Berkoff took one last look at the vacant skull-socket into which he had almost dropped. He still felt compelled to return to it but forced himself to walk on, resisting the urge to look back, because he knew that he would not be able to stop.

He picked up his pace, eager to put as much ground between him and the hole as he could.

When he'd turned a bend in the track, obscuring the view of it, Berkoff found he could think more clearly, as if his thoughts had not been his own, some dark cell in his mind calling to him. They said that people who feared heights didn't trust themselves not to step off the cliff. The death wish was buried deep but rose like a monster given the chance.

Berkoff considered the possibility that he'd had some kind of fugue state; a person could perform activities, make journeys, and have no memory of it.

There were precursors to such behaviour, surely?

He didn't think he'd been exposed to any undue anxiety or other stressors – other than Pitt, of course.

They say that if you think you're mad, you aren't, because the insane have no insight into their own illness.

His mind was gabbling to itself. Perhaps a short holiday somewhere sunny *was* what he needed.

He sighed[*]; *fat chance*.

Nevertheless, Berkoff decided that it might be a good idea to see Stephens, a friend who practised psychiatry – invite him for dinner or something, keep it low key.

Berkoff felt much better, having analysed the matter and come to a decision. He could see the roof of the centre now, just a quarter of a mile away. He took deep lungfuls of the moist, frigid air, picked up a bit of Hazel that had fallen on the path and swung it back and forth as he walked.

A small Holly tree partially blocked the path. He swung the stick to push it aside and heard something fall from its branches. He paused, pushed branches aside, red fruits pattering to the ground…and there, wearing the berries like bright clown buttons, lay a dead crow.

Berkoff always examined carrion in the woods, to be aware of any potential diseases that might threaten the wildlife. Besides, crows[†] were a protected species.

He knelt, reached into the bush and pulled the bird onto the path. It was a fresh corpse, although stiff, but perhaps that was due more to the temperature than rigor mortis. There were droplets of congealed blood on it. He looked into the bush again, used his torch to scan the area. There was no blood on the ground.

Berkoff turned the bird over. There were two large holes in it, deep in the thorax, but the bird had not been chewed or torn. A predator would have left little of the prey but feathers.

---

[*] Without farting, this time; threw that one in so that I could use the *fart* word again.
[†] Strange but true.

He pulled a specimen bag from the pocket of his coat, lifted the crow into it then sealed it. He scanned the area once more, looking for spoor – faeces, tracks, anything that might provide a clue to the killing – but found none. He frowned, continued on up the path.

Davis, the Ranger who'd been retained to manage the site until the centre was fully staffed in the spring, was having a sneaky fag on the doorstep of the centre. He stamped on it when he saw Berkoff approaching.

'Morning, doctor. Wasn't expecting you.'

Evidently, thought Berkoff, but said nothing. Davis was a valuable asset to the centre, had broad experience of both woodland management and wildlife conservation. He could puff on a water pipe loaded with hashish for all Berkoff cared.

'Would you open up the lab? I want to take a look at this.' He held up the specimen in its transparent shroud. Davis said nothing, stepped inside and held the door for Berkoff.

The lab was freezing. The heating was on a timer, just enough to prevent pipes freezing but not sufficient to make it comfortable to work in. It felt colder in there than outside.

While Davis prepared the instruments for dissection, Berkoff removed his gloves and broke the seal on the specimen bag. He pulled the bird out, grasping it by the head, to avoid handling the torso. The sharp beak of the animal pierced his thumb. It was only superficial, but already a bead of blood had formed. He walked over to the sink, turned on the tap, but nothing came out.

Davis turned to him. 'Sorry, chief. Water's off. I drained the pipes last week.'

Berkoff shrugged, sucked the blood off, oblivious to the possibility of infection from the corpse. Then he glanced sharply at the Ranger. 'Last week? Were you here on Tuesday night?'

'Well…yeah. Forecast was for frost. Didn't want to come in and find the place flooded.' Davis frowned. 'Why?'

'Did you see the headlines in this morning's paper?'

Davis shrugged again.

'Another murder,' said Berkoff.

'Fuck[*],' said Davis. 'Sorry,' he added, aware that his boss hated curses.

'Did you see or hear anything?'

Davis made a face that said: *it's woodland, doc*, but shook his head.

---

[*] Could have said *"Stone the crows!"* but not PC these days, what with them being protected and all that.

'Nothing?' Berkoff's tone was a little too strident. Davis was on the defensive immediately.

'Should I have?'

'I'm not *accus* – look, forget it. It's just rattled me, that's all. Until they catch the culprit, we'll just be keeping the place warm. So much to do.' He sucked at his thumb. It was bleeding more freely than it should. He wrapped a piece of gauze from the instrument tray Davis had prepared and taped it. His thumb began to throb.

'Chief?'

Berkoff looked up.

'You want me to stake 'im out?'

Berkoff gazed down at the bird, focused on the beak. A little fresh blood there. His. He had an irrational urge to throw the thing on the floor and stamp on it, keep on stamping until it was nothing but a red smear on the tiles. A vein throbbed in his head. A sudden flush of hot blood raced to his brain, raising a storm of black snow in front of his eyes. For a moment he thought he would pass out. He steadied himself, gripped the edge of the central bench that served as an autopsy slab.

'Yes. Please.'

Davis looked askance at the doctor. He spread the crow's wings, tacked a retaining pin into each and then did the same with the legs. It was supple, now, easily manipulated. 'Ready when you are.'

Berkoff nodded. He pulled the angle poise spotlight over the crow, switched it on. The flare of light brought a lancing pain behind his eyes. He turned it slightly away from him, screwed his eyes shut for a few seconds. When he opened them, Davis was staring openly. 'What?'

'You look like shit, doc,' said Davis. 'We can do this later.'

'No.' Berkoff picked up a calibrated slim rod from the tray and inserted it into the higher of the two punctures in the bird's thorax. 'Sorry. I don't mean to snap. I just need something to do.'

'No sweat. Do you need me for anything?'

'You could open a window. Damned stuffy in here.'

Davis did not try to disguise his confusion. 'It's only just above freezing in here, chief.'

Berkoff ignored this. 'Just a couple of inches. Please.' He was finding it hard to concentrate and the Ranger was becoming tiresome. Sweat dripped onto his hand as he bent over the bird, trying to read the measurement on the rod. 'Three centimetres.'

Davis opened the window then zipped his fleece. He returned to the bench, opened a notebook and jotted down the calibrations as Berkoff called them.

'Pass me the scalpel.' Berkoff held out his hand. Davis slapped it there, handle first.

There was a tension in the lab.

The first incision was deeper than necessary. The hollow ribs gave easily. 'Shit.' Berkoff put the scalpel down. 'Scissors and Spencer-Wells, please.'

Davis, now more than a little concerned about his boss's behaviour, placed the instruments on the bench beside the crow.

Berkoff used the surgical scissors to cut a flap of skin in a semi-circle, pulled it back to expose the organs beneath the ribs, then clamped the flap in place with the forceps. The little bones themselves had come away, leaving only lungs and heart; the heart had been pierced, as had the lower lobe of the right lung.

'Look at this,' said Berkoff.

Davis didn't like the way Berkoff's eyes were bulging. They were bloodshot, with a tinge of yellow to them. He looked as if he'd had a skin full - looked as if he'd been having regular binges for some time, in fact, but Davis didn't think that was likely. Until today, the doctor had never shown any indication that he had that kind of problem. He'd once lived with an alcoholic, so he knew whereof he spoke. He didn't know why he felt the need to do this, but Davis removed the scalpel from Berkoff's reach before leaning forward. 'What'm I supposed to be looking for?'

Berkoff hissed. 'Let's start by telling me what you see, shall we?'

Davis was not a man to be browbeaten. He was getting a little peeved and was almost at the point of walking away before he said something he would regret. Yet the doctor had been okay to work with until now and didn't ask for much, and everyone knew that academics were eccentric*. Definitely coming down with something, though.

'All right. Well…the punctures weren't inflicted randomly. Whatever caused them, they were meant to pierce those organs in particular. The depth of the punctures indicates a measured bite, not meant to go straight through the body… but a fox or a dog would probably inflict multiple bites, shake the prey about in its teeth, but the rest of the body is undamaged and I can only see two incisor punctures.' Davis took a small probe, dipped it into the heart.

---

* Not *just* because they all wear fleecy Happy Hippo PJs. Of course, they'll deny it.

He moved it around, the end of the probe pushing against the muscular wall, and then pulled it out. He repeated this technique in the lung.

'Clean. Not a drop of blood left in 'im.' He examined the wings. They were broken in several places.

'Okay. My guess is that the bird was picked up and held, like this.' He mimed the action, making a fist, then brought it to his mouth. 'Sick as it seems, I think we're looking at a human predator.' He thought about that for a moment but it was too disgusting. 'Or maybe a big ape,' he added, and then wished he hadn't*.

Berkoff nodded then smiled for the first time. 'Outstanding. Yes, the lack of residual blood spatter indicates that it was drained directly into something. Killed, then sucked dry on the spot. Very sick indeed, and all the more disturbing when we consider the nature of the murders in the vicinity. Did you know that there were no bloodstains at the site of each corpse?'

Davis swallowed. His throat bobbed. Berkoff noted this.

'It appears that we have a modern day vampire. Or thinks he is.' He watched Davis's reaction. A vein pulsed in the Ranger's neck.

'We should tell the police' said the Ranger.

'I shall be driving into Bath when I finish up here. I'll go to Manvers Street station.'

'Shall I bag 'im up?'

'No. Best to leave the specimen pegged out. I don't want to damage any evidence. If the police forensics team want to see for themselves, they'll have to come here.'

Davis glanced at his watch. Berkoff saw this. 'Relax. Just leave me the keys.'

Davis hesitated.

'It's all right,' said Berkoff. 'I'll finish up, you go home.'

Davis put the bunch down on the bench. 'I'll, um, see you tomorrow then.'

'No. No need. I'll meet you here on Friday.'

Davis needed no further prompting. He was on full pay, despite the lack of actual work, and if his boss didn't want him here that was fine by him.

Berkoff watched him go to the changing room.

No sooner had his assistant left, Berkoff collapsed to his knees. His buttocks vibrated as he let rip with noxious gas†; pain arced across his body,

---

* Because they aren't indigenous to Britain. Unless you count mortgage arrears counsellors, of course.

† Sorry, but it really *is* necessary to use farts like punctuation. Even saying the word *fart* makes people giggle. Of

as if he'd touched a live terminal. The pain sprang from his thumb which, even through the agony, he thought was ridiculous. It was merely a prick, no more than he could inflict with a pin, but he could see that the gauze wrapped around

his finger was soaked through and dripping. He heard Davis in the next room. He would be back in a few seconds. Berkoff stood up. The throbbing had eased a little. He applied more gauze to the wound, strapped it, and then wafted his hand through the stink-fog that still leaked from his arse.

The door to the changing room clicked and then swung open a few inches. He could see the Ranger naked to the waist, pulling his tee shirt on. Davis was shivering, yet Berkoff was filmed with sweat. It had to be some sort of virus; a fever brought on by an infection. But how? He knew of no pathogen capable of inducing such symptoms so rapidly.

He watched Davis preparing to leave; Berkoff noted the ripple of muscle, meat, the skin covering the bulge of biceps revealing thick blood vessels. There was barely any fat on him. The veins stood proud; dense; corded muscle in his neck seemed to push these veins into taunting prominence. Berkoff wondered what would happen if that thin covering of skin were to be punctured, releasing the fluids, jets of it spraying all over-

Berkoff shook his head violently. *A bloody great mess – That's what you'd get. Bloody great pools. Bloody great. Bloody blood.*

He almost shook his head again, as if this would shake these grotesque fantasies. This wasn't him.

Then a thought wriggled into his mind, in amongst all the sick images and perverse scenarios; he had been thinking of fugue states, earlier, and it occurred to him that if one were capable of committing certain acts without any clear memory of them, might he not have been involved in some way in the series of killings that year?

Berkoff tried to shake the morbid mood, but his behaviour over the past hour disturbed him. Davis had noticed; perhaps others had. He would have to talk to Stephens today. The only other alternative, if you took this line of thought to its logical conclusion, would be to lock himself in his own wine cellar, manacle himself to something solid until his thinking cleared, or someone in a white coat and a reassuring smile came to have him fitted for a jacket with lots of straps and buckles.

Which was ridiculous…wasn't it?

---

course, they'll deny it.

Berkoff made a mental note to check his diary against the dates of the murders; he kept a busy schedule, and if he was involved in those killings he would find out.

Satisfied that he now had a course of action to settle his mind on the matter, Berkoff was able to compose himself before Davis returned.

'I'll be off then,' said the Ranger. He frowned, sniffed.

Berkoff nodded.

Davis left, hesitated briefly by the door but evidently decided against further comment. Berkoff heard the main door slam, gravel crunch, and then Davis's car starting up.

Berkoff left the lab, went directly to the reception desk and picked up the telephone. He dialled, connected; it rang three times before Stephens's voice told him to leave a message after the tone.

Berkoff felt an impulse to slam the receiver back in its cradle, but this was too important to succumb to an infantile display of temper; smashing the 'phone was not high up there on the list of constructive action. Although he tried to control his voice, by the end of the message he was sure that his friend would be alerted to the fact that this was no casual invitation for a social visit; there was a tone and pitch to it that said, Come Quick, And Bring Lots Of Strong Tranquillisers.

Done.

He had told Stephens that he would call in at his home around four o'clock, to commit himself to the arrangement. His friend would be expecting him. If Berkoff were to be seized by a fugue state, he would miss the appointment, and he knew his friend well enough to expect him to come looking.

Berkoff sat back and rubbed his face. His hands came away wet, not only with sweat but fresh blood. By the reflection of one of the display cases in the room, Berkoff saw that his thumb had left crimson streaks across his face; but while this elicited a grunt of disgust, he found that he could not immediately look away. He was appalled to find that he was also excited.

CHAPTER FIVE

Monday 10.16 A.M.
Peat lands, West Somerset.

Pitt had his team erect the examination tent dangerously close to the site of the find. He wanted as little manhandling of the specimen as possible, and as few people to see it, including any of the hired help not directly involved in the dig. To this end the structure was in effect three tents, like a Russian doll* with a narrow margin of three feet between each shell.

At each stage, before one gained this inner tent, Pitt and Dr. Emmerson shed outdoor gear and put on protective suits to prevent contamination.

The examination area had, in its turn, a transparent inner sleeve. Tubes and hoses fed the thing with a gas mixture that did not include oxygen but might make you speak in a very silly voice. Hence, Pitt and Emmerson lumbered around the central table with diver's oxygen cylinders.

It was a curious set-up and most of the diggers had been asking questions. It was not normal practice, and the degree of secrecy was extreme. As Jason so whispered into Jan's ear.

'This is stupid,' said Jan.

'Then why are you here?' Jason pulled the outer tent flap closed. There were no other protective suits available, but they weren't meant to be there anyway. For this was a covert mission.

'What do you expect to see?' said Jan, who felt that one of them should be the voice of reason.

'I don't know. That's the point.' Jason unzipped the door to the next tent. 'Clear,' he said, beckoning Jan through.

'I know I'm going to regret this,' she muttered. It was a cliché, but also a prophecy of sorts, although she didn't intend it to be. Obviously. People say things like that without thinking about it. Just as they say things like: " It's quiet…too quiet." As Jason did, just before Pitt's strident tones rang out.

Obscenities. Criticism. Sarcasm. Hyperbole. Mimicry. All nasty stuff directed at the long-suffering Emmerson. Occasionally she would make a sharp retort of her own, but mostly it was Pitt's voice that they heard.

---

* Except Russian dolls don't have dried slugs, urine stains and fag burns on them.

'Why does she tolerate it?' Jan said. Her face had drained of colour. She mixed with the rugby crowd and was no stranger to foul language, but this was vitriolic. Personal.

'S and M, perhaps? Some couples are kinky like that.'

'You think they're a *couple*?' said Jan.

'They sleep in the same tent, babe. What d'you think?'

'Doesn't mean anything. Some people just enjoy talking to each other, deep into the night.' As soon as she said it, she bit her lip. Jason cocked his head to one side, raised his eyebrows, and gave her a bemused grin.

'Ah. I see. They're actually really into each other *intellectually*.' He shook his head.

She hit him. 'Don't call me "babe". Twat.'

The tirade in the innermost tent finished, and Jason judged it safe to move closer. They were at the inner shell, now.

'Can't we wait until tonight?' Jan did not want to think what kind of verbal assault they would suffer if Pitt discovered them at this point… assuming that he would stop short of actual physical abuse. Neither she nor Jason could be certain.

'This is our only chance. They're moving the stag this afternoon.' They crouched and duck-waddled as they navigated in the dark, the light from the inner tent effectively blocked from filtering out. Jason ran a finger over the surface of the shell. His face broke into a confused blend of delight and disbelief.

'It's like metal, but not,' he said.

'Articulate as ever,' said Jan.

He scratched his head then added: 'Do you think that the stag was infected, or something?'

'All I know,' said Jan, 'is that the whole set up gives me the eebie-jeebies.'

He continued along the dim passageway. The tent had a solid base. The groundsheet, integral to the tent, was of the same metallic material. Pitt had gone to a lot of personal expense. It wasn't standard kit for a dig, that was a given. A thought occurred. 'Jan, d'you think Pitt knew we were going to find something significant on this dig?'

'There's always a chance, Jas.'

'No. I mean, *knew*. As in, already prepared.' He scuffed his boot against the ground sheet. 'This is advanced stuff, bulky…and why pack an hydraulic hoist unless you know it's needed?'

'So he's anal-retentive, over prepared; so what?' She wanted to believe that it was that simple. 'Stop asking me what I think; I told you, this is stupid.'

They continued along until they were at the opposite side to the point where they'd entered. Jason stopped. There was a sound like an empty metal bin struck with a piece of wood. It was followed by a squeak of pain. 'Packed bloody air tanks, too. That's not just anal retention, That's full-blown constipation.' Jason rubbed his head and tried to be brave about it, but actually wanted to cry, as folk do.

'That's not air,' said Jan.

'How can you tell?'

'I was a nurse, remember?' She snorted. 'Sometimes I wonder if you listen to-'

Jason's hand slapped across her mouth. 'Shush. Listen.'

They could hear Pitt giving instructions to Emmerson.

'Get on to Johnson. We can't wait any longer.'

'But surely it would be better to wait until dark?' Emmerson was saying, echoing Jan's earlier misgivings.

'The specimen is unstable. Must I repeat myself? Get Johnson. Now.'

'Shit,' said Jason. 'Hide.'

'I thought we were already doing that.' The scorn in Jan's voice had no effect on Jason. He crept back the way they came, peeped around the corner.

Emmerson came out. She was wearing a boiler suit of a similar metallic material. She slipped out of this, left it in the inner tent, zipped the flap then let herself into the outer marquee.

Jason twitched a finger, gesturing Jan forward. 'This is our chance.'

'Yes, you keep saying.'

Pitt followed a few minutes later.

'Quick.' Jason grabbed her elbow.

'Leggo. You've got skin.'

Jason unzipped the flap, pushed her in.

On the ground lay two sets of overalls with matching helmets. Through the transparent inner sleeve they saw the Elk stag where it lay in an incubator. A small generator to the side provided power for red lamps; the tableau was like a high-tech holiday cottage in Hell.

'What's all this about?' Jason moved closer and his hand moved to the flap fastener. It wasn't a zip, but the kind of seal found on supermarket freezer bags. Air tight.

Jan slapped his hand away. 'You really don't listen, do you? Those canisters outside aren't breathable gas.'

'Then we'd better get suited up, hadn't we?' Jason grinned as he pulled on the larger of the two overalls. He slipped the helmet over his head. The face plate misted over immediately. 'Kind of stuffy.'

Jan shook her head. She turned a dial on the left side of the helmet.

'That's better,' he said. 'Come on. Last one in is a cauliflower fart.'

Jan shook her head again. 'That's it for me. I want to finish this degree. See you later.'

Jason barred the way. 'You've got this far. It'll only take a minute. I promise.' He pulled a face that was meant to be charming. 'Please?' he added.

Jan ground her teeth. 'You'll pay for this,' she said. 'Big time.' Suited up, they entered the inner sanctum.

They moved up to the plastic casket, fed by tubes. Liquids hung from drip-stands. Needles and tubes conducted the contents directly into the Elk. 'This is too creepy,' said Jan. 'He's feeding a two thousand year old Elk with – ' she leaned forward to read the label on the drip-bag – 'Jesus.' Her face had lost any colour it had. She stepped away from the incubator.

'What?' said Jason. 'What is it?'

'Shit. I'm gone. Sorry.' She left the examination area, didn't bother to seal it after her.

'Jan, wait!' He took one last look at the incubator, swore, and then moved to follow her. As he did so he noticed another table in the corner, near the generator. A notebook had been left there. He didn't bother to argue with his conscience, because his conscience knew it would get a severe kicking if it dared to utter a word of caution. He picked it up, left, disrobed, and sealed the sleeve behind him.

He caught up with Jan as she headed for her tent. She stumbled as she went and her shoulders shook. He seized her by the hand, swung her around.

'I'm *leaving*,' she said. 'That's *it*. I want no more to do with this.' She was frightened. Jason wasn't especially sensitive, but even he could see that.

'What was in those bags, Jan; what are you scared of?' He had to know.

'Plasma,' she almost shouted. 'You give it to trauma victims until a blood cross-match is done.'

'He's feeding a corpse *plasma*? Why?'

'How the fuck should *I* know?' She pulled her hand free. 'Why don't you ask him?'

Jason looked around. The rest of the team was busy in the trenches, doing what archaeologists were supposed to do. There was no sign of Pitt or Emmerson. He pulled the notebook from his jacket. 'I don't need to,' he said, wiggling his eyebrows. He pushed it back in his pocket, hurried over to Jan's tent. She followed him in.

Ow, was the noise Jason made.

'You punched me,' he said in a tone of disbelief. *'Again.'*

'You stole his notebook?'

'Not exactly. I'll give it back. Eventually.' Jason opened the book to the first page. Then he flipped to the next. And the next. He riffled the pages, exasperated. 'I don't understand a word of this.' He tossed it down. *'Bugger,'* he added.

Jan picked it up. She began to read. After a few pages, she closed the pad. Her hands were trembling.

'Are you going to share, or what?' Jason picked up the note pad again and took another look. It made no more sense than a computer manual.

'It's nothing to do with archaeology,' said Jan. 'I can understand some of it. There's a log of the drugs and other treatments he's given the specimen.'

'Bizarre,' said Jason, relishing the intrigue.

'They're resuscitation drugs.'

'He's trying to *revive* it?'

'That's what I said, fuckwit. Something else, too; that generator – it wasn't just for the lights.'

'Yeah, what about those? Why red, I ask myself?'

'Are you listening?'

'I await your wisdom. Hit me.' He sat, cross-legged like a Buddha awaiting *satori*[*].

'Maybe I will. Did you notice that the generator had paddles attached to it?'

Jason made the face that said Stupid.

'Electrodes. Come on, Jas, keep up. Don't you watch *Casualty*[†]?'

Light dawned. 'He's going to jump-start…?

Jan nodded.

Jason's mouth flapped. 'Get packed.' he finally managed to say.

---

[*] Enlightenment. Which reminds me of the Buddhist who walked into a McDonald's and said: "Make me One… with *Everything*." True story.

[†] English version of *ER*. George Clooney was never in it, though. He already earned more than the Roman Catholic Church (or not, depending on the likelihood of being sued for libel)., so we didn't give him a chunk of our TV licence fee. Would *you*?

'Fackin' ay,' replied Jan.

CHAPTER SIX

Monday 12 p.m.

Some called him Old Tosser. Others called him That Bastard. There were many other epithets of similar vulgarity, but none of them were ever used in the presence of The Gaffer; in his presence, he was Sir. The Gaffer was a legend in his own tea break, a detective's detective. He was a copper of the old school. His instinct for smelling misdemeanour, and the apprehension of the perpetrators of same, was unparalleled. Face of granite, thick white hair, a man familiar with psychosis and Gut Feelings.

This morning, for example, he'd felt that old feeling in his water. He'd been prepared to dismiss it as the raging bladder infection he'd been trying to shake for a week. Or perhaps it was the kidney stones. That is until now.

Detective Inspector Bratt took two Diazepam, washed them down with cold coffee. He ignored the stub of the cigarette he'd just put out in it, because his need was great. What he wanted were facts that he could make sense of, but the two uniformed Constables seated across the desk could only look at each other and fidget.

'Stop that,' said Bratt. 'This is not the headmaster's office.'

'No Sir,' said they, with a capital S.

'Where is she now?'

'Holding suite. We had to stick a board over the window.' The older of the two, Constable Barry Park, shifted in his seat.

'Stop fidgeting, man. Why did you do that?'

'My underwear is stuck in the crack of my arse, Sir.'

'No. I meant, why did you block the window?' Bratt lit another cigarette, pulled back a ball attached to a wire then released it, setting in motion another ball at the end of the row. Click, clack, went the desk toy.

'The prisoner appears to be photophobic, Sir. Can't stand daylight.'

'I know what photophobic means, Constable. I know all about phobias.' He lit another cigarette, apparently unaware of the one in his other hand. 'Have you arranged a psychologist yet?'

'The Custody Sergeant is attending to it, Sir.'

'Right. Now then.' The Inspector turned to the younger officer. 'You don't seem to have much to say for yourself. Perhaps you could enlighten me. Is this the same girl you saw last night?'

'Yes Sir, no doubt about it - but we had no idea she was hiding in the skip.'

'No. Well, you were busy apprehending the suspect.' He turned again to Constable Park. He stabbed a cigarette in his direction. 'You, however, were *with* her; how could she climb into a refuse skip without your knowledge?'

Park began to fidget, thought better of it, but could not prevent himself blushing. 'I, um, that is…don't know.'

'Are you on medication?'

'Certainly not, Sir.'

'There's nothing wrong with being on medication. No need to get defensive, son.'

'I'm not. I mean no, Sir.'

'You'll have to do better than this, Constable. I want a full report on my desk before you finish your shift. No "ums". No "ers". FACTS.' And for emphasis, the Inspector slapped the desktop. It stung like buggery.

'Yes, Sir.'

'Right. Now sod off.'

The two Constables stood to leave.

'Oh, and one more thing, Park. I want you to book yourself in to see Doc Stephens.'

'The shrink?'

'Psychiatrist, Park. That's an order.'

'But.'

'But me no buts. Either that or I'll suspend you.'

'Sir.'

When they'd gone, Bratt played with his balls for a while. Then he lit another cigarette. He took two more Valium, which was inadvisable, but it was better than playing with his balls all afternoon. He picked up the 'phone.

'Duty Sergeant.'

'That's me,' said the voice at the other end.

'Has the shrink arrived yet?'

'The *psychologist*,' corrected the desk Sergeant, 'is indeed here.'

'I want to talk to him as soon as he's finished with the lass. The place of safety order won't last much longer. I want to know if she's mad, bad, or safe to release.'

'Release?'

'That's what I said.'

'But she's barking, Sir.'

'That's not a politically correct label for the insane, Sergeant.'

'No, I mean she's *barking.*'

The Sergeant evidently held the 'phone up to face the holding suite, as they like to call the bare cells in your local nick these days. Bratt heard something howl, and then –

'Okay. I take your point. Keep her quiet, will you?'

'What would you have me do, give her a biscuit?'

'Don't be flippant. I won't have barking in my station. See to it.' He slammed the receiver down.

Click, clack, went the desk toy.

Now pleasantly stoned, DI Bratt pulled out a copy of *Wet 'n' Wild* and settled down to read the articles.

*

'So. How's our lass?'

Bratt reached for the toy that went click-clack but stayed his hand; you couldn't trust a shrink not to read too much into things like that. He might think the Inspector wanted to do unmentionable things to his mother. Even though the Inspector had never met the psychologist's mother.

'Barking,' said the shrink.

Bratt hadn't met this particular psychologist before. The name on his ID tag said Irving.

'You're a little young for this line of work, aren't you?'

In Bratt's experience, all shrinks were near pensionable age and dignified with it; this one looked as if his mum had only recently allowed him to start wearing long trousers.

'Excuse me?'

'I'll ask the questions, sonny. Where's Stephens?'

'Doctor Stephens is a psychiatrist, Inspector. I'm a psychologist. Is this relevant?'

'I said *I'll* ask the questions. How's our lass?'

'Barking', said Irving. He put a mark on his form, next to the bit that said *Is This Person Safe Amongst The General Public?* The tick was in the *No Fucking Way* box.

'Now you're repeating yourself. Why can't I get a straight answer out of anyone?'

Irving's mouth tightened, like his mother's did when he swore in front of strangers. It was a look that said You Have A Serious Problem My Lad. 'I don't know. Have you tried sticking to the point?'

'You're trying my patience, sonny. *Is she safe to release*?'

'No!' said Irving, a nervous laugh exploding from his throat before he could stop it. 'Absolutely not. She needs treatment.'

'Can you arrange it?'

'Of course, but it'll take a few hours. I'd like to talk to her GP, if that's possible. May I see her details?'

'If it'll stop you pestering me.' Bratt passed the Duty Sergeant's copy of the information he'd gathered.

'It's blank' said Irving.

'I know.'

'Well, no matter; we can still get her sectioned. May I use your 'phone?'

'No. It's *my* 'phone. Use the one downstairs.'

'Then if you'll excuse me.' Irving stood up to take his leave.

'Where are you going?'

'To make a call.'

'Sit down. We're not finished.'

Irving sat.

Bratt set the click-clack machine in motion. The psychologist raised an eyebrow. 'Have you ever met my mother?'

'No. Now let's get down to business. What exactly is wrong with her?

'She's incontinent, smokes too much.'

'No. The lass downstairs.'

'Oh' said Irving. 'Well, she thinks she's a wolf. And she can't stand daylight. She also smokes too much.'

'Does she. Does she. Who gave her cigarettes – has she had a visitor?'

'No. I mean *she* smokes too much. That's what happens when she's in direct sunlight.'

'That's what my Duty Sergeant said, too.' Bratt lit a cigarette. 'But he's an imbecile. Let's stick to what's logical. This young lady was apparently assaulted in the early hours of this morning. She hid in a skip until two bin-men found her.'

'Why was she brought here?'

'She attacked a dog warden.' He blew smoke. 'Allegedly.'

Irving dry-swallowed. 'I was in there with her…alone.'

'You don't think I'd risk one of my officers, do you? Anyway, this lass made a right old mess of the lad's face; bit off his ears. And the end of his nose. Eyebrows, too. Tore into his neck. The poor lad's comatose. Now, I want to know if she's legally culpable. Get your team together then let me know. Off you go.'

Thusly dismissed, Irving went.

Bratt reached for his copy of *Wet 'n' Wild*; the 'phone rang. 'What?' he demanded.

'It's DC Wood, Sir.'

'What's that to me?'

'You sent me to the hospital, Sir; to keep an eye on the dog warden.'

'Get on with it.'

'Yes Sir. He's conscious.'

'Then go and talk to him.'

'I did. He's delirious.'

'How would you know? Are you medically qualified?'

'No. But he said he was attacked by a-. Well, his exact words were…'

'A wolf?'

'Nearly there; a werewolf, to be precise.'

'A werewolf.' Bratt repeated the word, his tone flat.

'I told you he was delirious.'

'I'm coming over. Watch him, Wood. Don't let him out of your sight.'

'He's strapped to the bed Sir. Totally ga-ga.'

'We'll see about that. You tell him to pull himself together. I'll be there in half an hour.' Bratt slammed the 'phone down. The plastic cracked. He picked it up again. 'Desk Sergeant.'

'That's me.'

'Get me a new 'phone.'

He slammed it down for the last time, the pieces ricocheting. God bless Mr. Graham Bell; if a man couldn't vent his homicidal tendencies upon the infernal machines, the cells would be more crowded than a Soho[*] knocking shop[†] offering two for the price of one.

Two more Diazepam later he was heading down the stairs, trying to put his coat on back to front.

---

[*] An area in London famous for its wenches of negotiable *amore* and bookshops forbidden by Law to display their wares to the general public – unless you're 18 or over and unlikely to leave the goods on the shelf with the pages stuck together without paying for them.

[†] Knocking shop: brothel. No idea why it's called that. A Londoner would know, but of course they'll deny it.

CHAPTER SEVEN

PC Barry "Baz" Park was still no closer to finishing his night shift and had spent a frustrating hour on the telephone attempting to locate the appropriate department within the council's public services. He was passed from one disinterested body to another until he mentioned the matter of the dog warden.

'Oh,' said one voice. '*Those* bin-men. Actually, we've been trying to trace them ourselves. They made off with one of our disposal trucks.'

'Ah,' Barry said. 'Now, that simplifies matters. Would you furnish me with the details of the employees' addresses?'

'Of course. Do you have their names?'

'No.'

'So what am I, eh? Sodding telepathic?'

'But you said you knew.'

'I didn't. I said, "oh, *those* bin-men." I don't know them, personally.'

'Then can you put me through to someone who does?'

'Please hold.'

'No! Don't – ' Barry held the 'phone at arm's length, as if it had just been doubly incontinent in his ear, and swore at it.

'No need for abuse*, mate. You wanted some details of two of our employees?'

'My apologies, and yes, in that order.'

'And you are…?'

'Police Constable Barry Park.' He gave the voice his number. 'Will that do?'

'I suppose. We were going to report the theft of a truck, anyway. Will you beat them mercilessly before they get to the station?'

'No.'

'Pity.' The voice gave the names and addresses of the miscreants. Barry thanked him.

*

Finally on the road, Barry and his beat partner, Clive Feart, found the residence of one George Cloonie. They surveyed the street from the safety of their patrol car.

'Is it safe to get out?' said Clive.

---

* Untrue; when dealing with Public Services on the phone, it always comes down to verbal abuse. It's a Universal Truth.

'Looks like Beirut, don't it?' said Barry.

'Dunno. Never been to Beirut.'

'It looks like this street.'

'Glad I've never been, then.'

Clive ensured that he had his baton and Mace before leaving the car. He avoided several piles of dog shit on his way to the front door of Mr. Cloonie's abode by a sort of manic version of Hopscotch.

The door showed signs of recent attempts to gain forcible entry. Clive knocked, using the brass effect clapper cunningly crafted in the form of a penis. There was no response from within.

'Anyone at home?' he called. There was no answer. He turned to leave.

'Hold it,' said Barry. He pushed the door. It opened.

'Don't we need a warrant, or something?'

'Don't be insipid,' said Barry. 'We have reason to believe that a burglary is in progress, don't we?'

The door gave up its tenuous hold on life. The door frame split. Down it came, brass-effect willy and all. The Constables entered therein.

'It stinks,' said Clive.

'Probably that pile you just stepped in.'

'Oh *yuk*. Who lets their dog crap in the house?

'Who said a dog needs permission? Anyway, if the owner's done a runner, the dog needs to go somewhere.' Barry, the voice of reason.

'That's a big pile. All coiled up with a twisty end. Like a plastic joke turd.' Clive tittered*.

'But the dog is real.' Barry pointed. A pair of amber eyes glowed from the shadow near the stairs directly in front of them.

'Oh shit,' said Clive.

The dog smelled his fear and it reacted accordingly. A low growl greeted him. On the Richter Scale of Terror, it registered an easy four points.

'Nice doggy,' said Clive.

The nice doggy, however, did not feel like visitors. Not unless they were on the menu. And these two looked just like a take-away, delivered to the door.

It licked its lips.

Its eyes blazed.

Its hackles stood up.

It began to edge forward.

---

* Yes, there are people who chortle at such things. I've used them myself to devastating effect. Oh, mirth.

'You have a way with beasts,' said Barry.

The dog was uncomfortably close. It tensed to spring. It was big.

Clive backed up. The dog gave a warning growl.

'Keep still,' said Barry. 'It won't hurt you.'

'How d'you know it isn't trained to kill?'

The dog sprang.

'SIT!' Barry yelled.

The dog twisted in mid-air and landed just short of Clive. It raised a paw.

'Aw. Isn't he cute?' Barry shook the paw. 'How do you do.'

'Oh, please,' said Clive, wiping sweat from his brow. 'Who the feck are you, Doctor bleeding Doolittle?'

'No need for that kind of language,' said the dog.

Clive gaped. 'What the bollocks,' he said.

Out of the shadows stepped the lady of the house. 'My dog can beg, roll over, die for the Queen and chase bicycles. If you give him a biscuit, he might even *lick* your bollocks for you. But he doesn't *talk*, copper. What do you want?'

'Mrs. Cloonie? We're looking for George.'

'Who's askin'?'

'PC Feart,' said Clive. 'And this is PC Park.'

'Fart?'

'*Feart*[*]. F.E.A.R.T'

'That's what I said. Anyway, he ain't here. What d'you want him for?' The lady of the house rested her heavy bosom upon folded arms. A thin roll-up hung from her mouth and dropped ash upon the Special Forces tattoo on her forearm.

Clive couldn't help staring at a large, hairy mole on the end of her broken nose. 'We believe he is a witness to an assault. Do you know where he is?'

The good Mrs. Cloonie consulted her watch. 'Try the Pigs.'

'Watch it,' said Clive.

'The boozer. Up the road.'

'Sorry.'

'That's all right. Twat.'

'Sorry to've inconvenienced you, Mrs. Cloonie.'

---

[*] Yes, the *fart* word again. But it's a noun, this time, so it's allowed – all right?

'I'm not Mrs. Cloonie. The Cloonies live next door. You going to fix my door, or what?'

The two Constables looked at one another. 'We'll get someone to pop over,' said Clive.

She moved fast, did the lady who was not Mrs. Cloonie; she blocked the doorway with her not inconsiderable bosom. She could have made a good living as a bouncer in the city centre if it hadn't been for the huge melanoma on the end of her nose. 'No you bleeding won't. I wants me door fixed, NOW. It's not safe without a front door. It's like Beirut around here.'

*

'Where's Do-It-All*?' said Barry.

'On the way to –' Clive consulted his notebook. 'Ted Watts's place. We can pick 'em both up.'

They found the domicile of Ted Watts. It was a sad little shack that looked as if it had been tacked together with corrugated cardboard, papier-mâché, dried snot and toothpaste. It did not have a door knocker in the shape of a willy. This one was shaped like a cockroach. Clive knocked on the door, using his knuckles, afraid of using the door knocker in case he caused major structural damage.

The cockroach scuttled away.

No one answered the summons.

'Off to the Pigs, then,' said Barry. 'I could do with a pint.'

*

The Pigs was a fortified building, heavy on graffiti and not ashamed to wear its dried-on vomit, urine and petrol bomb stains with pride. The windows were old, stained glass of great beauty beneath toughened Perspex sheets. A sign swung high over the front door, the only indication that this was a hostelry. Barry and Clive went in.

The pub was the sort where conversation stopped when none-regulars risked a visit, but conversation was not conspicuous, being the kind of pub where people went in to do serious drinking. No one paid any attention to the Constables. The clientele were used to it.

'Two pints of Best,' said Barry.

---

* A super store where you can buy expensive tools and whatnots for smashing up your house.

'Best what?' said the landlord

'Bitter?'

'Wouldn't you be, stuck in a pisshole like this? I've been trying to sell it for years.'

'How about lager?'

'What's wrong with bitter?'

'Two pints of that, then.'

'We haven't got any.'

'What *have* you got?'

'Particular.'

'Okay. That one.' Barry pointed a finger at the single pump. It appeared to be an Inn of limited means.

'What is it?' asked Clive.

'Particular,' said the barman, and a bit pissy with it.

'That one. *That* pump. What is it?'

'Are you being funny?'

'Two pints of whatever it is, please.' Barry was used to being arsed about. It was the uniform. It said: Come Test My Patience To Destruction. The trick was not to let them know that you were kicking seven bells of shit out of them in the warmth and security of your own skull.

'It's *Old Particuler*. You deaf, or what?'

The barman went about his duties. The Constables glanced around the bar. Lighting had evidently been phased out through popular demand. It didn't have dark corners. The entire bar was a dark corner.

Spitting his defunct roll-up on the floor, the barman placed two perfectly poured pints of *Old Particuler* on the bar. 'That'll be fifteen quid, then,' said he.

'Try again,' said Barry.

'But this is Bath. All the select bars charge those prices.' He sighed and shook his head. 'We'll call it four, since you're officers of the peace. God bless you.' He took the fiver offered and did not give any change, an oversight raised by Clive.

'That's for the information,' said the landlord.

'What information?' said Clive.

'Don't you want to know where Ted is?'

'How did you know…okay. Where is he?'

The barman consulted his watch. 'Should be at the boozer by now.'

'Late, is he?' said Barry

'Don't know. He doesn't drink here.'

'How about George?' said Clive

'That'll cost you another quid.'

'But…' Clive began.

Barry shook his head. He placed the coin on the bar. 'Now, stop this foolishness. Where is George?'

'Dunno. Should be here by now. He's late.'

Clive's hand twitched where it rested upon his canister of Mace.

'Did you try the house?' said the barman.

'We did. She said to come here.' Barry kept his hand over the coin.

'Have you fixed the door yet?' said the landlord.

'No, we're on the was…how did you…'

'It was *my* house. The missus rang to say you'd be in. And Ted is an old mate. Just in case you were wondering. Telepathy is not one of my many talents. Which is why I feel compelled to ask you why you're looking for them.'

'They're witnesses to a serious assault,' said Barry. 'And that information will cost you a quid.' So saying, he pocketed the coin. 'Thanks for your help. Very public spirited.'

'I'd like a good hard wood. Oak. And a knocker shaped like a knocker, if you don't mind. That last one was too vulgar for my taste.'

The Constables took their pints to a table to await the elusive unemployed bin-man. The bench seat was lumpy, but Clive managed to punch two bum-shaped hollows into it. They sat.

'Nice place,' said Barry. 'My kind of boozer.'

They supped, exchanging police small talk, but Ted and George did not appear. What they heard, in hoarse whispers, from the table hidden beyond the old partition next to theirs, made up for it.

'Sunday night, I swear. Haven't been seen since,' one voice said. It was a whisky-soaked voice, ruined through years of abuse. *'I told 'em straight. You keep diggin' where y'shouldn't…'*

''Tis a bad business, Tom,' said a second voice that had been dipped many times in Sherry. *'But like you always said, "Rob the dead, there's yer bed".'*

'I never said that.'

'You did, Tom.'

'Crap proverb,' said Tom.

'But true. Unholy trade for a young man. You can forgive his Dad, being descended from a line o' grave robbers, but Joel...well, I always thought he would do better.'

'Ar,' said Tom. *'He was after training to be an undertaker. Y'can rob 'em before they gets too soft and smelly.'*

Clive nudged Barry. 'Did you hear that?'

'Yes. Keep your voice down.'

'Grave robbers!'

'Keep your voice down.'

'But…'

Barry nodded into the gloom. Pale globes of faces turned in their direction. Most had broken noses. Or cauliflower ears. Mainly both.

'Nice pint,' said Clive in an over-done stage whisper.

They rose to leave, having drained their glasses quickly.

'Thank Christ,' said the old gent they'd been sitting on.

Before they left, Barry leaned over the partition. He exchanged a few words, most of which Clive did not hear, and then Barry headed for the door.

'See if you can get one without a letter box,' the barman called after them.

Outside, Barry was a grim picture. Clive pointed this out.

'Your face is a picture. A grim one. Like one of them painting-by-numbers wotsits.'

'Come on,' said Barry. 'We're going out of town.'

'Where?'

'A place called Tepid Ashton.'

'That sounds like a thinly veiled pseudonym for a real village,' said Clive.

'Well, it isn't; and I've just had a tip-off.'

'What about our bin-men?'

'We've wasted most of the day on that. I've got something more solid.' He got into the driver's side. 'Buckle up, lad. Blue light and siren, I think.'

'Wicked!'

*

Peat lands. Monday, 14.00.

Jason and Jan were long gone when the cowpat hit the turbine in spectacular fashion.

'My notebook!'

'Jesus, Leonard, don't blow a valve. You obviously just put it down somewhere. Where did you last see it?' said Emmerson, choosing exactly the wrong moment to ask a question.

'If I knew that, you stupid girl, I wouldn't be standing here.' Pitt walked up to the incubator. All appeared to be as he had left it. 'Find out who's missing.'

'The students packed up an hour ago', said Emmerson; her tone indicated Who Gives A Shit.

'Then find out who left early, you moron.'

'Are you sure you can trust me to do that?' Emmerson left.

'And get onto the removal people,' he shouted after her.

His bleep went off. It was the pathology department at the Royal Infirmary. He pulled out his mobile and dialled the number.

'We've got another one,' said an unpleasant voice. The sort of voice that pulls wings off butterflies.

'I'll be there in two hours,' Pitt responded. 'Get the lights fixed.'

He ended the call and then sighed; not *too* much pressure.

CHAPTER EIGHT

Monday, 16.30

The holding suite* in any local nick has a high turnover of guests in any given week. They leave behind a smorgasbord of smells, ranging from expensive colognes to the earthier yet no less musky odour of good honest sweat. Mingled with such odours, indeed overlaying them, is the smell of fear. Humans cannot smell fear, but the current guest in holding suite number one had certain talents unavailable to the average guest at Manvers Street nick.

There was nowhere to hide from the sense of dread and foreboding in the cell. A lone female sat in the furthest corner away from the thin plastic covered mattress where the fog of terror lay heaviest. Curled in a foetal position, she whimpered constantly. Her senses were overloaded not only by the heavy atmosphere but also the incessant noises from all parts of the

* As they like to call the bare cells in your friendly neighbourhood police lock-up these days.

building. She could hear weeping from the cell adjacent to hers. Further down, someone was cursing. In another cell, a man was masturbating noisily. That last one had interested her briefly, but she had already touched his mind, her senses skittering around his brain like a spider exploring a house. He hadn't known she was there. None of them did.

What she had found was that they were prisoners before they were brought here, trapped in patterns of thinking, never exploring, never asking questions beyond the most basic concerns. There was little to differentiate between them; male, female, it came down to sex or security – will I keep my job? Will I keep my lover? What will happen to me today, tomorrow, when I get old? How do I get out of this mess? What can I acquire that will make this life worth living?

They were all so cut off from themselves, from each other, life histories sealed in bottles adrift in a black ocean. Occasionally they bounced off each other, and this they called contact. They would never know what possibilities swam around and beneath them, had no thought for what was above.

It was true. Everything that Melthus had told her. It was best just to think of them as food. Now that she had left the nest, it was the only way forward. She could not linger here. Melthus would be sending Collectors.

No. He will make this a personal matter. He *will come...*

The sun was setting. She did not need to see the dimming of the light to know this. And with the rising moon came power.

The building began to throw out a new pattern of vibrations. New thoughts collided off each other. *Conflict.*

Her strength was returning. She could pick out individuals without trying...like the little band of officials in the corridor. She knew their intentions before she heard their footfalls approach her cell.

She had planned to flee this place as soon as the door opened. They would be expecting a disturbed female, dangerous unless cozened and spoken to softly as if comforting a child. As if she was someone who had no control. For the first time since she had chosen to use this place to shelter from the day, she felt composed, even managed a wry smile. There was one among these do-goods, these arbiters of others lives, who interested her. Perhaps she would play.

'We shall see,' she said.

The door opened. The dull one, the one who had earlier described her as a mere pup, looked around the door. He said that she had visitors. As if she couldn't fathom this for herself. In they came - huddled, although they would not realise this, for safety.

'Hello,' said a tired woman. She had a cancer in her uterus, although the symptoms would not show for a while yet. Her husband was gone, and her evenings were spent writing letters he would never read. 'My name is Helen Carter. I'm a social worker.' She introduced the others. They all professed to be concerned for her well-being.

The one who called himself a psychiatrist, named Stephens: he drank to excess and could not pass a gambling den without breaking into a sweat.

A physician, Knowles, who took opiates and stimulants and secretly yearned to bed his friend's wife.

All so *concerned* about her health.

They were perplexed when their prisoner laughed out loud. They grew afraid when she didn't stop. She did not stop until she was satisfied that the balance of power had shifted. Their perceptions had changed. They were on the defensive.

'Where is the other one?'

The one called Stephens glanced at his cronies.

'Other one?'

'That is not an answer.' She had been sitting, her arms wrapped loosely around her bent legs, regarding them over her knees. Now she snapped upright, the movement faster than they thought possible. They started, drew back. The physician was wondering how fast he could get to the door.

Not fast enough, she thought. *Not even close*.

He had been looking at her, up to that point, his eyes and his groin as one. He was disappointed that he could no longer see the length of her legs, the bulge of her thighs.

'I think she means Craig.' Helen moved slowly toward the cot, sat on the mattress. She would leave traces of her tumour-smell on it.

'Don't be absurd,' said Stephens. 'She can't possibly know that.'

But he's not certain thought Caitlin.

Helen said, 'Will you tell us your name?'

Crafty, this one; she will fetch Craig if I tell her. No matter. One name is like another. I will give them something to call me by.

She smiled at the social worker. The smile was returned.

So easy to please. Like babes.

'O'Connor.'

'Good. It's a start.' Helen tapped on the door. The dullard answered. 'Will you ask our colleague to join us?'

'The guy with the big hair? He just left.'

Helen turned to speak.

O'Connor held up her hand. 'He will be back. There is a bag by the desk.'

Knowles thought he could hide a sneer behind his hand.

There was another voice, outside. Footsteps. 'Er. Officer? I left something behind. Or I think I did. Could've sworn I came in with my – '

'At the desk,' said the Sergeant. He had grown pale. He glanced at the girl. 'Be careful,' he told the others. 'I should have an officer with you. Don't forget what she did.'

'I'm sure we can cope,' said Helen, her tone curt.

The turnkey hurried off. 'You're needed,' he was heard to say.

'Me?' came the reply further down the corridor.

'You see anyone else about?' snapped the Sergeant.

Footsteps. Softer, more unsure than the others. Then he was at the doorway. O'Connor couldn't see him from where she stood.

'Someone ask for me?'

'Yes'. Helen gestured for him to enter.

Craig stepped further into the room. He noted the others, nodded, still unsure as to why he had been summoned. And then he saw her.

O'Connor reached out with her mind. In her eagerness to know more of him she was not as careful as she had been with the others. His head jerked back, eyes screwed shut. She realised her error, eased off, but the damage was done. He was wary of her now, although he would not know why.

When he opened his eyes again, his eyes were moist.

'Sorry,' he said, and then appeared to be confused, didn't know why he'd apologised. 'Do we know each other?'

'I know a little,' said O'Connor. 'Come. Sit.'

He moved to sit on the mattress, but she shook her head. She lowered herself to the floor, nodded to him. He glanced over his shoulder at the others.

'You need not heed them,' said O'Connor. She pointed at the duty Sergeant, loitering at the door. 'You. Take these' – she pointed with her chin – 'get them out of here.'

'We still have some questions, Miss O'Connor.' Stephens was uncomfortable with the whole situation – he didn't know why, just a feeling that this was not a healthy place to be just then – but more than that, he didn't like to be summarily dismissed. He was used to authority.

O'Connor knew, also, that he needed a drink.

'I will speak no more with you. Go.'

Knowles snorted, picked up his briefcase and shouldered past the Sergeant. Stephens shook his head. 'You're not helping yourself, Miss O'Connor.' He followed his associate, leaving Helen to excuse their abruptness.

'They – that is, we - we're only trying to help. Perhaps you can trust Craig here,' said the social worker.

'I am able to decide that. I need no help.'

Helen lowered her head, turned to the door.

'You should see a physician,' said O'Connor suddenly.

Helen gasped, frowned. 'Why do you say that?'

'Your bleeding. It is irregular, yes?'

'That's none of your business,' she said, but her voice carried no conviction.

O'Connor laughed. 'Do you not see the irony in that statement? You come to me, strangers, full of your own woe. Yet you claim to know what is best for me.'

'You don't understand,' said Helen. 'You are in serious trouble. We're trying to help you find a way through it.'

'Enough. You are the caretaker of your own body. Do as you see fit.'

Helen opened her mouth to speak but found she had no reply. She left Craig and O'Connor together.

When the door slammed shut, O'Connor reached out and took Craig's hand. She tugged gently, and he joined her, cross-legged, on the floor.

'Are you comfortable?'

'Yeah. Fine.'

'No. With *me*. I don't want you to be afraid.'

She knew that he was unsure of the situation, wasn't even certain that it was ethical to be alone without a chaperon, but she wanted to gauge his honesty.

'Well…no. I don't understand. Why did you want to see me? Did one of the others suggest – '

'No. I knew you were there. You interest me.'

'You don't even know me.'

'More than you think.'

'You're playing games.'

Sharp.

'Is that not the way between men and women?'

'That's ...you're talking about sexual courtship. I can't relate to you in that way.'

'Why not?'

'Because...' He blew air down his nose. 'I'm here in a professional capacity. I'm a psychiatric nurse. You're a client.'

'You? A *nurse*?' she said, incredulous.

'Yes. Is there something wrong with that?'

'You are offended.'

Yeah. Bloody right I am, she heard him thinking.

'No. Yes. Look, what do you want from me? You don't want help.'

'That is why I wanted to talk to you. You are direct. Honest. And you are the only one who has seen the truth. Those,' she said, waving a hand in the general direction of the door, disdainful, "'*professionals*." They wanted something from me. You ask, what is it that *O'Connor* wants?'

'*They* would have, too. If you'd given them a chance.'

'It was insincere. They will go home this night, away to their dismal lives. Did you know that Stephens is a drunkard?'

Craig was shocked. Not because it was a revelation. Most of his staff were aware of the problem but he hadn't allowed it to affect his work. Yet. 'How...who are you?'

'I am O'Connor.'

'That's just a name.'

'Hah!' She pointed at him 'You see? You cut to the meat. You are not shackled by the same modes of thinking as they.'

'You're not being fair. Sure, they have problems. *I* have problems.'

'But,' she said, interrupting him, 'you have not become defined by them.'

'This is getting us nowhere.' He made as if to stand. She was on him before he could.

'What are you *doing*?' he said, his voice raised.

She looked down at him, from her straddling position, his arms pinned to the floor. 'Are you a virgin?'

'What?'

'Am I the first?'

'Look, even if I was free to... to...please. Let's just calm Dow –'

She kissed him. He resisted. She ground her hips, her groin, against his. She could feel him responding. 'There. Is that not better?'

'You can't do that!'

'Why not?'

'Because I'm a run-'

'Oh, cease your babbling! "'I'm a nurse,"' she said, mimicking him. He had to admit it, it was exactly like him. Which was sort of scary, since his voice had once been compared to a diesel engine ticking over.

'What if someone were to come in?'

'What if they did?'

'I'd lose my job, that's what.'

'Your job would be such a loss?

'Yeah. Yeah, it would, actually. I like what I do.'

'And there is only one way to do it?'

'According to the *NMC* code of conduct, yes.'

'Who is this *NMC*?' she said, licking his face.

'The people who can get me sacked.'

'They would bundle you into a sack?' Again, O'Connor was incredulous.

'Are you really as thick as you make out?' said Craig, a slack and silly grin on his face. *This is a set up. Has to be. Some twat is winding me up.*

'I am not thick.' She released his hands, slipped her own down the length of her body. 'I am svelte.'

'Er.'

'You have bone,' she said, grinding herself against him again.

'So it seems.' He flopped down again. 'All right. 'I'm sexually attracted to you. But that doesn't change anything.'

She frowned. 'I don't understand. Why will you not mount me?'

Craig sucked air. He released it explosively, laughing so hard that his ribs hurt. She slapped him. Not as hard as she could have, because she wanted him conscious, but she had lost the advantage she had thought she had. She rolled off him, sat with her legs bent up before her as before, her arms tight around them.

Craig sobered. He had blown it. ' I'm sorry.'

'So you say.'

'No. Really. That was unforgivable.'

'I forgive you'

'But I hurt your feelings'.

'My feelings are not easily injured, Craig. You flatter yourself.'

'I've been accused of many things, but self-flattery isn't one of them. I feel like an arsehole.' He sat up, reached out his hand. 'Friends?

'You think that if I shake a part of your anatomy that this proves that we are friends?' She shook her head. 'You are a strange people.'

Craig lowered his hand. 'Where do you come from, O'Connor?'

'My name is not O'Connor' she said.

'Oh'.

'Oh,' she repeated.

Craig scratched his head. 'Listen, O'Connor, or whatever your name is…my colleagues will be expecting me. Do you want to talk again, or what?'

'I have never before met a man who would rather talk to me before mounting me.' And her voice was so flat, so emotionally devoid, that Craig felt his chest hitch. She looked up, her eyes suddenly sad. 'You are a strange one,' she said. 'I want to talk with you again.'

'Good.' His voice was gruff. He did not want to show how easily he could blubber. He hadn't known this woman fifteen minutes, yet she had affected him on a profound level. 'Then let me help.'

'How?'

'Give me something I can tell the others. We can make the law work for you.'

'I can leave any time I wish.'

Craig did not doubt it. If half of what he'd heard, read or experienced was true, she could have ripped his face off and used it as a hand puppet. 'I know,' he said. 'But let me do it my way.'

'Would I see you? Tomorrow?'

'If you like.'

'I like.'

'Then let's start again. What's your name?'

She narrowed her eyes. The giving of a name meant handing over power to those who knew it. If someone spoke a name, albeit in a crowded room, the owner of it would turn in response. And that was not the least of it.

And yet…

'Caitlin. My name is Caitlin.'

'And who are you?'

Caitlin paused; considered. He truly wanted to know. There was no going back.

'I am Wamphyr,' she said.

'Is that European?' said Craig.
Caitlin stared. 'Are you mocking me?'
'Um. No. Did I say something funny?'
Her mouth gaped. She put her head into her hands; her shoulders shook.
'Oh, look, I didn't mean to-'
Craig wasn't prepared for it.
She threw back her head and laughed.
'No need to come over all Errol Flynn,' said Craig.

CHAPTER NINE

Monday 16.30.

DC Wood greeted his Guv'nor cautiously, testing the tempestuous waters of the DI's mood swings with extreme caution. 'Good afternoon, Sir.'

'That's your opinion,' said Bratt. 'Where is he?'

Wood opened the door behind him. Bratt entered therein.

On the bed, cot sides up, was a body. It was secured to the side rails by leather straps, padded with cotton wool. Blood hung in bags by the bed; tubes connected, it appeared, to every orifice. The body had a head, swathed in bandages.

'He's quiet at the moment, Sir.'

'I can see that. Is he talking any sense?'

'Hasn't said much of anything since they gave him an injection.'

Bratt leaned over the body.

The man opened his eyes. He shrieked.

'I thought you said he'd been sedated?' said Bratt.

'I didn't. I said he'd had an injection.'

The shriek became a wail, a pitiful sound, the kind of noise they encourage you to vent in Primal Scream Therapy. This one did not suggest anger, or rage, or peevishness however; it spoke of despair, horror, a man lost in anguish.

'Seems upset,' said Bratt.

'He did have his face almost eaten off,' said Wood.

'Is that a rebuke, lad?' the DI demanded.

'No, Sir.'

'Well, it should have been. I'm an insensitive bastard. Go and get a doctor.'

While Wood went about his errand, Bratt took the wailing man's hand and gave it a bit of a squeeze. 'There, there,' he said.

'Aargh,' said the body. 'That one's broken.'

'My sincere apologies. Have you done wailing?'

'For now,' said he.

'Good. I have questions.'

'Have we met?'

'DI Bratt. I'm investigating the assault upon your person.'

The bandaged lump jerked. A nod.

'Did you get the bastard?'

'We have an individual in custody. DC Wood informs me that you saw your attacker. Can you give me a description?'

'It was horrible,' said the bandaged head.

Bratt paused, to allow the witness to continue. The pause lengthened into an awkward silence.

'A little more specific,' he said.

'I'd rather not.'

The body whimpered.

'Look, son, I'd rather not have a kidney stone the size of the Koh-I-Noor diamond, but life is a real turd-burger sometimes, isn't it? Cough it.'

'It had hair all over its face. Big pointy teeth. Big pointy ears.'

Bratt took out his notebook. *Big and pointy*, he wrote.

'A black, wet nose.'

Black and wet, scribbled the policeman.

'Fetid breath,' said the body. His breathing became more erratic.

Ate shit shortly before attack, went Bratt's pen.

'Not literally,' said the victim.

Bratt looked from his notebook to the body on the bed. He was a couple of feet away and wasn't even looking. There was no mirror on the ceiling. He crossed out the last entry. 'Anything else?'

'The eyes.'

The body swallowed. He said no more.

Bratt removed the get-well cards that hung like bunting along the head of the bed. Thinking of the victim as "the body" was somewhat ghoulish, he felt. A nameplate said that this was Kevin Costner, against all probability. Then again, his face *was* swathed in bandages. It could have been the Queen Mum, under that lot.

'Mr. Costner.'

'Hm?'

'The eyes?' Bratt prompted.

'Don't mention the eyes.'

'But I must.'

'Oh dear.' Kevin's lip trembled, setting the tube that grew from his mouth to wobble. 'It was awful.'

'I have so surmised,' said Bratt. 'But I must press you on this. What colour were they?'

'Gold.'

Light brown, wrote Bratt.

'No. *Gold*,' corrected Kevin.

Bratt went cold. Kevin's eyes were closed, his head tilted slightly to the left, away from him.

'How do you do that?' said Bratt.

'Do what, mate?'

'Bratt. Do what you just did.'

'Correct your notes without looking, you mean?'

'That was my point, yes.'

'Don't know. Just came to me.'

Must be a trick, thought Bratt.

'No, it isn't,' said Kevin.

This is spooky, added the DI

'It is, isn't it?' said Kevin.

Bratt put his notebook away and took a couple of Diazepam. Since his anxiety levels were now reaching critical, he added beta-blockers.

'That's a lot of medication,' said Kevin, still lying there with his peepers unpeeled.

I've had enough of this, thought Bratt.

'Don't go,' said Kevin.

'I have better things to do than play the straight man to your comedy routine,' said the DI.

'But I must tell you about the eyes,' said Kevin.

'Then do so. And no funny stuff.'

Kevin sighed. 'They were *gold*. I 'm not trying to be droll. They were golden and they *glowed*, like they were back-lit.' He turned to face the policeman. 'And the hands,' he said, swallowing hard. 'Ohmygod. They were long. Fingers like drumsticks.'

'Turkey or chicken?'

'No. *Drum*sticks,' said Kevin. 'The sort you play drums with. About a foot long, thin, and claws for fingernails. Strong. And I remember they had pads on the palms, these hands. They held my head, I couldn't move, hot breath, rotten, like old meat, and I struggled, but I couldn't…'

Kevin began to sob. Deep ones. Drawn from the soul.

'There, there,' said Bratt, unsure what that was supposed to mean. 'There, there.'

This man is stark, raving bonkers.

'You bastard,' said Kevin.

'So they tell me,' said Bratt. 'So, what you're telling me is basically what you told DC Wood. You saw a werewolf.'

'That's right.'

Bollocks, thought Bratt. *I can't file this.*

'Suit yourself,' said Kevin

A doctor came in, looking shagged out and in no mood for crap.

'Who are you?' said the medic.

'DI Bratt. I have enquiries to make. Got a problem with that?'

The doctor smiled but there was not a hint of sincerity. 'Perhaps I could prevail upon you to clear it with me first, Inspector,' he said, showing Bratt to the door by the elbow, as if escorting one of his elderly patients.

'Take your hands off me.'

'Out,' said the doctor.

'You can take medical authority too far, you know,' said DI Bratt. 'But since you're here…I wonder if you could prescribe me some decent opiates?'

'What?'

'He's not kidding,' said Kevin.

'You keep out of this,' said the DI.

'You're serious.' The doctor was visibly shocked. 'I couldn't prescribe opiates of any description without a good reason.'

'It's for my …sciatica. The pain, you see. From my arse all the way around to my bollocks then down my leg.'

'Are you describing your pain, or some kind of incontinence?'

'Are you trying to be funny?' said Bratt.

'He'll chin you, doc. Best do what he says. He's off his chump. He doesn't believe in werewolves,' said Kevin.

'I warned you, Mr. Costner. What kind of a name is that, anyway?' said the DI.

'Look, Inspector, I'm a busy man. Bugger off,' said the doctor.

'Those restraints, there. Has he been sectioned?'

'What?' The doctor paused in his DI-ejecting activities.

'A Section Three of the Mental Health Act, 1983. It's the only legal way to use physical restraints in the treatment of a patient.' Bratt smiled. He often did when he was bluffing.

'I'll fill out the forms,' said the doctor. He began to sweat, for it was he who had ordered the restraints.

'It's not as simple as that. You have to prove that he is suffering from some psychosis, and must have treatment to ensure his safety, and the safety of others. It allows you to enforce a course of treatment. In this case, restraints. Did you say that you were *going* to fill some forms? Haven't you already had him psychiatrically assessed?' The DI shook his head and sucked in air between his teeth. 'That's common assault, that is.'

The doctor licked dry licked lips that had suddenly gone dry.

'What kind of opiates?", he said.

*

Monday 17.00

Dr Berkoff had suffered pain in his life, but nothing so excruciating as the sun boring its way into his skin.

Even with the visor down, the drive home had all but blinded him. He staggered from his garage and then let himself into the house where he closed every curtain and blind. He had to lie down. Although the pain of his burned skin demanded relief, he did not trust himself to make it to the drug cupboard. There was no strength in his legs, and a creeping paralysis moved up his body. It was almost up to his chest.

His bladder let go. He could smell it, although he couldn't feel it. It was going to be too late…Stephens.

The pressure in his chest became unbearable. An atheist for nearly forty years, he now made deals with God. But God already had the upper hand, and all deals were off. Heaven is a Come As You Are affair; if he'd done anything to piss Him off, it was a little late in the day for a box of chocolates and promises.

His breathing became erratic.

The pressure on his heart finally stopped.

There was a light ahead. He felt he ought to go to it, but it was an awfully long way off. Still, he had nothing better to do, what with his body being dead and everything.

Yet the closer he got to the light, the greater the compulsion to return to his lifeless carcass.

But it's all over, Berkoff reasoned; *there's nothing to go back to. And here's this lovely bright light…time to go.*

Berkoff looked down at his body. It was closer than he thought. He hadn't made much progress toward that light after all.

Best give it some welly, then.

With all the force and focus of his intellect, he willed himself toward his goal. But the tunnel got no shorter. He knew that the light wanted him, welcomed him, but his plunge toward it became slower until finally he came to a complete stop. Something was pulling him back to his shell.

That *Something* now erupted from the corpse that lay sprawled on the bed, already growing cold. It leered up at the part of Berkoff that hovered above his own body. The body that…

*...That Thing just came out of...*My *body…*

Berkoff took a good,, long look at the present resident of his cadaver. It was black. Not deep blue. Not brown. *Black...*

…Black, like ancient dog turds - dry, but still lying around for the unwary.

This creature had a suggestion of eyes, or rather a twin glow roughly where eyes should be.

It was the overpowering smell that hit you. Perhaps this aroma was not detectable to a nose of flesh and blood, but on this plane – limbo, whatever – the stench was something you experienced holistically; it grabbed you by the balls and grinned in your face. Old, *old* digested meat. Or blood.

The Thing was thirsty.

'Hurry,' it said, voice as dry as an alcoholic's aftershave bottle. 'I thirst.'

What the hell are you?

'No questions. Join me. All will be clear,' rasped the creature.

Looks a bit too crowded already. I'll pass.

'Doctor, I have no time. Come. Now.'

…Dry, ancient turd-arms reaching out for the essence of Doctor Carl Berkoff, embracing him, pulling him into the soft darkness of the flesh…

'I have you now,' said the demon.

The essence of Berkoff, now no more than a whiff of bad cologne at the back of the bathroom cupboard, began to scream. But there was a new guy in town, and he was in charge. What remained of Berkoff was banished to a stony shore, deep in his cold brain, where he continued to scream. And scream. And scream some more.

*

The birth of a vampire is never an easy business. With the soul of Berkoff now trapped and helpless the demon got to work, checking out bodily functions. This it did with enthusiasm. The body on the bed that used to be Berkoff, but now something entirely different, rose two feet into the air, spun slowly on its axis then farted*, loud and noxiously, expelling all the gases that had built up in the intestines. It had been five hours since the demon had ensnared Berkoff's soul. Without it, this body would have been useless, since it required a human soul to reanimate it.

The demon was getting to grips with the mechanics and now it was all systems go. All that was left was a little creative hot-wiring. The heart was a none-starter†; a jump-start in the circuits was needed to get the old grey matter working. The demon searched for the right junction box, a collection of neurons, synapses and various other slimy bits of how's-your-father with which to accomplish his evil work, tutting and muttering to itself like a man looking for a candle in the dark…

…And found what it was looking for, took the ends of two sparking synapses that seemed to be going out of business and plugged them in to each other…

…The body convulsed. Excreta shot out of both ends. The body's face, bland and somehow younger looking in death, now twisted into muscle-tearing grimaces. Its tongue snaked out, lashed about a bit as if tasting the air, then slipped back into the maw which now boasted fine white teeth. Yellow bile dripped from them as his stomach ejected everything. When there was nothing left to bring up, he dry-heaved.

His stomach was rearranging itself, for it would be digesting a different kind of nourishment from now on. Fresh and hot. Maybe a hint of adrenaline.

The body ceased its violent seizures, easing off until it barely twitched. Eyes opened, bright gold in the dark. The Newborn examined its environment.

The place looked like a slaughterhouse. Excrement, expelled by the force of the convulsions, had pebble-dashed one wall. The other was decorated with the previous night's groceries. And there was blood, too. The anticoagulant in the puncture on Berkoff's thumb was still doing its work. Blood oozed constantly. It awoke a terrible hunger-thirst.

It had to be sated.

---

* Look, okay, it's overkill but this is what happens when a person Turns all right? FART.

† The demon was a newcomer to humour.

There were a few hours yet until dawn, and he must ensure that he fed before he took shelter from the day. Which was a bit of a downer, since he would have liked to take in a pub, club, or two. Get to know the city the way he never had before.

CHAPTER TEN

Tuesday, 13.00

Kevin Costner, troubleshooting darling of the dog patrol, knew that he would not don the uniform again. His last case had broken him. It was time to hang up his noose-on-a-stick.

An alternative career had not suggested itself. The only future he was moved to consider was that of the immediate, a future in which he tracked down the bastard who'd done this to him.

Justice, That's what mattered now.

There would be no suspended sentences, no community service for the arse-whore who'd tried to eat his face.

Kevin had a small armoury of weapons at home. He now understood why he'd collected the arsenal for so many years. It was to fight this cause; kill the face-eating son of a physiotherapist*. Not just the beast that had done for him; Kevin wanted *all* of them. This was his destiny.

He knew that there were more. He didn't know how he knew, he just did. They waited, sleeping, in the earth.

He would locate them. Burn them out.

Cleanse the land.

Kevin's temperature plateaued at 104 F.

They tried constant cold sponging, fans, and now they were going to wheel him to the bathroom and try an ice-bath.

Kevin's pulse rate pushed 230.

The doctor decided against a bath. Bags of ice-cubes, intravenous drugs, cold units of plasma; that was the thing. Chop, chop, nurses, at the double.

Kevin no longer cared. Kevin could see a light, like a torch beam at the end of a vacuum hose. *That* was the place to be…

…But not *now*. Kevin resisted the light. There was work to be done. He turned back to his body. They were giving him shots of electricity and because he had a lot invested in their success or failure, Kevin watched the medical team working hard with their needles and electrodes. He urged them on.

---

* Strong language indeed.

They could not hear his cries of encouragement. Though he yelled in their ears: 'Stick that Mutha to the hilt,' and 'Juice it to the max', it availed him not.

After fifteen minutes of plying their trade, the resuscitation team stood away from the body of Kevin Costner and noted the time. It was agreed that Mr. Costner had died at 21.09. There were no tears, or emotional goodbyes.

*

Kevin shook his head. Or had it in mind to - but that was all he was, now, wasn't it? Pure Mind. Somewhat limiting, when one is contemplating a career as a slayer of hairy wotsits.

He'd got an idea of the gear he'd wear, too: long leather coat, motorcycle boots – *and* leather trousers, since he was going for the Maverick Wotsit Hunter look (new this season, a must for the well groomed hard sonofabitch). It would include the wearing of many sharp edged weapons.

He had, in fact, a modest arsenal at home: a couple of flare guns, a hand held crossbow and a rusty Victorian revolver he'd found wrapped in old oilskin, buried in Box Wood. A Samurai style sword, too, like the one the hero used in Highlander. He was *born* to be a slayer.

But, oh dear. All is lost.

I'm having one of them astral near death whatchamacallits.

His body was cleaned up and shrouded as he watched.

Off to the mortuary with it.

…And here he was, feeling the pull of the light but determined to get back to his body, even if, from this angle, he was looking a little tubby these days. Those love handles would not look good in leather trousers…

…Yet there was something different about his body. Something he couldn't quite identify. He floated closer to it, the better to get a good look…

…And that was when his body sprouted arms…

…Arms that reached out and grabbed him.

What the shag is this? thought Kevin's Mind.

'You don't want to know,' said the vampire demon.

Get out of there, Kevin snarled, but this amused the entity no end.

'Your body has been prepared. Come.'

Kevin found himself in darkness. He knew that he was in a part of his brain that had been disconnected, the plug on the TV pulled; however, by degrees, the light improved until he could at least see.

His right arm twitched.

Somebody nearby said 'Close his eyes and pull that sheet over his face.'

A thin white cotton coverlet had been draped over him. His line of vision was cut off as the sheet was dragged over his eyes.

'Close his eyes, Gaz.'

'His face is covered,' said someone else, presumably Gaz.

'I know, but they're still open and it's creeping me out.'

The motion of the trolley ceased. They were directly beneath a fluorescent strip. Even through the coverlet, the light hurt Kevin's eyes. The strip became a sun gone nova as the cover was flicked from his face. Two grimy fingers, nails loaded with malodorous grunge, pulled down his eyelids.

'Better?' said Gaz, in the tone of one who does not give a toss*.

'Much,' said his mate.

The trolley continued to roll.

Now the morgue, as they like call to call it on TV cop shows.

'Cold storage?' said Gaz.

'No. Straight through. The Professor will do 'im now.'

"Do 'im?" thought Kevin, with no small degree of panic.

'Now?' said Gaz's colleague. He glanced at his watch, and it told him that it was just short of Too Late p.m.

The trolley jumped over a ridge. They went through a door and the temperature dropped. Kevin could not feel it although he could see the breath of the two porters blowing in the frigid air. They turned a corner. A double door. More light.

'Close his eyes,' said the nervous one.

'They *are* closed.' Gaz buzzed the door, impatient. It was dark in this stretch of corridor.

'No they ain't.'

The cover had slipped. Kevin could see; the darkness hid nothing from him now.

Gaz was reluctant to touch the corpse's eyes; they'd gone a funny colour. Brighter. Fish-eyed.

'Tape 'em,' said the first voice.

Gaz tutted but taped them anyway.

The buzzer indicated that someone had got off his arse to answer the summons. The porters manoeuvred the trolley through the doors.

More light.

---

* Be it a monkey's or something else entirely.

'Quickly,' snapped the pathologist. At least, Kevin assumed it was a paid professional and not some high priest in a necro-dismemberment cult. Not that you couldn't do both, mind, and Kevin thought the bloke looked the business:

Gowned up, one tall man, slight stoop. High brow, domed forehead. Strong, beak-like nose – narrow, like a blade. Dark eyes. Don't-screw-with-me eyes. You wouldn't ask him to give you a sick note. Not this doctor.

'Careful, don't drop him' shouted the pathologist, nearly causing them to do exactly that. 'That isn't meat you're carrying.'

Gaz mumbled something the Professor couldn't hear. But Kevin did. If his face had been his own, he would have grinned.

The porters trundled off with their trolley. There were footsteps. Lights dimmed. The spotlight directly overhead suddenly turned red.

The tape was removed from his eyes. He found that the pathologist was exactly as he'd imagined - even the spot of egg yolk that had congealed on his tie; neat trick, with his eyelids taped down.

There was a feral look in the Professor's eye. 'Can you hear me?' he said.

Kevin could, but he couldn't say so.

'I hear you,' went Kevin's voice…

…And Kevin's Mind said: *Oi. I didn't say that.*

'Do you hear them call?' said the Professor.

'Yes. They call,' said Kevin's voice, deeper than he remembered it; with this one, you could sell lager. Or perhaps a cough linctus of some kind*.

'And you are hungry,' said the pathologist, emphasizing the word. Not a question.

'I must feed.' The Kevin-body moved to get up, but the doctor pushed him back down again.

Kevin's Mind was more than a little outraged that he had no control of his body. None. He was a mere spectator. He could see through these eyes, smell, and hear - which was passing strange, because his eyes had never displayed such qualities before. In fact, he was discovering entirely new ways of experiencing the world. Each of his five senses was enhanced. He could

---

*In some pubs, there isn't a great deal of difference.

feel colour in his fingertips, see a smell with his eyes as well as his nose, could create an image in his Mind from a mere footstep.

A perfect hunting machine.

Restraints were secured around his ankles and wrists. Good thick ones banded with steel.

Oh, come on, thought Kevin. *Don't you think that's overkill?*

'Let me go,' said the demon.

'You will answer my questions,' said the pathologist.

'Your father shags sea-shells on Morecombe* beach,' said the demon-Kevin, his voice thick and phlegmy.

'No. Actually, he lives in a bungalow in Surrey.'

There was an embarrassed silence. 'I was speaking metaphorically,' said the demon.

'Whatever. The point is this.' The doctor reached up. A hood had been fixed to the spotlight; attached to this hood, several tinted filters. He adjusted a dial and the spotlight became brighter. The world went a Rosy pink for a bit when the demon closed his eyes, but each eyelid was peeled back and taped. The light was brilliant even with the red filter, but he could cope with it. It even seemed to enhance his eyesight until the Professor made another adjustment and the red orb became a welder's torch, burning into his eyes.

Kevin's Mind looked on at all this; he couldn't be blinded, but the demon was. It was suffering, he knew that much. The UV light was doing dreadful things to the demon-body. Possibly irreparable.

The Professor switched to the red filter once more.

'Do you see what I'm driving at? Do you understand the need to answer my questions with utmost veracity?'

'What does veracity mean?' asked the demon, after chuckling in what it hoped was a cynical and derisory manner.

'Do not play games with me,' snapped the doctor, his hand straying to the light switch.

'No, seriously. What does it mean?' said the demon.

'Truthfulness. Honesty.'

'But they're *sins*,' said the demon in a shocked whisper usually reserved for Sunday school teachers, for he had grown up in a tough neighbourhood. 'I couldn't *knowingly* commit a sin like that. They'd make my life a living hell. No joke intended.'

---

* Another reason for not visiting Morecombe on a Monday. You get a lot of that sort of thing. That's what a bloke in a pub once told me.

'None inferred. These others – where are they?

Again, the demon made with the maniacal laughter. It was on firmer ground, here. 'Close. Very close.'

The demon-Kevin strained against the straps, sniffing at the pathologist. 'You're no physician,' said the demon. 'And your name is Pitt. Professor Pitt.'

'Save your tricks for someone who is easily impressed,' said the Professor.

'You still wear that old *Hai Karate* aftershave you found at the back of your wardrobe – although, mercifully, not today*.'

The demon had another good sniff, as if he were snorting a thick green bogey back up his hooter, and then relaxed.

'You also have the smell. You've been treading on old hunting grounds, Professor.'

'Enough!' Pitt switched the lamp back to UV; the demon-Kevin stiffened, screeched, and smoked a little. When it returned to soothing red light, Kevin could see a length of wood in the good Professor's mitt. It was sharpened at one end. The bit digging between his third and fourth rib, in fact.

'How many have woken?' demanded the pathologist.

Hey now, hang on, no need to come over all Van Helsing, thought Kevin's Mind.

'Oh, per-*lease*, not that old Peter Cushing campery. It doesn't work, anyway. People think that any old wood will do. Just rip a leg off that conveniently broken chair, ram it in quick as you like… but it has to be a certain kind of wood,' said the demon, his tone suggesting a tapping of the side of his nose. 'Which, I note…' – sniff – 'ahh. Oh. That stake in your hand is the real bananas, isn't it?'

'I've done my homework. Where are the others? How many have woken?'

The demon-Kevin took some time to consider. It wasn't a particularly difficult question, but there were implications.

This guy isn't playing with round snooker balls, thought Kevin. *And if this demon thingy doesn't say something soon, that's my career as a wotsit killer down the shit chute.*

Can't let that happen.

'You will never find them without me.'

'Meaning what?'

---

* A lousy excuse for a Hannibal Lecter line. However, you *will* find a bottle of said cologne in your wardrobe – even if you never bought it. It's a Universal Truth.

'Meaning, I could take you there. Right into the nest.'

There was a short pause. The Professor narrowed his piggy eyes*.

'You'd do that? Against your own kind?'

'No. But this thing inside my head would,' said Kevin.

The demon-Kevin responded to this interruption by head-butting the edge of the trolley.

Kevin said, *ouch.*

The point had been made. The demon–Kevin had just told him to keep his thoughts to himself…

…*Which means*, thought Kevin's Mind, *that there's room for negotiation…maybe have some influence over the demon-body. A working relationship, even.* He decided to test the water, as it were.

Poke myself in the eye, thought Kevin's Mind.

The demon-body obeyed. The demon tried to resist, but as it had said, it took a human soul to animate the body. Which kind of shifted the balance of power, if you looked at it like that; Kevin was the engine, the demon was the shell, the gears, the seats and the upholstery. The demon lived to eat. Kevin needed to live, to fulfil his destiny as a Slayer.

It could work.

Something in his head went *twang*†.

'Super,' thought Kevin. Then, delighted, he realised he'd said it aloud too. 'Super,' he repeated, just for the sound of it.

'How many of you are there?' said the Professor.

'You just asked me that.'

'No. I mean, in *there*.' The Professor rapped his bony knuckles against Kevin's skull.

'Very droll.'

'Whom am I talking to now?'

'*Kevin*. I mean, the real one, not the demon thingy.'

The Professor gasped. 'Fascinating. You've retained your human identity. Can you control the demon?'

Can I? he asked the demon. Kevin felt It shrug.

We'll discuss terms later, It said. *Pay attention to the psycho, if you want to get out of here alive.*

---

* Yes, he had eyes that were piggy – he was a pathologist, after all.

† Like an elastic band smacking you in the eye, but without the tears. That's onomatopoeia for you.

Kevin nodded. 'It seems that we've got an arrangement. As long as I can keep him fed, he won't go stalking the fog-bound alleyways of Olde London Towne. In fact, I'll pretty much be back to normal.'

'But the beast may return at any moment?' pressed the Professor. He had a furtive, unpleasant look in his eyes – fleeting, but nevertheless there.

'Essentially, yes. But this demon has an interest in keeping me alive. It won't interfere unless dinner is cancelled.'

'And if it misses a meal?'

'Read the headlines the next day.'

There was another pause, just like the first one, but anyone with a basic understanding of human nature would have picked up the distinctive sound of someone mentally licking his chops. It was the sound of someone thinking that there were certain advantages to having a vampire for an ally… the Professor, he of the porcine peepers, had much need of same.

'I see. Then we had best keep you well fed. How does a litre of O Positive sound to you?'

'In a warm glass?'

'If you like.'

'Yes. Please. Though it be against my strict vegan principles, I say, pass the bottle, mine host.'

The pathologist tapped his stake against the palm of one hand. 'I must get you some clothes' said he, releasing the straps. 'I don't think I have anything in your size, here.'

'Are you calling me a fat bastard?'

The Professor indicated a mirror by the sink. Kevin went over to look.

The Professor walked into frame and laid his hands on Kevin's shoulders. But Kevin only saw the Professor standing behind him, his hands resting upon nothing.

No reflection, whispered the vampire-Kevin. *Happy now?*

Major brain fuck, thought the Wotsit slayer. 'Nasty trick to play, Prof.'

The pathologist shrugged. 'You have to accept what you are.'

'I know *who* I am. What do *you* think I am?'

'You are Wamphyr.'

Kevin paused. 'You mean…I'm no different from the Wotsit inside me?'

'It's important that you understand – you may still feel like Kevin Costner, but you are trapped in a symbiotic relationship with your demon.

Such relationships are usually unstable. You must, therefore, be eternally vigilant. Do not let it mislead you. Your soul depends on it.'

'Yeah, but…I'm still the good guy, aren't I?'

Exasperated, the Professor explained very slowly, in a manner he usually reserved for the hard of hearing.

'Your intentions are human, but the beast within knows only hunger and the desire to survive.'

'You even talk like Van Helsing. Can I have a long leather coat, almost down to my ankles?'

'I have a fat, idle wallet. You may bid me purchase as much leather, weaponry and essential fashion items as you see fit. You've obviously given the image thing some thought,' said the Professor, smothering a grin.

'Maverick Wotsit Slayer.' Kevin frowned. Something about the title didn't sit right on the tongue. A vampire-hero had to have something snappy.

'Too clumsy,' agreed the Professor.

'Wotsit Slayer,' said Kevin.

Pitt frowned. 'You will be hunting Wamphyri, not "Wotsits".'

'Maverick Wamphyr…no…'

'How about *"Slayer"?'*

'Hasn't that been done?'

'And will be again.'

'As in, "Unto each generation is born…"?'

'No. Be serious. That really *has* been done before, and you don't look like a cheerleader. I mean, there will always be others to take up the fight. You just happen to be singularly well suited to the role of Champion.'

Champion, thought Kevin.

The only person ever to describe him as a champion was an elderly lady, to whom he had returned a fur ball. He wasn't 100% certain that it was canine even now, but a victim of some twisted surgery, or a genetic experiment with fruit bats that had gone horribly wrong. She'd insisted on calling it Minnikins, but that didn't count, especially since he had felt sorely tempted to take Minnikins to see the wonderful aquatic wildlife down at the canal. The little bastard had bitten him twice while trying to coax it out of a cement mixer. He should have let the site workers continue to pour the concrete into the foundations.

But this was something else.

He *felt* like a champion. It was a pity that the mirror wasn't interested. His muscles – shit, yes, he had those, of a sudden – rippled and bulged *ad nauseam* every time he moved.

A creature like himself could do an awful lot of damage.

'You're taking a risk,' said Kevin, as he slipped into a white boiler suit and a pair of rubber Wellingtons*. To hide the scars, the Professor gave him a surgical mask.

With a disposable cap pulled low over his eyes, the burns inflicted by the UV lamp did not show. He could, he felt, be forgiven for bearing a grudge and the Professor didn't appear to be taking precautions at all – he had no crucifix around his neck, and his breath was not seasoned with garlic; of weaponry, nothing close to hand.

The pathologist was no fool; he carried with him a remote control. At the flick of a switch, the lights sprang into life – as if he'd anticipated Kevin's thinking. It was like having stadium floods all in one room. UV light.

'I never take risks' said the Professor. He turned them off again. 'A mere precaution. I have known other cases like yours; the host soul regains control of the vampire body. The demon cannot hunt. A vampire that cannot feed itself is a doomed vampire. The arrangement can have its advantages, if you know how to channel your appetites and new powers.'

'And you're volunteering to teach me,' said Kevin.

'I could; and you could help *me*. I will provide shelter and food, anything you need. You will help me eradicate this disease.'

'Suppose we do – eradicate them, wipe out the whole nest; what next? Me?'

'This isn't the only outbreak. There will be others.'

'That may well be, but I'm only interested in *one*, Prof : The Wotsit responsible for this.' Kevin waved a hand before his face; the scars, the missing pieces.

'You look fine to me,' said the Professor.

'Yeah. Like, that means a lot, coming from a guy who takes people apart for a living. The rest of us think that it's best to get through life without looking as if we've already had an autopsy.'

'There are compensations,' said the pathologist.

'Being?'

'Well, if *I* were a Wamphyr, I wouldn't cross you. You're a mean looking mother, as the colloquialism goes.'

---

*Harbouring a fungus that could wipe out humankind. Irrelevant, mind, so forget I mentioned it.

'I wish I could lay my hands on the bugger right now.'

'No. You don't. In fact, I think it's best you lie low for a while until your wounds heal. When I report that your body is missing, people will be looking for you. Granted, they won't be expecting the missing corpse to be walking around, but you'd better stay at my house for safety.'

Kevin's tone indicated his surprise. 'You're inviting a vampire into your house? You *must* be desperate for hired help.'

'Only for certain talents, Mr. Costner... '

'I'm hungry.'

'...And it isn't just *your* safety that concerns me. Wait here. I'll get you a snack from the blood room.'

The Professor left. Kevin ran his fingers over his face. His ears were still missing. His hair had been shaved off, in order to stitch his scalp. He felt the scars running down the right side of his face, the puckered skin where his flesh had sizzled like Alka-Seltzer. His mouth had sprouted outlandish dentistry. These beauties had grown to replace the old set of pearlies, and much bigger than the pansy pair they used for Christopher Lee.

The Professor returned. He tossed a bag of cold blood. Kevin managed to stop himself leaping at it, catching it in mid-air and impaling it. The urge to bite was almost too much to bear. 'Er. Do you have a glass for this?'

'A glass? Why, yes, I suppose.'

'Only, if I'm to get a grip on things, I need to start with the basics. Like resisting the temptation to get dinner on the hoof, as it were. Or catching Frisbees.'

'Excellent. Splendid, in fact.' The old guy seemed pleased.

'Yeah,' said Kevin. 'Awesome.'

CHAPTER ELEVEN

Monday 19.00...a few hours before. Hard to keep track, isn't it?

Wesil was enjoying his first meal on the acute unit of the neighbourhood cuckoo's nest. His room was en suite. There was totty everywhere he looked. Proper nurses, although sadly not in uniforms. Black stockings, though. Presently, he was giving himself a hand job on autopilot.

Pervs paradise.

The lamb stew he was eating was good. He'd forgotten what actual cooked food was like. Best of all, there had been no mention of a court appearance. In any case he had been detained for psychiatric reports and since this was a secure unit, everyone was happy.

The staff nurses gave him medication to keep him calm and free of the voices he claimed to hear: "Urging me to do things I don't wanna," as he so eloquently put it. The tablets lodged in his throat - he insisted on dry swallowing – and were easily dislodged by finger-tickling his tonsils. The only drug he accepted and swallowed were the little blue ones. He didn't know what they were but he felt pleasantly stoned, thank you very much.

He was on to a good thing, here.

Wesil detected raised voices. Real ones. Outside his room. He laid his plate aside and slipped off his bed, crossed the room to the little panel of glass in the door. He couldn't see much. An elbow. The back of someone's head, bobbing about; someone talking, animated and pissy with it.

'Where is he?' shrieked one voice. It had authority. It had timbre. It rattled plastic beakers on the coffee table, outside in the common room.

Someone suggested – it might have been the bobbing head – that things calmed down a bit. Let's all sit down, it said.

The response to this was an ear-splitting howl. A howl that belonged in ancient forests.

Wesil saw two burly guys enter the scene, stage left. They stood on the fringe of the group, watching. There were several voices, speaking at once. None of them sounded calm, or reasonable. A slap. Flat-handed against a bare cheek. Wesil only heard it, but he'd been slapped enough times to know.

At some signal, the two burly guys stepped forward and introduced themselves. Chris and Ethan were also nurses. Big nurses. And they were only here to help, they said. If Miss O'Connor would just take a minute to sit down, listen. There was no cause to get upset. She was here for her own protection.

There was a lull in the dialogue.

'I am here for *my* protection?' This voice was different to the others. A trace of the southern republic, there. Dublin, or thereabouts. Then there was laughter.

The beefy pair moved in. There was an injection to give, a voice, off to the right, said. And under Section 3 of the Mental Health Act, it could be given without the patient's consent. It wouldn't hurt (they said).

They couldn't have been more deluded, as it turned out.

Wesil had had such an injection. In his arse. It had kept him horizontal for about eight hours. Strong medicine.

'Don't you go gently,' said Wesil, to no one in particular.

But out there, things were quieter. The look on the faces now milling around – some were patients, come to investigate the noise – showed relief. Someone had a little white tray in their hands. The recipient asked what the tube and spike were for.

Yes, said Dublin, but what is a syringe? What *is* an injection?

Wesil opened his door. A circle of staff, waiting, tension in the cords of their neck muscles. At the centre of this group, standing in a relaxed posture, was the girl. *The* girl. The one who'd got him into this mess in the first place. Although it was kind of cushy in here, the cops now had his fingerprints. He had a record. And that would make his recreations that much more risky.

Dublin was slowly backing up. There was a door behind her. The room behind it was empty. They called it a "Time Out" room. It was where they put you so that you could bounce off the walls to your heart's content without harming anyone. Apart from your dignity, that is.

'But why do you want to pierce my skin?' she was asking. She seemed genuinely interested. 'Is it for some tattoo? I already have mine.'

To prove it, she lifted the hem of her smock-like leather dress. Beneath it there were indeed blue tattoos, intricate designs of Celtic significance; spirals, knot work. All very *Clannad.*

But it wasn't the tattoos people had noticed.

She was naked beneath the smock. No undies. Just the blue woad tattoos. Nothing, as your granny would say, to keep the weather out.

'Nice,' said Wesil. Aloud. He'd only meant to think it. Oh well. Too late to hesitate, as he liked to say. 'Erm. Yeah, babe. Very…*ethnic*. But they ain't looking to improve your collection. It's a drug they want to put in you.'

'Drug?' said Dublin, whom Wesil now knew to be O'Connor. Dublin suited her better.

'It's to keep you controllable. So they don't have to try too hard.' Wesil tapped his head with a finger. 'They want to do you over, Dublin. I know. They did it to me.'

The girl stared intently at Wesil. Her nostrils twitched. Recognition in her eyes. *I know you,* they said. *And we have unfinished business.*

She ran the tip of her tongue over lips that were already moist.

The erection that had begun to rustle into existence in Wesil's trousers now subsided. He had intended to incite some action, a little aggression into the tedium of reasonableness and peace that the staff tried to cultivate. Wesil now dearly wished that he'd stayed in his room and finished off the extended wank session that had been interrupted by dinner. She was aware of him now. Was there a lock on his door?

'That's enough, Weasel,' said the nurse in charge. 'You're not helping.'

'She deserves the truth.'

'Please return to your room.'

Wesil grinned at Liz, the matron, or whatever they called them these days. 'They'll pump you full of sedatives, Dublin, and you won't know Protestant from Catholic. Total brain fuck. Don't let 'em.'

The girl adopted a defensive stance, one foot planted ahead of the other, facing these people. The only escape was the room behind.

Liz realised what was about to happen. Too many people, for whatever reason, were converging on the poor girl, surrounding her. Closing in. No way out, only a door into another trap. What else to do but fight?

She was about to break up this little convention, leaving the question of the injection until later when it could be handled more discreetly. The whole procedure of explaining why the doctors thought she needed treatment and what form that treatment would take… it was usually conducted somewhere private. For some reason, the process had become a circus. Roll up, roll up, see the infamous Wild Woman thrash and spit and claw.

'Show's over,' said Liz, trying to disperse the other residents on the ward. The other staff realised what she was doing. They began to move about, doing mundane things like putting the kettle on, counting heads for tea and coffee, cigarettes offered, TV on. Within a minute, the throng had found other things to do. Only Liz and Dublin were left. She hadn't moved. The nurses, hovering close by, were uncertain of what to do next.

'I wish to know two things only. Where is Craig,' she said, counting them off on two fingers, 'and what is Protestant/Catholic?'

Wesil sniggered. He'd moved to a safe distance. Dublin put her hands on her hips, arms akimbo. She glared at Wesil. 'You mock me?'

Wesil sobered.

'You?' she said

Wesil did not have time to avoid the lunge. She appeared to clear ten feet of space, a coffee table, two chairs and a startled resident, without having the consideration to take a run-up for the leap. Her thighs bunched, she sprang; it was as quick as that.

'Get her off me!' squealed Wesil. 'Please!'

The two beefy bastards he'd seen earlier now materialised. One of them had a syringe; they each took an arm belonging to the girl. They later received treatment for multiple injuries. Well, being thrown twenty feet will do that. Even if they bounced.

'You're mine,' she whispered into Wesil's ear. She nipped at him, playfully, not enough to break skin. She rubbed her pelvis into Wesil's crotch. Her face suddenly registered surprise, then disgust, then amusement.

'Bitch!' yelled Wesil.

The shame. Not enough to emasculate him. He'd already been humiliated once. The growing yellow puddle beneath him was too much. His fear displaced, hate rose to take its place. She sat astride him. Her smock was damp, where it had absorbed Wesil's urine. She was openly scornful. Dublin spat as she got up. 'I want to bathe,' said she. 'Attend to it.'

Liz had enough sense to go along with grandiose behaviour, at least while the girl was so obviously unwell. 'There's a shower in your room,' said Liz.

'Shower? Do you not have baths? What happened to the spa?'

What planet is she on? Liz decided that a tour of the ward's facilities might defuse things. She invited the O'Connor girl to follow.

'Kitchen. Feel free to use it as you will.'

'And this door here?'

'Treatment room. It says so on the door.' Liz watched, bemused, as O'Connor traced the black letters on the metal panel.

'Next room is the linen cupboard. Next to that, the bathroom. There's a utility room, too. You can wash your clothes.' Liz walked on. 'This is the off –'

The girl had gone. The door to the bathroom clicked shut, the bolt switch thrown.

'You can't do that,' said Liz. 'Please. Open the door.'

'I need no assistance.' There was the sound of heavy clothing slapping against tiles. Then mumbling; footsteps approached. The door opened. O'Connor was frowning. 'There is no water. You tricked me.'

Liz went in. O'Connor did not bother to cover herself. She watched as the nurse laid hold of some metallic contraption and wrung it. Hot water spewed forth. 'There's bubble bath and shampoo. Towels on the rail. Enjoy.' Liz left her to it. Outside, Wesil was trying to peek through the door. Liz knew it was unprofessional, but he made her skin itch. Repugnant. She wondered about the history between Mr. Weasel and O'Connor. 'Have you met before?' Liz nodded in the direction of the bathroom.

Wesil did not answer.

They stood there a few moments. Wesil did not like the ward manager. He disliked intelligent women on principle. He hated women in authority more so, and she knew that he felt that way.

'Catch you later,' said Wesil. He walked off and sat next to a depressed individual, a guy who bore a striking likeness to Uncle Fester. Wesil begged a cigarette, then sat watching the bathroom door. He didn't care that he was being obvious. They thought he was a creep, anyway.

The psychiatrist arrived. He looked exhausted, but his day wasn't over. Liz took him into the office. She said something to him, but Wesil could only see her lips move. The pair of them looked over at him, then returned their conversation.

*

'I shall have to look into this,' said Dr Stephens.

'I can't be sure,' said Liz.

'But the circumstances surrounding their admissions…the girl, for example.'

'O'Connor,' said Liz.

'She was discovered yesterday morning. In a rubbish skip. For some reason, a dog warden tried to noose her and drag her off to his van. She attacked him.'

'Sounds reasonable.' Liz smirked.

Stephens gave her a look. 'She tried to eat his *face*. Ripped into his neck. He's in the Infirmary.'

'How does this connect with him,' Liz said, a barely perceptible nod in Wesil's direction.

'There was an assault this morning. Sexually motivated. The arresting officers didn't get a full description of the victim, but the circumstances fit.' Stephens checked his watch. Liz guessed that he wouldn't be here long.

'We're still trying to get some details on her, but apparently there are no medical notes. At least we have a name.' Liz pushed the file across the desk. There wasn't much in it apart from the Section documents.

'Ye-es. O'Connor. Well, we'll see.' Stephens shrugged.

'You think it's a falsie?'

Again, Stephens shrugged. 'All I can suggest is that you keep those two separate. I'll make enquiries at Manvers Street tomorrow.'

'This is a small unit,' said Liz, hating to state the obvious, but doctors could be obtuse sometimes.

'Then get extra staff. I'll have a word with your line manager. Get agency staff, if you have to, but don't leave either of them alone. I'll get back to you as soon as I –' Stephens glanced at his watch again. 'Er, actually, I won't see you. Not until tomorrow. I have an appointment, and I'm already late.' He left the office, a sheen of sweat on his face and a fine tremor in his hands. He stuffed them into his pockets.

*

Wesil was hovering close to the door when Caitlin opened it. She flung it wider, grabbed Wesil by the shirt and lifted him off his feet. She carried him to the bath and dropped him in it.

The doorway was crowded with the delighted faces of his fellow residents. Here was entertainment.

Caitlin wore her leather smock, now almost black with the water it had soaked up. It looked as if she had worn it in the bath. Suds dripped from it, from her. The doorway cleared as she approached.

Wesil sat in the bath water, now tepid, and thought it was time he showed Dublin real humiliation. And he wasn't talking about his own. 'You'll get yours,' he shouted. 'Hear me?'

But all he heard was laughter.

*

Melthus greeted his day in a relatively good mood – relative to waking up during painful, invasive surgery, that is. His good humour was short lived. It was the latest update from the Pitt household that did it.

If the news had come from any other quarter Melthus would have doubted its veracity, but his protégé was more reliable than hotmail.

There had been a long silence.

Long.

Dufus waited. As Melthus's right hand man, he was accustomed to the meteorology of his Lord's moods, which tended to range from Gale Warning to Hurricane Alert.

'This is…unexpected,' said Melthus. He stood facing the rock in his private chamber.

Dufus had already suspected as much. He remained still, listening to the echoes that bounced around the caverns. There were howls, roars, screams and arguments – all normal background noise in the nest.

At length, and a goodly length it was, Melthus turned to his second in command. 'Return tonight. Costner must be dispatched.' He spat, as if the name of the Professor's latest ally had left a nasty taste in his mouth. 'A creature that will turn upon its own kind cannot be suffered to live. Be sure that *she* understands this.'

Dufus nodded. 'She is equal to the task, my Lord.'

Melthus shook his head, hidden beneath the cowl of his black robe.* 'Let me be clear on this. She merst not engage him dahrectly. If there is opportunity to eliminate him, she should use any means available; but the Professor must not suspect her. Not yet.'

'Of course,' said Dufus.

'On the erther hand, you will remain at the Man-air† until the creature is dead. Be bold.'

'I will breach the household defences and make it so,' said Dufus.

There was a sound not unlike the grinding of teeth. 'Ah said be *bold*, nert stupid. Lucy will see to the defences, as always. You will wait and observe until the time is right to strike.'

Dufus bowed, turned to leave.

'One more thing,' said Melthus.

---

* Standard costume for evil masterminds.

† Manor. The accent, you see.

Dufus paused; sweat rolled off the end of his nose.

'If there are...*visitairs*...anyone taking an ernhealthy interest in the Man-air...ah want no more surprises. Do ah make mahself lucid?'

Again, Dufus bowed. It didn't pay to nit-pick the finer points of spoken English. Not if you wanted to keep your throat where it was most comfortable.

'Now leave me. Ah fahnd mahself in bad hum-air.'

Nuff said, thought Dufus. One of the (few) benefits of being Melthus's Chief of Security was knowing when to make a rapid exit, and Melthus at least gave fair warning.*

Now, if he could find somewhere to shelter close to the Manor, he might be in with a chance of a good hard shag with the lady of the house before the hunt began.

* Just the once.

CHAPTER TWELVE

Monday 22.30

Pitt's house was situated out of town, on a hill that commanded unobstructed views over the valley to Box. 'On a clear day,' the Professor was saying, 'you can see the Westbury White Horse; to the left, just across the valley, is Solsbury Hill.'

'That so?' said Kevin. 'Thanks for sharing.'

'Ah. Yes. Forgive me,' said Pitt.

Kevin had little interest in the scenic opportunities of the wall-length French windows. The opportunities for glorious sunsets weren't a happening thing any more.

He had eaten well from Pitt's stock of O Positive. He didn't ask where the Professor got it. For now it was enough that he had the patronage of a man who could protect him, feed him and, most important of all, equip him.

Kevin stepped back from the dressing mirror, tilted to take in his entire reflection.

This is going to take some getting used to, he thought, staring hard at the space that was supposed to be looking right back.

He turned to Pitt, who had somehow managed to acquire everything Kevin had requested, including some of the more exotic ordnance. Hollow tipped bullets filled with Holy water weren't usually required for bagging rabbits in this part of Wiltshire. 'How do I look?' said Kevin. He had already been practising The Flourish. His black leather coat reached to his ankles; leather jeans tucked into high biker boots were cut to allow free movement. It's hard not to preen when you *know* you look Bad.

The belts strapped to his waist were festooned with daggers of an unusually wrought design, antiques by the look of them. Wooden stakes, phials of water blessed by a priest (a personal acquaintance of Pitt's) and various gadgets of an incendiary nature made up the bulk of his armoury. There were pouches filled with various herbs: Monkshood, Dried Roses, and Hemlock. He doubted the usefulness of so much muesli in close combat but Pitt said he would explain it all later. For now, Kevin hefted the hand held crossbow.

'I mentioned weapons training earlier, but this is hardly the time-' Pitt began to say.

There was a sound like a ruler twanged off the edge of a desk.

A six-inch bolt carved the air, neatly parting Pitt's Barnet.* The bolt embedded itself in a large book propped in the oak case standing against the wall behind Pitt.

'Sorry,' said Kevin.

'Perhaps we should set aside the weapons for the moment,' suggested the Professor. The bolt had done more than create a new hairstyle. A thin rivulet of blood ran from his widow's peak hairline.

'Sorry' repeated Kevin.

'No damage done,' lied Pitt, and Kevin knew this too. He was finding that he knew a lot of things about people. Pitt, for example, was fretting about the book that now sported a feathered shaft sticking from its leather bound cover; he frowned, picked up the bow.

'Where did you get all this stuff?' said Kevin. He reached behind, grasped the hilt of the sword that was strapped there. The sound of steel clearing leather was just the sort of sound he could get used to. It felt *right*.

'It belonged to an acquaintance of mine,' said Pitt, but Kevin knew that this was a partial truth.

'You have a lot of generous acquaintances,' said Kevin. 'This, um, “friend” of yours – into hunting, shooting and such, was he?'

'You could say that.'

'Come on, Professor. Level with me. I'm not the first to use this stuff, am I?'

'Let's leave that for another time,' said Pitt. 'There are many things to discuss in the days to come. For now you should rest.'

Kevin stretched. New muscle bulged, but he felt stiff and heavy. His body had been undergoing radical renovation and his reserves of energy were quickly depleted. Although the sun was a few hours from rising, Kevin could feel it; a great sphere of nuclear flame, lurking there in the darkness below the horizon. He shuddered involuntarily.

'I'll show you to your rooms,' said Pitt. He led Kevin from the study into a short passageway. A door at the end of it took them down a long flight of steps that should have brought them out onto the ground floor. It grew colder the further they went. Pitt flicked on lights as they descended.

'As you may have guessed,' said Pitt, 'these stairs go much deeper than the foundations of the house.'

'No shit,' said Kevin.

Barnet Fair: hair. Cockney rhyming slang. It isn't supposed to make sense.

'It's just a precaution. I thought it best that you had an alternative point of egress.'

'Eh?'

'There's a secret passage leading from your suite. It opens out near Ditteridge.'

'If you say so,' said Kevin. All he wanted to do was sleep. Possibly a snack, first, to stave off any urges he might feel during his slumbers.

The stairs ended at another door. This one was heavy, made to stay shut. Pitt murmured something under his breath, made a strange gesture with his index finger. The door swung open, untouched. Pitt stepped to one side. 'Please,' he said, waving Kevin through.

He shrugged, stepped into the darkness beyond the door. Pitt followed him in.

'Nice place,' said Kevin. He didn't need light to see his new accommodation.

It was filled with bookcases. Strange specimens, frozen in various snarls and grimaces, hung on wooden trophy shields along the walls. Weapons from different eras took what little wall space was left.

Pitt clapped his hands. Torches ignited in their sconces.

The flare of light made Kevin wince. The flames sent uneven light skittering across the room. Shadows cast by the hunting trophies moved as the torches flickered, blown by a warm current of air. Kevin felt it, raised his head and sniffed.

'Convection heating,' said Pitt. 'A furnace in one of the basements has a pump. All the hot air is conveyed through shafts under here.' He pointed at a grille in the stone-flagged floor. 'Which isn't really for your benefit. It's to prevent the books going mouldy, you understand.'

'Cosy,' said Kevin. 'Where do I kip?'

'This way.' Pitt led his guest through a door. Beyond it was a long passageway, doors off to the left and right. 'Bathroom,' said the host, nodding at the first on the left. Kevin looked inside.

It was cavernous. His own bathroom, back in Twerton, could have been slotted in many, many times over. A walk-in shower, big enough for a football team, the shower heads all positioned just so. Pitt turned a knob on the wall by the shower. Steaming jets of water converged at the centre of the shower room.

'I guess a bloke can get pretty sweaty, hunting and killing werewolves,' said Kevin.

'Ah. Werewolves. Interesting. Perhaps we should explore that misconception tomorrow. But yes, the slaying of the, ah, undead can be a messy affair.' Pitt took Kevin by the arm and guided him to the wardrobe. Well, at least that's what the Prof. called it. To Kevin, it was a large dressing room. Racks of clothes hung ready for use. There was a lot of black leather and the room was rich with its smell. It had a male feel to it. Rows of steel cabinets, fronted with armoured glass, held weapons of pedigree. Two-handed swords, short swords, long daggers, axes; crossbows, longbows, arrows and bolts of different colours and material. An old blunderbuss, set alone from the rest of the arsenal, gleamed. It had history, that gun. Kevin moved to retrieve it from the case.

'I think,' said Pitt, gently but firmly removing Kevin's hand from the cabinet's handle, 'that it would be best if we save any more potentially lethal gunplay until we get onto the range.'

'You have a firing range?' said Kevin. He shouldn't have been that surprised. The house seemed to have everything a Wotsit Slayer could want or need.

'In the morning,' said Pitt. He nodded at the huge gun in its case. 'It's not loaded because it has a hair trigger. It could go off just lifting it out of the case.'

'Ideal for home defence, eh?'

'Oh, I can personally attest to that.' Pitt led Kevin from the room. They made their way along the corridor, pausing now and again to look into other side rooms. It was all on the same grand scale. There was even a kitchen and games room.

But the bedroom…that was something else.

'This is something else,' said Kevin.

' I'm glad you like it.'

'No. I mean, it's something *else*.' Kevin looked around the cell. Unlike the other rooms this one was dank, chilly, airless, and had glow-in–the-dark fungi all over the wall. In the centre of the room, a long box rested on a stone plinth that wouldn't have looked out of place in a cemetery. It wasn't especially ornate, but it was well built. There were brass hasps for securing the lid to the casket.

'It's a coffin,' said Kevin.

'What were you expecting?' said Pitt, exasperated.

'A bed would do. Nothing Laura Ashley.' Kevin raised the lid. Hinges squawked. Kevin glanced at Pitt. 'That'll have to get fixed.'

Inside the coffin, there was a lot of silk. Black. A small cushion, like a hassock used in Church, nestled at one end, 'Isn't there supposed to be a little pile of Transylvanian soil in here?'

'Are you Transylvanian?'

'No.'

'Then you're already treading on your Mother soil. Unless you're planning two weeks in Benidorm there's no need to carry dirt of any kind around with you.'

'All that stuff is true?'

'That and more,' said Pitt. 'We have much to discuss, Kevin; Lore, Legend…'

'Van Helsing stuff,' said Kevin.

'If you like. But you need to know it.'

'When do I get to use some of this gear?' Kevin unsheathed his sword, swished it around a bit. 'Sorry,' said he, neatly nicking a piece of skin from Pitt's left ear.

'All in good time,' said Pitt, holding a handkerchief to staunch the blood. 'The fight begins in here,' he added, tapping Kevin's cranium. 'You must be prepared. Because They'll be prepared for *you.*'

'Is that a capital T for "They"?'

'Yes.'

'Tough bunch?'

'Most certainly.'

'Then I'll get some sleep.' He slammed the lid shut. 'But not in here, Prof.'

'It is customary,' protested Pitt.

'If you're Transylvanian, maybe. I'll kip on the couch tonight. You might like to get a little man in to fix this place up a bit.' Kevin left the master bedroom.

Pitt watched his guest as he returned to the study. Kevin took a run and a jump, twisted in mid-air and landed flat on his back on the old leather couch. A small dust storm blew around him.

'I'll have that little man see to a bit of spring cleaning, too, shall I?' said Pitt.

Kevin did not reply. He was already deeply asleep, oblivious to sarcasm. Pitt moved closer. He leaned over him. His hand gripped the handle of his favourite stake, holstered beneath his jacket.

'Whut?' said Kevin. He didn't know what had woken him but he was ready to fight. His heart hammered. Well, no it didn't; obviously, that wasn't going to be a happening thing. His breathing was fast, however (but only out of habit), and his veins coursed with adrenaline.

'Just testing,' said Pitt. 'Your powers are growing.'

'Nice to know,' said Kevin. He knew that the Prof. wasn't just keeping his trousers up, that his hand, beneath his jacket, was even now sweating where it gripped the shaft of Holly. 'Now, if you would be so kind as to piss off – I get awfully cranky if my sleep is disturbed, yeah?'

'Goodnight, Kevin,' said Pitt.

'Watch the bed bugs don't bite,' muttered the Slayer.

CHAPTER THIRTEEN

Monday, 22.00

Jason's bed-sit. A malodorous, depressing affair. Yellow wallpaper, that might once have been white, curled and hung from bare plaster here and there. A threadbare rug on the floor did its best to hide a large and unpleasant brown stain. The rug itself harboured several such stains and possibly some livestock.

Over the bricked-up fireplace, above the single bar electric heater that he couldn't afford to use, a mantelpiece was cluttered with various esoterica picked up on his travels; small glass water pipes, objet d'art in their own right, did their utmost to brighten up the room. Posters hid other stains on the walls, apart from one. This stain bore a striking resemblance to Kylie Minogue in full moon posture. It was a very big stain, as if Kylie herself had stripped off, rolled around in something browny-fag-ash in hue, then plastered herself to the wall; perhaps she had[*]. Jason was staring at this image from his bed, his hand down the front of his trousers, when Jan walked in.

'Are you fantasizing over her *again*?' said she.

'Just releasing a pube from my foreskin,' he said. 'How may I help you?'

'You know why I'm here. Where's the book?'

'Safe.'

Jan moved directly to a pile of festering underwear. She selected an ice-hockey stick from the general debris strewn around the floor and used it to sift through the lad's soiled clothes and empty burger cartons. There it was. Partially covered now by a pair of stiff boxer shorts, she hooked it out and batted it across the floor to where Jason lay on his bed. 'Let's have another look.'

'Pointless. What we need is someone who can understand and translate for us.'

'Like…?'

'Dunno. You know anybody from your nursey days?'

---

[*] Stranger things have since happened. George Bush Junior got elected President after several recounts and a record of dubious doings in his youth as long as a credit card statement. Allegedly.

'No. But I've got the next best thing.' Jan dropped her duffel bag on the floor, pulled out a large volume. '"*The Art and Science of Forensic Pathology*"' said she, reading the title. '"*A Writer's Guide*".'

'You want to turn our jolly escapade into a novel?'

'Twat. This is science made easy. Well, easy enough for your average pulp writer. Comes with translations.'

Jason sat up, patted a space next to him on the bed. Jan joined him, opened both books. 'This bed smells doggy.'

'Life goes on,' said Jason, uncomfortable. Female friends tried to mother him. He was sure there was an Ideal Woman out there who just loved to shag and enjoyed the smell of old sex. Or at least, the smells of old ejaculate and curry.

This was the first time that Jan had not backed off when he indicated a desire that she should join him on his mattress. She must be serious. 'Go on then. Let's take a look.'

They read the notebook from cover to cover. Jan's medical knowledge and the Writer's guide weren't much use.

'Some kind of Voodoo necromancy,' said Jan, her nose wrinkled. 'Creepy.'

'Archaeology it ain't' agreed Jason.

'An extension of his other areas of expertise, perhaps,' added Jan. She knew that Pitt was active in many fields of learning. He had several doctorates - one in archaeology, for which he had the chair in Bath University, and a doctorate in forensic pathology. He was a pioneer in the field of Cryptozoology, too, the study of life forms that departed from the norm. Legendary beasts, mostly. He'd once been to Brazil seeking the infamous Chupacabra, the Goat-Sucking Kangaroo that had a penchant for, strangely enough, sucking goats*. But Pitt did not have to explain himself. They, Jason and Jan, did.

'The university would just love to get a hold of this,' said Jason.

'Why?'

'Well, I doubt they'd consider this sort of research as prestigious. Wouldn't do their image much good. Or Pitt's.'

'He isn't funded by the university for these expeditions. *He* finances it all.'

---

* Of their blood, in case you were wondering

'But he uses his students to do his donkey work,' said Jason. 'And what about the specimen itself? Is it legal to unearth a corpse, even a two thousand-year-old Elk, and keep it yourself?'

'He has his own lab. Better equipped than the one at the faculty, actually. I saw it once.' Jan left that one hanging in the air. Jason bit.

'You?'

'Me. Why not?'

'Invited you over for a little extra curricular tuition, did he?' said Jason, eyebrows beetling up and down.

'He was showing a group of us. Said that he hoped that, among us, there'd be one or two who would eventually get to work in such an environment. It was kind of suggested that he'd picked our little group, that he might consider hiring anyone who met his standards.'

'This sounds like an ego-wank to me,' said Jason, snorting.

'Well, you'd say that wouldn't you?' Jan was suddenly prim.

'Are you saying that I'm scholastically challenged?' said Jason, his tone suggesting deep emotional injury.

'I'm saying that Pitt isn't just an obsessive scholar. He's committed.'

'Probably will be when people hear about this,' said Jason, tapping the notebook. 'I mean, a one-off experiment, sick as it is, on a dried-out carcass is one thing; conducting such procedures as a regular habit…what next? Grave robbing?'

'Apparently,' said Jan. They had found references to human remains, similarly preserved. 'There must be a reason. He isn't *just* a crackpot. Everything he does, he does with a specific goal in mind.'

'Most serial killers do.' He frowned. 'Do I detect a note of adoration here?' said Jason.

'I *respect* him,' said Jan, her words clipped. 'As a man of learning.'

'Would you work for him, if he offered you a job when you graduate?'

Jan paused. 'Possibly,' she said, in a quiet voice. 'It would be great experience.'

Jason didn't pursue it. In truth, he was a little jealous. He returned to the notebook, as a change of topic. 'But do you think he should be doing stuff like this?'

'Why shouldn't he? He's paying for it.'

'But it's a significant find. It belongs to everyone.'

'Such nobility' said Jan, fluttering her eyelashes.

'He's a pompous twat,' said Jason. 'The Elk should be somewhere where it can be properly examined, straight from the peat. God knows what evidence, what information he's destroyed since he got his mitts on it. Filling it with plasma. Yeuk.'

Jan had to admit it; he was right. And how many other archaeological finds had he removed to his private lab? The notebook indicated five; three of these had been small animals – a hare, a badger, and a fox. The other two had been human. One, a female, was around twenty years old when she had died. The other, a child, had been barely out of infancy when something cut short its life. Any one of a number of predators could have caused the death of the specimens; however, puncture wounds seemed to crop up in all cases.

'What do you think he does with them, when he's finished his experiments?' said Jan.

'I guess McDonalds would cut a deal.'

'No. Seriously. D'you think he stores them?'

Jason shrugged. 'Maybe.'

'I'd like to get in there, have a look,' said Jan.

Jason shook his head. 'Come off it, Jan.'

'I didn't say I *would.* I just think it would be…interesting.'

'Then shine like a star; get your first class with honours and go bang on his door.'

'I've got another year before finals,' she said, impatient, 'and I'll probably have forgotten all about this by then.'

'No,' said Jason. 'You won't.'

Right again, thought Jan. *The boy knows me too well*. 'Nothing we can do about it, anyway,' she said. But the way she said it left Jason with no illusions.

'You wouldn't,' said Jason, a little concerned. Creeping around a tent was one thing. Breaking and entering was another.

'No.' Jan shook her head. 'You're right. The proper authorities would best deal with any investigations.'

'Hah,' said Jason.

'What, hah?'

Jason huffed. 'By "proper authorities", you mean the university?'

'Of course.'

'Pah!'

'People don't say "pah" anymore.'

'Bollocks, then. The university isn't going to break down his door on our say so. This is one of those situations that have to be handled more directly, yet with overtones of the clandestine, not least surreptitious.'

'I think the phrase you're looking for is "covert operation"' said Jan. She was trying very hard not to appear smug. Men were so easy to manipulate. It helped if you knew that they were trying to get into your knickers.

'Give that girl a tongue job. Yes. Someone should just go there. Do whatever it takes. Expose him for what he is.'

'Gather evidence,' said Jan, as if entering into the spirit of it, 'take pictures of anything we see.'

Jason, who'd been thinking more along the lines of smashing things and spray-paint graffiti, said 'Er. Yeah. That kind of thing.'

'Not us, though.' Jan shrugged, as if she'd lost interest. 'Are you going to offer me a drink?'

'If you like. I have live drinking yoghurt. It's very nourishing, I'm told, but it still tastes like baby sick.'

'It's month old milk and it's growing legs,' said Jan, who occasionally took pity and cleared the communal fridge out.

'I wish you hadn't said that. I drank half of it about an hour ago.'

The banter stalled. There was no getting around it. An unspoken something fizzed in the air, like the smell of Jason's intestines. They'd already thought about it. Discussed it. It would take but the flatulent eruption of a microorganism to break the silence and push someone into making a rash suggestion.

Somewhere in the room, unseen, an Ebola virus feasted on a microscopic piece of Tandoori chicken and farted*.

'I've got a crowbar,' said Jason, and then wished he hadn't.

'I've got a credit card,' said Jan.

'For inserting into locks, thus precluding the need for my jemmy?'

'No. Paying for the bloody damage you'd cause. Men.'

'You have a better idea?'

'I do,' said Jan. 'Sit up, take your hand away from my arse and listen closely.'

'My hand is nowhere near your arse,' he said, moving it anyway.

'Pitt is the kind of man we don't want to upset. Too much. Agreed?' said Jan.

* Micro-organisms are allowed to fart, too, I suppose. They must do. Otherwise, what do they do for fun?

'Too late for that,' said Jason, picking up the notebook and waving it in her face.

'He doesn't know we have it. I'll make a copy and return the original,' said Jan. She put her hand up before he could say it. 'Yes, I know, he'll be waiting for someone to sneak into his office and do just that.'

Jason's face crumpled. Bright ideas didn't often visit his mind, and then only for a quick coffee. These days, he was lucky to get a Christmas card. That was probably why he hung out with Jan. She had bright ideas all the time. *And* she sent him Christmas cards. She also had a nice pair of –

'Are you listening?' Jan challenged him.

'I am. And, as usual, you are lengths ahead in this race we call thinking. Do continue.'

'Our main concern is to gain access to Pitt's lab without facing a magistrate . To this end,' she said, with her didactic expression now in place (slight frown, stares into distance, counting off the points with her fingers), 'to this end, I suggest a subterfuge.'

'Ah yes,' said Jason, nodding sagely, 'subterfuge.'

'In short, we get his house keys.'

'Do what?' said Jason, heading for Panic Valley.

'With a bunch of keys, we could be in and out without leaving a trace. Always assuming you don't break anything.' Jan gave him a look. 'Or daub obscenities.'

'That would be moronic,' agreed Jason.

'How about tomorrow night?'

'Eh?'

'I'll get the keys tomorrow morning. We're in the practise lab all day. Pitt's holding forth on excavation technique.'

'Evidently unhappy with our expertise,' said Jason.

'Whatever. He usually remains in the lab over the lunch break. That's where you come in.'

'Oh.' It was the sort of "oh" one vents when suspicion becomes confirmation.

'When we break at twelve, I want you to wait ten minutes. Then call him – internally. Use a 'phone at the porter's lodge. Make any excuse, but get Pitt out of the lab. I'll be waiting. As soon as he's gone, I'll sneak in and get his keys.'

Jason stared. 'You're serious.'

'Of course I am.'

'But you can't.'

'I can.'

'What happens when he discovers his keys have been stolen?'

'He won't know. Not straight away.' Jan grabbed her old duffel bag, rummaged in it, fished out a ring of keys. 'I drop these in his pocket. He won't realise until he gets home.'

'He will when he finds he can't get into his car.'

'Emerson drives him.'

'But when he gets to his front door?'

'He won't be home until late. Tomorrow, after lectures finish, he's off to some symposium in Glastonbury.'

Jason sighed. He saw it all, now; she'd already planned it. They had fled the field, as it were, and arrived back four hours ago. On the journey home Jason had thought that she was withdrawn, afraid of the consequences of their theft…*his* theft.

But no. Little Jan, she of the teasing tits, had been working it all out in her scheming little brain. Sneaky shit.

'So you see, there's nothing to worry about.'

'There's always something to worry about,' said Jason, gnawing on a fingernail. He had nothing more to offer in the way of argument or reason. He looked out of the window. It was snowing.

'Get some rest,' said Jan, patting his knee. 'Full day tomorrow.'

Jason grunted. It may have been a yes. Jan thought so. She stood, and made it the door without treading in anything that stuck to her shoe. 'When are you going to clean up?' she challenged him. Did a lot of that, did Jan.

'Much too busy, what with scheming and trespassing. You know how it is.'

'You should do something about that stain on the wall.'

'I will. I've already contacted the Vatican. I'm expecting a team from the College of Cardinals to verify that this is a holy thing, the very image of The Minogue.'

'I don't think the Pope is into blonde totty,' said Jan.

'Bollocks he isn't. He's infallible, they reckon.'

Jan knew deep concern. His quips seemed only half hearted. He usually laughed at his own wit. 'Jason?'

'Yup,' he said, still staring out of the window. The snow was sticking.

'Are we going to do this or are we just warming the air with our breath?'

'You're really excited about this,' said Jason.

'Aren't you?'

'Yeah, but *my* nipples don't stick out like that when I get horny for something.'

Jan blushed but, against the odds, didn't throw a heavy object at him before she left.

'Bloody hell,' said Jason. 'There may be hope.'

*

Frank "The Sting" Kemp once had an affluent lifestyle, and the City of Bath had been the ideal place to enjoy it.

If there was one good thing to say for the wealthy it was that they were always looking for a quick way to become wealthier – and that, for Frank, was the key to his own good fortune.

Of course, he had feelings about his new life as a gopher for the Wamphyr Lord. Like the spices in a good curry – something he sorely missed – these feelings were mixed. On the one hand there was no further need to risk a spell at Bristol's biggest government hotel. As much fun as the scams were, there was always the occupational hazard of a smart Mark; if you ran into one of those, it was possible that they might take it too personally. There were some dodgy rich bastards who would like to see Frank wearing concrete Wellies, and there were social circles he avoided even now.

This is where his confusion arose; although he had no further use for his plush-seven-bed-multi-garaged-heated-swimming-pooled crib in North Wiltshire, or access to his bank account, he knew that he could take what he wanted from anyone and no bugger could stop him. What he missed most, all things considered, was the thrill of The Scam; the buzz that came with a successful Sting was more satisfying than sex. Well, almost.

Certainly it was better than bunny blood – especially since myxomatosis had been introduced by the local farmers. Diarrhoea was nothing to snigger about when all you had was a hole in the rock to shit in. If it hadn't been for the grudge bearing control freak he now served, Frank would be making full use of his crib a few miles up the valley. In truth, he was prepared to risk going AWOL – perhaps a few days, here and there, to test the water (and Melthus's security measures) – before he did a runner.

Melthus had summoned him, though. It was as if the old bastard had known. Of all the things that could persuade him to stay (assuming that Melthus actually needed to use persuasion), this was it.

'Ah have need for a criminal of the scheming mind-set,' Melthus had said. 'You will have to do.'

Oh flattery.

'There are Newborn who may need assistance to come to the nest. However, there are…complications. You are accustomed to dealing with agents of the Constabulary, I am told.'

Uh?

Oh.

'Cops, you mean? Yeah. Kind of.'

'Very well. This is what I want you to do…'

CHAPTER FOURTEEN

Monday 23.00

It had taken a few hours to ascertain whether the Anglican Church still used the cemetery in Tepid Ashton, which was a disappointment given their arrival at the bone yard with blue lights and sirens.

'Kind of steals your thunder, don't it?' Clive commented.

The chapel itself was locked. This was probably just as well; a good fart* in a downwind would have brought the entire structure down.

Eventually, the two Constables found someone who explained that the parish of Tepid Ashton was one of several that came under the See of Bristol. The Rural Dean had appointed someone to hold services, but they hadn't met him yet. 'Wainwright,' the churchwarden said. 'He has the living of Box.'

'Really,' said Clive. He'd never understood Church Speak. He left the talking to Baz, who did. He was Welsh. It was enough for Clive.

'He means that Wainwright's main parish is Box but has responsibility for organizing services in the outlying districts when necessary,' said Barry.

'Some job.' Clive hefted the keys on the iron ring. He wanted to get a look inside the chapel before midnight. It was no less dark at this time of night, as the month turned toward mid-winter, but… things happened in churchyards around midnight. Or did you have to walk anti-clockwise around the chapel, patting your head while reciting a *Megadeth* album backwards?

'No,' said Barry, who knew his young partner and others of like mind. The English, he thought, had never got the hang of religion. They confused it with chocolate eggs and the ghost of the Black bleeding Monk, or the Grey friggin' Abbot, and misquoted bits from the Book of Revelation. All a bit Winnie-the-Pooh meets Damien Thorn.

They were after grave robbers, although they didn't mention this to the churchwarden. The churchyard had had only one recent burial. A young lady, name of Sarah Fortes…Fergu…Far†... couldn't remember the rest. Couldn't miss it, though. It was the only plot with a fresh memorial and newly turned earth. Why? Was it important?

'Probably not,' said Barry, beginning to doubt the verisimilitude of certain information gathered at The Pigs. He remembered the name, and thought that the lass had been buried with indecent haste for a murder victim.

---

* I suppose some people may consider that this stopped being funny at page 55: wrong.

† No. Not this time.

Farquaarson. *Sarah Farquaarson.* 'Many thanks.' Barry tipped the churchwarden a salute, took Clive discreetly by the elbow and propelled him back to the churchyard.

'Why don't we just chuck it in for today?' said Clive. It was late, they still hadn't clocked off at the station and overtime had not been granted. He was getting cold, hungry and frustrated in his own time.

'Because,' said Barry, and left it at that.

They entered the cemetery by the gate, although the wall surrounding it was barely four feet high. Stone had been taken over the years. There were gaps in the boundary that owed much to water features and rockeries in gardens around the district. 'Hardly secure,' sniffed Clive.

'Well observed,' agreed Barry. 'You'd think they'd put some electrified fences up.'

'Ah. The piss take,' said Clive. 'Right on cue.'

Barry had a torch. It was a very big torch, the biggest that Mag-Lite could make and still leave a hand free to release your partner's bra strap. He pulled this out of his coat pocket.

Clive had one, too. His wasn't as big. His face bespoke no small degree of Mag-Lite envy.

They were alone in the cemetery. There were no lights. Wisps of mist wove between headstones, trees and weeds, luminescent. The nearest houses were all dark, no one around to call *Crimestoppers* or order a pizza. Or hear a scream for help.

'Come to the Dark Side,' said Clive. He held his torch, double handed, pointing at the sky. He switched it on. A beam of light appeared, special effect laser sounds courtesy of Clive's missing front teeth. 'Pish-oom,' he said, waving his light sabre. 'Whirr-rowrr.'

'What the fuck are you doing, Clive?'

'The Force is strong with you, Skywalker.'

'Stop pratting about.' Barry switched his torch on.

'Pish-oom,' said Clive.

Barry ignored him.

They did not have far to walk before they found what they were looking for. And a lot more that they weren't.

'I thought he said there'd been only one burial?' said Clive. 'Willawobble. Rurr-rup. Whir-rowrr.'

'Stop waving that torch about.' Barry concentrated the beam of his own torch on the pile of earth.

'Aaargh,' said Clive. His light sabre no longer cut the night air into chunks, although it was cold enough to require a power tool of some kind. It was almost tangible, the air up here. It hurt your sinuses to inhale through your nose. But Clive wasn't thinking about that. He was thinking that he might have broken something.

'What are you doing down there, Clive?' said Barry with exaggerated patience.

'Is this someone's idea of a joke?' said the injured party.

'I told you to stop pissing about.'

'But an open grave… bloody irresponsible.'

'Is there a coffin?' said Barry.

'What?'

'A casket. Since you're down there, have a look.'

Clive did. 'No.' He tried to get out of the hole, slipped, fell back in. As he hit dirt, something sounded hollow, and it wasn't his heartfelt oath to get a proper job. There was indeed a long box between his feet. It was mostly filled in, the hole, but now he saw that bits of wood lay around. 'Have a look at this.'

Barry stood by the grave, his torch directed into it. He could see footprints in the loose soil. Not the sort left by Wellies or police issue boots. Whoever had been stamping down this soil had to have been barefoot.

'Leave it for now,' said Barry. He held out his hand for Clive, pulled him up and out. 'We might need a cast of those prints later.'

He turned his attention to the pile of earth. There was too much of it to belong to the last resting-place of Sarah Farquaarson. The hole wasn't deep enough. 'We have several possibilities. One, the churchwarden was lying. Two, he wasn't aware that someone had been digging holes elsewhere.'

'He might be high on angel dust,' said Clive.

'There is also the matter of the whereabouts of Joel and Dad Sampson.'

'Who're they, Baz?'

'They'd be the grave robbers, Clive. Remember?'

'Come to the Dark side, Luke. I am your father.'

'And they haven't been seen for a couple of days. Are you starting to see a pattern emerge here?'

Clive holstered his light sabre. 'What do you want to do?'

'Go find some liquid plaster,' said Barry, as if this was a reasonable request at eleven o'clock at night.

'Any particular brand, colour, consistency?'

'There's a pottery up the road. Potters use plaster to make moulds,' said Barry. 'Step lively, Clive. It's almost midnight. And you know what happens in graveyards at midnight. Woohooharharr.'

Clive needed no further prompting. By quarter to, he was back. The potter had come along for the ride. 'It's resin,' explained he. 'Quick setting. I thought I'd better assist the police with their enquiries.'

Not someone to scoff at one so public spirited, Barry thanked him. In fact, the potter turned out to be more than that. He was a faucet of information, as opposed to a mine of it. In a mine you had to pick at the bits you wanted and hammer it out. However, once turned on, the potter needed a new washer to turn him off again. Barry listened…and, as the potter spoke, he became aware that he was abnormally tired…

…And the man's voice was all that he could think of.

'Tragic,' he said, as he laid slats of wood to isolate the best complete footprint. The potter mixed up his casting solution and poured it into the mould.

'How did she die?' said Barry, rubbing his eyes.

'Murder, they do say[*].'

'Who says?'

'The locals.'

'Around here?' said Clive.

'Well, yeah.' The potter made the face that says *Duh*. 'Sarah was local. Bit of a wild one, Sarah.' The resin had set. The potter, who introduced himself belatedly as Frank, knocked the slats away and turned the cast over. A perfect print had been lifted. The resin had picked up some of the crystals of ground frost, making the bas-relief print glisten.

'Anyway,' resumed Frank, 'some bizarre cult got her, I do reckon.[†]'

Barry looked at Clive, and Clive looked right back.

'Cult?' said Clive. 'What kind of cult?'

Frank shrugged. 'One of them New Age things. You know. Prancing around in robes on Glastonbury Tor, sort of Cult.' He was admiring the quality of his handiwork. 'Is this a scene of crime thing, or what?'

Barry gave him the fish eye. *This man likes attention. He gets his rocks off by close proximity to officialdom. I bet he isn't here just to help.* 'We don't know yet. This cult,' he said. 'Where do they meet?'

---

[*] An outrageous lampoon of Wiltshire dialect. In case you were interested.

[†] They don't really talk like that. Well, mostly. Then again, they *do* drink a lot of cider.

Frank laughed. ''Tisn't like going to Chapel, officer. They meet in secret.' He caught Barry and Clive giving him a look. 'Not that I'd know,' he added. 'But some odd things have been going on. You know about the *Phantom*?'

The officers nodded.

'Well, the victims all died in Box Woods, yes?'

Another nod.

'Well, guy I know says that the bodies were found exsanguinated.'

'Come again?' said Clive.

'Drained of blood,' said Barry.

'And more,' said Frank. 'Did you know that at least one of the bodies disappeared from the mortuary?'

'We did,' said Barry. 'But that information wasn't released. Or the bit about exsanguinations. So who's the friend?'

'Can't say,' said Frank.

'I can make this more formal, if you prefer.' Barry pulled out his handcuffs.

'Can't say because I was lying. 'Twern't no friend. 'Twas me.' Frank puffed out his chest. He seemed oddly pleased about it.

'You? *You f*ound out all that? How?' said Clive, notebook in hand.

'I was there when each of the bodies was hauled away – in the woods. Most of Box was, come to think about it. You could've sold tickets. They couldn't find any tracks or footprints – the police, I mean.'

'Okay. What about the missing bodies?' said Clive, his pen busy.

'I work part time as an occupational therapist up at the Infirmary.' Frank made a face of the guilty type. 'I put on my white coat one morning, to start work. I got a call to ask me to go and accept delivery of a load of clay. I didn't bother to take my coat off. You wouldn't believe how differently people treat you when they think that you're a doctor. I passed them on the corridors. Catch someone's eye, they nod at you; you ask a question, you get an answer. Respect, see? And all I had to do was put on my white coat.' Frank began biting his thumbnail. 'Is this still unofficial?'

'For now,' said Barry. He put up a hand to silence Clive, who was about to object in the strongest terms. 'This could be useful.'

'Right. Okay. Anyway,' Frank continued. 'I, um, decided to go walkabout in this white coat. There were parts of the hospital I've always wanted to see.'

'The parts with locked doors?' said Clive.

'Yes. It's an amazing thing, to be able to move about like that, unchallenged. Well, I ended up at the mortuary. There's a hell of a fuss going on. Pathologists, doctors, technicians and some blokes I'd never seen before. They turned out to be detectives.'

'Then what happened?' said Barry.

'I kind of hung back, slipped into the pathologist's office. There were case notes.'

'Which case, exactly?' said Clive.

'*Phantom* victim…last week, maybe. Anyway, the body was missing and there's all these coppers saying things like, "you must have made a mistake, doc. She couldn't have been dead." And the pathologist, he went apeshit…but, like I said, I found case notes. In his desk.'

'*In* the desk,' said Clive.

'And you read them,' prompted Barry.

Frank shook his head. 'Not in great detail. All those long Latin words and medical terminology made my eyes water. But I know what exsanguination means. There was another bit I understood, too. The wound in her neck, presumably the fatal injury, showed indications that it was healing. That last bit was underlined. Which made me think.'

'Oh, you did, did you?' said Barry, in the sad tone of one who may soon have to perform an unpleasant duty. He fingered his cuffs, held discreetly out of view.

'You see, I recognised the name. Sarah Farquaarson. I'd never seen the inside of a mortuary before. To be honest, I was disappointed – nothing like *Quincy* – and I wasn't expecting the smell -'

'Just cut to the interesting bit, Frank.' Clive said, pen busy.

'Well, naturally I started thinking.'

'Naturally,' said Barry. 'Where's all this leading, Frank?'

'All right, don't rush me! It was damning – I mean, I know I'm not medically trained or nuffing, but it seemed to me that the "corpse" was showing signs of life. Maybe she wasn't dead. That wouldn't do the pathologist's career any good, would it?'

To Barry, this didn't add up. The Forensic Pathologist had pronounced her dead at the crime site. Nevertheless, the tale was intriguing and he allowed the potter to continue.

Frank's eyes glistened as he told his story. He was clearly enjoying spilling his guts. Barry wondered if the man was on medication or something.

He was admitting to offences that carried a stiff penalty. Perhaps now would be the time to caution him. It seemed only fair.

'Frank, slow down. This is taking the piss. You can't expect me to listen to all this without warning you.'

'Noted, officer. But somehow I don't think you'll be arresting me.'

'You must be mistaking me for a clueless git, mate.' Barry stroked his chin, as if thinking of a way to proceed. He leaned toward their informant's ear, the better to whisper into it. 'My partner here, for example: he hasn't made an arrest in the past forty-eight hours. I think we need a bit more than your assurances to keep him in his cage.'

'Feckin' 'ell Baz, let him talk,' said Clive, constantly scribbling.

'My point,' continued Frank, 'is this; the pathologist didn't say anything to the police about this file. I saw him give a different set of notes to the detectives. When the rozzers had gone-'

'Ay, watch it,' cautioned Clive.

'-When the *police* had gone, the pathologist - I don't know how he knew, but he told me to hand over the missing file.'

'Which you did, being the sort of man you are,' prompted Barry.

'Well…I told him I would if…if he'd arrange for me to have a proper doctor's coat and ID and a steffosope.'

'Steffosope,' wrote Clive. Then he paused. 'Steffosope?'

Barry waved his partner to silence. 'So what did he say?'

Frank shook his head. 'He went apeshit. "Are you trying to blackmail me?" he says; "Yes," says I. " And then you'll get the missing file". Well, he went bugshit, didn't he?'

'As opposed to apeshit?' said Clive.

Frank ignored him in much the same way that you try to ignore the fact that the bit of food stuck between your teeth has legs.

'He threatened to tell the police. I suggested he do what he must do. Then I walked out.'

Frank paused to light a cigarette. He started taking heavy pulls on it. Rapid, successive drags. And he was sweating like a bank manager at the Pearly Gates.

'Next day,' said he, 'a box turns up at the workshop. It's a white coat. Badge. Everything. Even a steffosope.'

'How d'you spell that again?' said Clive, frowning.

'And did you use them?' said Barry.

'No. I didn't have the nerve. What if I was roped in to help in an emergency? I could kill someone.'

Barry nodded with relief. 'That's the one thing you could've said that would redeem you.' He put his cuffs away.

'But I did wear them the once.'

Barry paused, his fingers straying once more to his irons. 'Go on,' he prompted, cautious.

'I used it to get into the mortuary. I wanted to see if there was anything…I dunno...'

'Something you could use against him?'

'Yeah. In case he went to the police anyway.'

'So you found something?' said Clive, and his tone was hopeful.

' Aye, I did. But it wasn't criminal, exactly. Just some stuff about the wildlife centre, up in the Woods. Financial stuff. The pathologist had his finger in a few other pies, too. Very busy man. He funds all kinds of things out of his own pocket – the centre, archaeological digs, even an expedition to South America by some cryp. Crypto. Crypto-somethings.'

Frank was lighting another cigarette.

'But I was caught. He walked in while I was going through his desk. He threw me out.' Frank blew smoke down his nostrils. 'And *that's* why I'm telling you all this, because I believe he really will tell the police. He plays golf with the chief Constable. I wanted to tell you my side of the story before I got a knock on the door.' He shook his head. 'It's been freaking me out for days.'

'Is that all of it?' said Barry.

'I think.'

Barry nodded thoughtfully. 'All right. Thanks for the information. We'll take things from here.' He turned away from Frank, making it clear that he was through listening to tale telling. The pathologist had some answers to give but Barry wasn't interested in what he got up to in his spare time.

'Although there was one other thing,' added Frank, apparently oblivious of the concept of Quitting While You're Ahead. 'While I was rooting about in his desk, I found a box file full of news clippings. All about the *Phantom* murders. And others.'

Barry rolled his eyes then turned to treat Frank to his grade A Copper's Stare. '*Others*?'

'Yeah. You didn't know that there've been other murders, occasionally, over the years? They were all the same MO – bloodless victim, no tracks – and all in rural areas, isolated spots.'

'Really. Now, *that's* fascinating. And you say this pathologist keeps all his records at the hospital?'

'Weeell, maybe not *all.* If poor Sarah can go walkabout…' Frank left the sentence unfinished and managed to look outraged.

'What's the name of this pathologist?' said Clive, looking up from his notebook.

'Pitt. Bartholomew Pitt, I think. Or it might be Leonard.'

'They're not exactly similar, are they? Which is it?' Clive snapped. It was too cold to be hanging on the words of some creepy twat in the backside of Wiltshire.

'There's no call for personal abuse,' said Frank, his lip trembling. I'm only trying to 'elp.'

Clive paled. 'Did I actually say…'

'It's been a long day,' sighed Barry. 'Frank, I apologise for my partner's lack of social skills, but stick to the point.'

'It was Len. Leonard.'

'You've been a great help, Frank,' said Barry.

'Pleased to,' said Frank. 'Pleased to.'

'And now I'm arresting you,' said Barry.

'What?' yelped Frank.

'For talking a load of bollocks, for a start. If Miss Farquaarson woke up on Dr. Pitt's autopsy table, why is the casket in her grave? What really happened, Frank? What did you forget to say?'

'They'll throw the book at you. Impersonating a doctor? Tut, and tut.' Clive wiped dribble from his chin but his pen did not stop.

'No, listen. All right. Sarah didn't just walk away.' Frank licked his lips.

'I know. You smuggled her out, didn't you?' said Barry.

Clive's pen applied ABS brakes. 'What?'

Frank narrowed his eyes and stared at Barry. 'Yes. And the answer to your next question is twenty grand. *Twenty thou*, just to drop her into a box and bury her. It was the last place anyone would think to look.' Frank sniffed. 'I reckon her parents called in a few favours, to avoid awkward questions. Like, every murder victim had to have a post mortem, yeah?'

'Twenty thousand,' repeated Barry. 'I hope it was worth it.'

Frank shrugged. 'I thought I'd got away with it until I saw you two show up. I knew you'd find the grave, see. Like those other two.'

Clive's eyebrows met in the middle. 'I think I lost you three paragraphs ago.' He threw the pen over his shoulder.

'Sarah Farquaarson, Clive. Only daughter of Mr. and Mrs. Theodopolous Farquaarson, of the *Giblet And Offal And Other Slimy Bits* dynasty (catering and parties by commission). They paid Frank to smuggle their daughter out of the mortuary and save her from the last indignity.'

'At last, someone we can arrest' said Clive.

'Yes, young Obi Wan. Charge him. Impersonating a physician will do to begin with. We'll work up to body snatching from there.'

'But-' said Frank.

'But me no buts. Don't worry. You'll probably get off with a community service sentence.'

'But I'll still be convicted! I need that job at the hospital. Pottery doesn't pay like it used to. They all go to *Argos* for their china these days.' Frank's voice had taken on a whining, pleading quality.

Barry made a noise that sounded, much to Frank's relief, like "hmmmm".

'I suppose…nah. You wouldn't go for it.' Barry took out his handcuffs.

'Wait! *No*. Tell me.'

'Well…we could dispense with the whole court thing, and the media coverage – body snatching is right up there with kiddy fiddling, you know – and then there's the fine.'

'Fine?' croaked Frank.

'Yup. Hefty one. Serious offence, see?' said Barry.

'So. Assuming that we could skip the, um, actual *convicting*…?' Frank prompted him.

'We could go straight to the community service.'

'What do you suggest?' said Frank.

'Weelll…we could start right here.' Barry kicked some dirt at the edge of the curiously shallow grave of Sarah Farquaarson. 'You know of any other burials in the past couple of days?'

'Nup. I know Wainwright. He despises funerals. If there had been one, he'd have been griping about it down at the Quarryman's Arms.'

'Do you have a spade?' said Barry.

Frank gave him a look which indicated that he suspected something brown and organic was about to fall on him from a high altitude. 'I do,' he said, slowly.

'Then let's work off your debt to society.' Barry smiled at Frank.

Frank looked a bit sick.

*

Tuesday 18th 2001 07.00.

'Shit,' said Clive.

The grave had been opened. Fully opened. Grey light* on the horizon. Almost time for brekkie. But Clive didn't think he would want breakfast this morning.

'Notice anything odd?' said Barry. He was looking into the grave.

'Apart from two mutilated stiffs, where there shouldn't be any, sort of thing?'

'*People*, Clive. Please. One's Joel Sampson, the other's his Dad, Dougal. I liked 'em.' Barry removed his cap, ruffled his hair. 'There's no smell.'

'They've only been there a couple of days at most, Baz.'

'Still,' Barry said. He began looking for tracks around the graves, but there were no more footprints in this frost-hardened earth. Even his boots barely made a mark. 'No blood.'

'I noticed.' Clive blew into his hands, for the meagre warmth that was in it. 'Change of MO for the *Phantom*, eh?'

They were waiting for the forensic team. DI Bratt was coming over. He had to square things with the Superintendent at Corsham nick, who, Bratt informed them, was livid. He should have been informed, he told them (at this point, Barry had to hold the mobile 'phone from his ear). They had no warrant to exhume a grave, even an unidentified one.

'We don't know it's the *Phantom*,' said Barry to Clive.

'But the neck wounds – like, you wouldn't be able to clean up that much blood. No tracks, either.'

'Ah,' said Barry, raising a finger, 'but we have.' He held up the rubber cast.

Which is mandatory for a Monday morning, but since this was Tuesday…well, frankly, I'm baffled.

'Could be anybody's. And no one commits that,' said Clive, jabbing a thumb at the two corpses in the single grave, 'in bare feet.' He smirked a smirk that would have earned him a smack in the kisser in other, less tedious circumstances.

'Clive, we know sweet bugger all; somebody was planted last week, and she isn't here now.' They looked at Sarah Farquaarson's headstone.

'Do you think it *was* a cult?' said Clive. 'Some kind of twisted ritual involving traffic wardens and meat packing assistants?'

Barry gave him a weary look. It was too late – or possibly, given the hour, too early – to berate his junior partner for his sense of humour. He hoped it was a joke, at any rate. He was tempted to be worried about Clive, sometimes. Like his tendency to speak his thoughts aloud at inconvenient moments. 'Do I really need to answer that?'

And, thought Barry, *I already regret not arresting Frank. Too,* too *convenient to find him tonight. I must be getting too old for this job.*

Clive shook his head. 'I dunno, Baz; they use all kinds of 'orrible stuff in Satanic rites.'

'You're an expert, are you?'

'I know a bit,' said Clive, who'd seen all of Denis Wheatley's films, and actually read his books, even without the use of helpful diagrams.

'Then you'll do the talking,' said Barry. 'But first, find Frank. He was trying to climb out of the hole a minute ago.'

The first of the Forensic team's vans drew up just beyond the cemetery wall. The crew in the back jumped out. They unloaded rolls of something or other. As work progressed, the something or other turned out to be a large tent…and a tent within that…and a tent within that.

Bratt arrived ahead of the Wiltshire police. He made straight for Clive and Barry. He looked angry. Extremely angry.

'Still want me to do the talking?' said Clive.

'Are you going to quote *The Devil Rides Out*?'

'But it all fits! Look…'

'I'll handle this,' said Barry.

Bratt stood before them; he was trembling. A vein pulsed, just below his left eye. He did not say anything.

'Guv'nor?' prompted Barry.

'Shut up! I'm just trying to remember what I was going to say to you'.

'Was it bad?' said Clive.

'There were many swear words.'

'I'm sorry we didn't find the bin men, Sir, but-'

Bratt closed his eyes and snorted. 'Don't. Even. Start.'

There was an awkward silence. The two Constables watched the scenes of crime bods doing complicated things with tent pegs.

'Bradshaw is going to make my life utterly miserable for this,' muttered Bratt. Then, aloud, and for the benefit of his junior officers, whom he always regarded as partially deaf, he said 'Piss off out of my sight. Get some sleep. I want you in for the midnight shift tonight. That's *tonight*. Understand?'

'Yes, S-'

'And I want a full report by the time I next see you.'

'Yes, S-'

'Still here?'

The weary Constables slogged the hundred yards or so to their jam sarnie, each lost to their own personal despair, wondering if they would have a job to go to upon the evening.

Strangely – or perhaps not – they thought no more upon the curious disappearance of Frank; they saw nothing untoward as they pulled away from the kerb, avoiding the growing number of interested locals rubbernecking over the wall. Possibly because the untoward bit was happening elsewhere. Not far away.

*

The coroner's driver saw movement at the corner of his eye, to the right, but that was all he saw. The fist that punched through the window was too fast, and while the engine ticked over, the passengers at the rear of the van were seized.

Frank slipped his shades from his eyes as he grunted with the weight of his load. There was a lot of smoke, now, and clothes and skin began to smoulder as the weak winter sun clawed its way bloody mindedly into the cloudy sky. He poked around in the undergrowth around a bank of earth, a few hundred yards from all the activity. He found what he was looking for and, with one last look around, he pushed through the screen of bushes to the hole in the earth behind it, two pairs of legs belonging to Joel and Dougal Sampson, grave robbers extraordinaire, trailing behind until they too disappeared into the shrubs.

A thoroughly nasty man, our Frank, and no mistake.

CHAPTER FIFTEEN

Tuesday. Late afternoon.

Unaware that they were fugitives from justice, George and Ted had squandered the past day and a half in a frenzy of substance abuse. Thus, if they had they known such, they would not have given a toss.

'Interesting phrase, that,' said Ted.

'What? Pass me that joint, my old mucker.' George had his feet up. Their biker friend, whom they knew as Dai (and they saw no reason to disbelieve it), had treated them royally. The skeletons of a Chinese take-out for three lay all around. It had been a strange twenty-four hours, for sure, what with discovering the dog in the skip – or rather, the dog that was *not* a dog, because a canine had no business using language like that. And the terrible injuries. Not to mention the loss of their employment. And the purloining of the means of said employment did not rate a mention, either.

It was all too depressing.

'To give not a toss. What kind of toss, anyway? The toss of a coin, perchance, or some other handy object? Or the masturbatory kind?' Ted was genuinely interested, but then he *was* stoned off his face.

'I think you'll find it's an old kind of currency, bud. Used to be a grope. It became a toss with the introduction of pounds and shillings,' said George. He was unaccustomed to bullshit, but he found that he was quite good at it.

'So what's a toss worth, then?' said Ted, impressed with his colleague's knowledge of mediaeval currency.

'With inflation…today's prices…about a tenner.'

'You're both talking bollocks,' said their host, Dai the biker, except he didn't have a bike (at *present*, he told them) and got about the city by hijacking commercial vehicles. 'And deliberately straying from the point. You said the dog was smoking when it came out of the skip?'

'It started smoking as soon as the lid was lifted,' said Ted.

'Certainly *sounded* like a dog,' said George. 'At first, anyway. But it was definitely an arm that shot out and slammed the lid.' He belched, tasted bile, took a sip from his bottle of Dirty* and swallowed. He licked beer foam off his lips. 'To be honest,' – George leaned forward confidentially – 'there

---

*Bottle of Dirty: Newcastle Brown Ale. The best reason for living in England

was more than a hint of the eldritch about the whole thing. That was not a normal creature we caught.'

'You don't know how close to the truth you are,' said Dai.

'Do *you* know the truth of it?' asked Ted. Not that he wanted an explanation, unless it came with pictures and a happy ending. 'Do yer? Ay?' Belch.

'Not all of it. Not yet. But I'm close.' There was a bit of a pause.

'Close to what?' said George.

'Something I wish I didn't have to face up to. No one else has a clue about what's going on. Who's going to do it, if not us?'

'Right on,' said Ted, thinking that that was how the younger generation spoke these days. 'Respect,' he added.

'Close to what?' persisted George. 'And *do* what?'

'You'd better want to know,' said Dai, suddenly solemn.

'Did you say, “us”, just now? Ay?' said Ted to Dai.

'I owe you both an explanation,' said he. 'You might find it as difficult to swallow as the Chow Mein Special, but it's all true.'

And so, with evident emotional strain, Dai told them about his girl, the argument in the Woods and the harsh words that had sent them both flouncing off into opposite directions. Of the night spent waiting for her to call, only to discover that a body had been found in the Woods late the previous day, after sunset, by a Reverend Wainwright. 'The life had been drained out of her,' said Dai. He picked up a bottle of scotch that had been doing the rounds, tilted it to his mouth and finished it off in one long swallow. 'Huge bite to the neck.'

'What did you tell the police?' said Ted, a frown creasing his brow.

'Nothing,' said Dai. 'I haven't spoken to the police. I was with her shortly before she died. We'd had a major blow-up; like, I'm going to tell the cops we'd all but knocked each other's teeth out just before she got...killed...'

'But they'll find you,' argued Ted. 'They'll talk to her mates. Her mates will tell 'em she was seeing you. The police'll think it's a bit strange that you didn't come forward.'

'Sound logic, Ted, and I'll not argue. That's why I'm on the road, right now, innit?'

'Yeah, right,' said George, looking around at the comfortable room in which they had spent the entire day rolling big fat roonies and swallowing beer. Even the fire was real, a big open hearth with logs. It practically demanded that someone should start the drunken bollock-talk with ghost stories. It had a good feeling about it, this house. Like the man, really. Both Ted and George had enjoyed his company.

'This isn't my house,' said Dai. I'm out in a couple of days.'

'Shame,' said George. 'Your friend's place?'

'No. My mate's crib is around the corner and several miles up the road. I think the Jones's live here.'

'You know the Jones's well, then?'

'No. That's why I've got to be out in forty-eight hours. They'll call the cops when they see the state of this place.'

George took his feet of the table.

'Then we are truly bonded by our misfortune,' said Ted, coming over all Winston Churchill.

' Aye,' said Dai. 'The cops would nick the lot of us, so they would. But listen, lads. I have a plan.'

'Oh, good,' said Ted. 'Best to have a plan, ay?'

'Let's hear it, Bud,' said George.

'We find the *Phantom*.' Dai took a deep pull on the number he was smoking and blew rings out of his ears. It was a strange way to fill another pause, but better than lots of boring narrative.

'Is that it?': George.

'Ay? *We*?': Ted.

'Obviously, we shall need to fill in the details.'

There was another pause, just like the other one, but longer. Dai did not perform tricks with smoke, either.

'Details. Yes. Such as, where do we start? What are we looking for?' said George.

Dai sucked in air.

'What?' said George.

'Exactly,' said Dai, pointing at George.

'Uh?'

'What,' repeated Dai. '*What* are we looking for. Not *Whom*.'

'If you're going to start with ghost stories I'm going home,' said Ted. 'Okay in daylight, bad idea at night. Especially after such extravagant use of Category C drugs.'

'We'll turn a light on,' offered George.

'No, we won't,' said Dai. ''Leccy's off while the Jones's are in Spain. I don't want the neighbours to know I'm here.'

'But there's a bloody great rubbish truck parked on the lawn. Isn't that a giveaway?' said George, with the suggestion of a guffaw.

'People park stranger things around here. And not necessarily on their own lawns.'

George nodded, conceded the point. Hadn't they had to jostle for the space with an armoured patrol carrier that very morning? 'Ted, it grieves me to distress you, but I like supernatural stuff. Carry on, Dai.'

The biker began by discussing the facts known regarding the *Phantom's* modus operandi. Everyone in Box village knew about the blood, or lack of it, and the absence of any tracks or other clues to explain how the victim got there.

'Don't mention neck wounds,' Ted pleaded.

'Of course,' said Dai. 'Now, when a major blood vessel in the cervical region is compromised, it's nothing you'd want to stick on a greetings card, innit? Blood doesn't just ooze. It jets,' he said, miming great geysers of blood from his neck, 'all over the place. Likely, the surrounding trees and bushes would be covered in it. You could try to clean it up, but you could never be sure, could you? And why bother if you were going to leave the body where anyone can find it?'

Ted and George shrugged. Such matters were beyond their experience.

'Furthermore,' said Dai, rolling another roonie, 'logic dictates that the body did not get there by flying.'

'Evidently,' agreed George. It seemed a safe point upon which to concur.

'Wrong,' said Dai. 'Because, as Sherlock once said, take away the impossible, and whatever's left, even if it's impossible, must be possible. Or something. Don't quote me. I'm ratarsed.'

'But if you take away the impossible, you have no explanation at all, in that case. People can't fly,' said Ted, wrestling with the logic of that statement.

'Yeah. Well, old Sherlock was known to say other things, like, "Go and score us a couple of rocks of H, Watson," and "Pass me that syringe, will ya?"'

'Holmes was a crack head?' said Ted, scandalised.

'This is so far off the point, I wish I hadn't said anything,' said Dai. 'All I'm saying is the victim had to have been transported to the site by some means. If they didn't walk, drive, drop in by helicopter or beam down from the star ship *Enterprise*, they must have…levitated.'

'Isn't that like council tax?' said Ted, filling in the space where a bit of a pause should be.

'No. It is a Yogic phenomenon. When the Yoga master reaches oneness with his mind and the cosmic beat of the universal heart, levitation has been witnessed, innit?'

'So,' said George, 'you're saying that all of the victims were Yoga masters. Well, should be easy to trace the killer, then. "Sobviously some bitter and twisted old Yoga instructor, knocking off his students because they've attained oneness, and he hasn't. It all fits! Well done, Dai.' George clinked his bottle of Dirty against Dai's empty scotch bottle.

'No, George. You have a remarkable mind, don't get me wrong, but sometimes you give me the impression that you're thick as pig shit. What I am in fact saying, is, that we have to look at the whole problem laterally. Take an indirect poke at it. Because pure logic, at the end of the day, when all's said and done, is…' Dai searched for the right phrase.

'Twatty bollocks,' said Ted.

'Inadequate,' corrected Dai, 'is what I was going to say.'

'No. Twatty bollocks. I know what you're trying to say, Dai. I'm going home.'

'Stay, Ted. Hear him out.'

'Don't wanner listen to spooky stuff.'

'He's not suggesting anything of the sort,' said George.

'I am,' said Dai.

'He is,' said Ted. He sat down again in a bit of a huff, and scowled at them both. 'Go on, then. Let's hear it.'

'You've heard the rumours about the Beast of Bodmin, and other yarns about big creatures killing cattle and sheep.' Dai let the question dangle in the air. While he waited for a reply, he sparked up the jay he'd been rolling then helped himself to another bottle of malt from the Jones's drinks cabinet.

'They're escaped cougars, or something, aren't they?' said Ted.

'They had a big cat tracker checking that line of enquiry,' said Dai. 'It wasn't a cougar, lion, leopard, cheetah, or anything of a feline nature.'

'Then the Beast of Bodmin does not exist, QED.'

'And yet the sheep continue to die, Ted. The problem does not go away because the logical explanation fails; no, *something* is killing wildlife and livestock, and it isn't a sheep dog with ideas above its station. Sheepdogs do not drink up to a gallon of blood at one sitting.'

'How about two sittings?' said Ted, who wished that he could go home and turn all the lights on. He had been drinking beer, whisky, vodka and tequila. He had sucked cannabis resin and skunk, in water pipe and rollie, but he could not totally overcome the sick feeling of dread and helplessness when he thought about what had happened that morning. Certain facts had to be dealt with. He never lied to himself, or others, because he knew that he didn't have the memory to be a good liar. Indeed, his first and last romance, an unrequited love affair involving a disinterested and unimpressed Careers Advisor Lady, had ended when Ted had finally pestered her into going for a drink. He had hired a car for the occasion. He wanted to show her that he was a man of means. 'Nice wheels,' said the Careers Advisor Lady. 'But…a Ferrari? Am I supposed to be impressed?' 'Well, yes,' Ted had replied. 'The guy at the shop said it was a fanny* magnet.'

'Ted, please, don't digress. A dog does not sit at a torn neck, drinking the stuff like it was on tap. Even a sheepdog, psychotic as the breed is known to be. No, gentlemen. I think I know what lies behind those stories, just as I feel you will agree, once the facts are laid bare, that my theory is the only one that makes sense. Innit?'

'He means, it was a vampire,' said Ted, blurting it out. 'Oh God.'

'What?' said George. 'The Beast of Bodmin is a vampire? That was never on *News at Ten.*'

'Nosferatu,' said Dai, shaking his head wearily. 'Forget about the Beast of bloody Bodmin. That was just an example. Wamphyri, is what I'm talkin' about. The Undead. Cheers for stealing my thunder, Ted.'

'Sorry, but I had to admit it. What I saw this morning…It's going to keep haunting my every waking hour until it's all out in the open,' said Ted.

'Not to mention every sleeping hour,' said George. 'You'll never be able to rest, knowing what you do.'

'Yeah, thanks a lot, George. There's always insomnia to look forward to, ay?'

'Come on now, lads. No need for rancour. What we need to do is pull together the facts we know and act upon them.' Dai grinned then pulled hard on the joint. His grin grew wider.

George and Ted, after no small degree of differing, if not bickering, finally agreed that the Thing In The Skip had been a girl. A slim girl, dressed in a short leather skirt. Nice legs. Athletic. Only the upper half of her body

* Note for American readers: it doesn't mean bottom, in England. Oh no.

had been covered in the warden's tarpaulin as she was hauled, kicking and screaming, from the skip. Her legs had been smoking, beginning to scorch, and there hadn't been time to have a closer look at her. Only the importunate dog warden had seen her face close up, and that had turned his mind.

'He kept saying something about werewolves,' said George. 'Of course, we didn't pay much attention at the time, what with the ambulance and the paramedics and all the blood. But what if he *did* see something…something beyond our ken?'

'Eldritch and beyond our ken,' repeated Dai, clapping his hands. 'Brilliant. You're both getting into the spirit of it.'

'What's he on about?' said Ted.

'Dunno,' said George. 'He's never met our Ken. I rang him this morning to see what he thought. It was beyond him. Straight as a die, our Ken is.'

'But the fact remains,' said Dai, 'that you have dared to face the truth. Knowing what we know about vampires, what would you say would be the likeliest outcome of being bitten by such a creature?'

Dai looked at Ted. Ted looked at George. George ignored them both and settled for a good long toot on the big fat number now being circulated.

'Okay, Dai.' George puffed the yellow smoke down his nose as he spoke. 'What're you suggesting – we go up to the Infirmary, like ghouls, wait for him to die then stake 'im with a big stick?'

'Yes,' said Dai. 'Discreet surveillance. We go in, like normal visitors. We watch. If he dies, we follow the body. We get to the body, we stake it through the heart. Then it's head off, and make with the petrol.'

'What was that last bit?' said George.

'Oh. I thought you knew.' Dai shook his head. 'You can't just stake a vampire. To be really sure, you have to stuff a rose down his gob, cut off the head then torch the lot.' He sniffed. 'Easy.'

'You've done this before, then.' George looked doubtful.

'Nnno. Not as such.'

'It'll be one way of finding out if we're right, though,' said Ted. 'Even if it turns out we don't need to do 'im in, or whatnot, we'd know for sure whether vampires exist.'

'*If* we do it right.' Dai looked from George to Ted. 'Could be a long wait. We'll have to be alert.'

'We should do it in shifts,' said Ted.

'This is exciting,' said George. 'Do we need crucifixes?'

'Probably.' Dai nodded.

'Do you have any?' said Ted.

'No,' admitted Dai.

George stood up, picked up a small table then smashed it against a wall. All four legs came off. 'Will these do for now?'

Dai nodded. He took the items from George, reached behind his back for the Buck knife he kept there in a pouch on his belt. He flicked it out and began sharpening the chair legs into something far more intimidating.

'You usually carry a knife?' In George's experience, only soldiers, surgeons and psychos did so.

'Very useful tools. Good for cutting yourself free when your ride falls on top of you,' said Dai.

'That's biker talk,' confided Ted to George.

'You'd know,' scoffed George.

'Actually, yes,' said Ted. He rammed his shirt sleeve up his right arm as far as it would go. He poked a nicotine-stained finger at the tattoo there. 'See?'

George narrowed his eyes. 'Maria Gives X-treme Head?'

'Not that one.'

'Oh. Who're the Slightly Desperates?'

'My 'bros,' said Ted. 'Cardiff chapter.'

'You're a Hell's Angel?' said George.

'It was a long time ago,' said Ted. 'And the past is a foreign country. And all that.'

Dai had finished hacking. 'One each' he said, throwing a sharp stick at his compadres. 'And one for reserve.'

'In case we miss?' said George.

'In case he don't go down with three in him.'

'You think he'll fight, then?' said Ted, nervous.

'Wouldn't *you*?' Dai shrugged.

Ted stood. He looked at the wall clock. It was twenty past eight. 'We'd better do this before I can change my mind,' he said. 'Let's move out.' And so they did.

'No one stakes anything unless I say,' said Dai, as they climbed into the disposal truck.

'Bossy boots,' muttered George.

CHAPTER SIXTEEN

The Manor, Tuesday evening

Lucy Emmerson watched the shadows slide across her wall and pulled herself out of the stupor she'd drunk herself into. These days, if she wanted to get gloriously bladdered, she had to work at it. Something to do with the acceleration of her metabolism, a side effect of her Curse.

Of course, The Monthly Curse had taken on a different meaning since those early lunar cycles when she had to deal with the panic of her first bleeds, compounded by the horror of finding pubic hair in the most embarrassing places. Armpits and groin she could handle, but around the end of the month she had to avoid shaking hands with anyone.

But she had learned to control that now. She had had help. Guidance. It had taken a long time to find someone who could guide her through the confusion and dread she had been facing every month for the past forty years. Lycanthropy wasn't something you learned to live with. It was something that you had to *own.*

Lucy tipped the bottle of malt and emptied it down her throat as she crossed to the window. The old tosser was in a bit of a lather. That was happening quite a lot lately, and a rare smile, one that touched her eyes, spread so far across her face that it hurt. He was so distracted, of late, that he hadn't noticed her absences from the Manor or the gaps in his defences that allowed her to entertain private guests at night.

Soon, then. Time is short. The rite will place me above this miserable existence amongst fools. Forever.

It was true, what her mentor said: You Don't Give A Name To The Pig That You Eat.

Which is probably bollocks, thought Lucy. *A lot of farmers do. But the meaning is clear: best not to think of them as anything but food. They can give you heartburn. Fatal heartburn.*

She threw the empty bottle aside, ignoring the crash and tinkle, and then opened another bottle of malt.

*

Tuesday 20.30.

'I'm really not sure about any of this' said Ted.

'Here,' said George, handing him the jay.

Ted sat next to his new buddy, in the cab of the refuse truck that they still hadn't managed to return.

'Taking his time, isn't he?' said Ted.

'He's just checking to see where the stiff is kept, is my guess.'

'The mortuary, surely.' Ted's eyes met across the bridge of his nose as he drew in smoke.

'Not necessarily. Might be in the chapel of rest waiting for relatives. If corpses can be said to wait.'

'They still do that in 'ospitals?'

'Dunno, but they wouldn't display the dearly beloved wrapped in sheets on the bottom shelf of the fridge, would they?'

Would they?

The jay was passed back and George had a good toot.

'Strange bloke,' said George.

'Who, Dai?'

'That's the geezer. I mean, until yesterday morning we'd never met. Is this not so?'

'It isn't. 'Tis, I mean.'

'And has he not become our best buddy in but a few short hours?' said George

'All hours possess the mandatory sixty minutes,' said Ted, 'but I see your point. Then you will be wondering, as I am, why we agreed to accompany him on this fool's errand, ay?'

'We're hunting vampires, ain't we?' said George, but his tone carried no conviction.*

'Are we? Looks to me like we're sitting here in a stolen truck, while our Dai goes trespassing in the Infirmary.'

'Like henchmen, you mean?' said George, pinching his face to see if it was still there.

'That'll be the way of it. Getaway drivers, or some such,' said Ted.

'Yes. My thoughts are yours, Bud.'

'Indeed.'

'Indeed.'

They sat smoking in silence.

Unlike the consequences of vehicle theft

'And then there's the category "C" drugs.' Ted shook his head, woe writ large upon his face.

'Yes. There is those lads. Are. *Are* those lads. The category "C" ones,' said George, who tooted greedily on same.

'I fear that we've been seduced into a twilight world of substance abuse, larceny and hanging about in car parks,' said Ted.

'Beats the shit out of emptying bins,' said George. 'Well, we don't have to fret about that palaver anymore. We have thoughtlessly wrecked the unemployment figures. They take a dim view of that, down at the job centre,' continued he, before Ted could interrupt. 'There's a little man who works it all out on a calculator. At the end of each working day, the tally of the unemployed is written down and carried somewhere important in a big red briefcase.'

'Where?'

'Straight to the Prime Minister's gaff, I 'spect. Anyone collars him on the doorstep in the morning, he's got the latest figures at his fingertips.'

'In his memory,' corrected Ted, lighting a fart and then giggling until he tasted bile.

'Yes. Just a metaphor, Ted.'

'They do that every day?'

'The Department of Employment is a demanding mistress,' said George.

'Is that another metaphor?' asked Ted, lighting another fart.

'Now you're getting the idea,' said George.

'Hm,' went Ted. 'You're very talented in the metaphor department, aren't you, ay, George old mate?'

George dismissed the compliment with a modest wave of his hand, spilling ash and red-hot blims* into Ted's lap and igniting more gas.

'Bet you can fit a suitable metaphor to any circumstance,' added Ted. 'My crotch is on fire.'

'If so pushed,' agreed George, flobbing† into his friend's lap. The small blaze went out.

'Now, supposing Dai came running out of that door over there with a small posse of security guards chasin' 'im, ay? Thank you, George.'

'Then I should likely liken it to a rabbit flushed from its warren,' said George, without hesitation. Or was that a simile?

---

* Blim: a bit of red hot cannabis resin that falls out of your jay and burns your chest hair. So I'm told.

† Flobbing: coughing up lung butter and spitting it out. Try not to think about it.

Ted made a face. 'What if the small posse was actually a *big* posse – say, about ten big lads – and Dai looked as if he was shitting himself?'

'Then I would liken him to a paedophile at a paediatrician's parley,' said George, 'parley being the alliterative alternative to a learned conference, symposium, or such like.' Yup. That was a simile, all right.

'It lacks a certain urgency,' said Ted.

The cab door, driver's side, was flung open. Dai scampered up. 'Lock your door,' he said.

'You seem a little breathless, Bud,' said George.

'It's the fleeing from justice that does it,' gasped Dai. He turned the ignition. It coughed like a TB victim sucking a Fisherman's Friend.*

'More choke,' said George. 'It's cold.'

Dai gave it more choke.

'We have ignition,' said Ted.

Dai threw all of his weight behind the wheel, turning it to the right.

'The exit's to the left,' said George.

'I know. So are the patrol cars.'

'Hospital security have patrol cars?' said Ted, impressed. A career in institutional policing beckoned. 'With flashing lights and sirens and stuff?'

'No. That'll be the cops.'

'The *cops*?' said George and Ted, with no small degree of alarm.

'Oh my,' wailed Ted, espying the crash barrier around the car park. The one that Dai had chosen to ignore.

'Oh deary me,' uttered George as the truck tested the crash barrier to destruction. A squeal of tires, metal (and Ted) ensued. An insane rush down the grass embankment on the other side. A squeal from George, too.

A police patrol car appeared at the broken barrier. And then a squeal from Dai, and the tires too, got their pennyworth.

'We've got to ditch this,' shouted Dai above the din of screaming diesel engine and police sirens.

'Whenever you're ready,' screamed Ted, already fumbling at the door handle.

'Not yet!' said George, grabbing a fistful of overalls. He hauled Ted from the open door just as it hit the wing of a Porsche Cabriolet. The door slammed shut, still wearing a lot of expensive Porsche bodywork. The truck shed it as Dai hauled on the steering wheel again. They were on the Bristol

---

**Fisherman's Friend: Strong throat lozenge. In case you were wondering.

road, heading toward the city centre. They could hear the sirens closing, but still distant.

'We can't hide a thing this size,' said Ted.

Dai floored the accelerator. Horns beeped and middle fingers were raised. Traffic lights were of no consequence.

'Why do people raise their middle fingers?' mused Ted between whimpers.

'It is an Americanism,' said George, armchair traveller.

'What's wrong with two fingers, ay?'

'Because people don't have a sense of history. The English longbow men would raise their two fingers to the French, to show that they were intact. Fair put the willies up 'em that did.'

'The French chopped off fingers?'

'If they caught an English archer, yes,' said George.

'*Bastards*,' said Ted.

'It's another good reason for hating the French,' explained George, lest a reason was needed.

'But what does a middle finger mean?'

'I believe it means "sit on it,"' said George, testing his memory of *Happy Days* re-runs.

'Doesn't really compare, does it?' said Ted, flicking two fingers at anyone who looked remotely French - Citroen or Peugeot drivers - and choosing to ignore the rate at which the truck was passing the other traffic.

Dai swung the wheel again. The truck heeled hard to the left, flinging the driver and passengers to the right.

'Vicky Park,' said Dai.

'It's closed, this time of night,' said Ted.

'That's the idea.' Crash, went the truck's front bumper. And crumple, too.

'Those spiked railings look terrible lethal,' said George. There was a horrible screech, like a Banshee having her first shit after a haemorrhoidectomy. Something hit the floor from beneath.

'Just keep your head down, said Dai.

'Hold on.' George removed a spiked railing from his left nostril. 'That's better.'

And indeed it was. For if the spike had still been up his hooter, the forward momentum as Dai leaned on the brakes would have skewered George.

'Like a Koala at a cuddly creatures craniotomy convention,' said the near-skewered.

'Another metaphor?' queried Ted, shaking his head with admiration.

'No. That was another simile. I think.'

'Everyone out,' said Dai. 'And follow me.'

George looked at Ted. Ted looked at George.

Sirens approached.

'Run,' said George.

'Like a bad dose of diarrhoea?' said Ted.

'Ted, shut it. Follow that dangerous individual.'

CHAPTER SEVENTEEN

Dai led them to a pub. It was as good as any place to dally, with cars and 'copters polluting the air outside.

A stray searchlight beam pierced the smoke and half-light of the public bar. A man dressed as Al Johnson, caught in the spotlight, went down on one knee and began waving his white-gloved hands. 'Mammee,' said he.

Groucho Marx scuttled past, shaking a cigar at his mouth. He didn't say anything, however, as his vocal mimicry was crap.

'What kind of bar is this?' said George.

A Jedi Knight sidled past making "vrrrming" noises and brandishing a neon strip light.

'It's unique,' said Dai. 'Everyone here is perfectly sane, I assure you.'

A Boris Karloff look-alike trundled past, dragging six-inch platform-booted footwear as he did so. He turned his flattened, riveted head in Ted's direction.

'What are you staring at?' said Frankenstein's monster.

'Great attention to detail,' said Ted, nodding and smiling before that fearsome green countenance.

'Thank you,' said the monster, a voice straight from the grave. 'Squirt.' The creature teetered on its platform hobnails. It bent down until it was face to face with Ted. 'And who are you supposed to be? Harvey Keitel?'

'No. That's me,' said George.

'So it is,' said Mr. Stein.

'I'm Elvis Costello,' said Ted.

'Crap costumes,' said the Karloff wannabe. 'Get a life.'

Dai called from the bar. Ted and George exchanged brief but frank opinions with the sad git in the monster make-up and then went to see what Dai was so excited about.

'Best we hold up here awhile,' said the biker. 'They found the truck.'

'Well, they would, wouldn't they?' said George.

'They're combing the streets.'

'For you,' said George. 'They're looking for *you*.'

'Thank you for pointing that out.' Dai picked up one of the three pints he'd bought. His hand was shaking.

'I put this shirt on only three days ago,' said George.

'Sorry. It's only beer.'

George slapped Ted away when he attempted to suck the stain. 'It'll wash out.' He turned to Dai. 'We've got to get you away from here.'

'Too risky.'

'But you missed my point. They're looking for *you*. Not *us*. We could walk out of here, get some transport.'

'You have a car?' said Dai. Hope gave clarity to those drug-and-alcohol-glazed peepers.

'No.'

'Van?'

'Nup.'

'Motorbike?'

'Nnnn….ooo.'

'Truck, lorry, land train?'

'Alas, no.'

'Tandem?'

'Ah,' said George, raising a finger.

'You are kidding, aren't you?' said Dai. 'Please say you're kidding.'

'Actually, I don't have a conveyance of any description. But I know a man who does.' He picked up his pint and downed it without coming up for air, as befits a man. 'See you lay-tar,' said George, when he'd done coughing up smoker's phlegm and lung tissue. 'Sorry about the beer.'

'Better a face full of Dirty than see you drown where you stand. Adios, muchacho. I'll be looking out for you.' Dai ordered himself a drink and a cloth for his face.

George pushed through a small crowd of Butt Ugly Martians and threaded his way to a gaggle of Star Trekkies dancing around their handbags. At the fringe of this group of jigging Essex astronauts, avoiding the stamping white stilettos, Ted swung his pants. He was not, as is commonly described, a mover. More a case of centrifugal force following the drunken sway of his hips, thus rearranging his sizeable paunch into more pleasing shapes.

'Will you piss off?' snapped a particularly beautiful member of the *Enterprise's* bridge crew.

Ted gave up his attempts at seduction. 'George,' he said. 'What ho.'

'Ted. You need some fresh air, my son.'

'She told me to piss off,' said Ted. 'Grizzle.'

'Forget her,' said George. 'Groucho over there told me she once slept with an entire Klingon skittles team.'

'Then I'm well shot of her. Let's go do something illegal, ay?'

'Steady, boy.'

'I don't care anymore,' said Ted. ' I'm reckless, I know.'

Wyatt Earp, bearing a tray full of hot cocoa, caught George's eye. 'A word, Malcolm, if you will.' George drew the mustachioed lawman aside.

'What's up, George?' said Wyatt.

'Ah. It *is* you. For a moment there I wasn't sure.'

Mr. Earp had a day job. When he wasn't mercilessly hunting scumbags and slaughtering them like dogs, his alternative persona, one Malcolm Morris Maraschino Mortimer, held the position of Chief Buyer at the municipal dump. What exactly he bought, or did, to earn the magnificent salary he received, no one knew. George had once got a sneaky at some of the papers on his desk. If people knew that the council had been buying in rubbish from other boroughs to make up the quota for their own, questions would be asked. This information, in the hands of the unscrupulous, could have been used for blackmail. But George, though in some ways more than unscrupulous, had not the wit to understand the significance of the information.

Yet guilt is a strange thing; it starts off as a tiny egg in the soul. With a bit of care and a lot of attention, fretting away at it, the egg hatches and becomes a maggot. The maggot sets to work eating the living spirit of the individual until, fat and bloated, the grub explodes. And you don't ever want to see part-digested soul all over the place.

Malcolm, who had seen CCTV footage of the bin man getting a shufti at Exhibit A (as they would later refer to the documents at Malcolm's trial), assumed that any conversation with George was fraught with innuendo.

'How's the buying business then, Malcolm?' said George, leering.

'What d'you mean by that?' said Malcolm, sweating like a very sweaty pig indeed. 'All right. What do you want?'

'Oh,' said George, affronted. 'I was only asking.'

'Yeah, yeah,' said Malcolm. 'So what is it this time?'

'Well, since you mention it, I do have a problem.'

'No more weekends in Bognor, George. People are getting inquisitive.'

'No. Really. That last trip was marvellous and *so* unexpected.'

'Yeah. Right.' Mr. Earp sucked his adhesive moustache.

'But at the moment I need transport for a very, very, very, *very* important job. You know how it is. Never a set of wheels when you need 'em.' A thought occurred. It just sprang up, unbidden. 'What are you driving these days, Malc?'

Malcolm did that thing with his bottom lip that people do when they don't get the present they hoped for but a totally inappropriate really crap gift instead. 'A Porsche, as if you didn't know. Here.' Malcolm pulled keys out of his Versace cowboy jacket, tearing the lining, but Malcolm did not care. He threw the car keys on the bar top. 'Take it.' He shuffled off. He didn't exactly say "Boo Hoo", because people don't. Not unless they're being sarcastic. Neither did he go, "Waaah", but lip-tremble and grizzle-grizzle he most certainly did.

'Act your age,' someone commented to him, which broke him down into a right old bawl.

'What's up with him?' said Ted.

'Dunno. Generous bloke, though. He seems to like me for some reason, but all I've ever done is make small talk.' George threw the keys in the air and caught them. 'Can you drive?'

'Not legally.'

'I know. But I can. And I've got the keys to a Porsche. Come on.'

They fought their way through a murderous re-enactment of the Battle of Bosworth. The Sealed Knut had a grudge match against the Chipping Sodbury Senseless Slaughter Society. Finally, they made it to the door.

'Do you know, I clean forgot to ask what colour and model of Porsche young Malcolm drives. Or, indeed, where it is parked.'

'Too late now,' said Ted. 'He just ran off - strange, that. He was muttering "boo hoo" and "waaah".'

'Sensitive chap.' George stopped a man in full knightly armour. 'Is there a back door to this place?'

'Befn ne kibble awy,' said the knight, neatly parrying a vicious broadsword thrust to the groin.

'Pardon?' said Ted.

The knight did something complicated and very impressive with his sword. His counter-thrust hit his opponent in the throat. The knight paused in his combat, flipped up his visor. He was smoking a roll-up.

'Behind the skittle alley,' he said, then ducked as a two handed bastard sword swept the air above him. 'That would have taken my head clean off. Thanks. I owe you one.'

'Are those swords real?' said Ted, reaching to touch the knight's fine blade.

'Of course. Not much point in battle re-enactment with toys, is there?' said the knight.

'I suppose not,' said Ted. 'Don't you worry about killing someone?'

'I let *them* worry about that. They know the risks.'

'I daresay. Don't the police get twitchy about all this?'

'Natch,' said the knight. 'I've just done ten years for decapitating a pike man.'

'Ah,' said Ted. 'I remember the case. Well reported by the media.'

'It was a fair fight,' said the knight.

'You sneaked up behind him in a MacDonald's,' said Ted.

'War is hell,' said the knight. 'Now if you'll excuse me, that bastard over there just spilled my pint.' He flipped his visor again, gave vent to a blood coagulating war cry then charged through the Essex Trekkies.

'Bath is a very strange place of late,' said Ted, to no one in particular.

*

Ted and George took their leave to search the streets for Malcolm's Porsche. They passed many police vehicles, plods on the beat, and overhead a flying machine chopped the air in a rotary fashion. No one paid any attention to them. They looked, after all, as if they had just finished a long, hard day's toil and therefore *couldn't* have been breaking every traffic law in a stolen refuse truck, could they?

They found the Porsche. It was the one they had hit just twenty minutes before. There was a large gap in the offside front wing. Further up the road the remains of this missing section lay strewn and somewhat misshapen.

'It might not be Malcolm's,' said Ted.

George slotted the key into the door. 'Nice thought, Ted.' They climbed in.

Well, no: you don't climb *downwards*.

You *bend* a lot, to get into a Porsche.

The seating did not sit well, as it were, with George's considerable paunch.

But they managed.

And they parked at the rear of the pub.

Ted got out, stretched, and thanked God.

'My driving isn't that bad,' said George.

'You drove most of the way in reverse,' said Ted.

'But you said you'd always had a morbid fear of a *head-on* car crash.'

'And then there was the hand brake turn.' Ted trembled violently.

'Well, that car was parked right across the road,' said George. 'Bloody inconsiderate.'

'It was a police road block' said Ted, stamping a foot.

'Keep your voice down,' said George. There were many people about; people who had business in the locale, people passing through, en route from whence to thence, and people who'd just come out to see what the fuss was all about. And when people are nosing about like that, with police milling around saying rhubarb, rhubarb, into their little radios, they tend to notice things like two grubby-looking bastards climbing out of an abused, expensive sports car. The two don't fit, you see. Unless you surmise that the two sweaty gits have half-inched the motor. Which someone did. In a very loud voice.

'Ooh, ooh, officer. Car thieves. Oh look, do.'

'Shut up, Len,' said George, who recognised the shrill tones of his former work colleague, even if delivered by a burly commander of a Klingon battle cruiser. 'Or I'll belt you one,' he added, when he was sure that all that muscle was foam padding.

'George? Is that you?'

'That is self evident,' said he. 'What are you doing skulking at the rear of a pub?

'There's a skittles match going on. I'm minding the door.'

'They need a minder for a skittles match?'

'Big money riding on this one,' said Len, suddenly whispering.

'Why are you whispering?' said Ted, whispering.

'Because it's illegal,' said Len.

'Then you must recall that old saying,' whispered Ted.

'The one about a bird in the hand?'

'I mean, the one about people who live in glass houses,' said Ted, tapping the side of his nose. 'If you catch my general drift.'

'Come,' said Len, warmly. 'Enter herein, oh do.'

Ted and George did so enter.

And that was when the unpleasantness started.

CHAPTER EIGHTEEN

Tuesday 21.30

Jason had decided on a chilled night in. With a full night planned for the following evening, tonight was for roonies. Or perhaps the old hubbabubba. Maybe another tab of Goofy, but he wasn't sure he was in the right mood for much more. Too much weird shit was going down, and he didn't want to start seeing munched-up Elk coming out the walls.

Pitt had not tracked them down yet. This was of some considerable relief to Jason. It had been a daft idea. Petty theft wasn't ingrained in him and he hadn't entirely squared the nicking of the Professor's notebook with his conscience.

And so here he sat, with all of his good intentions for a little academic work down the old shit-chute; he was already spaced-out, mellowed up, juiced and fried sunny side up. He caught himself giggling at the thought, stopped himself with some effort and decided he needed distraction. The news was on. Turn it up.

Usual stuff: unconfirmed sightings of Santa stealing lingerie, Christmas lights officially lit, holidays looming, and that suited Jason. What he needed was time – not to think, preferably. Quite the opposite.

The talking head on the screen was full of woe.

Apparently, a man had been arrested for indecent exposure. Not exactly usual, but bloody silly in this weather (the exposure, not the arrest).

Another man had been admitted to hospital after being attacked by a feral dog. In a rubbish skip. Now, *that* was unusual. But people threw all sorts of things out with trash, so not that surprising, really. He was about to turn over to another channel.

What's this?

Live bulletin?

Turn it up louder. The crockery from meals long forgotten rattled on the dining table. Someone was bound to complain.

Sod 'em.

Some bloke had been found trespassing in the Infirmary. Not the locker rooms or nurse's quarters. The mortuary. Pursuit through the hospital, car chases, sirens, helicopters.

Refuse trucks?

But the next bit was what motivated Jason to grab his mobile 'phone. The correspondent was interviewing the pathologist, who reported the theft of one of the mortuary's current residents. The deceased's name was not mentioned, naturally, but a body was a body.

Jan was taking her time. Six, seven, eight rings. Finally…

'Jan?'

'What?' Her voice was heavy, slurred and pissy.

'Turn the TV on,' said Jason, his words tumbling out so that he had to repeat himself twice before she understood.

'I was sleeping,' she snapped.

'Turn it on. Channel five.' Jason held up his phone to the TV. There was a bit of feedback down the 'phone link when she eventually located her remote and flicked on her set.

'Oh my god,' said Jan.

'The camera loves him,' said Jason.

Pitt was telling the interviewer that he didn't actually see the suspect stealing the body, but the presence of a trespasser seemed too coincidental. The correspondent remarked that a more significant coincidence lay in the fact that it wasn't the first corpse to go walkies. Hadn't there been a recent incident involving *two* missing bodies? But Pitt would not be drawn and a spokesman interrupted, letting the pathologist off the hook.

'He wouldn't,' said Jan, although she didn't sound convinced.

'Why not? The guy's a nut. Out there where the 'buses don't run, an ant short of a picnic, an onion short of a pickle, an equation short of a Unified Theory. A – '

'Have you been dropping acid, Jas?'

'Good gracious no,' he said, toking hard on a ten-skinner.

'Well, it's very interesting. Thank you for sharing. Goodnight.'

'You aren't seriously intending to sleep?'

'I'd put money on it.'

'Jan, it has to be *tonight*.'

'No. Frigging. Way.'

'It's the only way.'

'Says you.'

'You know I'm right.'

'*Balls*,' she shouted at him. The lass had a fine chest. And then some.

'I'll be around in ten, then, ' said Jason. 'Dress for action.'

'Piss o – '

Jason broke the link.

Pitt's face filled the screen. But the interview was over. Those were the sports results, weren't they? Coming out of Pitt's mouth? Pitt, now making eye contact with Jason. Pitt leaning toward the camera…

…He was *into* the camera…

…He was *out* of the screen...

…And here he was, grabbing Jason by the lapels.

'I'm watching you,' said TV Pitt. *'You and the whore-bitch. You stole my notebook, you thieving swine. I want it back.'*

'Gerroff!' screamed Jason, and as he struggled to free himself from the Pitt monster, James walked in. James the whinger, James the thumper on walls and ceilings, James the philosophy student and all-round pain-in –the-arse-house-sharing-nightmare-from-Nuneaton.

'What are you doing?' said the outraged resident, leaning to turn the set off.

Jason looked up. The trip shattered into a billion multi-coloured atoms that floated around and finally settled on James the Just, who now resembled a prophet of the Old Tradition. When he spoke, he spat bits of locust and honey.

'Armchair aerobics,' said Jason.

'You're on acid.'

'You've got a kangaroo living in your beard.'

'You're off your face.'

'You're absolutely correct. Now piss off.'

Old James pissed, and off went Jason.

And, suitably dressed for inclement weather, away he tripped to see his co-conspirator. Pitt did not put in any more appearances.

At least for the moment.

*

'That was all very unpleasant,' said George. 'Not least unnecessary.'

'I didn't start it,' said Ted.

'Yes you did. You pinched their balls.'

'So?'

'Look, I know I told you that the Essex Trekkie had been gang-banged by a Klingon skittle team, but *really*...is that any way for a grown man to behave?'

'Yes.'

'But they weren't even Klingons,' said George. 'They were Romulans.'

'Does that matter?'

'You have to know your Klingons from your Romulans, innit?' said Dai. He was scrunched up on the rear seat of the Porsche, which, as anyone who has ever been a passenger in such, will testify is singularly unsuited to the purpose.

'Anyway' said Ted, nursing his bruised knuckles, 'it was the Vulcan who got me in the end.'

'The old death grip will get you every time,' said Dai, nodding sagely.

They were driving aimlessly, looking for a suitable spot to stop and evaluate all that had happened. Dai had had to get out several times to be sick.

'My driving is not that bad,' said George.

'We drive on the left hand side of the road in the United Kingdom, innit,' said Dai. 'Watch that cyclist.'

There was a bump, and a clatter, and a man wearing a beret, stripy tee shirt and waving a string of onions rose up, bleeding profusely. He bit his thumb at them. 'Sacre bleu,' swore he.

Ted wound down his window, leaned out and waved two intact English longbow man's fingers in his direction. 'Where are we?' he enquired of George when he'd finished making his contribution to international relations. They had turned off the London road, past Batheaston, and were now heading uphill.

'Bannerdown Road. There's a lay-by at the top,' said George. 'We'll stop and Dai here can stretch his legs.'

And in due course, so it came to be.

The hill was long and unlit, with a double bend that George enjoyed so much that he reversed and did it again.

'That was fun,' said Dai, emptying his stomach once more.

'I thought so,' said George. They were standing at the lay-by. Across the road, over a low dry stone wall, open fields; the moon was full-ish and the pastoral scene was serene to the extreme. Said George.

It was also freezing. As Dai pointed out.

'Where next?' said Ted, modifying the fresh air with old shag.

'Well, Dai's place is out,' said George. 'So's mine. The missus won't be in a listening mood.'

George rifled through Dai's pockets while the poor man retched. 'Ah,' said he with glee. He found the roll-ups and transferred them to his own pockets, save for one, which he lit. 'What about you, Ted?'

'Alas, my modest abode has been condemned.'

'I'm sorry to hear that, buddy. Subsidence?'

'No. It was condemned before I moved into it and claimed squatter's rights. The man from the council told me it was designated a Site of Special Scientific Interest. The wildlife, you know.'

'Wildlife?'

'The pest control guy said that there were species that he was forbidden to exterminate. And a few heretofore unknown to zoology.' Ted shook his head sadly. 'They've given me a week to vacate. I don't know where to go.'

Dai had finished his business in the bushes. 'This is all fascinating stuff,' he said. 'But we need to find somewhere to pass the night.'

'And transport,' said George. 'The police at the road block got my number.'

Dai cast a critical eye over the Porsche's bodywork. 'Bad luck. They'd never have spotted us, otherwise.' Something in the rear suspension went twang.

'Then let us mosey along,' said Ted. 'My nadgers are getting frost bitten.'

Dai leaned against a tractor that had been parked there. He patted his pockets, frowned. 'Is no-one interested in what transpired at the Infirmary?'

George and Ted exchanged a look. 'The consequences speak for themselves,' said George. 'You were caught. You ran.'

'And yet there is much detail to bore you with.'

'Let's get in the car. It's too cold out here.' Ted opened the door to the Porsche. It creaked. Then it fell off. 'Oh.'

Dai groaned.

'All is not lost.' Ted stepped up to the tractor. 'Room for three, I think.' The door was not locked. 'Come on, who's going to steal a knackered, manure-bespattered tractor? On a lonely unlit road? On an evening serene to the extreme? Ay?'

It was a tight fit.

'Anyway,' said Dai. 'There I was, tippy-toeing along a dark corridor. No one about. I followed the signs to the morgue.'

'Yeah,' said Ted. 'Skip to the interesting bit.'

'So I get to the double doors. It's a buzzer lock. The kind they have in house flats. There's a light on in there. A red one. But I can't see anyone, so I punched in the number on the lock.'

'Hold on,' said Ted. 'You knew the number?'

'Yeah. I used to shag a student nurse who used to shag a mortuary technician.. She gave me the combination.'

'Unbelievably convenient' said George. 'But continue, do.'

'So, I'm in there. The autopsy table is vacant, but there're these steel straps fixed to it. Work that one out.'

'Restraints? On a desiccation table?' said George.

'Verification, perhaps?' said Ted.

'That's dissection and vivisection, chaps, respectively and in that order, innit. So, anyway, I looked through the worksheet on the clipboard, and there's no mention of wotsisname.'

'Kevin,' said George. 'Kevin Costner.'

'That's the guy. So I'm thinking, he ain't dead yet. Must be still in Intensive Care. I went up to see if he was receiving visitors.'

'That's a relief,' said Ted. 'So we can forget all about this vampire stuff.'

'No,' said Dai. 'Because when I get up there, the nurse in charge tells me "Unfortunately, Mr. Costner passed away earlier this evening."'

There was a bit of urinary incontinence from Ted, then George said: 'So where is he?'

'There you have it. My point exactly. The stiff should've been either in cold storage or on the table, and I'd already checked. But unfamiliar as I am with the layout of these places, I'm thinking, I must've missed something. So I went back down there. Guess what I found?'

His audience shrugged slowly.

'These.' Dai fished out a little polythene specimen bag.

'Teeth?' said George, examining the contents.

'Uuuurgh,' said Ted, with more than a suggestion of disgust. 'They've got blood on them.'

'There's a bit of cabbage stuck in that cavity, as well,' observed George.

'And they're all intact,' said Dai. 'Even have the roots on.'

'Bloody Nora,' said Ted. 'That one needed a filling something chronic.'

'But dental hygiene aside,' said Dai, rolling his eyes upward, 'what does this tell you?'

His audience shrugged individually but simultaneously.

'Well, when a vampire is born, the body is refurbished, innit?' said Dai.

'Huh?' said his audience. As one.

'Out with the old and on with the new.' He jiggled the bag, causing the abandoned gnashers to clink together. 'This is all that remains of the old Kevin.'

'That's amazing' said George.

'But total bollocks anyway,' said Ted. 'How do *you* know so much about the doings of vampires, ay?'

'Yeah,' said George, wearing a frown that bespoke consternation. 'How *do* you know all this stuff?'

'Ah,' said Dai. 'Y'see, there's something I haven't told you.'

'Do share,' said they, expecting the worst.

They weren't disappointed.

Dai cleared his throat noisily. 'Well, the night I had the row with my girl, I didn't go very far. I followed her.'

'Go on,' they said.

'Well, you know, what with the woods having a reputation – the murders, and everything. I couldn't just bugger off and leave her there, could I? She lived up in Tepid Ashton. Miles away. So I was still lurking about when it happened.'

Ted pressed his hands against his ears and made humming noises. George had gone very pale. He tooted on his jay like a steam locomotive trying to clear its sinuses. A cascade of red-hot resin grains dropped onto his chest, burned through his overall and set his chest hair alight. He patted the flames out and passed the joint to Dai.

'Thank you Humphrey*. So. There I was. Sarah's bawling her eyes out and I'm thinking, shit, I've got to do something. I'm just about to get up and walk over…when it happened.' Again, Dai paused to allow questions.

'You keep saying that,' said George. 'What happened?'

Dai drew a deep one on the roonie. 'It all went quiet. You know. Usually there are owls hooting, animals scurrying about, innit? Busy places, woods. But as I say, suddenly it's silent. Then I hear this voice.'

'Don't tell me. "And then it happened".'

'It did, George. I thought, fuck, she's on her own. But as hard as I try, I can't move. Can't move a friggin' muscle.' Dai had the complexion of a corpse that had been left in the sun for too long – sweaty, rubbery and a little green around the ears. He closed his eyes and let smoke blow down his nose, tipped his head back. Something wet rolled down the biker's cheek.

'Steady on, lad, said George. 'You don't have to say anymore. You saw the murder.'

'Aye. I did. But you have to understand. There was nothing I could do. As I listened to that voice, I could see Sarah…and this bloke just appeared, out of nowhere.

'Ummm. Hmmm. Da da dee de dum. Tra la la,' went Ted, his fingers buried up to the first knuckle in both ears.

---

* Bogart: "Don't Bogart that joint." Dope smoker's parlance. Apparently.

'And I could see that Sarah was paralysed. Like me.' Dai sucked hard on his smoke. His eyes were bloodshot. 'The voice. It was all I could think of. And it was saying things to her. To *me*. In my mind. Terrible, terrible things. Making me want to walk up there and let him…' Dai choked. 'He took Sarah by the shoulders. I thought he was going to rape her. I could've handled that. I'd have castrated the bastard. But he leaned forward and there's this animal grunt and Sarah started squealing and I couldn't, *couldn't* move a muscle and I can see her struggling and there's this sucking gurgling noise and I'm trying to run but can't and then… then he's gone. And Sarah's lying there. Her throat…'

George patted the distraught man on the shoulder. 'There was nothing you could do, Dai. You're a natural, dyed-in-the-wool coward and no mistake.'

'I should've been able to resist,' said Dai, his voice tired and low. 'She's dead, and it's my fault. I haven't even been up to see her grave. I can't face it.'

'But you still haven't explained how you know so much about vampires,' said George.

'That's the thing. The stuff the voice said. Promises that it wouldn't hurt, that soon she wouldn't feel any pain at all, not ever, and everything would be made new. He said that she would enjoy a new body, a better body, one that couldn't decay or grow weaker with the years, never get wrinkled and ugly and…shit. At the time, even through the horror, I'm thinking, "hmm, good deal."'

George was studying him when he looked up. 'So you've made it your personal quest to hunt the bastard down,' he said, after another round of sobs and "there, there."

'Yes. Wouldn't you?' Dai rubbed angrily at his eyes. It shouldn't have been possible but they were more inflamed and puffy looking than before. 'I knew you'd understand.'

'We've got to find the tosser and put a stake through his ticker,' said George. 'But first there's something you've got to do.'

'There is?'

'Yes.' George found that the keys to the tractor were under old Naan bread that the owner had used for wiping down the windows. He started the engine.

'Have you finished your story?' said Ted, tentatively removing his fingers from his lugs.

'Yes.'

'Where are we going?' said Ted.

'Tepid Ashton,' said Dai. 'Tepid Ashton cemetery.'

George put his foot down on the accelerator and pulled off the lay-by before Ted could make it to the door.

*

'This is not a good idea,' said Jan. 'It can wait. I can get the keys tomorrow.'

Jason had been hammering at her window for at least ten minutes. Eventually she had opened her curtains and, seeing Jason perched on a tree limb, deigned to lift her sash and stick her head out.

'No it can't. Something is afoot,' he said.

'Piss off, Sherlock. It's freezing out there and I'm knackered.'

'Look, come on. You want me to fall to my untimely death?'

'Who said it was untimely?' she said.

'Let me in.'

'No'

'It's dangerous out here. I'm risking multiple injuries.'

'If you come in here, what's the difference?'

'Ah.' He wobbled a bit on the branch. 'Humour. Like it. Oh, please.'

Jan harrumphed and retreated.

'Jan?'

'Climb in,' she called from her bed.

'What?'

'Your choice.'

Muttering dark and unseemly things, Jason somehow managed to reach the sill – just before the limb creaked, snapped and sagged. He dangled there for a bit, his legs thrashing for a foothold. Finally he simply dragged himself in. He fell into an untidy heap.

'What is this untidy heap?'

'My bundies,'[*] she said.

'Pooh.'

'Cheeky bastard. Make yourself useful. Put the kettle on.'

Jan kept a tray of the necessaries on a table by her bed. While he made coffee, she plumped up her pillows, sat up, the quilt swaddled up to her chin,

---

[*] Underwear

and shivered. 'How do you propose we get in without keys,' said she, stifling a yawn.

'I don't know. I'm making this up as we go along.'

'No. As *you* go along.'

'Jan, bodies are going missing and Pitt, as we know, is heavily into do-it-yourself resurrection. We have to do *something.*'

'Okay. If you feel like that.'

'Really?'

'Yep. Take the notebook into the cop shop. Tell them everything.'

'But they'll lock me up.'

'That's right.'

The kettle boiled. Jason ladled out coffee granules and sugar and added water and milk, as you do. But he took his time over it, trying to think of a plan.

'I could cut a hole in a window, release the catch, and we're in,' said Jason.

'It's taken you five minutes to put coffee into two mugs and that's the best you could come up with?'

'You have a better idea?'

'As it happens, yes.' She sipped coffee.

'Go on then.'

'Simple. Pitt has a live-in caretaker. He takes delivery of goods and such. We ring the bell. Door open.'

'Brilliant,' said Jason. 'Except for the obvious. The mail doesn't operate this time of night.'

'The stuff he has delivered doesn't come by mail. He has some kind of private courier service. *"Windbreakers"*, or something like that.'

'So all we need is a parcel with a *Windbreaker* label on.' He rubbed his chin. 'A bit thin on the ground, I'll wager.'

'I've got one,' said Jan, all smug smile and wobbly chest.

'You do?' said Jason, admiring the wobble.

'Yeah. I keep all my crap in it. You remember I said I'd been to his lab. Well, there was an empty one thrown out with the rubbish.'

'So if we tape it up-'

'-And leave it at the gate-'

'-Knock the door, Mr. Caretaker comes out –'

'-Then we nip in while he's picking up the parcel. Magic. Jan, I'm giving serious consideration to letting you have my babies.'

'I don't baby-sit,' she said, wrinkling her nose.

CHAPTER NINETEEN

Tuesday 23.00

Caitlin was getting used to people thinking that she ought to be locked up. This cell was even worse than the one at – what did they call it, the *station?* – because in this one there was no mattress. Just four bare walls.

She examined the door. It was covered in some resilient fabric, the like of which she'd never touched before; it had been padded. For her own safety, they kept saying. We don't want you hurting yourself (or anyone else). She knew that they feared her. They shouldn't have tried to stick her with that spike. She could sense their concern, though, even as the male nurses wrestled to restrain her. It puzzled her.

It had been the Weasel's fault. He'd been lurking in every corner, every room she'd been in. She could sense his hunger: sexual frustration, lust, but hatred overlaying both.

His hatred *flared* from him. His aura was black.

She would have to do something about him, but for now she was content to wait. Craig was coming in to see her.

Right now, the Weasel was still hurting from the punch she'd given him. He had gone down, soundless. It was only when he regained some of the breath he'd lost that he'd begun to squeal.

She had a right to defend herself, she'd said to the staff that came running.

Did he assault you in any way? Liz had asked.

No. But I know what he was thinking.

You can read his thoughts, then?

Can't *you*?

It was then that the one called Liz – she appeared to be some kind of matriarch, of which Caitlin approved – became worried. Shortly after that, the fight - brief, but no one had been too badly hurt. The males had bruised egos. Amongst other things.

Caitlin had agreed on what they called "Time Out". It was supposed to calm people down. But how could they be calm, in a room that reeked of madness and anguish and despair? And anger. Lots of that.

Call Craig, she'd said; tell him to come. Then I will go and sit in this room of yours.

Caitlin was becoming increasingly frustrated. She could feel the Moon, already high in the sky, and she had not eaten. Although she could resist the Change, if she did not hunt in the next twenty-four hours she would have to break out of here. The door would be no problem. She decided to sit, cease this prowling from one wall to the next, and entertain herself with thoughts of making the Weasel's life altogether more unpleasant.

She had barely devised her first strategy – it involved rope, pain, sharp sticks and more pain – when she felt Craig approaching. A league or more. Travelling fast. Caitlin walked to the door, banged on it twice. Then she stopped, listened; Liz, just outside the door. She opened it a crack (the door had not been locked), and peered out.

'…If Miss O'Connor wishes to see you, I'm sure she will find you,' Liz was saying.

'She can do what she likes,' said Wesil, petulant. 'I don't wanna see her.'

'Then why are you standing right outside her door?'

'Can stand anywhere I likes,' said Wesil.

'But not here. We're not idiots, Mr. Weasel,' she said, deliberately mispronouncing his name. 'We've noted your - shall we say, *interest* - in Miss O'Connor. You would be best advised to leave her alone.' Her tone was cold, her words clipped.

Caitlin smiled to herself.

'What you going to do, little girl?' said Wesil. He had manoeuvred himself so that Liz's back was against the wall. Now he was pressing all of his weight onto her.

Caitlin sensed the disgust and the revulsion, but…a flicker of fear there too. Liz struggled to free herself. '*Mr.* Weasel…'

'Come on little girl. Little nursey. What's the wee ward manager going to do now, heh?' Wesil's face was blood-swollen, his eyes wide and wild. His smell was raw and musky, overlaid with rotten sweat and a foetid, cloying odour. He looked, with the spittle frothing and running at the corner of his mouth, as if he was about to orgasm.

Liz tried to push him away, but he had her arms pinned tight to her sides. She attempted to bring her knee up into his groin. Wesil thought she'd try something like that. A knee in the balls. Little bitch. He pushed harder against her. He was not particularly big but the nurse was smaller than him. And it was only making him more excited, her struggling like that. Soon, he was going to shoot his load and he would make sure she felt it.

His climax built and he was close to release. He ignored his victim's twisted face, the fear and the disgust etched there, and his thrusting rhythm grew more frantic. *Yes. Yes. Ye-*

'Aaaargh.'

'Aaaargh?' repeated Caitlin. '*Aaaargh*?' She shook her head. 'Do you call that a scream of agony? Put some effort into it, boy.' She tightened her grip on his testicles. He had been so intent on his own ejaculation, he hadn't noticed that the door to the Time Out room was wide open…

'OOOAAAiiiagh. Agh. Agh.'

'That is much better,' said Caitlin. 'Now, I believe that the nurse prevailed upon you to stand elsewhere. You do see the wisdom of this, do you not? Scream twice to signify a yes.'

The corridor was filling up with residents from the other rooms. They watched, impassively, waiting for whatever happened next. There were a couple of girls there. They giggled when they saw what Caitlin was doing. 'Go on, girl. Castrate the bastard,' said one giggler.

And Caitlin thought that that was a wonderful idea. It would solve a lot of problems. So instead of squeezing twice, to elicit the "yes", Caitlin just squeezed. Harder. And harder.

Liz wriggled out, a little sob escaping her. She stood there, trembling, hesitating. Caitlin knew that she was trying to hold onto what little dignity she had left; yet still she felt that she should do something to control the situation. Caitlin looked at her, drew the nurse's eyes to hers. They were bloodshot, tears pouring from them, and they were wild and painful to look at.

'Listen to me,' said Caitlin. 'Go and find assistance. Let others deal with this.'

Liz opened her mouth to say something, but then simply nodded and walked away. One of the giggling girls helped her.

Wesil was still screaming. He had filled his pants for the second time in two days and it had been her fault. Even through the agony, his hatred blazed white-hot. Which was a mistake, for if he had shown the slightest feeling of remorse, Caitlin would have released him. Instead, the pain scaled new heights of possibility. Something popped down in his scrotum. His bowels exploded. Urine ran freely. To finish off the general effect of massive trauma, he vomited, sending a Jackson Pollock splash across the rapidly growing puddle of fresh sewage beneath his feet.

The other residents had begun to move away, afraid of what was taking place. It had been funny, seeing the dirty scrote having his nadgers tweaked, but now…some of the male residents were very pale, and they started backing off, horrified.

But Caitlin knew only one kind of justice and once you'd decided that guilt was rightfully apportioned and a sentence passed, it had to be done. Caitlin felt the second, remaining testicle shoot out from her grip. It had retreated up into his body. Such things were possible for adepts of certain fighting arts, but Wesil unfortunately happened to be lucky. This day. There would be no reprieve if she caught him again.

Craig was here!

She released the Weasel, as she thought of him. He was no longer screaming. Instead, he slithered about in his own mess and crawled off to his room.

Behind her, Caitlin sensed movement. She spun, crouching as she did so, her thighs bunched up beneath her, ready to spring. Her fingernails extended. She could feel her teeth begin to grow, but she fought that impulse. She reminded herself that she had not eaten, did not know if she could stop if she became caught up in more combat.

'Caitlin?' said Craig.

'Where have you been?' said Caitlin, sharply.

'What are you, my mother?' Craig frowned, stepped toward her. He froze. Caitlin retracted her claws, but it was too late.

Craig blinked, rubbed his eyes, and shook his head. *Must be the light*, she heard him thinking.

Caitlin stood. 'Do not think of me as your mother,' she said. 'Although I sense that they were merely words. For a mother would not be permitted to do this.'

Craig had time to utter something foolish, like “whoa”, before she launched herself at him, wrapped her legs around his waist and locked herself securely in position. She kissed him deeply.

Craig fell back onto his arse when she jumped off him. 'What *is* that you've got in your mouth? A bleeding eel?'

'Did you not enjoy?' she asked, innocence on her open face.

Craig picked himself up, dusted imaginary fluff and whatnot from his clothes. He jerked a thumb behind him. 'I'd like you to meet these ladies and gentlemen, Caitlin. They're doctors.'

Caitlin saw them now. Huddled together like frightened sheep. She gave them an appraising look. 'I did not ask to speak to them.'

Exasperated, he said 'Caitlin, look, it's enough I've been dragged back into work for this. All they want to do is ask a few questions.'

Caitlin sighed. 'Very well. You will come too?'

'I'll be right behind you.'

The ladies and gents from the assessment team broke like the Red Sea before an Old Testament oil slick, allowing her and Craig to pass. They were frightened. They'd seen more than they'd wanted to. As Craig passed one of the team, he felt his elbow grasped. He turned. 'Dr Stephens?'

'A word,' he said. He guided Craig further down the corridor, where the smell of fresh excrement wasn't so all pervading, and it was clear that Stephens wanted to get something off his chest. Craig knew that without the benefit of ESP.

'Perhaps,' said the psychiatrist, 'you could explain the meaning of "What is that you've got in your mouth?" hmmm?'

'Ah,' said Craig. 'You heard.'

'We all did,' said Stephens. His words were clipped.

'Yes.' Craig wiped sweat from his palms. 'Well, my relationship with Caitlin – '

'Relationship?'

'Well, no, obviously not, when I said *relationship*, I meant…' Craig realised he was babbling. 'Look. Dr Stephens. The only reason I'm here is because Caitlin wouldn't comply with treatment unless I came to see her. Since I first met her, she's–'

'What?' said Stephens.

'Well, she won't tolerate bullshit. She knows if you're being insincere. I don't know how, but she does. She is impulsive-'

'We were standing right behind you, Craig.'

'-And, I don't know, she's taken a shine to me and she doesn't trust anyone. I'm sorry if I offended you or any of the team, but it was my first honest thought. I was taken by surprise.'

'We all were. Relax, Craig, I'm just telling you to tread carefully. Don't get too involved. Do you know what I mean?'

Craig let his breath out, his shoulders slumped. 'Yeah. Yeah, I do. Don't worry doc. I only want to help.' If Stephens saw the pained wince on Craig's face when he said that, he did not indicate it. 'Let's join the others,' said Stephens. 'Before world war three starts.'

*

Wesil watched them all go. He closed his door.

Above everything – the pain, the humiliation, the hatred – there was now a deep and abiding fear.

He wedged a chair under the handle then staggered over to the window, clutching at his scrotum as he went. He struggled with the catch, tried to open it, but it barely cleared a foot. He just didn't have the strength to force it any further.

Weasel snarled in pain and frustration. He had to get out of here. Get right the fuck out, as far as his mangled bollocks would allow. He could get to a hospital, another one, get his mashed testicles sorted out; they could do wonders, these days, couldn't they? Bollock transplants. Even stitch someone else's cock on. A bigger one. Imagine what he could do with *six* inches…

But there would be no escape tonight. Not with him having less strength than a bottle of shandy, with shite all down his legs and trousers steaming. He stripped his clothes off, left them where they fell. Let the nurses deal with it. Naked, he pulled the chair from the door. He opened it a crack.

The corridor was dark now. He slipped out, padded quietly to the bathroom, let himself in and dropped the latch. There was a light switch. He flicked it on. Blinking against the harsh flare of light, he looked down at his groin. What he saw there made him whimper.

Gone, was his first thought. *All gone*.

She'd ripped off The Plasticine Man at the root. All that was left was this huge ballooned sac of blood and pureed right bollock.

But, with a wave of relief, he noted his foreskin drooping from his shrivelled old man. He couldn't be bothered to have a bath – Jesus, he didn't know if he could even get *into* it – but there was a shower cubicle. He would sluice off all this crud, and then…

…And then he would do exactly nothing. Because if he went near her again, or any of the bitches in here, he would die. Nastily, probably. He had no doubt about that. The best thing would be to continue to act like a loony, tell the good souls what they wanted to hear and get out while he still had anything between his legs. Besides, he really did need treatment. He had to go out there and show them.

This is what the psychopathic bitch did to The Plasticine man. Lock her up. Put her in a straightjacket and lock her up.

A thought occurred. As it grew, forcing other notions of hatred and revenge aside for a moment, he decided it was the funkiest idea.

He let himself out of the bathroom, walked up the corridor until he'd passed the steaming puddle of mess he'd deposited there, then got down on his hands and knees. He crawled on, sobbing, crying out for help.

Residents began to leave their rooms. When they saw it was Wesil, crawling along with his scrotum hanging like a cow's udder, they began to laugh.

The things I go through for that bitch, thought Wesil, and moved steadily toward the interview room.

*

The interview was brief and to the point. It had to be. Caitlin didn't like questions unless she was doing the asking.

'I have to remind you,' Stephens was saying, 'that you are detained under Section Three of the Mental Health Act. If you are not compliant to the treatment prescribed it may be necessary to enforce it against your consent.'

Contrary to all expectations Caitlin did not smash the place up. The team had taken seats close to the exit, poised to dive for it if necessary, but the only indication that this statement had found disfavour was the whitening of her knuckles as she gripped the arm of her chair. Tongue and groove joints creaked under the strain.

'I will not be pierced by spikes,' she said.

'Pardon?' said Stephens.

'She means needles,' said Craig.

Caitlin reached out and placed a hand on his thigh.

'Er,' he added.

Stephens's left eyebrow rose to meet his hairline, giving it the old Roger Moore.

Craig moved his leg away.

Caitlin looked at Craig. He was squirming, she knew. Just as she knew that he was under constraint not to respond. She could feel that he was closing himself off to her and she couldn't have that.

'I wish to speak to *him*' she said, pointing at Craig. It was a long, slender finger ending in a sharp fingernail, but not in the pampered and manicured sense; it looked as if it would be useful in close combat.* The team, too, looked at the finger and then at Craig, who seemed utterly transfixed by it.

'The rest of you, *out*,' said Caitlin.

'I have no wish to be confrontational, Miss O'Connor, but it is in your best interests to listen to what we say. Is there someone that you would like us to contact?' asked Stephens, determined to stand his ground.

Caitlin sniffed. 'Not one you would care to meet.'

'A relation, a friend?' Stephens persisted.

'Neither,' said Caitlin. 'Forget my words. ''Twas but a poor jest.'

'Miss O'Connor, please. Is there anyone you can call in an emergency?' Stephens was exasperated; he was also more than a little afraid.

'Do not concern yourself,' she said. '*They* already know where to find me. And I'd best be far from here when they do.'

Craig didn't know why but he suddenly believed that this would be an excellent idea. A feeling of dread laid its cold grip on his guts. This would be a bad place to be if *They* came to visit. Oh yes.

Caitlin smiled at him. Yes. He felt it too. He had the Gift, but he didn't know that yet.

The team began to collect their papers and pens and briefcases together, fidgeted in that "We've done all we can, let's get the hell out of here" manner. They had explained her detention. The client did not give any indication that this was understood. It was up to the staff of the Intensive Care Unit to do their job.

Craig paused at the door as they left…

…And realised his mistake too late. The door slammed shut of its own volition, and suddenly he was alone with Caitlin. Her smile was feral.

'Is it wrong to be wanted, to be sexually desired?' she asked, apropos of nothing.

'Why does it all come down to sex with you?' said Craig.

'It doesn't. Not all of the time. There are other needs.'

Something in the way she said "other" warned Craig not to go down that path. She had refused meals both at the local nick and since her admission to the psychiatric unit. She would take only water and then only directly from the tap. 'Anyway', he said, 'the point is, as I'm sure you are aware, I can't respond to you.'

---

* It was.

'You are aroused all the same,' said Caitlin.

Craig's mouth flapped. 'How do you...what do...' he flustered. Embarrassed, out of his depth, wondering how the hell she was getting into his head (*that* freaked him out), he screwed his eyes shut and shook his head. 'As long as you are an in-patient, and I am involved in your care, there is no question of *any* physical relationship. You either deal with that or I'll refuse to have any further involvement with you.'

'You think so?' said Caitlin.

'I know so.'

'You think that I cannot find you if I so wish?'

Craig could not think straight. His resistance to her was futile, like a picket fence against the tide. He was floundering and at the end of his professional tether. He overcompensated by becoming terse and aloof. 'Even if you found me I wouldn't be at liberty to...to...'

'Shag me hard?' said Caitlin. 'I think that is how you put it.'

'Do you want my help?' he demanded, half rising from his seat. 'Do you want *anyone's* help?'

'I need no one. But I want *you.*'

'What you need,' said Craig, now standing with his arms folded, 'are friends. People to act as your advocates. You're facing some serious charges.'

'Pah,' said Caitlin. 'I was merely protecting myself.'

'You all but ate the face off a council worker,' said Craig, in a tone that spoke of disbelief.

'He was assaulting me.'

'He was trying to *help.*'

'His hands were everywhere,' said Caitlin, bored with this turn in the conversation.

'He didn't know that there was a person in that skip. He thought it was a dog in there. Strange, that. Still maintains that his injuries were caused by a were...' Craig stopped himself. He didn't want to plant any more delusional ideas in her already busy brain.

'A werewolf,' said Caitlin.

'Er. Well. A dog, at least.'

'Werewolves don't exist,' said Caitlin. 'Not anymore,' she added, too quietly for Craig to hear.

'But you don't deny you attacked him.'

'I defended myself. He was trying to hurt me.'

'He was doing his job. But why – *how* – could he mistake a dog for a woman?'

'A wolf is not a dog,' snapped Caitlin.

'Whatever,' Craig said, his voice a little too strident. 'Fact is, the end result was the same.'

'He was dragging me from shelter. Surely that is unjust?'

'Shelter? From what?'

'The milit…' Caitlin stopped, thought about it. 'A rapist.'

'Yeah. I heard about that. But…all night? You stayed in that skip until the bin men came.'

'Why should you care?'

'Why didn't you go with the policemen?'

Caitlin gave him a look of the incredulous kind. 'The *militia* locked me in a *dungeon*. Now I am here. You will have noted the locks on the doors. Is this how you protect your women folk?'

'You're manipulating the facts.'

'And you are not?'

The two of them were head to head now, yelling into each other's faces.

'Do you want to get out of here?' said Craig, when they'd been silent for a while.

'I can leave when I wish.'

'Then why don't you?' said Craig, shaking his head once more. He shrugged. He wasn't achieving anything here.

'When it becomes necessary.'

Craig made a gesture with a hand, inviting her to elaborate. 'Yes?'

'When necessary,' was all that she would say.

Craig chewed on a fingernail. 'Can we compromise here?'

'What is your suggestion?'

'I'll get you some escorted leave. It may take a couple of weeks and you'll have to prove that it's safe.'

'You mean allow these "nurses" to shove their spikes into my flesh? I don't need their medicine.'

'Then show them you don't need it. Communicate. *Chill*, for God's sake.'

'And I will see you again?'

'I think I can swing it.'

'You will be this escort?'

'I can't promise that.'

'Try.'

'I can't.'

'Try.'

Craig raised both palms, conceding the point. 'Okay. Okay, you win. But nowhere private. In public. I'll escort you on short trips. No touching. If you have to be restrained at any time in the next fortnight you won't see sunlight for a long while.'

'At least we agree on something.'

'What?'

'No matter. Very well. I agree to your terms,' she said, as if negotiating Craig's surrender. 'Up to a point.'

'No exceptions.'

'Not even the Weasel?'

'Weasel?' Craig narrowed his eyes. 'Who…oh. Yeah. Wesil. Caught exposing himself, I believe. He tried that with you?'

'Perhaps you would arrange for him to have his wounds dressed,' she said.

'What wounds?' Craig's voice sounded tired.

'He does not merit it, but I suppose a man does not deserve to bleed to death either. That would be a waste.'

'What are you saying? What have you done?' Craig's voice rose, and it was unsteady.

'His gonads, Craig. He is lucky to have anything left. I'm sure he would appreciate some strong draught to ease his pain. I could make such a potion,' she said. 'Do you have mandrake, a little hemlock?'

At that moment the door opened. There was no knock to forewarn them. The visitor found them still head to head, toe to toe, within that personal space reserved for intimacy. During their argument, Craig had not realised how close they were. They were like opposite poles of a magnet. A magnet that did not merely pick up nails; this one would move the stars from their courses and cause meteors to collide. He stepped back, putting some distance between them.

'Sorry,' said Ben, the Charge Nurse. 'Could I have a word, Craig?'

Caitlin nodded at Craig, as if giving him permission.

'What's the problem?' he said.

'Got a bit of a crisis,' said Ben. He opened the door wider behind him. Craig stretched to peer around it.

Out in the common room, a group of residents had gathered. They were looking at something on the floor, but Craig couldn't see from where he was standing.

'I've got to go' he said.

Caitlin nodded. She lingered by the door, watching.

Craig approached the group, Ben close behind. The residents parted.

'Oh my god,' said Craig.

'Help me,' said Wesil. 'Please.'

He gibbered, and where he sat on the cold floor something large and purple and bulbous nestled between his thighs, like a beach ball with acne and bum fluff.

'You ever see a scrotum expand like that?' said Ben.

'That has to hurt,' said Craig.

'Did you hear what he did to Liz?'

'Later,' said Craig. 'Let's get this guy seen, first. Where's Stephens?'

'Already gone, squire. Said he was late for an appointment.'

'Who's the duty doctor?'

'Already spoken to him. He'll be along in a bit.'

'He needs emergency treatment,' said Craig.

'He needs a few minutes alone with a couple of the guys,' said Ben, whispering. 'If you'll pardon my momentary lapse in professional ethics. Liz is pretty shaken.'

'How long does it take for a scrotum to fill right up?'

'Don't know. I suppose I should get a calculator and do the maths. It's the sort of information that a doctor might ask for.'

'You'd better get right on it, then. I mean, I wouldn't want to administer painkillers if it interfered with the rate of scrotal expansion. That would mess your sums up a bit, wouldn't it?'

*

'Bitch,' said Wesil.

'Uh?' Ben turned toward the injured man. He followed the look of pure hatred aimed at some point behind him. Glancing over his shoulder, he saw Caitlin close the office door.

'Bitch,' said Wesil once more. Then he vented one more groan of agony and lost consciousness.

CHAPTER TWENTY

Tuesday 23.00

Joel and his Dad had not slept in the same room in years. Not since the days when Joel had kipped and dreamed his cherubic little dreams at the foot of the parental bed. But, as his Dad told him at the time, “You're sixteen years old, lad. It's time we stopped those 03.00 a.m. feeds, don't you think?'

Well, no; it wasn't that bad. Joel was at least three years old before his mother told him that he could no longer breast-feed but learn to use chopsticks like other maladjusted children.

But they did not wake in the parental bedroom. They woke in an unlit, damp cellar of some kind.

'Dad?'

'Son?'

'There's a tap dripping.'

Plink. Plink. Plonk. That's the best that onomatopoeia can do.

'Dad?'

'Yes?'

'Where are we?'

Joel's Dad had already been giving this some thought while his son, mercifully, had still been sleeping. 'The quarry, Joel. We're in the quarry.' For such he had concluded. Once – a long time ago – he had dallied with the idea of a proper job. One shift of back-breaking toil had put the kibosh on that notion.

'How long have we been here?'

'Buggered if I know. Did you sleep well?'

'Well…no. Terrible dreams. I dreamt,' said Joel, his throat suddenly dry, his tongue feeling like the stairwell carpet at home. 'I dreamt I died, but then…' Joel cut his stroll down memory byway short.

'Aye, lad. I know.' For Dad had dreamed the same dream. The last part, in particular, had been about as nasty as a nightmare can get. Nastier. Because he couldn't be certain that the nightmare was over, even now. He didn't feel that he had full control over his body. For example, he knew that he was hungry. He had obviously slept for a long time but while his first thought had been to grab a big greasy breakfast at Spike's (parties and functions catered for), his body yearned for something altogether more exotic. Images of steak, bloody and rare, made him drool. When he subtracted the steak, leaving just the blood, his stomach growled and he bit his lip, as if he'd accidentally chomped upon an imaginary slice of beef. He felt the twin holes with his tongue…

…For out of his toothless gums had appeared a fine pair of incisors. They had grown in response to his hunger. Which was pretty weird, when you thought about it. That, and the fact that he did not need illumination to see his exact whereabouts.

'Ouch,' said Joel.

'Joel?' said Dad.

'I bit my lip.'

'Were you, by any chance, thinking of a raw T-bone?'

'Not exactly. A turnip, in a rich beef gravy.'

'How rich?'

'Pretty rich. Mainly blood, actually. Yeeuk.'

'And your teeth?'

'Give over, Dad. I brushed them this morning.'

'No, fool. Have a feel.'

There were lip-smacking, tooth licking noises in the dark. 'Ouch,' said Joel, and 'Oo. Ar.'

'Oh dear,' said Dad. 'Oh dear oh dear oh dear.' They were silent for a bit, for which Dad was grateful.

'I feel sick,' said Joel. 'Sick, and light-headed.'

'You aren't going to take your pulse, are you?' asked Dad. Joel was in the habit of checking his pulse; show him a shovel, and his fingers were at his wrist. Give him a flight of stairs, he would swear that his heart had skipped a beat.

'Dad!' yelped Joel.

'I told you,' said Dad, shaking his head.

'I'm having a heart attack! Dad! Dad!' squeaked the son.

'You've already had that,' said his old Pa. 'There's really no point in making a fuss.'

'But-'

'Joel. Look at the facts, boy. We're dead.'

'But-'

'Do you know anything about the undead, lad?' The Dad kept his voice nice and even, not wanting to add fuel to his son's rising hysteria.

'Well…yeah. Lots.'

'A pity you didn't apply this knowledge before you started shagging that lass.'

'I *wasn't* shagging her,' snapped Joel.

'Only because there wasn't room. Anyway, it's all hacademic now. We's vampires, boy. Get used to it.'

'A wise approach.'

'Thank you, son.'

'I didn't say anything.'

'Yes, you did.'

'Didn't.'

'Did.'

'And it's *Wamphyr*.'

'Only if you've got a speech impediment, son.'

'Who's got a speech impediment?'

'What?' said Dad.

'What?' said son.

'Good evening' said a voice: deep, sinister, and altogether creepy.

'AAAAArgh,' said Joel.

'Calm yourself,' said that voice again. 'You have nerthing to fear. Apart from moi. And if you are obedient, as ah'm sure you will be, there will be no necessity to see mah nasty sahd.'

'Did you say, "*Nerthing* to fear"?' queried Joel.

'Ah did.'

'You're French, ain't ya?'

There was a sudden and unpleasant stillness, the sort you get when you know that the joke about the actress, the bishop and a box of altar candles has either gone roaring off at twenty thousand feet or you really have dropped a social fart.

'Fronch?' spat the voice. '*Fronch*? Ah am Belgian, monsieur.'

'Whatever,' said Joel. 'Show yourself.'

And the voice became flesh.

'How did you do that?' said Joel.

'You will lairn, mon ami. But for now, you merst eat.' The voice emerged from the shadows which, considering that the cave was unlit, was quite a nifty trick. Joel wished he hadn't invited the Belgian to reveal himself. He would have a hard time trying to forget. 'I am Melthus,' said the Belgian.

'Is that a skin complaint?' said Joel. '*I've* got a skin complaint.' There was a hint of pride in there, and Joel felt that at least it was common ground.

'An occupational hazard, in a profession such as yours,' said Melthus.

Joel could see as well in the dark as his Dad. But try as he might, and mightily did he try, he could not fix an image of the man Melthus. When he *did* try, the details became foggy. He knew that Melthus was man shaped, in general, but the particulars swam about a bit. Joel's eyes began to water. 'I've got a headache,' said Joel, feeling his pulse.

'You must nourish yourself,' said Melthus. 'Here.'

Two rabbits thumped to the ground. They squeaked a bit. Being alive, and all.

'Bunnies!' cried Joel.

'Food, you daft twat,' said his Dad.

'You would do well to listen to your father,' said Melthus.

'How're we gonner cook rabbits down here?' said Joel. He looked around. 'Oi. Melthus.'

'He's gone, ' said Dad. 'And good riddance.'

'He scares me,' said Joel. 'Here, bun.'

'Don't play with your food, boy.'

'I'm not *eating* him.' He stroked the rabbit's ears. 'He reminds me of Mr. Buggles.'

The old man's eyes rolled upward.

'Nice, er, ickle rabbit,' said Joel. 'Lovely, fat, vibrant creature. That's a fine pulse you've got. Healthy. A bit fast, but you don't like being tossed on the floor like a slab of meat, do you? No.' Joel licked dry lips. 'A piece of *raw* meat. A hint of fat. Crushed peppercorns. Lots of gravy.'

'Stop it, boy,' said his Dad. 'Pass me the other rabbit.'

'...Rich, dark gravy. With bits of coagulated blood in it.' Joel shuddered. *'Good, red blood, spiced with bunny adrenaline.'*

The rabbit that was a dead ringer for Mr. Buggles squawked. It was a brief squawk.

'Mmmmf. Mmmnf. Rrrrfff,' said Joel.

'Don't talk with your mouth full, boy,' said Dad, between bites.

'I said, "Aack, this is disgusting",' translated Joel. I'm drinking *bunny blood*. How low can you go?'

'Get used to it,' said his Dad. 'This is it. From now on, you get your food on the hoof.'

'I'd rather not.'

'*I* don't want to go down that road, boy, but wise up; this little snack is just to keep us going. I have a feeling we'll be expected to hunt bigger prey,' said his Dad. He managed a sigh. It was a strange feeling, filling his lungs with the dank, malodorous gas that passed for air down here. Stranger still to have to make a conscious effort to remember what his lungs were for. 'Like I said, I don't want to go down that road.'

'But don't vampires feed on young virgins?' said Joel.

'I don't thing sexual availability has anything to do with it.'

'Because if it's a virgins-only diet, we're gonner starve.'

'Steady lad. Don't worry. Blood is blood. Did you ask Mr. Buggles there if he was a virgin?'

Point taken. 'Still,' said Joel. 'I wouldn't mind seducing a virgin or two. Just to test my vampiric hypnotic powers.' He wiggled his fingers and eyebrows. 'Woo-oo.'

'Best practice on something less ambitious first,' said Dad. 'Like a field mouse, or a vole.' Dad gave his son a clout. 'Blithering idiot. You're coming home, boy. We can live off black pudding if need be. Blood we can get from a butcher. I ain't bitin' *anybody*, hear me? And neither are you, you little perv.'

'Ow! Da-ad! Leggo!'

But Dad did not hear his son's plaintive cries. For he had come to a decision. They were getting out of there. The sooner they got back to normal, with four walls and a fire in the grate and a glass of Dirty at his elbow, the better he would like it. This vampire malarkey wouldn't be as frightening as it seemed in this lightless, wet dungeon.

The only thing more frightening than this place, and that bugger Melthus, was having to explain to the Missus.

It would need tact, diplomacy, cunning, economy of truth and a heavy dose of subterfuge; his Missus could see through a lie like a whore's nightie.

'There'll be no mention of this to your mother,' said Dad, already sweating heavily at the thought of it. 'She won't be having Undead under her roof.'

'We have to be invited in, anyway,' said Joel.

'Don't be soft,' said Dad. 'It's going to take my considerable experience of lying through my teeth just to stop her slamming the door in my face, and you want an *invitation*?'

'That's the way it works, Pop. A victim, once inside their home, is safe unless the vampire is given permission to enter.'

'I think that rabbit's drained, lad. Put it down.'

'Still a few more drops.'

'Leave it, boy. It sounds disgusting.'

'Sucking comforts me; you know I gets anxiety attacks.'

'Ee gods,' said Dad. 'World tremble. A neurotic vampire. Joel, your public is not ready to meet you yet. What you – both of us – need, is time to think.'

The tunnels had no end. They wove through the bedrock, beneath streets and houses, fields and brooks. The two Newborn could have wandered deeper into the labyrinth without knowing it. But they had other senses, now, and not least of these was the draw of the moon. Dad could feel it. He followed the air currents, sniffing. 'Up here,' said the old man. He began pulling at boulders that had blocked the mouth of a tunnel.

'Watch where you're chucking that,' Joel complained, dodging a boulder the size of a watermelon.

'Give us a hand, then.'

Between them, father and son shifted enough good Bath stone to build a decent bungalow. Or a small house. Half a dozen outside loos or sheds, possibly. Whatever your architectural fancy happens to be. But they shifted great blocks of it. They'd have made a good living, quarrying, but the door to that career was now firmly shut. As were many doors in normal life. Unless they could get permanent night work, times were going to be hard.

'But we *have* permanent night work, son.'

'Dint say anyfink.'

'Look, the worst has happened. There's nothing we can dig up that's worse than us. Think of the advantages.'

Like, you could do your fair share of the digging, thought Joel.

'That ain't fair,' said Dad.

No. It ain't. I've been carrying you for years, you old scrote.

Thwack. That's the sound of an unexpected, open palmed slap across the lughole. 'Ow!' was the noise Joel made when his lughole exploded.

'Old scrote, ay? Bin carryin' me 'ave yer, all these years?'

'Ow! You're reading my thoughts,' Joel said, in the tones of one who has just caught someone sniffing his soiled underwear.

'So what?'

'It's like reading someone's diary, that is.'

'Aye. Done that, too.'

'You really are an old bastard. A rotten, scrotey old bastard. A rotten, scrotey, *smelly* old bastard. A rotten, scrotey, smelly, *nosey* old bastard. A rotten, scrotey, smelly –'

'Shut your cake hole for five minutes. I can hear something.'

There were steady drips of water, but that had become a mere background noise. Nevertheless, behind all the noises conducted through the rock – a 'bus or lorry thundered along a road, somewhere, and a pneumatic drill hammered far away – another sound could be detected.

'Sounds like wind,' said Joel. 'And it isn't me.'

'And rain,' said Dad.

'And a door. A loose door, rattling in its frame.'

'Yes.

'And a spider. Muttering to itself as it spins its web. A flatulent spider.'

'I didn't hear that. That's amazing.'

'I didn't, either. I'm pissing about.' Chortle, went Joel.

'Move those rocks, you little shite.'

And move more rocks they did. Until finally…

'Godzilla's goolies,' exclaimed Joel. 'A door.'

'A trap door.' Dad pushed against it. 'A padlocked trap door.'

'Oh. What a nuisance.' Joel pushed. Hard. Timber creaked and timber broke and the trapdoor all but flew off its hinges.

'You first,' said his Dad. For once, Joel didn't mind being volunteered. He felt strong, invincible. As his Dad had said, there was nothing they could meet that was worse than him.

Yea, though I walk through the back streets of Twerton, I shall fear no evil, for I am surely the meanest motherfucker in the valley. Any valley. Any fucking city. Boy, do I feel sexy tonight.

Having finished this blasphemous misquote, he started to muse upon it. 'Dad, d'you reckon we're evil?'

'Evil is as evil does,' quoth his Dad.

'No. Seriously.'

'I *am* serious, lad. We've bin robbin' graves for years. You think that deserves a Community Action Award?'

'That's just bad behaviour,' reasoned Joel. ' I'm talking about real evil.'

'Just get through that trap door, son, and we'll talk religion later.'

Joel reached up, grabbed the edges of the open trap door and pulled himself up. However, he miscalculated the effort required. 'Whoa,' went Joel, doing a fair impression of a vertical take-off.

'Stop pissing about, boy. Help me up.'

Joel did not reappear. Dad hauled himself up, surprised at how easy this was. No explosion of arthritic pain, no grind of bone upon unprotected bone.

His limbs and joints were supple, well-muscled tools that did his bidding without complaint for the first time in twenty years.

Dad found himself in a room, as would be expected, but this room induced in him a mortal dread. Which was daft, considering he was no longer mortal. 'Joel? Joel, where are you?'

A kick to the side of the head told him where his errant son had gone.

'Come down from there,' hissed the Dad.

''M stuck,' came the muffled reply.

Dad looked up. He could see a goodly part of his son, save for his head, which had penetrated the ceiling.

'Get me down.'

Dad grabbed the dangling legs and pulled. When this did not work, he swung to and fro, feet off the floor, until a splinter and a groan above signalled success. The two almost fell back through the trap door.

'That hurt,' said Joel, plucking long splinters from his neck and face.

'Anything up there?'

'Some kind of shop. I dunno. There's windows and another door.'

'Well, let's get this one open first,' said the Dad, indicating the portal in the far wall.

'What's that hanging on it?' said Joel.

'Just open it.'

Joel dutifully complied. The closer he got to the door, the greater the sense of terror. He was within three feet of it but no power on earth or beyond could take him any closer. Even stretching a hand toward the doorknob proved to be a feat in itself. He touched the knob and a fizz of white-hot energy blew his hand away.

'It's wet,' said Joel, hopping about and blowing on his hand. 'Someone's rigged it to the 'leccy supply. Bastards!'

'No. 'Taint that. Look.'

What had appeared to be no more than the gap between door panels now became obvious. 'It's a Cross,' Joel said, backing away. 'Oh shitty-do.'

'There's your answer, then,' said Dad.

'I'm evil?'

'We, lad. We.'

'Ferkin' ay!' said Joel. 'I really *am* the meanest mothefu-'

Thwack.

'That doesn't mean I have to tolerate language like that, boy.'

Joel's bubble burst. His Dad had a habit of doing that.

'Looks like the only way is up,' said Dad, raising his eyes to the floorboard ceiling. 'Do you think you can widen that hole?'

Joel flexed his fingers, biceps, and any other muscle that was handy. 'No problem.' He jumped, grabbed, pulled, and planks broke. It was the work of less than a minute to create an exit. 'Done,' he said, dropping to the floor. He glanced at the door. The Cross was glowing. 'I want to be far away from here,' he said.

'Then let us depart.'

*

The upper room was a strange affair. There were glass cases with bits of rock, dried plants, mounted insects, and various animals that bore testimony to the taxidermist's art.

'Weird,' said Joel. 'Who'd wanna buy stuff like this?'

''Tisn't a shop,' snapped Dad. 'I know where we are.'

Joel put his fist through the glass counter. He pulled out a chunk of rock, hefted it in his hand then threw it through another display case.

'Stop that!' growled the Dad.

'Just havin' fun,' sulked the boy.

'It's vandalism.'

'Yeah,' nodded the vandal, exploring other avenues of delinquency. 'That's why it's fun.'

Dad shook his head. You tried to raise them right but in the end it was all down to them. 'Let's just go,' he said.

But Joel was busy. Dad heard him mooching around in the next room. He heard the boy call.

'Look at this,' said Joel.

Dad entered the room. It smelled of hospitals.

'What?'

Joel nodded at the table in the centre of the room. Spread-eagled across it, fixed firmly in place by metal pins, was a crow. 'Ee,' said Joel. 'Someone's been messing about with a dead bird. That's sick, that is.'

'Tis called "*desiccation*",' said Dad, who knew a bit about the doings of scientists. Not much. Just a bit.

'I think you'll find that's *dissection*, Pop. But it's still sick.' Joel removed the pins. The body remained spread-eagled. 'So where are we?'

'This is the wildlife centre, up in Box Wood. I 'eard about it.'

'But why the trap door? The cross on the door? Holy water on the ferkin' door handle?'

'All good questions, boy, but nothing to concern us. We're gone.' And so said, no sooner done. The Dad pushed the main door open. The lock fell with a sad little clunk onto the gravel. 'That was strange,' he said. For, having fixed an image of himself opening the door, he had apparently crossed two rooms without putting one foot before the other.

'That'll be your new vampire powers,' said Joel. 'The Undead can *move*.'

'There'll be no more mention of our predicament,' said Dad. 'Now, home, boy.'

'But mum's bound to notice.'

'Shut up and pull your teeth in,' said Dad, attempting same. Tooth retraction, however, proved to be a tricky exercise.

'My dentures don't fit anymore.'

'That's because you don't need 'em.' Joel tapped a sharp fingernail against a healthy white pearly. 'You've got a new set.'

Dad's face lit up. 'Of course. Oh joy. Oh *bliss*.'

'Mum's going to notice that.'

'No she won't. I'll tell her I've been in the dental hospital having screw-ins put in.'

'They can't do that.'

'I know. But your ma don't. Which is how we'll leave it.'

Joel cast a doubtful glance at his Dad. 'That's the story then, is it? We've been at the clinic?'

'It solves the problem of explaining where we've been. What time is it?'

Joel gave his Timex a shufti. 'Just after midnight.'

'What's the date?'

'Give over, Dad.'

'The date.'

Huff, said Joel, and pressed a little fiddly button on his timepiece. 'Oh,' he said.

'How long've we been out of it?'

'Only twenty four hours.'

'Buggeration.'

'Well, we could say it was touch-and–go, as they say in the medic movies.'

'We're talkin' dental surgery, boy, not a heart transplant.' Dad sighed. 'No matter. I'll tell her they left something behind when they stitched me up.'

'In your gums?'

'Don't quibble,' said Dad. 'Anyway, it happens all the time.'

'I don't think so, Dad.'

'Look, you little shi-'

Car headlights swept the windows of the centre, illuminating the far wall behind them. Father and son ducked.

'See? I told you to get a move on.'

'No you didn't,' said Joel.

'Did.'

'Didn't.'

'Did so.'

'Did.'

'Didn't.'

'Hah!' said Joel, punching the air. 'Gotcha!'

Thwack.

'Someone coming. Quick.'

'Quick?' said Joel.

'*Hide*, you silly sod.' Dad scanned the available options. Across the clearing surrounding the building, bushes and rocks offered the likeliest cover. A car door slammed. Feet on gravel.

'I'm right behind you,' said Joel.

And again, no sooner said than done. They made no sound, those Undead feet, nor was there print or track to mark their perambulations within or without.

'Who is it?'

'How the shite should I know?' said Dad. 'Some scientist bod, p'raps. Who else would be up 'ere, this time o' night?'

'Vampires, for one', muttered Joel.

'Shh.'

They watched the tall figure as it crunched gravel. The man stopped and froze when he reached the mangled door. Then he unbuttoned his coat and began searching inside it.

'What's he doing?'

'I'm not the fount of all feckin' wisdom, lad, much as I'm flattered that you think so. Now shush,' said Dad, putting a finger to his lips.

The tall man withdrew his arm from the recesses of his coat. His hand gripped a large crucifix. In the other, a short rod of some kind. Pointy at one end, it was.

'Shit,' said Dad.

'What?' asked Joel.

'Shit shit shit.'

'What what what? Who is he?'

'Someb'dy who knows what he's doing', That's what what what.'

The two fugitives ducked again as the man turned around. A torch beam hit a tree trunk above their heads. It swept the bushes then moved on. 'This is fun,' said Joel.

'That's all your generation thinks about,' muttered Dad.

'Cause that's all there is,' said Joel, a little testy. Why did his Dad always react to the mere mention of the word "*fun*"?

'There's also twenty miles between us and a warm bed, lad.'

'No problem. We can just change into bats, like, and–'

A clout cut the flight of fancy short.

'Sounds like he found the hole in the floor,' said Dad. 'We'd best be gone.'

Joel stood up and screwed his eyes shut. He flapped his arms.

'What are you doing?' said his Dad, wrinkling his nose and knotting his brow in bewilderment.

'Shush,' said his offspring. ' I'm about to transmute.'

'Well, do it later.' *Dirty little shite*, thought Dad, giving him a look.

Joel opened his eyes. He looked at his arms, which were still the size and shape they had always been.

'Disappointed,' he grumbled.

Dad looked across at the Land Rover. The lights were still on. Exhaust plumed from the rear, the door left open and the keys still in it.

'Fun, eh?'

'Uh?'

'You want fun?'

'What?'

'*Fun*, boy. You want some?'

'What?'

'Follow me.'

*

Pitt had expected a break-in at some point. An unguarded building in the woods was bound to attract the moronic sooner or later. Easily fixed.

But he wasn't prepared to find that certain defences had been breached. The sheer tonnage of rock in the tunnel below should have been enough. Ever cautious, he'd had the basement room subdivided. The room with the trap door was protected. He hadn't considered that a crucifix would be necessary on the ceiling. In retrospect, a similar safeguard should have been fixed to the trapdoor.

A right balls-up, thought Pitt. A muscle twitched in his face. His nose wrinkled. *How could I have overlooked it?*

He would have to do something about this before he left. Taking out a slim bottle from his coat pocket, he dribbled blessed water over the trapdoor and all around. A little more on the door, too. He fixed his crucifix to the hole in the ceiling, as well as he was able, returned to the upper rooms and proceeded to empty the remaining Holy water around the gap in the floorboards.

With all this done, Pitt left the centre. He thought about nailing the main door shut, but decided that it was pointless.

Pitt had been hoping that this particular access point to the tunnels would be safe enough. At least until he was prepared. This development had thrown him somewhat. He would have to get the basement filled in with concrete, which was going to be difficult to explain to Berkoff. At least his usual contractor could be relied upon to remain silent - for the right remuneration, of course.

If nothing else this incident emphasised the need for precaution, and it had proved that his theory was correct. Melthus was still down there swelling the ranks of his army and some of them were just too damned impatient to get out into the cold fresh air. It was important now to find as many access tunnels as he could. They would also have to be filled in. Holy water, cement and sand aggregate should do the trick.

He was still worried about his missing notebook; too many details in it to let it go. He already had a list of those who were on site when it had been stolen and he meant to see each one individually. It was just another problem.

Yet his latest acquisition put all of his anxieties into perspective. *Now* he had a weapon. *Now* he could achieve something, instead of rooting about in the earth looking for evidence.

But it's still a risk. Kevin said so himself. I must be desperate.

When the battle began, people were going to die.

He would have to justify his actions, his suspicions; show them proof. Make them listen. He had archaeological finds - tangible evidence – but now he had a *live* specimen, living under his roof. All that was left was the fight.

Still, Kevin Costner is hardly a name for an action hero. "Kevin the Slayer" isn't going to strike fear into the heart of a monster. We'll have to work on that.

Pitt returned to his car, deep in his musings. He climbed in, dropped into the driver's seat and let out a heartfelt chestful of cold air which, if not meant to be a symptom of relief, certainly sounded so. He reached up and touched the little pentagram that dangled from the rear-view mirror by a silver chain. Just for luck. Something he did when he felt he'd had a close one - road rage, fender benders, uncomfortable questions from the University Board, and brushes with the Undead (which amounted to the same thing, in his opinion).

People assumed that he was aloof, impervious to the problems that plagued lesser mortals. But Pitt knew fear and he felt it now. In the shrinking of his scrotum, the clenching of his gut and the crazy tingling in his fingertips, he felt the fear.

But he swallowed it. He didn't allow himself to chew it over, making him too scared to think. That would be too easy, giving into it. Even if he dearly wished that he could abandon the work, bury himself in respectable studies, organise none-controversial digs; lock, bolt and douse that front door with blessed water and break out the crucifixes. That had its own appeal and he had given it serious consideration many times, but then, as now, he ate the fear whole.

Why, then, did he feel the hair on the back of his neck bristling like the hackles of a pissed-off Rottweiler?

*

'But we don't know where he's going,' whispered Joel.

'It don't matter. Anywhere's better'n the woods. You want that Melthus geezer looking for you?'

'Nuh.'

'So shut it.'

Joel sulked. 'Bet I could've flown. If I'd really tried.'

'Shut. It.'

CHAPTER TWENTY-ONE

Night Shift. Wednesday 19th 12 a.m.

'I ought to suspend you both,' said DI Bratt.

PCs Park and Feart shifted uneasily in their seats.

'But I won't.'

Park and Feart expressed their gratitude.

'Aren't you going to ask me why?'

'Why, Sir?' said Feart.

'I'm glad you asked me that, so I'll tell you. I have a new assignment for you.'

Park and Feart looked at each other in a way best described as Oh Shit.

'Indeed,' said Bratt. 'Deep shit. Deep, deep shit.'

Click-clack, went the DI's balls.

'Before I tell you what your new assignment is, may I take this opportunity to commend you on your initiative. You detected a crime that would have gone unnoticed for some time.'

There were mumbled thanks from the two Constables.

'The recovery of two murder victims has shed new light on the *Phantom* murders. And the footprint cast is being analysed by forensics as we speak. Very well done. And in the light of this, I have arranged to have you both transferred to CID. Congratulations, detectives. However…'

Bugger, said the glance exchanged between Barry and Clive.

'…As you are aware,' continued Bratt, opening his desk drawer, 'after your illegal exhumation of the deceased, the bodies were to be taken to the mortuary. That much we know. There were at least twenty witnesses who will testify that they saw the mortal remains of Joel and Dougal Sampson bagged up, boxed and loaded into the coroner's van. Do you agree that this is so?'

Barry nodded, Clive made a confirmatory noise.

'And yet,' said Bratt, taking a small brown bottle from the drawer and shaking a pile of little yellow tablets into his palm, 'the mortuary technician and the attending forensic pathologist did not take delivery, as it were, at the intended destination. Between Tepid Ashton and the autopsy room at the Infirmary, the bodies disappeared.'

This much Clive and Barry did not know. They had returned to the station on Tuesday morning to write their reports before finishing what had been an extraordinarily long shift.

'Disappeared?' said Barry.

Bratt swallowed his medication. Click-clack, went his balls.

'That is correct. Indeed, the van was found just yards around the corner. What is singular about the case is that the driver of the coroner's vehicle was found with his neck snapped – and, I might add, with such violence that the fellow's head was almost ripped clean off.'

Clive swallowed whatever had been lurking at the back of his throat and Barry opted for the dazed look.

'Well?' said Bratt.

'Sir?' said Clive.

'Why are you still here? Get out. Out out out. As detectives, the First Rule of keeping me happy is to know that I want my slightest whim satisfied five minutes before I tell you. Now scoot.'

They scooted but, at the door, so close to a clean and swift exit, Bratt bade them pause. 'One more thing,' said the Guv'nor. 'This "Frank" you interviewed. Local potter, you said.'

Park and Feart nodded.

'His fingerprints were recovered. We got a match.'

Clive grinned; Barry raised his brow.

'He disappeared.'

Barry could not admit to surprise.

'Six months ago,' added Bratt. 'Interesting that he should happen to be at home when you called, don't you think? It would bear further policemanly investigation.'

DC Park and DC Feart nodded agaian and immediately vacated their Guv'nor's office.

*

Lucy was more than up for a shag. She was also more than happy to have a hand in Kevin's demise.

'I can take him,' said Lucy.

'I know you can,' said Dufus, enjoying a post-coital ciggie. 'But Melthus was…emphatic. Just stay in the background, watch and listen, make your reports. For now. Don't move on him until you can be sure of a kill.'

Lucy snarled.

'Hey, I'm just the messenger,' said Dufus, showing his palms. 'Look, it won't be much longer. The Solstice is upon us.'

Lucy retracted her fangs.

'Got a bit of drool on your chin,' said Dufus.

She wiped it off. 'I suppose it can wait,' she said.

'Good. Fancy another shag?'

'You have to ask?' she said, straddling him.

'Gentle or rough?'

Ruff, she replied

*

'Detectives!' said Clive. He punched the air. 'Yes!'

'Yeah,' said Barry.

'Gimme five,' said Clive, holding up a palm, slapping for the use of.

'Jubilation. A wonderful thing. But I draw the line at high fives.'

'Miserable git,' said Clive, but he did not allow his partner's lack of spontaneity to ruin his moment of glory. He hopped about a bit. Hopped, skipped and punched his way to the locker room, in fact.

Barry removed his uniform, carefully folding it and placing it in his locker. Standing there in his novelty underwear, he was a forlorn sight. Which Clive did not understand. And said so.

'I like being a beat copper,' was all he had to say on the matter.

'But this is the big time!' enthused Clive. 'Come on, Baz, don't be a wet fart. Think of the totty!'

Barry shook his head and pinched the bridge of his nose. 'Clive. Clive, Clive, Clive. I know you're relatively new to the job, your probationary two years, and I know that all the young bloods see their time in uniform as a mere stepping-stone to plain clothes; but there's more to policing than undercover work and growing your hair longer. Some of us *want* to be on patrol. It's why I joined.'

'That's not the reason you're pissed off, though, is it?' said Clive, putting his new detective skills into effect.

Barry managed a smile. 'Have you any idea what it's going to be like, working under Bratt?'

Clive considered this. The DI's reputation for eccentricity was well earned. One might even say that he was renowned for it. Some detectives had pleaded to transfer back to uniform rather than endure the DI's tirades. More DC's had been referred to the psychologist, during Bratt's long reign of terror, than the rest of the division put together.

'Still a good detective, though,' said Clive.

'The man is ruthless,' said Barry. 'He'll drive us both into the ground until this case is solved. And he'll call you out. Any time of the day or night, whatever you're doing, he'll expect you to be there.'

'It'll be worth it,' said Clive. 'And I don't have to stay with CID indefinitely,' said Clive. Which was true enough. He'd already made plans to make Special Branch by the time he was twenty-five.

'True,' said Barry.

'But?'

'Many a broken man has said the same.' Barry finished dressing. Even in his jeans, V-neck pullover and cheap stockman coat, he still gave the impression that he was in uniform. Which Clive admired.

Some people are born to be coppers, he thought; *as a baby, Baz probably formally cautioned his mum for using artificial milk.*

Clive himself wore a snazzy black suit and collarless white shirt, shoes brightly polished, cufflinks gleaming. 'How do I look?'

Like a Jehovah's Witness, thought Barry. 'A real Dandy,' he said.

They reported immediately to the canteen, as any self-respecting cop with time on his hands should. Over a greasy breakfast, they considered their next move.

'What's our next move?' said Clive, spearing a sausage.

'Good question. A detective's question.' Barry wiped a fried slice over the egg that had dripped on his coat. 'First, I suggest we pay a visit to the mortuary, find out what forensics have to say about the coroner's driver.'

'Do we have to?' said Clive, replacing the sausage on his plate. He didn't like autopsy rooms, especially since an awful lot of so-called corpses seemed to be surprisingly mobile of late; he'd heard about the latest absconder. The dog warden had still not been located. He wished he'd never seen all those zombie films.

'I doubt you'll actually see any cadavers,' said Barry, munching a bit of fried kidney.

'It's not that I don't have the stomach for it,' said Clive, shameless with this falsehood. 'I just don't see how it'll help us.'

'We're after a serial killer,' said Barry, slicing a piece of liver. 'And the driver is the latest victim. There may be evidence, some clue to point the way.'

'But he had his neck snapped. All the others were' – Clive paused to swallow – 'drained of blood.'

'The culprit didn't have time to feed,' said Barry. 'There were police everywhere. You don't take the time to rip a man's throat out and drain him.'

Clive did not like blood, a curious phobia for a police officer. Anything related to the workings of the slithery bits within the human body made him bilious. There was a reason why God had put all that slimy stuff inside. It was to allow folk to go about their lives without the risk of repeated vomiting.

Barry shoved his fork into a sautéed ox testicle and transferred it to his mouth. 'Furthermore,' he said, wiping seminal juices from his chin, 'there may be traces of the perpetrator. Skin under the fingernails. Hair. Clothes fibres. It may give us a clearer picture of what we're dealing with.' Barry swallowed the testicle and began to tuck into the roast pig's heart.

Clive had lost all interest in his sausages. He was aware as never before of what they said went into them: lips'n'arseholes, specifically. In any case, watching his partner devour a plateful of offal was perversely fascinating. Perhaps he might be cured of his aversion to all things organic. And then, as Barry started work on his black pudding, a thought occurred.

'Hang on,' said Clive. 'You said, "feed".'

'What?'

'Feed. You said the Perp didn't have time to *feed*. What's that all about?'

Barry looked up from his plate. 'Did I say that?'

'You did. You also said that forensics might tell us what we're dealing with. Not whom. *What*.'

'Did I?'

'Stop stuffing your face for a minute, Baz. What's on your mind?'

Barry forked the last mouthful, a lamb's eyeball, into his busy gob. He dabbed at his mouth with a paper napkin, drained his tea mug, and began to roll a ciggie. 'Clive, who do you think killed Joel and his Dad?'

'The *Phantom*,' said Clive, without hesitation. 'Same MO.'

'Yes yes. But consider the nature of their business. What were they doing shortly before they died?'

'Robbing a grave.'

'Exactly. And where was the body of young Sarah Farquaarson?'

Clive shrugged.

'Come on, detective, you'll have to do better than that.'

Clive made a sound that said he was becoming exasperated. 'P'raps it was stolen.'

'For what reason?'

'Well, Frank said she was involved in some cult or other. Maybe they nicked it. For nefarious reasons.'

'Frank. Yeah, interesting you should mention him. I ought to have brought him in for questioning. Where did you find him, by the way?'

'Walking down the high street, stretching his arms and saying "another hard day at the potter's wheel".'

Barry shook his head. Something about Frank didn't smell right at all. 'Anyway, nefarious or not, removing a corpse would leave clues. Footprints, a vehicle to transport the body. Now, it's possible that someone came along with the sole intention of stealing Sarah's corpse and this someone discovers Joel and his Dad interfering with it. But it would have to be more than one person, which would preclude the idea that the *Phantom* is a lone operator. It stretches the imagination to consider how one nutcase manages to perform his evil work without leaving tracks, but several? I don't think so.'

'Who says that there was more than one?' said Clive. He thought that it was a reasonable question.

'Clive, it's one thing to overpower a single terrified female. But Joel is a big man. A bit of a wussy, but still a man. Even a coward will fight when his life is threatened and his Dad would not have stood by while his son was done in. There would have been a bit of a ruck, don't you think?'

Clive frowned. The business of detecting was a whole lot more complicated than he'd thought. There seemed to be a lot of actual thinking involved. 'Well yeah, I s'pose.'

'Did you see any sign of a struggle?'

'No.'

'And there was frost on the ground that night. There were no tire tracks when we arrived, were there?'

'All right' said Clive, leaning back in his chair and ruffling his coiffured Barnet. 'So it wasn't the *Phantom* who did for Joel and his Dad. What are you suggesting?'

'I'm not going to spoon feed you anymore,' said Barry, standing up. 'We've got plenty of time before we see Bratt again. Let's pop along to the mortuary.'

'I don't mind being spoon fed,' said Clive. 'And you still haven't explained what you meant by “feed”'.

'That's right. And until you get your brain working on both cylinders and come up with a few ideas of your own, I shall not reveal my thoughts on the matter.'

'That's not fair.'

'*Life* is unfair. Now move your bottom. Mortuary, then we'll go see Pitt.'

'Pitt?'

'Yeah. I understand he's overseeing the autopsies on *all* the *Phantom* related cases. Interesting, that, don't you think?'

The two detectives left the canteen and proceeded, in a copperly manner, and Infirmary-directed fashion.

*

'Let me get this straight,' said Clive to the mortuary technician. 'Mr. Costner died, but you don't have the body.'

'You don't know any of this? Don't you people talk to each other? We've had police all over the place most of the evening.'

Clive hated that, being referred to as You People. It really caught his pubes in his foreskin, that did. 'Okay. We'll leave that for now. But why hasn't the driver-'

'Mr. Lumley,' said Barry, referring to his notebook.

'-Mr. Lumley been examined yet. This is a murder investigation.'

The technician looked at Clive as he would at a lump of brown sticky stuff on his shoe. 'Then he'd be at the forensic mortuary, wouldn't he?'

'But Professor Pitt is doing the autopsy isn't he? And he does his forensic work here.'

'That's true. But Pitt told me he had to postpone it until tomorrow. Eight o'clock sharp. It wasn't urgent.'

'Wasn't urgent?' Clive repeated. 'This is a –'

'-Murder investigation,' said the technician, holding up a hand. 'Yeah. You said. Look, pal, I just work here. I follow orders. If you ask me, all the bloody murder victims should be done at the forensic lab. But Pitt has a lot of clout. He could do an autopsy on the Queen mum's dinner table if he wanted. '

Barry rubbed his chin. 'Did you say *all* the victims? Including Sarah Farquaarson?'

'Nup. Her family had connections, and they weren't keen to have a *common* pathologist getting his grubby paws on their daughter – especially since some of the bodies in his care have gone missing.'

'And he's still allowed to practice…' said Barry, doing more of the old chin rubbing. 'I think I need to look into that.'

'You look into whatever you like, mate. Like I said, I just work here. You want to see the stiff?'

Clive did not like this man. Short, his girth as great as his height, his chubby cheeks red with broken capillaries. A big fat cigar in his big fat mouth, his stupid Hitler Barnet and his twatty glass eye.

'I can't help it. I lost the bugger when I was a kid.'

Barry whispered in Clive's ear. 'You ought to try not to think aloud, detective.'

'Bugger. Sorry, Mr.…?'

'Just Mister to you, shit face. I'm just telling you how it is. It's not my fault.'

Barry intervened. 'So is Mr. Lumley here, or at the forensic unit?'

'Yeah,' he admitted, in a tone which suggested reluctance. 'He's here. But he should be at the other place. As if I haven't got enough to do. I hate murder victims.'

'Yes. That's very humanitarian. If you would be so kind as to show us.' Barry was already weary and they'd only just started the shift.

The obstreperous midget led them to the rear of the autopsy room. He opened up the cold storage unit and pulled the late Mr. Lumley out on his tray, like the butcher's cut of the day at the bargain counter. The body had not yet been wrapped. He flicked the sheet off the corpse's face.

'You could have laid him on his back,' said Clive.

'He *is* on his back.' The technician grabbed the head and turned it the right way up.

'*Jesus,*' said Clive. 'When the Guv'nor said his neck was broken, I didn't realise…' He turned away. 'Oooargh.'

Barry patted his colleague on the back. 'Would you be kind enough to fetch a bucket for detective Feart, please? Thank you so much.'

The technician shook his head, as if dismayed at the calibre of police officers nowadays, but waddled off to get a suitable receptacle.

When he'd gone, Barry gave the body a closer examination. He pulled the sheet completely off the body.

Mr. Lumley had not been prepared for autopsy. He was still in his black suit, the one he'd been wearing when he met his Maker. He was evidently someone who'd taken a lot of care in his appearance. The suit was spotless, pressed; the shoes, apart from the grit and dirt they'd picked up from the ground, were immaculate. The tie was knotted just so. The shirt was possibly new; the collar was crisp, no sign of wear. None of these items had labels.

Barry frowned. He took a roll of Sellotape from his pocket and tore off a strip. He applied the sticky side to an area on the left side of the corpse's face, close to the neck. He removed it, complete with the skin sample attached to it, stuffed it into a specimen bag.

Lumley's countenance was not at peace.

Perhaps it had been that that had tickled Clive's razz reflex. 'You all right now, mate?'

'Thbit. Ack. Yes. Think so. I 'ate being 'ick.'

'Take your time.' You couldn't blame the lad, thought Barry. He looked at Lumley again.

The man's face was a white as his shirt, but that was normal enough. It was the look of surprise that struck him. Not as in "What a lovely pair of breasts madam, but please put them away, this is a public highway." More like, "Which part of the deepest ocean did *you* slither from, Quasimodo?"

For whatever those wide goldfish eyes had seen had etched itself upon the blank canvas of his face. The nostrils were flared. The mouth was stretched wide, but not like a mouth open to scream; it was stretched sideways.

The chin, square once upon a time, had disintegrated. Teeth had been knocked out. The jaw had been dislocated, forced out of the hinge socket and outward so that the skin was stretched, as if he was sucking a gobstopper and it had got stuck at the side. There was dried blood inside the mouth and the tongue had all but disappeared.

Barry took a closer look at the heavily damaged right side of the face. The cheek was close shaved but a single hair stuck out. It didn't match the colour of the man's hair.

The technician returned with a steel bucket. He threw it down with bad grace. Barry clutched at his chest. 'Was that absolutely necessary, you evil little bastard?'

'What did you say?'

'I said, do you have a pair of tweezers, please?'

'Harry frigging Corbett![*] Don't you people carry your own equipment?'

'I'm so sorry. I plucked my eyebrows this morning, and do you know, I put my tweezers and mirror down and I completely forgot where I put them! Aren't I a silly girl?'

'No need to take the piss,' said the technician. 'What d'you want 'em for?'

'I have a nasal hair that tickles every time I breathe. Would you?'

The technician scowled but walked off once more.

'Clive. Are you done yet?' said Barry

'Yeah. Think so. I'll never eat sausages again.'

'Probably for the best. You know what's in 'em, don't you?'

'Don't say it.'

'Lips-'

'NO. Please.'

'-and arseholes-'

'-Bastard-'

'-And noses-'

'-NO-'

'-And eyelids.' Barry pulled a face that shouted disgust. 'And *ears*,' he added.

If this had been meant to test Clive's mettle, then Clive had the victory. He pushed all thought of anything of a retchly sort from his mind. He was a professional. 'There. See? Nothing you can say can hurt me.'

'And then there's the minced penis, bollock bag-'

'Shit.' Splat, went something into the bucket.

Barry shook his head and chuckled. He really was a git sometimes. Being the nice, reasonable one was no fun. He ought to do things like that more often.

'Your tweezers,' said the technician. He glanced at Clive. 'Oil me up with festering lard,' said he. 'Ain't your mate finished yet? What's he been eating?'

'Canteen sausages.'

'Oh. Poor chap. That explains it. Well, go on then.'

[*] Harry Corbett. Famous for having his hands stuck up the arses of a cloth bear and a puppy.

'What?' said Barry. He was waiting for the ribald little oik to bugger off while he completed his unauthorised removal of forensic evidence. Pitt would not be happy.

'The nasal hair. I've never seen anyone actually pull one out before.'

'You don't say. I thought everyone had. There's really not much to see.'

'It'll hurt.'

'Yes,' said Barry cold-eyeing the vertically challenged fiend.

'Go on, then.'

Barry had to the get the little bastard out of the room. He didn't want him telling Pitt what he was up to. He brought the tweezers up to his left nostril. There *was* a hair there that had been tickling and he would really prefer to snip it off, but the technician was eager to see this.

'It's no good,' said Barry. 'I need a mirror.'

'Do I look like a frigging shuttlecock?'

'I'd be grateful. This is going to hurt. A *lot*.'

'All right. But I'm getting mightily wanked off with to-ing and fro-ing.' Off he went.

Barry pulled the single hair from Lumley's grossly bashed-in cheek, put it in a specimen bag then covered the body. He pushed the tray back into the storage unit.

'Time to go,' said Barry, grabbing Clive by the scruff of the neck.

'Ay. 'Ang on.'

Barry hauled him out, eager to be gone before the sadistic, foul-mouthed excuse for a human being returned.

*

The sadistic, foul-mouthed excuse for a human being could not find a hand mirror anywhere and he really wanted to see what the traumatic removal of a nasal hair did to a man's dignity. There was an old store cupboard in the sluice room. Perhaps in there.

The sluice room was in a part of the building he didn't like. There were pipes and ventilation ducts there that made loud noises when you least expected them. He didn't like loud noises. Not unless he was trying to frighten the crap out of someone else.

He hurried along the dark stretch of corridor.

There was a loud metallic clang. He jumped. A squirt of adrenaline buzzed along his arms, leaving unpleasant pins and needles sensations in his fingertips.

'Bastard heating,' he said.

The sluice room was in darkness. He flicked on the light switch. It wouldn't work. Not didn't; *wouldn't.* Because he believed, as the North American Indians did, that all things possessed spirit, or *Manitou.* If an inanimate object didn't do what it was designed to do, it was just sheer bloody-mindedness as far as he was concerned. People went to great expense to buy long life light bulbs, but it was unnecessary. Ordinary bulbs did not just blow. It was done out of malice. Later, he would rip the bloody thing from its socket and give it a damned good thrashing before he stamped on it.

Yes. The sadistic, foul mouthed excuse for a human being had very dark thoughts indeed. A torturer of insects, a ripper of wings from butterflies, as a child he did not leave drawing pins on other kid's chairs at school, oh no; he pushed sharpened nails through flat pencil erasers to see what *that* did to a person's dignity.

What fun life was!

And, oh joy! A mirror!

In his wicked glee the wee monster did not notice that one corner of the room was darker than a shadow should be. Or that it now moved. Not until he walked straight into what he thought at first must be a brick wall.

'Ooyah[*],' he said. 'Sorry,' added the little arse. 'Didn't see you there, doc.'

But it wasn't a doctor.

''Ere,' he said, doing his best Dick Van Dyke cockney. 'What's your game then, John?'

It wasn't Mary Poppins, either.

'You're not supposed to be in here, mate. Go on. Clear off.'

But it wasn't his, or anyone's mate; and he wasn't the sort to clear off when commanded by a five-foot, foul mouthed, sadistic little tosser.

'Aaaaaaargh![†]' said he. Because when someone says, 'Where is Costner?' and you don't have a clue, and when that someone somehow twigs that you don't then expresses his disappointment by lunging at your throat… you don't *say* anything.

And yes, people really do say things like that. Honest. Well, they do when they walk into solid objects. 'Aaaaaaargh!' s so old hat.

Some people have no style.

You run.

'Erk,' said the little tosser. An improvement on aaaaaargh, but not much. There was a meaty, gristly noise, then a squelch, and even that sound you make when your nose is running, you can't find a bit of clean sleeve and you have to snort a six inch semi-solid bogey to the back of your throat.

The door to the autopsy room slammed.

The intruder dropped his meal, as one might toss aside an empty Burger King carton.

The Burger King wrapper that used to be a sadistic little tosser now gurgled and staggered, glugged and stumbled, and in so doing somehow found himself back in the autopsy room. But the dynamic duo had gone, leaving only a pail of sick.

'Baaah-leeerks,' he rasped through his ruined throat. And then, because he had no style…

Yes.

He kicked the bucket.*

---

* Now you can't feel sorry for someone like that, can you? Eh?

CHAPTER TWENTY-TWO

Lucy watched her lover as he slipped between shadows, using the route she had marked for him earlier. Fresh urine was so much easier to use than a map, and she could weaken the Manor's unseen traps as she went. The Professor had taken to using new ones every day and she had to adapt. It would be inconvenient for Pitt to find a charcoaled corpse on his lawn; the Professor was at the height of his powers and it wouldn't do to alert him. Then again, it would be a fresh challenge; it was the closest thing to fun without exchanging body fluids these days. Mere "watching and listening" didn't tweak her adrenal glands.

Now, with Dufus out of the way, the Professor poking about in the Woods and Simmons the caretaker somewhere deep in the bedrock, feeding the furnace in one of the many sub basements, she had the Manor to herself.

She had been putting in a little surveillance overtime since Kevin's arrival; from what the Professor had been saying, Lucy had recognised an opportunity for some authentic malice.

Weapons training.

This is too *easy.*

A sloppy grin had formed, and there it stayed as she moved about the house, meddling with this, fiddling with that, and tweaking things in places most people with a healthy sense of danger would fear to tread.

This done, she returned to her room with a warm feeling of evil glee. As she climbed the staircase her thoughts of mischief took a happy side-turn; she paused, considered, and finding her conclusions more than satisfactory she returned to the ground floor.

In the kitchen she crossed to the bin and had a bit of a rummage. The elderly remains of a can of pilchards was just the thing.

Perfect.

There had been a series of horrifying encounters and cattle mutilations in the fields around the village; there were rumours, and tales, and tales of rumours, but none of them came close to the real horror. Lucy, however, was on nodding terms with this particular creature of the night, and there was only one thing more tempting to it than livestock…and she was laying a trail of it now, all over the driveway and the Professor's favourite parking space.

Pitt would be home soon, and it was a fine night for a silent predator.

'Here, puddy tat; here kittykittykitty…'

*

...And so it came to pass that as she returned to the house, light flared at the far end of the drive. The Professor couldn't have timed it better...

*

...As a pair of luminous yellow eyes caught the glare of approaching headlamps. The eyes blinked, and the brain behind them fizzed and switched to Stalk And Maim mode. The smell of festering fish had pushed all the right buttons...and oh, look, here was *real* prey. It was dressed in tweeds and already had the smell of fear upon it.

The creature crawled on its belly, ready to spring...and slash...and rend...and...

...What *were* those Things lurking in the back of the vehicle?

The shadow beast paused to consider; it had smelled such Things before, all too often on its own territory. As much as it detested Them, it knew well enough not to engage something until it had been observed in combat. It had noted the drained corpses around the woodland across the valley; deer could run far and fast when fleeing feline tooth and claw. It was the same smell that wafted up from the holes and fissures in the bedrock thereabouts, and this particular puddy-tat kept its distance. Better to wait in the shadow by this drainpipe and watch.

The tweedy man-creature had made it to safety (curse it), but the Things were larking about at the gate. There was something different about these two. They gave off a slightly different odour to those Others who visited the Manor (more frequently of late).

Never one to turn away from free entertainment, the maimer of cattle followed the pair for the fun that might be in it, oblivious to the fate that was said to await a creature of curiosity...

It was worth the bother.

*

'What's up Prof?' Kevin said.

Pitt sat in the armchair across from the couch where the vampire lay, still rubbing sleep from his eyes. They were glowing in the semi-darkness,

'Have you breakfasted?'

'Still a little *early,*' snapped Kevin. It was only half past one. 'I thought I might try for a *full night's sleep.*' He sounded peeved.

'No need for shirtiness.'

'I told you. I get cranky when I'm tired.'

Pitt drank deeply from his glass of brandy. His hands shook, and although he was never really a healthy pink he looked particularly washed out; there were shadows in his eye sockets and beneath his prominent cheekbones.

'We must accelerate your training,' said Pitt, after long silence.

'Why?' said Kevin.

'Because the Nest has been breached.' He wiped hair from his face.

'The Nest?'

'Them. The Tribe.'

Pitt did not need to elaborate. The demon inside Kevin knew.

They would come.

Although Kevin was deep in the bedrock of Colerne hill, in his subterranean bachelor pad, sooner or later they would find him and try to claim him, to take his place in the Tribe.

'Bugger,' said the Slayer of Hairy Wotsits. 'Bugger bugger bugger.'

'We still have time,' said Pitt. 'If you're up to it, we should begin your weapons training.'

'Fine by me,' said Kevin, now fully alert. 'I'll just grab a bite from the fridge and I'll be right with you. '

They were an unlikely partnership, Pitt and Kevin, but they had become companionable in a short space of time. As they strolled to the place Pitt had designed for the previous tenant, the Professor leading the way, Kevin drank his O negative from a pewter tankard. It had a glass bottom to it and as he drained the last few drops he could see a crimson-tinted Pitt through the glass. The old buffer was looking worried. He was wringing his hands but Kevin didn't think that the Professor was aware of doing this.

They came to a door. Pitt unlocked it, stood aside to allow Kevin to enter first.

As he stepped across the threshold, something cut the air in front of him. An ordinary person would have been sliced in half lengthways by the blade that swung across from the right, triggered by the pressure pad beneath the stone flag inside the doorway. Kevin rolled, came up in a crouch just in time to hear the click behind him. He rolled again and the crossbow bolt that sped from the wall missed him, hitting the opposite wall then clattering to the floor. He remained where he was, flat on the cold stone, listening. Pitt had closed the door and locked it.

So. He'd been tricked. Pitt had intended to dispatch him from the beginning. Or perhaps he had been unnerved by his experience at the wildlife centre? Pitt had filled him in on what had happened as they made their way to this room. Maybe Pitt didn't trust him anymore. It was a risk, having a vampire as a lodger, even one that still had a human soul capable of controlling the demon within.

Do not be fooled, said the demon inside Kevin's head. *Mortals have been hunting our kind for millennia, since the dawn of Man. You must be wily, cunning; never trust a human.*

'Yeah,' said Kevin aloud. 'As if *you'd* know. I'm human and *I'm* okay.'

You have a strong spirit. An exceptional will. It was your desire for revenge that made you strong enough to resist me.

'Whatever,' said Kevin. 'Just tell me how we're gonna get out of this mess.'

Simply follow your instinct. Do what you are already doing. If you can make it to the far wall, you will understand. And then I will show you a trick or two, said the demon.

After a series of close calls involving more sharp edges, thrusting spears and vibrating wooden stakes than a mediaeval Anne Summers party, Kevin stood with his back to the wall. The darkness was total but, as before, he could see as easily as if it was daylight.

'What now?' said Kevin. He could see the metal poles that stretched from ceiling to floor. Attached to them, brackets that looked as if they ought to hold something.

Face the wall, said the demon.

Kevin obeyed. 'Now what?'

Place your palms against it.

'Done.'

Now climb.

Kevin hesitated. 'That's the plan? Climb?'

Trust me.

'It's sheer rock,' said Kevin.

This is true.

'Are you taking the piss?'

Climb.

So climb he did. One hand at a time, cautious at first, expecting to drop at any moment. Eventually he felt the ceiling against his head. He clung to the wall with his hands, his toes barely touching the rock. This was fun. And he still felt strong. Before the change, a brisk walk would have had him panting.

'What now?'

This is the best bit, said the demon. *Put your hands on the ceiling.*

'No way.'

You are Wamphyr, said the demon. *Try to* act *like one. Do it.*

So he did. He refused to be shamed by something that looked like a fossilised jobbie.

I heard that, said the demon. *I can't help it. I was made this way.*

'Made?'

I am literally Hell spawn, the lowest in the hierarchy of Hell.

'You have social classes in Hell?'

And then some. Like, you have the original Fallen Angels. They're your nobs. Dukes, Archdukes, Princes, Barons.

'Like, up here?'

Where d'you think you lot got the idea? Not all of your human aristocracy began life on Earth[*].

'So where do *you* fit in?'

I, and others like me, were an experiment. The Boss decided He'd have a go at creating life Himself. We were the result. Tried to create a soul but it all went a bit pear-shaped. We can exist in human form, but only if the body is dead and inhabited by a human soul. Tricky, catching a spirit as it leaves the body. It's the pull of the Light.

'Do you lot always succeed?'

Ninety nine times out of a hundred. Pure souls go straight to the Good Place, no problem. Just about everyone does, really – unless we get to 'em first – but people like you…too strong a tie to life, you know? Unsettled business. Either that or they don't realise what's happening until it's too late.

'Well, I suppose I knew I wasn't that good.'

Good enough to go the Good Place.

'Really?'

Yes. But not now. Possibly not ever. Wamphyr aren't easy to kill, and until that happens you and I will have to make the best of it. Now, what d'you say we quit gassing and get some work done, yes?

Well, you have to wonder.

Kevin put a hand on the ceiling. Then the other. When he realised that he wasn't going to fall he was scurrying along the ceiling and around the walls like a big fat hairy house Boris*.

Got the hang of it?

'Is that a joke?' Kevin dropped, landing lightly upon his feet.

Demons don't have a sense of humour.

'We'll have to do something about that.'

Dream on.

Kevin felt great. Top of the world. And hungry.

Good, said the demon. *So feed me.*

'Can I open that door?' There was only one way out of the chamber, and it was iron-banded Oak.

Easy peasy.

'It's heavy.'

No problem. Take a run at it.

Full of confidence and *joie de mort*, he pulled back then ran full tilt at it.

'Aaaaiiii!'

What's that *supposed to be?* said the demon.

'War cry.' And then he hit it head on.

'Ark,' said Kevin, then dropped like a stone. Or like a Wamphyr with a bump on Its head the size of a tennis ball. But the door, apart from a slight crack, remained intact. 'I thought you said it was no problem. Ooh.'

Did I say that you should nut it? What's wrong with a kick?

'Oh me,' said the Slayer. 'Oh my. My poor head. I need a doctor.'

Oh please.

The lump on Kevin's head shrank rapidly. Inside ten seconds, Kevin's crowner was no more. 'That's dead good, that is. Does it work for acne?'

I'm hungry.

'Shut it.' Kevin backed up again. 'A kick, you say?'

A Bruce Lee job.

'I always wanted to do that.'

Well, now you can.

'How?'

You watched all the Lee films.

---

* The sort that creep up out of the plughole while you're having a shower.

'A misspent youth. Always at the pictures.'

And the Van Dammes.

'Wang Yu, too.'

You can do all of that and more.

'Can you fix me up with Claudia Schiffer?'

As an hors d'oerve, perhaps.

'I don't think I can do Bruce Lee.'

Listen, bud, said the demon. *My last incarnation was a Shaolin monk.*

'No shit. You get to be reincarnated?'

The Boss insists on it. Anything good enough for the One ...A bit of one-upmanship, you might say. He's a big kid, really.

'Who?'

My Imperial Lord. Satan. Terrible temper, though.

Kevin thought about all this. Was it possible that he was discussing metaphysics and theology with a demon living inside his head?

Yup said the demon. *I mean, come on...who's going to know more about the afterlife than a wee devil?*

'But that's the point. You've got a biased opinion. How would you know who goes where, and why? Like, what's Heaven like?'

Look, I'm really hungry. Starved. All that exercise.

'I'm on it. Just tell me. How do you know?'

You got the rest of your life to listen? The demon sighed. *Look, Paradise is great. You'll love it. If you get there. If you die. And I know all about it because it's all the Fallen Ones talk about. Endlessly. Talk about homesick.*

'But they can never go back. That's tragic.'

Serves 'em right. They had it all and they blew it. All they have to do is apologise, but will they? Will they bollocks.

Kevin was stunned. He had a million questions.

Save 'em.

'Listen, I can't keep thinking of you as just "demon".'

It's what I am.

'You need a name.'

If it'll get you out of that door, okay.

'Right. Boris it is, then.'

Oh no, hang on a minute ...

But Kevin, thus decided, began his run-up. Five feet from the door he jumped. 'Wassaaah!'

Oh shit, said Boris the demon.

'Aark,' said the Slayer, for solid Bath stone is formidable indeed. Kevin viewed the corridor outside the room from an inverted perspective.

'I'm so sorry,' said Pitt. 'But I heard a bang on the door. I thought you'd finished your workout.'

'You bastard! You locked me in!'

'Again, my apologies. It's been so long since it was last used. I must get the latch fixed.' He took a closer look at it and frowned. 'This looks new.'

'I think I broke both my legs,' said Kevin.

Don't be such an arse whispered Boris the demon.

'Are you ready for your weapons training now?' Pitt said, testing the latch again.

'Whut?' Kevin blinked hard.

Pitt pressed a switch on the wall. 'Just engaging the devices,' he said, then stepped inside the room.

Kevin groaned, stood up then staggered to the door. He leaned against the wall. His hand strayed to the wall switch, the red one that said Clear Room Before Pressing.

Go on, said Boris inside Kevin's head. *Turn it on.*

He was tempted. Lord, he was tempted. And it would teach Pitt a lesson. His finger twitched. It would be soooo easy.

A bead of sweat rolled down his face.

Go ooooooon. You know you want to.

Kevin trembled. Yes. He couldn't deny it.

You believe all that crap about the latch not working properly? Bollocks. That was a test. He was testing you, see if you were cracked up to be a slayer. No skin off his nose if you didn't make it. One less vampire. Off with your head while you're lying there with your guts split open, trying to heal; a stake through the ticker, a handful of Roses in your cake hole, and into the furnace with you. Go oooooon.

'No.' Kevin took his hand away. 'No, I won't. It's not my way.'

Damn, said Boris.

'You arsehole,' said Kevin. 'That was horrible. You nearly made me do it.'

No. You did. Another inch and my Lord would have had you.

'Charming. Are you always going to be like that?'

It's in my nature. Now please, let's go and eat.

'Nag nag nag.' Kevin wondered off back to his flat, picked up another couple of bags of O Positive and filled his tankard. When he returned to the training room there had been some changes. 'What the -?'

'Ah. Replenishing your energy reserves. Splendid.'

Kevin burped. 'What's all this?', he said, waving a free hand to encompass the chamber.

The steel poles in the room were festooned with every diabolical weapon devised by a mediaeval psychopath. Morning Stars, maces, double-edged blades, scimitars, felchions, broadswords and - *crème de la crème* - bloody great sticks with nails in them. 'So *that's* what the brackets are for.'

'Come on in, my boy. It's quite safe. For now.'

Kevin walked over to Pitt. 'Are you trying to kill me?'

'I'm sorry. I had to test you earlier. Or rather, to prove to you that your instincts are true. How do you feel?'

Actually, pretty good thought Kevin; 'Lousy,' he said. 'What's all this for.'

'To build stamina. An hour in here should work up a sweat.'

'Well, take it easy. See you later.'

'Very funny, Kevin.' Pitt passed a practise blade to him.

'It's got a lot of notches in it.'

'It's had a lot of use.'

'You must tell me about the last Slayer sometime. I'd just love to find out how he died.'

'I doubt it,' said Pitt, his voice dropping.

Kevin took a closer look at the equipment, narrowed his eyes. 'What're the melons for?'

'While you dodge, parry and counter strike I want you to see how many of them you can split. When you've done those, all the machines will automatically shut down.'

'Ingenious.'

You can always rely on a human to think up something like this, said Boris.

'Shut up,' said the Slayer.

'Excuse me?' said Pitt.

'I was talking to Boris.'

'Boris,' repeated Pitt, his tone flat.

'My demon,' explained the Slayer.

Pitt frowned. 'You talk to your demon.'

'Can't shut him up.'

'I don't think that's a good idea.'

'Tell me about it.'

'No. Really. You share a body with a demon from Hell.' Pitt regarded him, eyes slitted, rubbing his chin.

'I know. Hell spawn. One of the lower classes. A working guy,' said Kevin. 'Just like me.'

'It will whisper things, try to draw you to the evil side.'

'Believe me, I know. But Darth Vader he ain't. I'll be ready for him next time.'

'Hmm.' Pitt walked away, a worried frown upon his Peter Cushing brow. 'We shall see.'

'Oh Prof?'

'Yes?'

'I'd like you to see this; leave the lights on.'

Pitt stepped into the safety of the corridor. He switched on the machine.

'Wassah!'

*

'That was impressive,' said Pitt. 'Twenty seconds.'

'Easy peasy.'

The split melons lay about. Holes appeared out of the ceiling, metal arms descended with small brown hairy things clasped in their claws.

'Coconuts?'

'Let's see how you cope with a smaller, harder target.' Pitt closed the door. The lights went out. The machines began to move.

'Wassah!'

*

'Fifteen seconds,' said Pitt. 'Have you any martial arts training?'

'I learned from the best. Lee, Van Damme…'

'Wang Yu?'

'Of course. And a Shaolin monk.'

'Not David Carradine.' Pitt had serious doubts about the effectiveness of martial skills learned from Hollywood.

'Another one. You wouldn't know him. Knocked about in the eighteenth century.'

'Interesting,' said Pitt. 'We must discuss this later. Enough fruit carnage, I think; now, the firing range. '

'Lead on McDuff.'

*

'Any armed forces training?'

'Boris?'

SAS combat experience, said Boris. *Forgot to say. Didn't last long.*

'Can't you be more specific?' said Kevin.

Sorry. Official Secrets Act, and all that.

'Kevin?' Pitt prompted him.

'I could tell you but then I'd have to kill you,' he said. 'But yes, lots.'

The firing range was about a quarter of a mile long. The targets – those paper cut-outs of grunts charging with a rifle in their hands – all but disintegrated from the centre outward. Kevin blew smoke from the barrel of his GPSMG.* 'Anything bigger?'

'Don't even ask.'

'What?'

'You were about to ask me for a general electric mini gun. No. Absolutely not. In any case, against vampires a stake, crossbow, blade and flamethrower are all you need.'

'Aw. Shit.'

'This isn't a game, Kevin.'

'That's your opinion.' Kevin grinned. His fangs grew.

Pitt stepped back. 'Kevin?'

'It's all right, Prof. It's the buzz. The merest hint of combat and I can feel the change.'

'Explain.'

'The wolf form - but unless I'm actually hungry, I can control it.'

'That's just as well. Your martial skills would not be much use to you in that form.'

Pitt gave him an appraising look.

---

* General Purpose Sub Machine Gun, although it's difficult to say where "general purpose" comes in. You could use it to open tinned food, I suppose. Or prop a door open. Pretty useless, compared to a screwdriver.

'What?'

'You have the skills,' said Pitt, rubbing the side of his nose. 'All you lack is experience.'

'But Boris said-'

'Never mind about *BORIS*,' said Pitt, suddenly sharp; 'he is *Hell spawn*. It has never fought its own kind. You must.'

And that, more than anything else that had happened in the past twenty four hours, sobered Kevin Costner like a douche of cold water to a drowning man. 'This is going to be really bad, isn't it?'

'Yes. I'm afraid so.'

'When do I start?'

'We begin the hunt on the eve of Midwinter.' Pitt checked his watch. 'I would rather that we had more time to prepare you but…'

'I'm scared.'

'Good. You should be.' And as Kevin the would-be Slayer walked solemnly back to his couch, Pitt watched him go.

But are you scared enough? he thought.

CHAPTER TWENTY-THREE

Meanwhile, some time previously, on the same Tuesday night...

Jan parked her car behind a big black van that had some kind of twirly ventilation thing on the roof. The van hid her car from view but she could see Pitt's house, an ancient pile that had much in common with the Brick Shit House School of Architecture. It had crenellations on top that once upon a time may have seen English longbow men firing at French tourists.

'Did you know that the now rarely used two finger fuck-off tablet originated in mediaeval times?' said Jason.

'Someone's coming. Duck,' said Jan

'Where?'

'Land Rover.'

'There's a duck driving a Land Rover?'

'Get your head down! It's Pitt.'

Bonces were bowed.

'Get your face out of my lap, Jason.'

'Mmmm. Warm. Cosy,' said Jason in Homer Simpson fashion.

Pitt slewed his car onto his gravel drive. He jumped out, ran to the gates and locked them behind him. Then he disappeared behind a wall for a moment before he ran back to the car and took off, gravel spraying, turned a right hander and was lost from view.

'Shit,' said Jason. 'He was in a hurry.'

'And shit again. Those gates are electrified.' Jan sighed. 'Oh well.'

'That sounded like, "Oh well, best go home".'

'Did you hear what I said?'

'So the gates are electrified. Is that going to stop us?' said Jason, slapping the steering wheel. He would have preferred to slap Jan's thigh but that would have cost a lot in remedial dentistry.

'Well, yeah,' said she.

'There's a wall.'

'It has razor wire, broken glass on top and barbed wire nailed to it on the other side. Want to come back for coffee?'

'You give in too easily. Let's just wait a bit.'

'Jason...'

'I have faith in a Providence which shapes our destinies. And we didn't get this far for no reason.'

'We got this far because you're a tea leaf and we're both nosey bastards.' But she did not, for the moment, start the engine.

'Big place,' said Jason. 'I wonder where he gets all the dosh?'

'He has the Professorship at Bath University, he's a practising pathologist, and he sells artifacts that he finds on expeditions to museums and collectors all over the world. He has numerous business interests but, most important of all, he doesn't have kids. He must be pulling in at least a million a year, after tax.'

'Still. He spends a lot, too.'

'It might also be due to his shares in a South African diamond mine.'

'That'll do it. He doesn't happen to hob-nob with the Thatchers, does he?' Jason huffed air, just to watch the white plume that resulted.

'Are you trying to make a point?'

'Well it *is* cold.'

Jan turned on the engine, switched on the heater. 'Now sit there and stop complaining. This was *your* idea, remember?'

Jason blew on his hands and rubbed them together hard enough to make fire. 'Anyway, whenever an English archer met a Froggie, he'd raise two fingers to show that his shooting hand was still in full working order, thank you so very much, so just you give me an excuse, any excuse.'

'Yeah. You were saying.' She yawned.

'Am I boring you?'

'Yes. But it's okay. Carry on. The radio's broken and I like a bit of meaningless background noise when I'm sitting in a freezing car waiting for something to happen at one o'clock of the morning hour.'

However, if this was meant to shut him up, she was wrong to the utmost degree.

'You can just imagine it, can't you? “This here's an English longbow. It's made of Yew for extra tensile strength and an arrow can penetrate armour at two hundred yards. It's probably the most powerful bow in the world. It could take your head clean off. In all the confusion, blood and mayhem of mediaeval combat I clean forgot how many arrows I fired. Now, you have to ask yourself a question, punk; do I feel lucky? Well, do ya, punk?” '

'Dum de dum de dum,' said Jan in a singsong voice.

'Personally, I prefer a Webley forty-five,' Jason said, aware that he was droning on. 'Snap action for faster reload. Highly accurate. Robust. As issued to officers in the First World War. It's the weapon of choice.'

'You certainly know your penis symbols.' Jan peered into the freezing fog that had unaccountably begun to form outside. 'Jason, shut up for a second. There's something going on over at the gate.'

*

Pitt drew up outside his house, wasting no time in locking his car before running up the steps. He slammed the door behind him.

'Seems nervous, don't he?' said Joel.

'He sensed us, but he didn't twig we were here,' said his Dad. 'I could read him like a copy of the *Beano*.'

'Which is to say, easily and without moving your lips?'

'Precisely. Let's go home, boy.' He popped the rear hatch and they unfolded themselves from the narrow space. 'You know, this undead lark has its compensations,' he said. 'That would have hurt like buggery.'

'Yeah. You keep saying.'

They walked back along the drive in silence.

'Oh look. A locked gate.' Joel tittered. 'We're trapped'.

'Quit your tomfoolery,' said his Dad. 'Just open it.'

Joel flexed his new vampire muscles.

'Will you stop doin' that?'

'Can't help it. I feel invincible.' He walked over to the gate. 'What we need, on a night such as this, is a bit of eerie mist.' Joel closed his eyes and concentrated. When he opened them a fog of satisfying density had distilled from the cold, damp air. 'There. That's better.'

Joel looked up at the gate. It was fifteen feet high, made to keep out anyone with a fear of heights. There didn't seem much to deter the determined prowler, however. He reached out and grabbed a pair of bars.

The white flash caused Dad to fling up his arms to shield his sensitive undead peepers. Purple dots obscured his vision for a few seconds but when he opened them, he saw something that made him guffaw with amusement.

'It's not funny,' said Joel. He lay in a smoking heap twenty feet away, his clothes a mess of charred polyester and wool/viscose mix. Small fires ignited upon his person. He rolled around until they were out.

'From where I'm standing, it's ferkin' hilarious. That'll learn ya, you great wazzock.' And his Dad guffawed again.

Joel stood up. His legs were a bit wobbly but he would not be beaten. A frozen puddle cracked beneath his boots.

He put his boots back on, which were nice and warm now, a minor compensation for almost being cooked on the spot. He scooped some iced water from the puddle then threw it at the gate. It did not fizzle, flash or vaporise. 'It's safe. Must've blown the circuit.'

'You're a real live wire,' chuckled his Dad. 'A proper bright spark. A-'

'Give over, father.' Joel grabbed a bar, pulled. It did not budge. He grabbed another bar with his wet hand but this did not result in further aerial acrobatics. He put his back into it. 'Come on, pop, give us a hand.'

'But you're *invincible*,' said Dad. 'A regular He-Man.'

'You want to go home?'

'Oh, all right.' Dad lent his not inconsiderable strength to the task in hand. They were rewarded for this team effort by a gratifying snap of the mortise lock. The bolts also gave up the unequal struggle to keep the trespassers in. In the stillness of the early hour, the sound of their vandalism was like gunshots.

'*Quiet*,' said Dad, putting a finger to his lips. 'People have to get up early for work, you know?'

'Yeah. People with *proper* jobs. I wonder what *that's* like?'

They opened the gate, stepped through and surveyed the street. Ahead, a narrow lane - a high wall to the left, a row of old cottages to the right. On the corner, where the lane bent to their right, a primary school. The lane continued until it narrowed even further. There were more cottages down there, but not many. A big black van with windows of the same persuasion was parked next to the cemetery wall. Behind that, a smaller car, its windows steamed up. Joel stared at it. There was a young couple in it, and the bloke, at least, was as randy as. His mind was like the rear room of a porn merchant's.

'Cor,' said Joel. 'That's a bit public, innit?'

But Dad didn't reply. He was staring at the van.

And the van, he swore, was *looking right back*. He didn't have to try very hard to know what was happening in the smaller vehicle. The two kids in it were paying Joel and himself a lot of attention, but their real interest was in the big house. Perhaps those steamed up windows had nothing to do with unbridled libido. However, when he tried to focus on the occupants of the black van, he found that his thoughts bounced right back. Which hurt.

'What's up, Pop?'

'Nothing. Just keep moving, boy. Walk slowly. Don't look at the van.'

'What, that one?' said Joel, loud of voice, pointing.

Smack, was the noise that bounced down the high walled lane.

'Ow!'

OW, came the echo.

'What did you do that for?'

WHAT DID YOU DO THAT FOR,FOR,FOR...

'You're a total prat. Come on.'

'My ear's getting a callous on it', Joel muttered.

....*PRAT,PRAT,PRAT...*

They walked straight on and up the lane, turned left at the vicarage on the corner. There was a square, of sorts, with a fenced off bit of turf and a memorial testifying to the village's war losses. A few threadbare wreaths were still leaning against it.

'Quaint, innit?' said Joel. 'Why can't we live up here?'

'You got a spare hundred grand?'

'We could squat.'

Dad shook his head then sighed. 'We're still miles from home.'

'Where are we?'

'Colerne,' said his Dad. He'd had business in the cemetery, before Joel was born.

'It'll take us ages to walk.'

'Then we'd better start.'

'Hold on,' said Joel. I'm hungry.' He looked about. To their left, a small grocery store.

'Don't even *think* about it,' his father warned him. Joel had a larcenous streak longer than a mail train.

'But there'll be sweeties and…meat.'

'You'll have the rozzers here. We've got enough problems.'

'I'm *hungry*.' Joel walked over to the shop; two doors separated by a broad window. There was no time for finesse.

Crash. Tinkle. Jangle-jangle.

Joel stepped through the ruined door. He made straight for the fridge, grabbed packages of meat then turned his attention to the confectionery. He stuffed as many tubes of Smarties into his pockets as possible then vacated the premises. He did not seem concerned by the decibels of the burglar alarm, which hadn't yet drawn anyone to their bedroom windows. People didn't bother, usually. They assumed that it was someone else's job to call the police.

However, on this particular night, the good burghers of the village were flicking lights on inside a minute.

'You bloody fool,' said Dad.

'Don't panic. Watch this.' He closed his eyes, did Joel, and a proper pea-souper rose up. A real can't–see-your-hand-in-front-of your-face job.

'Brilliant. Now we can't see where we're going.'

'Who said that?' said Joel.

CHAPTER TWENTY-FOUR

Jason wiped a circle in the condensation on the windscreen. 'Did you see that?' said Jan.

'I did.'

They looked at each other. Then they looked back at the gate.

'He was on fire,' said Jan.

'That was an amazing backward somersault,' said Jason. 'I liked the arm flapping. I thought they only did that in cartoons.'

They watched the mist curling around the two figures as they wrestled with the gate. They both gasped when they heard what sounded like gunshots.

'That gate was specially made,' said Jan. 'Pitt bragged about it. Titanium mortise. Titanium-Vanadium bolts and padlocks.'

'Hefty geezers,' said Jason.

'I don't like this,' said Jan. And she didn't; no, not one bit.

'Who are they?'

'I never saw burglars trying to break *out* before,' said the brains of the pair. 'And they're not carrying anything.'

They saw the younger, bigger of the two men look around and point.

'They've spotted us,' said Jason.

'They can't see. The windows are all steamed up.'

'I hope they don't come over this way. I have a very bad feeling about this' said Jason.

The older man cuffed the younger a good one across the head.

'Definitely not burglars,' said Jan.

'I was thinking along the lines of Laurel and Hardy.' Jason dry-swallowed. 'In an unfunny kind of way.'

The two men walked on and Jason and Jan breathed again. 'I want to go home' said Jason.

'Uh-huh. Gate's open now. You woke me up for this, and now you're going to pay.' She opened her door, got out, walked around to the boot and opened up. Jan returned with a box, two by two, with a *Windbreakers* stamp on it. Jason got out. Reluctantly.

'Let's get this over with,' he said.

They left the car where it was, Jason carrying the box, Jan checking every shadow. There was no sign of anyone loitering with dubious intent. Just a large dog.

'Where'd that dog come from?' said Jason. 'Wasn't there a second ago.'

Jan spotted the narrow alleyway to the right of the gates, the area in deepest shadow. They approached the driveway. The dog watched them.

'I didn't know that Alsatians grew that big,' said Jason.

'German Shepherds,' said Jan.

'At this time of night? Where?' Jason almost dropped the box when she hit him.

'They don't,' said Jan. 'Grow that big, I mean.'

'That one did.'

'That isn't a German Shepherd.'

'Even I can see that. He isn't wearing shorts or even carrying a big stick with a loop on the end.'

'Crook,' said Jan.

'Yeah, all right, don't labour the point. You already called me a tea leaf.'

In a fit of pique, or possibly extreme anxiety, she hit him again, and this time he *did* drop the parcel. There was a depressing tinkle when he picked it up and shook it. 'There goes your dinner service for four,' he said. 'Never mind. *Argos* does some good stuff.'

The dog that wasn't a German, or indeed a Shepherd of any nationality or breed, watched them intently. Its eyes were golden… not bright yellow…or brown…or anything in between.

Almost a metallic gold.

'What's the nearest relative to a German Shepherd, Jan?'

'His mum and dad, I suppose.'

'Seriously.' Jason had bad, *bad* vibes about this, and they were coming off the dog in waves that you could surf on.

'I'm trying not to be serious. That thing scares me,' said Jan

'It's a wolf, isn't it?'

'Don't be silly.' But Jan wasn't convinced. She was pretty sure that wolves were smaller; even Irish Wolfhounds weren't that big.

'It is, though.'

'Don't say that,' said Jan.

'It isn't wearing a collar, Jan.'

'Keep moving. And don't let it smell your fear.'

'You want me to walk over there and stick a peg on its nose?'

'Good. Humour. Keep it up, Jas.'

'I think I may be experiencing the gastric precursor to a spot of intestinal hurry,' said Jason, and then farted*. 'Sorry.'

---

* That one was entirely justified, don't you think?

'There are many bushes with conveniently shaped leaves in the grounds,' she said. And although she was making with the quips thick and fast, which was itself an indication of how scared she felt, her voice quivered.

'Nearly there,' said Jason.

But to be there, they had to pass within four feet of the nearest living relative to a German Shepherd. And it wasn't his mum or Dad, nor uncle or sibling, not even a distant cousin who didn't bother to send Christmas cards…

…Wasn't, in fact, a wolf at all. But Jason and Jan didn't know that, for if they had, both would have filled their kecks where they stood.

'I can't walk any closer,' said Jan.

'Yes you can' said Jason. He took her by the elbow, just to be sure.

'Let's turn back.'

'I don't think that it would be wise to turn our backs on it.'

'It's drooling,' said Jan.

'Dogs do that. It's expected. When they've got time on their hands they stand around on street corners and drool.'

'Why isn't it blinking?'

'Eh?'

'It's been staring at us like a perv at a peepshow, but it hasn't blinked once.'

'You called it a perv. I think it heard you.'

Thus it seemed. The beast began to growl. It sounded like heavy furniture dragged across bare floorboards. Jason farted again* – a wet one, he suspected, with no small degree of dismay.

They were ten feet away from the gates. The wolf-thing was now on its feet. All four of them.

'My, what big teeth you have' said Jason.

'Shut up, Jas.'

'I'm trying to be friendly.'

'You're not the one wearing a red hooded coat.'

'Eh?'

'Never mind. You probably never read the usual children's literature.'

'That's right. If there wasn't a pair of knockers by page three I lost all interest. I took regular periodicals.'

'National Geographic?'

---

* That one was, too; a wet fart is a serious business. Only funny if it happens to someone else.

'Jahoobies' said Jason, 'and *Wet and Wild*, for preference. Although the latter turned out to be about waterfowl in Norfolk. Nice doggy.'

It was crouching, pre-lunge style, its haunches bunched and quivering. Which, somewhat bizarrely, given his predicament, reminded Jason of a girl he'd once met*.

'Go,' said Jason.

So Jan went.

And the doggy, which was not nice or even affable after a few drinks, leapt…

…Just as Jason cowered, holding his box up for protection….

…And there was an OOF…

…And the obligatory crash, which could have come straight from the BBC's stock of amusing sound effects…

…And an irate creature, presently exploring the wonderful world of lamp post sniffing and cat chasing, shook Its terrible head. But the box was jammed upon it. Bits of broken pottery with fragments of a brightly coloured design glazed upon them flew there, thence, hither and here, but as hard as It tried It could not free Itself. It worried at the box with Its paws.

Jason was not by nature a cruel chap. When other schoolboys were pulling girls pigtails, or inflating frogs and newts with bicycle pumps, Jason had been content with a locked door and a copy of *Wet and Wild*.†

But this beast had destroyed the unopened boxed dinner set for four that Jan's mum had insisted she would need as a student…and, once it was free, would come looking for them for another go…

'Ahh, sod it,' said Jason, and then took a running kick at the dog's arse.

Even the emerging forests of post-glacial Europe, or the primaeval wilderness of the North American continent, had never echoed to the wolven cries that issued from the Thing that now had Jason's Reeboked foot clenched between Its thighs. As the lupine monster vainly attempted to suck Its aching and swollen bollocks better, Jason had no choice but to hop along with it.

'Help,' said Jason. 'Ja-an. HELP?'

Jan's face appeared around the wall.

'Quick,' yelped Jason. 'Undo my shoelace.'

'Don't be bloody stupid.'

'I can't get my foot out. Quick. *Do* something.'

Panic. Dear oh dear.

---

* Which, having no relevance here, we shall not pursue further.

† This wasn't about Norfolk wildfowl. He lied

Jan was clearly terrified. Which made her next move all the more heroic.

A cat had turned up to see what all the fuss was about. It was black and it had a green collar and it had a Don't-You-Mess-With-Me cast to its evil yellow eyes that would have put the wind up Jan if she hadn't already been pushed to the limit of terror. It was a ratter of the first order, a scrapper that would not stop short of disembowelment if it felt in the least bit pissy…

…And its owner had strapped a nice new flea collar onto it.

So it was not merely pissy.

It was looking for something to kill – like an antelope – but they weren't native to England or Wiltshire in particular, and it had already scared off what remained of the deer herds that had once grazed on its turf. Ergo, it was looking for worthy prey.

It had no notion of danger.

It cared not for Things that went bump in the night – because it was usually she: No-No, The Wildcat Of Watergates, Wiltshire.

And tonight No-No felt like a challenge.

'Here *puddy*,' said Jan.

It gave her a Look.

Touch Me, it said; Go On. Try It. And Then Count The Stitches.

Jan rooted about in her pockets for something that might remotely interest a homicidal feline. Alas, her pockets did not yield a haunch of antelope, or sheep, or at a pinch a generous portion of Postal Worker's *gluteus maximus*.*

However, what she *did* have, and which never fails to please, was a bit of cheese.

She pulled out the sandwich. She tried to remember when she'd last worn this coat. Since it was an anorak, and bright scarlet, she guessed it must have been a very long time ago; the state of decomposition on the sarnie bore this out*. Needless to say, to a cat - that denizen of the dustbin, raider of rubbish and trawler of trash – it smelled like the Second Coming.

'Meow?' said No-No. Or something like it.

'It's yours if you don't take my hand off with it,' said Jan.

'Assistance!' yelled Jason. 'Anyone? Oh help?'

'Here kiddy-kiddy.'

'*Rowwrrr*'.

Bum meat

It's best not to describe it in any detail.

'Jumping Jesus of the Jewellery Quarter!'* screamed Jan. The rake of claws had damn near taken her index finger off at the first knuckle.

The cat had lost all interest in the human now. Munch, gobble, masticate, devour. Eyes closed. Cat heaven…

…Which made it that bit easier to grab it by the appendage furthest from its terrible maw.

'Rowwwrr?' said No-No.

'Coming through,' yelled Jan at the trot.

It was like holding a sack full of rabid ferrets, lost in atavistic sex frenzy. It thrashed and hissed and spun on its own axis so fast that its tail would forever wear a kink, a souvenir of the night that it did battle with a Thing from the Underworld.

'How did you get such a unique and fascinatingly deformed tail, grandmother?' No-No's descendents would ask.

'Ripped the froat aht of a bleeding demon, didn't I?' she would say.

Which is exactly what happened.

'Oh my god,' said Jason. 'It's horrible.'

'That poor dog.'

'Where did you find that thing, Jan?'

She shook her head. 'It found me.'

'Then I suggest we leg it. It looks as if it's nearly finished. And then, I fancy, it'll be looking for fresh prey.'

And leg it they did.

And nearly ran in to Pitt's caretaker. 'Big chap,' said Jason.

'Used to be a doorman at Alcatraz. Kept the rough element *in*.' Jan parted the branches of the Holly tree that they had had to dive behind. The shaven head of the caretaker was already wet with the mist, moonlight giving it a sheen, accentuating the Cro-Magnon bumps and ridges of his skull. His fists dragged across the gravel, making a merry sound as it tinkled against his brass knuckle-dusters; his huge back and short powerful legs disappeared into the fog.

'A silver-back male; magnificent isn't he?' said Jan.

'That tattoo on his head. Did it say, "Open This End?"' said Jason. He waited a few more seconds until he was sure that the man had gone. 'Come on. This is our chance.'

* I have no idea what this means.

They rounded the last bend and, as they approached the front of the building, they heard the pitter-patter of little paws.

'Did you hear that?' said Jan.

'You know that I did.'

'Then run,' said Jan. 'For the love of God, Jas, run like the wind.'

It was close. No sooner had they reached the relative sanctuary of the door and slammed it behind them, they heard the frantic scratching and yowling of a moggy apoplectic with rage. The door shook and rattled in its frame. Jan went to the spy hole.

'What's it doing?' said Jason. He noted the tremble in his voice and hoped that Jan hadn't.

'It's pacing,' said Jan. 'No. Tell a lie. Now it's considering attacking a statue of a rampant Gryphon.' She was silent for a moment, then: 'No. I don't believe it.'

'What? What?'

'It's sharpening its claws. It's horrible. There's a great chunk of dog flesh stuck in its teeth.' Jan turned away. 'We'd better do what we came here to do. Mighty Joe Young will be back soon.'

'We'll have to open the door. He'll suspect something's wrong if we don't.'

'But the cat…' She returned to the spy hole. 'Oh. Hang on. It's stalking a Rottweiler.'

'There are dogs loose?' said Jason, his voice rising in pitch. 'You didn't say *anything* about guard dogs.'

'Maybe they're a recent acquisition. Anyway, it was daylight when I last visited.'

They took a quick look around the hall. It was light, airy; there was a lot of marble, black basalt pillars and onyx columns. Even the banisters were crafted from stone. There were wall sconces for torches, but up-lit lamps were fixed to them, a concession to the twenty-first century. A wide spiral staircase led up, and up, and up. It was dark up there.

'Through here, as I recall.' Jan walked toward a door, one of four leading off the hallway. She listened at it and then turned the handle. Steps led downward. 'Oops.'

'Oops? Come on, Jan, which door?' Jason stood at the spy hole. 'I can't see the cat. I think…'

There was a very *un*Rottweiler-like whimper and a yelp. Jason saw it bolt across the drive, the cat riding on the dog's back, making liberal and lethal use of its claws.

'It's busy. I think I can open the door now. Have you found ours yet?'

Jan had opened and checked all but one. 'This is it.'

Jason opened the front door. Howls screeched through the night.

'Quickly,' said Jan. 'Through here.'

There was a short passageway, a door at the end. A metal one, with bolts on it, and a big, big lock with the sort of key they used to have for dungeons back in Merrie Olde Englande. There was also a metal rod of the kind that downtown New Yorkers use to brace their door on the inside.

'Do we really want to go in?' said Jason.

'This was your intention, wasn't it?'

'Our. *Our* intention. All right. Let's get to it.'

They disengaged all the security devices, turned the key. Jason slowly pulled the door open. Inside, a laboratory of the mad scientist description: benches groaned beneath the weight of beakers, retorts, condensers and lots of coloured liquids bubbling away over Bunsen burners.

'This place is fantastic!' said Jason in exclamatory fashion.

'Pitt undertakes research for private companies. Can you see why I'm tempted to work here?'

Jason wandered around picking up this, that and the other. He pretended to drink a beaker of green, smoking liquid, clutched his throat then sank out of view behind a bench.

'Stop clowning. There's more to see. Through that door.'

Jason replaced the beaker, followed Jan through to another room. This one had a metal cage in the corner and an unidentifiable smell pervaded the air. An extractor fan whirred in the background. In the centre of the room was a table with metal bands at each corner; the top of it was recessed so that it formed a shallow sink, grooved channels leading from the centre to drain holes at the side of the table.

'Tell me that this isn't what I think it is,' said Jason.

'Okay. It isn't a dissection table.'

'That's what I thought. Does he know that specimens are supposed to be dead before he starts work?' Jason ran a finger over one of the metal bands. 'This is made of the same stuff as the gate. He's a cautious guy, ain't he?'

A noise, again not immediately identifiable, came from the cage. Well, not so much a cage as a strong room; one might keep one's most precious treasures in there. Or something you didn't want to break *out*. That thought put the wind up Jason.

'Jas?' It was Jan's voice. Jan's voice with an unpleasant ring to it, rising in pitch, tremulous. 'Look at this.'

So he looked.

And this is what he saw.

The upright cupboards that could so easily be mistaken for strong boxes, the sort used in bank vaults, were in fact caskets standing against the wall. Eight, in all. Labels identified the contents. Each one bore not a description but a name: David Stapleton said one. Sandra Johnston said another. Richard Jacobs next to that, and so on.

'This is cosy,' said Jason. 'Perhaps Pitt gets lonely at night.'

'I recognise the names,' said Jan. She looked at Jason as if pleading with him to disagree, to offer an explanation. 'They're all victims of the *Phantom*.'

'Why do they all have red lights on the doors?'

'They're cold storage units.'

'Hold on a sec.' Jason took a camera from his pocket. He fiddled with it, setting the flash. 'Right. I'll get some pictures, then we're out of here.'

'No,' said Jan. 'Not just the caskets. We've got to get a look inside.'

'Are you feckin' serious?' said Jason. 'And it's locked, anyway. No key.'

'Pitt has a small office at the back.'

They followed the cage around to the left; the flash on Jason's camera went off, eight times, auto zoom focusing on each label.

There were two more doors. One led into a Spartan little room – a desk, a chair, and a filing cabinet. There were papers on the desk, three metal drawers on the side. Jan opened the top drawer. There were keys in there, each on a little plastic fob. Jan selected one and then, curious, she sorted through them and took two more.

Jason tried the filing cabinet. It was locked. 'Is there a key for this?'

'We don't have time for that.'

'We won't get another opportunity.' He held out his hand, wiggled the fingers. She found a key, tossed it to him. He threw the camera to her. 'You make a start. I'll join you in a minute. Scream if you need me.' He almost grinned, but it became a grimace.

While Jan went to open the cage door, Jason opened the file cabinet. Most of the files related to private research projects commissioned for commercial purposes, but in the bottom drawer Jason found files bearing the names he'd seen on the caskets. He pulled them out.

Jason knew he didn't have time to read through them all. Each file contained details of the circumstances in which each murder victim had been found. There was more of the same medical gobbledygook he'd found in the stolen notebook. He removed the top sheets from each file with personal details relating to each victim. He rolled these up together, secured them with an elastic band and then found a pocket for them. He replaced all the files to the drawer, locked the cabinet, put the key back in the drawer.

Jason took a closer look at the loose papers on the desk. They were concerned with one of Pitt's recent ventures, a wildlife centre in Wiltshire. Box Wood, to be exact. There was a folded sheet. He opened it up, laying it out on the desk. It was a blueprint for the design of the centre. There were some odd features in it. Another of the loose papers proved to be an ordnance survey map of the Wood; there was another map, too, of Colerne and outlying districts, including Bath itself. Across the surface of all of these were little X's, but the significance of these wasn't obvious. Jason shuffled the lot together, shoved it all inside his coat. He left the office to join Jan.

Things became somewhat surreal shortly afterward. It began with a humungous and cataclysmically smelly fart.*

Jan wasn't taking pictures of the residents in the cage. He found her behind door number two. Shortly after, he wished he hadn't.

'Boo,' he said.

'Prat,' was the response.

This room was like an accident and emergency theatre in a general hospital. Most of the bits and bobs you'd expect to find in such a place were there, even down to the smell which somehow touches something in the soul and reminds us of our mortality.

'Poo,' said Jason, and: 'Friggin' fakirs in fancy frocks, Jan, that's 'orrible.'

In the centre of the room, strapped down to a table, he saw what looked to be an oversized set of bagpipes, made of leather, sans tartan.

'Our Elk,' said Jan.

'And still dead. I guess necromancy is a dying art.'

The Elk was no longer protected, as it had been at the dig site. No incubator. No tubes ran into it. No bags of plasma.

---

* Essential to the plot, I promise you.

'Do you think Pitt keeps plasters around here?' said Jason. He'd cut himself, just a nick, caused by a piece of dinner service shrapnel that had penetrated the box.

Jan took pictures.

Jason sucked at his wound.

Jan laid a hand upon the neck of the beast.

Jason poked it. He glanced at Jan. 'What are you doing?'

'Nothing,' said she, too casual.

'You were checking for a pulse, weren't you?' He have her a good hard glare.

'Well…no…don't be bloody silly.'

Jason was impressed with the size and state of preservation of the body. A bit of a connoisseur of wildlife, was Jason, being of the opinion that each representative of every species was an ambassador of its kind, so he didn't have much truck with flea-bitten mongrel breeds or runts of the litter. But this was a magnificent beast, and the table upon which it lay was barely big enough to take it, although it took up most of the space in the room. The head on the thing was of like gargantuan persuasion. If, as the myth goes, shoe size was an indication of penis size, then surely, likewise, the antlers on the thing must have guaranteed a good time for any two thousand-year-old Elk totty.

It was a monster.

Jason pulled back the upper lip of the stag. It had curiously bright teeth. They could have sold toothpaste. Jason didn't recall such fine gnashers when he had first found it. Perhaps it had been dirty water. Maybe Pitt had given them a bit of a scale and polish…well, he *was* obsessive.

He ran a finger over them. They were smooth, with no sign of wear. He withdrew his finger; perhaps it wasn't such a good idea to fiddle about with the dubious oral hygiene of a corpse, even one as well preserved as this one. Especially with a cut on his finger. Then –

'Shit!'

'What?' said Jan. She was taking photographs of the stag, proof that Pitt had stolen the find – although, given that he had funded the dig himself, "stolen" might be difficult to prove. Did the Crown own it? Or would the Queen prefer not to have it stuck over her mantelpiece?

She paused in her musings. Jason had stepped away from the table, suddenly paler than he had been. He pointed at the creature's mouth. 'It swallowed,' he said. 'I saw it.'

Jan looked from him to the stag's mouth, then back at Jason. 'Swallowed,' she repeated, and her tone suggested Bollocks.

'It did! It did!' Jason stepped back another pace, pointing at the beast.

'It's been in the ground for millennia, Jas. Don't be stupid.'

'But it *did*!' He stamped a foot to prove his veracity.

'Let me see.' She probed the Elk's mouth with her finger, pulled the lower jaw down a little. The tongue lolled - plump, leathery, but more to the point, lifeless. 'Swallowed what?'

Jason stared down at his finger. Blood had seeped through the handkerchief he'd wrapped around it. It was a deeper wound than Jason had thought. It dripped, leaving crimson splashes on the tiled floor.

Blood on the stag's gums…

…And now that she took a closer look, blood on its tongue.

The tongue moved.

Shriek. Blasphemy. Curses.

'Jeez Jan, it's *alive*.'

'Don't be bloody stupid,' said Jan again. She backed up all the same.

'Look! Look!'

The left eyelid fluttered.

'Jesus,' said Jason, half blasphemy, half plea.

A groan erupted.

'It's just the warmth of the room,' said Jan, sounding more reasonable than she felt. 'Gases escaping, skin tightening.'

As if to confirm this, the aforementioned botty-burp exploded from its anus. The stub of a tail vibrated as the fart rasped on. And on. And on.

'Hoo-ee,' said Jason, waving his hand before his nose. 'At least we know it's a vegetarian.'

They backed up, partly due to fear, partly to give the stench room to expand. It was like a solid wall, pushing them back. 'Must have had a kebab before it died,' said Jason. 'Come on, let's get out of here. We've got enough photos.'

They left the room.

'Sorry about that.' Jason gave Jan the look that says, I'm A Prat And I Know It. 'Must be the Goofy I had earlier.'

'Let's crack those caskets open. We've been here too long already.' Jan unlocked the cage. She entered, approached the first casket. A Mr. Swittering was the current resident. She reached for the button that said Do Not Press.

The crash from the next room stayed her hand. Jan froze. 'Must be bloated with gas,' she said.

'Yeah,' said Jason, eyes a-bulge. 'Hell of a flatulence problem.'

In the rutting season, the glens of the highlands echo with the roar of the deer stag. It is a roar that says, "I am gorgeous, and I am horny." Impressive it is, and the ladies think so too. Other males, less confident around girlies, slink away to wait their turn for a shag-fest in another season, perhaps when their acne has cleared up. Or, feeling cocky (as it were), they issue a challenging cry and indulge in the deer equivalent of shoulder barging, arm wrestling, or a bit of a ruck.

This roar was nothing like that; this roar said:

HELLO WORLD. I'M BACK, I'M PISSED OFF, AND I'M *HUNGRY*.

With a capital aitch.

'They say that charcoal biscuits can help,' said Jason.

The door vibrated. It was the impact of something big and heavy that did it. The sounds of gas cylinders crashing to the floor and other bits of equipment going the same way issued from the room.

'Let's *not* open any caskets,' Jason said.

He grabbed the hand that Jan held out, finger poised to push the big red button, and hauled her out of the cage. Legs quivering, they slowly backed out of the room watching the other door as they went.

BELLOW, went something behind it.

Smash, went a pair of hooves against the door. It was buckling.

'What did you say the door was made of?'

'I didn't,' said Jan. She sounded very young, of a sudden.

'Looks like Titanium/Vanadium to me. It should hold, shouldn't it?' Jason desperately needed reassurance.

'You want to stick around and find out?'

'Uh-unh.'

They left. Just as the Titanium/Vanadium door gave up.

SNORT, went the Something as they slammed the exit behind them and ran…

…Through the Jekyll and Hyde lab, out through another door…

…Another crash signalled the demise of yet another barrier between the frightened and It. Most definitely an It. Capital I, as in Irate.

'Pitt will go apeshit *and* bugshit when he finds out,' said Jason, sliding bolts, bracing the metal rod against the door. 'And the other shits in between.'

'Let's just go.' Jan was trembling. She had bitten her lip so hard that it bled.

They reached the end of the short corridor just as the first charge almost took the door completely off the frame. Only the bracing rod held it in place.

They were out through the last door and into the hall as the It charged through.

It came at a gallop.

Its bellows were terrible to hear and sapped the strength from their legs as Jan and Jason turned to run through the entrance hall.

The front door was opening wider…

Jan skidded, turned left. 'In here.'

Jason did not argue, for to argue there must be thought; he was already beyond that and looking for a corner to sit and dribble in. The next door opened on to stairs. Going down.

Behind them, It galloped.

There was a squeal of the pant-filling, terror-stricken type; but it was neither Jan nor Jason, for they were fleeing as only the panicked can. Down and down they tumbled, barely able to remain upright. It didn't matter where the steps took them, only that it was away from the terrible screams above.

'Oh God, oh God,' said Jan, over and over.

'Fuck, fuck, fuck, fuck,' said Jason, his personal mantra in times of trouble.

At last, the noises of maiming and general destruction grew faint until, finally, they were no more.

But still they ran, down, ever down.

'Door,' said Jason, reaching the last step. 'Big heavy door.'

Jan opened it, entered therein without pause, and Jason followed.

If they had been expecting anything, it wasn't a furnished room. Jason swore, as he was wont so to do. The two looked around them. It had the look of someone who didn't get out much, someone who had missed most of the twentieth century and, hence, innovations such as the vacuum cleaner, *Ikea*, *Argos*, and *Allied Carpets*.

'What a tip,' said Jason.

He looked up at the walls. In the flickering light of the wall torches, weapons hung in brackets. They hadn't always been used for decoration, he could tell; there were double headed axes, claymores, scimitars, and daggers – enough to stock a mediaeval arsenal.

Jan made a noise that sounded like Eek.

'What is it?' she said.

'What's what?'

'That.' She pointed at a head mounted like a trophy. It was dried up, grotesque, and vaguely human. It stared back at them with eyes that hated everything they saw.

'I had an aunt who looked like that,' said Jason. 'Every Christmas we had to give her sherry and mince pies. Then she'd force me to kiss her.'

'You're always so disparaging about your family. It couldn't have been that bad.'

'It was almost rape,' he said, and then shuddered. 'She had these big jutty-out teeth. But nothing like those.' He reached up and touched one of the long incisors.

Jan couldn't look at it anymore. She toured the room, inspecting bookshelves.

Some people, when they visit a house, will get up and have a nose around the room they're left in while the host is busy with tea making, or some such[*]. They may pick up knick-knacks, adjust pictures that look as if they need adjusting, or browse amongst the video collection - perhaps amuse themselves with the host's taste in music. *Peters and Lee* is always guaranteed to raise a titter or two. Or *Black Lace*. Or *Brotherhood of Man*. And let us not forget *Bucks Fizz* , *The Glitter Band*, and just about any Seventies Folk outfit.

Jan liked to take a peek at the literature people kept – whether pornographic, creative fiction or factual, the books that people read said something about them…but the books that they read and re-read until the spines gave out said more.

In one bookcase, behind glass, there were many of the latter: big, dusty, much consulted tomes. They had curious titles. She took one down, turned to the title page. *'"An Historie Of Thee Lyckanthrowpe,"'* it said, and she read it aloud.

'Eh?' said Jason. He couldn't take his eyes off the snarling, macabre trophy head.

'Look at this stuff,' said Jan, her voice breathy in a pre-orgasmic way. 'They must be worth a fortune.'

Indeed, most of the volumes were rare first editions. But these were mere paperbacks compared to some. Several pre-dated the invention of the

[*] Presumably not to switch on the CCTV

printing press. The ancient vellum crackled as she opened one such book. It was bound in leather that had worn through to the wood of the cover leaves.

Jason looked over her shoulder. 'Joanna Lumley's legs,' he said in wonder. 'It's a work of art.'

It was illuminated with tiny paintings. The inks had faded but it was easy to imagine the brilliance of the colours when the book had first been written. It had the look of the *Book of Kells* about it, but this one differed in a significant way.

'That's horrid,' said Jan, tracing a gnawed fingernail over the illustrations.

'Can you actually do that to a human being without being violently ill?' said Jason. The script was adorned with scenes of degradation. Of every human base act, there was a representative picture. 'Is it a book or a do-it-yourself manual?'

'That isn't funny' said Jan.

'Friggin ' right it isn't. Put it away, you'll catch something nasty.'

It did not make for light reading. *Any* reading, in fact, since it was written in Koine, a form of Greek not spoken or written for two thousand years. Jason picked up a more recent tome. This book had a bright dust cover.

'*"The Bumper Fun Book Of Lycanthropy"*' he read aloud.

'Piss off,' said Jan.

'No. Really. Take a look.'

Although they were at least a hundred feet below ground level, a thunderous crash vibrated through the rock ceiling; some glasses that had been left on a tray began to rattle. It reminded them of the danger they were in. They replaced the books, closed the cabinet door then looked for an exit.

'That's a relief,' said Jason, espying just such a portal. They were through it faster than a Vindaloo through an alcoholic's anus.

'More doors! The fun just keeps on coming.' Jason opened them as he went - bathroom, kitchen, etc. - the usual. No nasty surprises.

'We don't have time,' said Jan. 'Jason! Come out of there' she hissed at him.

'Just wondering if anyone's using the place.' He opened the fridge door, having returned to the kitchen in search of food to steal. Some people suffer from boredom eating; Jason ate to give his stomach something to do other than digest itself. Terror, he found, gave him awful acid reflux. 'Did I say "no nasty surprises"?'

'I don't want to know.'

'I think you do.' He reached into the fridge. His hand came out with a bag of red stuff.

'Put it back,' said Jan.

'It's blood.' Jason examined the label. It had the Infirmary stamp on it. 'O Rhesus Positive, transfusion, for the use of.'

'I want to leave. *Now.*' Jan turned and walked off.

Jason pocketed the bag. More proof. Of what, he did not know. Yet.

They came to another door. Jan opened it. A corridor stretched left to right, lit by burning torches.

'He's totally into the Gothic look, isn't he?'

'Must be difficult to get electrical cable through solid rock. Come on Jas. Left, or right?'

'Left.'

'Right it is then.' Jan walked off. The passageway ended at another door of the fortified kind.

'This is a man who likes his privacy,' said Jason.

There was a wall switch next to it.

'Don't touch,' said Jan. 'Please don't touch.'

Jason shrugged. He *liked* pushing switches. He opened the door.

'Shag me backwards,' was his choice of metaphor.

'Shit with sugar on,' was the phrase that Jan opted for.

Jason moved to step into the room.

'I wouldn't do that if I were you.'

Jason froze.

Jan went EEK.

'Turn around. And close the door. If you want to live.'

And so, given the options, they turned. Pitt was standing there, all glowering looks and Peter Cushing presence. 'You two!'

'That's us,' said Jason.

Pitt approached, slowly, with what could be accurately described as menace. 'I suppose I shouldn't be surprised,' he said. 'I believe you have something that belongs to me.'

Since there were several somethings in their possession they thought it wiser not to ask him to specify. Behind Pitt, another figure lurked in shadow.

Pitt stood before them. Or rather, *over* them - about as over as you can get without actually levitating. Or hanging from one of those block and tackle pulley thingies that the aristocracy use for kinky sex.* He sighed. There was much shaking of the head. 'What am I to do with you?'

'You could escort us from the premises,' said Jason. 'After we promise that we'll never, ever, cross-our-hearts do it again. *Honest*.'

Jan didn't say anything, but she looked at her shoes a lot.

'Come with me,' said Pitt.

'And if we don't?' said Jason, while at the same time knowing that they would.

'Allow me to introduce you to my associate.' Pitt half-turned. The lurking figure lurked some more, but moved toward them as he did it. Which isn't easy.

'It's a fair cop,' said Jason.

*

Lucy had been very much in the background since the arrival of Kevin, but that needed no great skill in the art of camouflage. Being part of the background was her default state in the Professor's household.

She had almost given herself away, though, while observing tonight's bungled burglary. She had known them immediately: Jason, Janet, the newest and most incompetent recruits to the criminal underworld . The same sweet aroma of fear had been easily picked up by Lucy's preternaturally sensitive nostrils back at the dig, when the notebook had gone missing; she had simply chosen not to reveal the identity of the thieves. Watching the Professor tearing his hair out was easy entertainment, but Lucy was intrigued all the same. What would they do with the notebook? What motivated them to start prying in the first place?

Lucy had met the two trespassers before. They were always willing volunteers for archaeological work of any kind and easily exploited by academics like Pitt. It was perversely satisfying that the Professor's prize exhibit for the forthcoming Christmas Lectures had wreaked such damage. She would include a detailed account of the fiasco when she made her report.

Downstairs, the Professor's dogsbody, Simmons, was bleeding with quiet determination all over the stone tiles. She almost giggled aloud, just as she had earlier as Jan and Jason fled the monster they had roused.

Would this mean an end to the Professor's private crusade – a visit from

* Allegedly

the police, perhaps, in the early hours…or a more lethal strike from those others?

She had been aware that the Manor had been under surveillance for months; it was comical, really. Black vans with the twirly bits on top were so Seventies Cop Show.

Lucy stepped further into the shadows. Standing by a window, she lifted the sash and felt the familiar restlessness brought on by cold night air. Moonlight etched the bushes and statuary in sharp, black relief; somewhere in the fields beyond the garden, a Rottweiler fought for its life as something malign and feline clung to its back, riding the fear of the enemy and relishing it.

Lucy could not contain it any longer. She had to escape the suffocation that came with living in the Manor. She barely had time to shed her clothes, dropping them out of the window to collect later; she watched them land on the frost that crusted the grass and then leapt to join them.

The fabric disguised the imprint of two lupine feet as she landed, the metamorphosis completed before touching the ground.

In the instant that she felt her thighs bunch to absorb the fall, she sensed that the Professor had been busy with his defences. Still, it did not concern her.

She had learned a lot from Melthus.

CHAPTER TWENTY-FIVE

'You're late, ' said DI Bratt, startled out of his doze. He wiped the little puddle of dribble from the desk.

Clive couldn't help himself. His hand strayed to his own chin, staring at the slithery runnel on Bratt's.

The DI wiped his sleeve across his mouth. 'Sit, ' he snapped.

Clive and Barry, Twenty-First Century answer to Sherlock and Co., sat.

'Where have you been? '

'The mortuary, ' said Barry. 'Sorry, Sir; my idea.'

'Was it? Was it? '

'It was. It was.'

'Good. That's why I made you both detectives. Find anything?'

Click-clack, went the DI's balls.*

'Yes Sir. Several things.'

'Then let's have a look.'

'I left them with Parsons,' said Barry. Parsons was the Chief Bod in charge of examining fiddly bits and pieces found on murder victims. 'That's why we're late.'

'Nothing else?'

'Sir?' said Clive and Barry, individually and together.

'I only mention it since the mortuary technician was found legs up. Throat torn out. And, curiously, a bucket load of puke.'

Clive blushed.

'But we'll leave that for now. Any news on the dog warden, wotsisname? '

'Costner. Since you mention it, Sir, it seems that Professor Pitt has mislaid the body.'

'Mislaid? Mislaid? I didn't know about this. Don't we people talk to each other? '

'Um, ' said Barry, tactfully omitting to mention the evening news.

Clack, clack, went the balls, an indication of Bratt's consternation. The Click eventually caught up, however, when the DI took some more of his little yellow pills.

---

*He didn't think that this was tedious or irritating in the least – all right?

'Well, at least you're in plain clothes. Well done. Apart from you, Fart. You look like a Jehovah's Witness. When I say plain clothes, I don't mean costume.'

'That's Feart, Sir. F.e.a.r.t.'

'Is it? Is it?'

'It is. It is. Sir, do we have a lead on the Sampsons?'

'As it happens, yes. In your absence we manage to function, Fart.'

'That's F.e.a.r.-'

'Shut it. About an hour and a half ago, just after you left, we had yet another call. Two reptiles matching the descriptions of the deceased.'

'They've been found? Well, that saves us a job,' said Barry.

'No. No, it doesn't, Park. They were at the scene of a crime. Shop raid. Several savoury slices and some *Smarties,* if you'll pardon the alliteration, but that's what it says here.' Bratt held up the incident sheet and flicked the page. 'Explain that if you will.'

The DCs gave a look that was vacant.

'Shame. I was hoping that you could. Beats the bejasus out of me. Still, it'll keep you both busy for the rest of the night. Get out of my office.'

'Sir?'

'Fart?'

'That's – '

'Constable, get on with it.'

'Where did the theft take place?'

'Oh. Yes.' Bratt looked at his sheet. 'Colerne. *The Happy Shopper.* Now, That's a jolly venue to launch the criminal career of the undead, isn't it?'

Again, Clive and Barry exchanged a look.

'Are you two in love? ' said the DI.

'That was a look of puzzlement and astonishment both, Sir, ' said Barry.

'Why? You've nothing against homosexuality have you? '

'No Sir. But you said "undead".'

'I did? I did? '

'You did, ' said Barry

'Meant nothing by it, I'm sure. Now, why are you still here?'

DCs Clive and Barry stood to leave.

'Where d'you think you're going?'

'Sir?' said they.

'I forgot to give you a copy of the incident sheet. See if you can clear up any other incidents in your travels. Park?'

'Sir.'

'What's the menu in the canteen?'

'Offal, Sir.'

'I know that. It's the cook. But what's on the menu?*'

'Giblets,' translated Barry. 'From various beasts of the field.'

'My favourite. Do you know what they put in sausages, by the way?'

Barry wisely shook his head.

'Good. I'd hate to know. Now get the hell out. Stop wasting my time.'

And so they left.

'I hate him, ' said Clive.

Barry just patted him on the shoulder.

*

"Do Androids Dream Of Electric Sheep?" a chap once wrote. Fair question[†].

So, what does something supposedly soulless *do* while he-she-it is taking the zeds? Dogs dream. So do cats. You can see them, little legs jerking away as they chase cats-mice-bicycle wheels in green happy fields. Occasionally a whimper, too, which proves that, yes, they can also have nightmares. Strange, then, that Judaeo-Christian doctrine has nothing to say about the spirit of the beast.

Then again, neither does it mention the existential angst or the neurotic dream life of the undead. Most of what is known about your average vampire is the stuff of legend, of myth, stories told in the midst of winter on long, cold, dark nights when it is easy to believe any old shite. Hollywood cares even less about the accuracy of its representation of those that feed upon mortals, just so long as it makes you too scared to get out of bed for a wee-wee in the middle of the night.

Melthus cared not a fig for such fiction. Neither did he give a dried prune, date, sultana, currant or those vacuum packed fruits that are supposed to be a substitute for a king sized *Mars* bar or *Snickers*. Melthus knew about healthy eating; it came fresh, hot, and by the pint. And he dreamed about such

---

[†]Not to mention a fair old money-spinner since the sci-fi novel earned a packet as a cult film classic under the name of *Blade Runner*. But that's sci-fi. Hollywood. In the film, the question was never asked.

things as can satisfy a man's hunger. It gave him a decent appetite when he woke up at sunset, scratching his head and making lip smacking noises.

He also had nightmares, and because he was, essentially, Hell spawn, these nightmares were real doozies. They served as a reminder of Home, which is why a vampire tries *really* hard not to fall prey to the howling mob and sharp pointy sticks.

Melthus also had some wonderful dreams. Dreams of power, of becoming Lord of this earthly realm. In a time so long ago that he sometimes forgot his own origins, Melthus's host body had belonged to a man of honest farming ancestry. Farmers of livestock, mostly; sheep, specifically. Melthus dreamed of a life in which he did not have to hide beneath cold, leaking rock with the sound of the 21a to Chippenham rumbling overhead; a life in which mortals were served as cattle should be, fresh from the field and the barn, as peasants in those far-gone days were – dirty, and sweaty from their labours. In his dreams, mortal folk would be farmed just like sheep.

Well, a man had to dream.

But some work hard to make their dream come true.

Melthus greeted this fine evening in Advent with a smile. His dream would soon be within his grasp, a tangible thing. With a little industry and perseverance, he would have the Roman city in his grip, the population converted. And then he would show this bloody country what fear was.

How would he achieve this?

Mathematics, that's how.

One vampire takes a meal. The meal becomes a vampire. He bites another. Even at this pace, the contagion spreads at an alarming rate. Now, given that a vampire of even modest appetite [*]will feed at least twice a day, and those two meals go on to eat possibly three or even four times a day…

…Get the picture?

Within a few days, Great Britain would be a dangerous place for tourists and itinerant Hansom Cab Lamp Fitters. Bad news all around, really, what with all the airports and seaports… because a nation of vampires will quickly realise that its own food source is rapidly depleted.

Caution, then, thought the WamphyrLord Melthus; *create just enough of our own kind to make life comfortable.*

Which made it all the more important to keep tight control of the Newborn, keep them close to the Tribe; understandable, then, that he went

---

Say, a she-vampire who wants to slim down to a size zero.

apeshit, bugshit, and all the shits in between when he heard the news. The loss of Newborn was not conducive to secrecy.

'*Fahnd* them!' shouted he, being in a proper lather. 'They can't get far. They will be weak still.'

'And the traitor, Caitlin? And the one called Costner?' said a minion.

'Ah have dispatched Dufus to find Costner,' said Melthus in his stereotypical and outrageously lampooned Froggie accent. 'He will fahnd 'im. As for Caitlin, ah will attend to 'er mahself.'

The assembled Tribe said, *Oooh.*

'Go now. There is leetle enerf of the night remaining. Fly, mah children. Ride the winds. Dawdle not, nor tarry, or piss about in general. Bring zem to me.'

The assembly bowed at the knee, then dispersed, finding their evil way through tunnels and passages that honeycombed the Wiltshire, Somerset and Avon countryside; up, and up a bit more, until they surfaced, climbing from the earth through potholes and bore holes, manholes and drains.

Tonight was a night to bolt the doors, hang the garlic and prune those boughs of Holly hanging in festive bunches to commemorate the season. A night to huddle together, light every lamp and if the loo was an outhouse, to tie a knot in it or cross the legs. Or pee into an empty milk bottle. Whatever. It was not a night to be outdoors.

Unfortunately, this was the week before Christmas.

And Bath City was rockin'.

*

They'd offered her sedation, those fools with their syringes and spikes. She had to sleep, they said. Sleep helped to heal the mind.

But Caitlin could not sleep, for the night was her time. She paced the common room of the Secure Unit. Up, down, up, down. Sometimes she varied this with a twirl or a hop, a skip or a jump, but mostly up, down. Up. And down.

And then she paused in the middle of a complicated pirouette she'd learned from a dancer at the Court of Munster. She landed on her bottom; her teeth clicked and she bit her tongue. She swore in Gaelic.

'They come,' she said.

'Who?' said Ben, one of the staff working the graveyard shift .

'Them. The Tribe.' She was suddenly on her feet, fast enough to startle the nurse.

'Tribe?'

'My people.' She left the common room, ran to her room. There, she strapped her sandals to her feet, wrapping the leather thongs around her legs.

Angus, another nurse, waited by her door. 'What are you doing?'

'I am leaving this place.'

'Miss O'Connor, I don't think…'

She was past him before he realised that she'd moved, which didn't just startle him. He flattened himself against the wall of the corridor and gaped, his heart a-gallop. 'Oi. Hang on a minute. You're on a Section Three. You can't just…'

But Caitlin could.

'Angus,' called Ben. 'What's all the noise?'

This nurse felt a minor hurricane of stale, smoky, common room air as he stood at the office door, like the passing of something moving at abnormal speed.

Crash, went a heavily reinforced door.

'Ben, stop her!'

'Whom?'

'O'Connor. The girl.'

'Where?'

'Through that mangled, now superfluous security door if I'm any judge.'

'Door?'

'Dozy git,' said Angus, pushing past the befuddled Ben.

Angus ran. This was going to be impossible to explain. Well, the impossible generally is. He ran, and once outside the building, he ran some more down the narrow road outside. He didn't run far. It was obvious that the girl was gone.

Angus and Ben searched the car park and circuited the psychiatric unit, checking corners and bushes.

'Sod it,' said Angus.

'I'll call security,' said Ben

'Call the police.'

'Police?'

Angus turned upon his colleague. 'Yes. Then call the duty manager. Tell him we've got a client AWOL.'

'What will you be doing?'

'I'm going to have a bit of a sit down.' Angus would much rather have had a big fat roonie and a lie-down, but that would have to wait.

'Who's that?' said Ben.

'What?'

Ben nodded, staring past Angus. Angus turned.

A fog had formed. In the space of a few minutes, thick mist that could hide a man until he was standing next to you.

'Good evening, monsieur.'

Angus made a sound similar to EEEEEEG, and then swallowed fog.

'Shall we go in?' said the man.

'You scared the bollocks out of me,' said Angus.

'Indeed?' The voice that came from the man sounded as if it had been soaked in something thick - thick and probably smelly. Angus hoped that the man wouldn't stay.

'What do you want?' said he. He regretted asking that question almost immediately. He'd really rather not know.

'Ah believe you 'ave a guest.'

'Got lots of those. Who are you?'

'You could call me 'er spiritual father. Ah seek Caitlin.'

Angus looked at Ben. Ben looked right back. Then they both gave the stranger the once-over. In an appraising sort of way.

'Shall we go in?' repeated the strange one.

'I don't think…' Angus began.

'Perhaps ah am not making mahself understerd. Inside. *Now*.' He made a twiddly gesture with his fingers.

'Why's he getting twiddly with his fingers?' said Ben.

'That's hypnotic how's-your-father, that is' Angus explained.

'Ah. That explains this compulsion to do exactly what he says without further malarkey.'

'Let's go put the kettle on,' said Ben. 'Walk this way, Mr….?'

'Melthus. You may call me Melthus. For now. Later, you will call me Lord.'

'Ah,' said Ben. 'Haristocracy.'

'Harry who?' said Angus.

'Shut up,' Melthus commanded.

CHAPTER TWENTY-SIX

Wednesday 19th 03.00

'While I understand the need to facilitate the grieving process,' Ted was saying, 'why do we have to do it now?'

'Because we're travelling in a stolen tractor,' was George's reply. 'How far d'you think we'd get in broad daylight?'

'I don't know if I can do this.' Dai was crouched, most painfully, in the rear of the tractor's cabin, head in his hands. 'I don't. I can't.'

'You must. You can. And since you are a fugitive this is the time. Come, Dai. We'll be right behind you.' George opened his door and jumped out.

''Twill end in tears,' said Ted, shaking his head.

They had parked at the gate to the cemetery. It was three of the morning hour and a heavy frost had given the ground the appearance of wearing a dusting of snow.

'We don't even know where she's buried,' said Dai.

'Then we look for the most recent interment.' George had found a torch in the tractor. 'Like that one. Dai?'

The weeping biker walked onward. He stopped at the grave then bent to read the inscription on the headstone next to it. His weeping – silent tears until now – became sobbing

''Tis a terrible thing to lose the beloved,' said George. Ted nodded mutely, shedding a tear of his own.

'Ay, George.'

'Ted?'

'Who do you reckon would be walking around a cemetery in their bare feet?'

'I sense that there is good tangible evidence for such a bizarre enquiry.'

'Observe,' said Ted, pointing a nicotined and bitten finger. George pointed the torch beam at the ground. There were indeed footprints. A great many. All in a straight line. Dainty, female type prints. Fresh. They led away from the grave.

'Hmm,' went George.

'AAAAAARGH,' Dai went. 'Bastards!'

Ted's eyes rolled wildly. 'What? What?'

'The *wankers*,' shouted Dai.

'Steady on, old son.' George joined the bereaved at the graveside.

'Gone.' Dai's voice was a ragged thing, full of woe and outrage. 'They took her.'

Down went the torch beam. The resting-place of young Sarah Farquaarson was vacant. Even the coffin had gone.

'What's all this yellow tape?' said George.

'Funny. Hadn't noticed that. And then there's this big square of cleared ground.': Ted

'Like a tent, or some such, has been erected – in the past twenty four hours, too, I'll be bound.': George.

'Why would you want to be tied up, ay?' said Ted. 'Why George, why?'

'A figure of speech, my friend.'

'Like, " Go To The Foot Of Our Stairs"*?'

'Just so.'

'No. Really. Look.'

George looked.

A lone figure stood beneath a Yew tree: a young woman dressed most unsuitably for inclement weather.

'Barely got a stitch on,' said Ted. 'Why, George, why?'

''Tis a scanty frock to be wearing without a vest, or other appropriate under garment. Perhaps she needs help?'

'Ay, I don't think that's a frock,' said Ted, who knew what a shroud looked like.

'Lads?'

'Dai,' said George.

'What are you nattering about?'

'The young lady, yonder.'

'What young lady?'

'That…oh.'

'Where'd she go?' Ted looked left, right, fore and aft. Then, foolishly, up and down.

'Big dog, innit?' said Dai.

'Where?' said Ted.

'By the chapel.'

---

* A nonsensical phrase meant to convey amazement, surprise, disbelief. Or possibly just for the hell of it.

The lads looked. 'Oh my,' said Ted. 'That *is* an over-large pooch, and no mistake.'

'Bright eyes,' said Dai.

'Must be taking Bob Martin tablets,' surmised George.

'Don't think so.' Dai huddled closer to his companions. 'Shit. I think it's seen us.'

'That's a given,' said George.

The dog trotted toward them. It was bigger than they had thought.

'Oo. I have a feeling in my water,' said Ted. 'And it isn't a bladder infection.'

The dog stopped. It sat. It appeared to be staring at Dai.

'Good eye contact,' remarked George. 'Have you two met?'

Dai did not reply. His face had gone slack.

'Wipe your chin, lad,' said George. But the little Welsh motorcyclist, who didn't own a bike, drooled on.

'Ay. George. Want to know what I think?'

'What's that, Ted?' said George.

'We should leave. Pronto. As they say.'

'Who says that, then, Ted?'

'The Italians I think.'

George gave Dai a nudge. 'The Italians think that we should leave.'

Dai grunted.

'Come on. Slowly does it. Best not startle the doggy.'

'I think that the only way to startle that thing is to present George Bush with a prestigious comedy award,' said Ted.

'Or a stick of dynamite up its jacksy. Although I for one would not be so bold. Let us depart,' said George.

'And hasten in the doing' said Ted.

Dai, however, would not budge.

'Shall we leave them to their mutual yet wholly unnatural yearning?' said Ted. 'Ay?'

'That would earn no merit, should prizes ever be awarded for good thinking, Ted. No. Grab an arm.'

Between them, arms were seized. There was much pulling and tugging and Dai did not resist. The dog, however, growled.

'Distant thunder, do you think?'

'No, Ted. Although it does remind me somewhat of heavy furniture dragged across bare floorboards.'

The dog was up on all four paws once more. Hackles were raised.

'The hair is standing up on my neck,' said Ted.

'Mine too. Must be an atavistic response to an ancient threat.' George shivered.

'Eh?'

'An ancestral memory, Ted. A lone hunter, confronted by the wolf.'

'Didn't know you hunted, George.'

'I don't. But primaeval man did.'

'Don't mention the word "evil"' said Ted.

'Evil?'

'I said not to mention it*.'

'Uuuuuurgh,' said Dai.

'Don't do that, my biker friend.' George shivered some more.

'Um, did you say, "Wolf"?'

'Yes Ted.'

'Why did you say that. Why, George, why?'

'Because that's what it is.'

'No.'

'Yes.'

'You're scaring me, George.'

'Uuuuuuuurgh,' said Dai.

'That was a longer Uurgh than before. Let's move a little faster, George. Uuuuuuuurrrgh'

'Don't labour the point, Ted.'

'I'm not. He just dribbled on my hand.'

The wolf circled them. Teeth were bared. Long teeth.

'Not your European or Northern American species,' said George. They kept moving. Then, suddenly, it was gone.

'It's gone.'

'So it has, Ted.'

'I want to use the toilet.'

'You should have gone before we came out. Keep walking.'

They were almost at the gate, and had every right to breathe sighs of relief.

'Oh bugger,' spake George.

'It's back. It's going to attack us. Why, George, why?'

---

* See? It *is* worth keeping them in circulation. Oh chortle. Larf.

'I think it wants Dai.'

'Why, George, why?'

But George did not respond, for George was legging it.

'For shame!' called Ted. 'Cowardy cowardy custard.'

'Uuuuuuuuuuuurgh,' went Dai, and then he dribbled once more upon Ted's hand.

'Uuurgh,' said Ted, wiping it on Dai's trousers.

'Gibble,' said Dai, showing a broader vocabulary.

'I think I've pooed my pants' said Ted.

The Wolf crouched. It sprang. And so, too, did George.

Grrowrr was the sound rumbling from the Wolf's chest.

'Bonsai!' came the war cry, directly behind.

There was a single, keck-filling shriek that lasted for mere seconds but felt like minutes.

Dai blinked. 'Uurgh?'

'He's feeling better,' said Ted. 'George?'

'That was the single most terrifying moment of my life' said he, picking himself up from the ground. 'And it isn't over. Pass me your Buck knife.'

'I don't have a Buck knife, George.'

'I was talking to Dai.'

'Ugh.' Dai moved woodenly. Which is to say, unlike plastic, or metal, or some other man made material. Stiffly, anyway, which is another adverb but what the hell. But he reached behind him, pulled the knife from its belt sheath then threw it to George.

George opened it and set it to a useful purpose.

'Why are you removing the head, George?'

'Following instructions, Ted. 'Tis the only way to kill a vampire.'

'Why do you assume such, George?'

'Because when I had it in my torch beam, it did not cast a shadow.'

'Ay? You didn't mention that before. Why, George, why?'

'Because you would have been terrified, Ted. And I needed your assistance to move our large Welsh friend.'

The head came off. A stench of putrefaction filled the frigid air. George staggered back, his hand across his mouth. The Wolf lay still, as only a headless Wolf may.

Ted noticed the stake sticking out of its back for the first time. 'Ay. Nice work,' said Ted. 'If I may be so bold.'

'Got any Roses, Ted?'

Ted patted his pockets. 'Alas, no.'

'Then we must remove the body to a safe place until we find some.'

'Try some of mine,' said Dai. He reached into a pocket and pulled out a handful of dried petals.

George took the aromatic mitt-full and then stuffed them into the beast's mouth. No sooner and no later done, a strange transformation began to seize the Wolf.

'Oh God,' said Ted. 'Look.'

'I know, mate. Look away. And you, Dai.'

But Dai was already on his hands and knees. He was sobbing as he took her hand. 'Sarah,' he gasped. 'My little Sarah.'

Ted and George looked away.

'Evening, lads,' said Barry Park

'Oh shit,' said George.

'You're nicked, you are,' said Clive Feart.

CHAPTER TWENTY-SEVEN

Berkoff returned to his sad pile of a house in the guise of a sad pile of a man.

He'd run most of the two miles from the supermarket, although pursuit had been half-hearted at best. Perhaps that was because no one really wanted to capture a loping, long-toothed slavering dog-thing. You could catch something nasty off something like that. Sweaty dog bollock syndrome, for example. Or something.

This *Lycanthropy* business was trickier than he'd imagined. How could he have known that a hiccough, halfway through the Change, would leave him stuck between man and beast? Yet here he was, in a bit of a lathery sweat, drooling down his best tweeds and his clawed toes protruding through his new brogues. It hurt to run like that.

And he'd *had* to run. Bath wasn't generally cursed with stray dogs but they seemed to come out of nowhere – dirty, flea bitten, flaky mutts that recognised, somehow, that there was a stranger on their turf and they weren't having any of it. One of them had tried to mate with him – but then, a Jack Russell will mate with anything.

Berkoff swore, but the best that he could do was something that sounded like "Frassin' rassin' grassin' Dick Dastardly tee hee hee."

Which pissed him off no end.

Frustrated, and still hungry, he rampaged through his drab rooms, smashing this and that and a photograph of him shaking hands with Mickey Mouse, a treasured memory of happier times. But those memories belonged to another Berkoff; all he wanted was to feed, to feast upon living, running tissue, to gorge himself upon shivering fear-spiced prey, seeking out the dark places and becoming one with the night, a terrible shadow haunting the corners and back streets of the city.

Why, then, had he been caught shoplifting in *Somerfields*?

It wasn't as if they were known for their cut-price offers on whole bull's blood. The pimply youth at the meat counter had given him a Look. The nerve of him.

'A gallon of what?'

'Bull's blood. Pigs, at a pinch, but I won't go any lower down the food chain than a lamb.'

'What do you think this is? Psychos R Us? Piss off.'

So Berkoff had given the boy a Look of his own.

'Is that supposed to be scary?'

Which is when Berkoff, mighty hunter of the mortal, had sidled off and found a way into the back of the building, the jeers and scorn of the security bods still stinging his skyscraper-sized demonic ego.

And there he found what he sought: big gallon drums of blood. It wasn't hot, but even a lukewarm burger will do when needs must. It was in cold storage, ready for the blood sausage maker to practice his craft, but it would suffice.

Halfway through one such drum was he when the pimply youth caught him swigging from the container, guzzling away as if fresh bull's blood was going out of fashion. Which, in a very real sense, it had. In the Neolithic period, probably.

'Oi. Youse,' said the acned one.

'Are you French?' said Berkoff, spraying his meal.

'Well, no, but…'

Berkoff had given him The Finger. Because a proper two-fingered salute would have been a waste.

'Having trouble Malcolm?' enquired a pheasant plucker's mate, who was busy plucking pheasants in another room.

'Come and have a look at this,' called Malcolm the bespotted. And so the pheasant plucker's chum came and looked.

'You're not the regular pheasant plucker,' noted the Malcolm.

'Indeed not. I'm a pheasant plucker's mate. And I'm only plucking pheasants because–'

'Heard it,' said Malcolm, somewhat tersely.

'I was about to say, my mate has come down with a bad case of *Dhobi's Itch*. Who's this?'

'He's a sad old perv who's about to get his kidneys kicked.' Thus spoken, the impetuous lad made the appropriate moves to achieve this end.

Combat!

Berkoff's teeth had responded right on cue. As did the Change – a natural reaction for any self-respecting vampire. It kept one's options open: rip out the throat or run like fun.

'EE,' said the pheasant plucker's mate, whose name Malcolm did not know. 'That's 'orrible.'

'It's not that bad. I saw something really gross once. There was a big hairy toe in the Beluga caviar.'

'No.'

'Yes. And there was this long green bogey in the Calamari…'

Growl, went the Berkoff-Thing.

'Security,' called the pheasant plucker's acquaintance. 'Oh help, do.'

'Having trouble?' said the over-large security person, suddenly appearing from his favourite skiving place. He crushed a cigarette out on a hanging haunch of beef*.

Rowrr, was the noise Berkoff made as he hurriedly finished the dregs of his gory repast. *Groo-aaarhg*, he added.

'Didn't I throw him out five minutes ago?'

'Go get him, Marion,' said the grossed-out, pustule-ridden lad.

'The name's *Wayne*, Malcolm.' Wayne shrugged his shoulders, tough guy style, set his peaked cap upon his close-cropped head and looked very menacing indeed. It was enough for most shoplifters, anyway. 'Stand aside.'

'I *am* standing aside.'

'Then stand aside a bit more. Move along. There's nothing to see here.'

'I beg to differ,' said the pheasant plucker's mate.

Berkoff finished, wiped his snarling snout upon his sleeve and then threw the empty container at the security man, who swaggered forward to apprehend the miscreant.

'Ow!'

Grrrrr.

'Stop pissing about, Marion,' said the pheasant plucker's mate.

'I told you,' warned he. Then he turned to the thief. 'You want to watch where you're chucking empty drums of whole bull's blood, mate. You could take someone's eye out with that.'

'He's getting away,' remarked the pheasant plucker's buddy.

'Not while *I'm* on duty.' And thusly said, the man who would be called Wayne rushed at Berkoff, who now resembled something that even Rolf Harris would be tempted to stuff in a sack with a brick tied to it.

Which is when Berkoff had learned the error of rushing his food. He burped; his belly hitched. He hiccoughed…

…The Change stopped short. He was left with arms and legs flapping uselessly in his brown tweed suit. Flight seemed to be the only recourse. To flee, perchance to raid the cold meat store again. He bumped into a late

---

Important note: this is a fictitious branch of *Somerfields*, so no need for libel action. No, honest.

arrival for the night shift, but Berkoff was on his misshapen feet before any organised pursuit.

'You're late,' said the pheasant plucker's mate.

Oh, the ignominy of it. To be run off like a dog with its snout in a bin bag. He would return to see them, one day. But not tonight. There was little enough of the night remaining, and Berkoff had had a long day. He checked his answering machine for messages. There was only one. Stephens. Calling to say he couldn't make it. Some emergency. Possibly pop around in the morning. More likely the evening. He'd ring again. Maybe.

The message was a day old. Berkoff erased the message then grinned. Tonight would be fine. Just in time for breakfast. He headed for his bed and then, remembering the state of it, decided to kip in the spare room instead. Perhaps he would be back to normal when he woke up.

Or perhaps that itch behind his ear was a touch of mange.

CHAPTER TWENTY-EIGHT

Wednesday 19th December 2001.
Really, really late.

'Do you believe in the undead?'

Pitt, against all expectations, was taking the burglary very calmly. He'd taken his students to what he called "the lounge" in the complex of subterranean chambers beneath the Manor. He stood facing them, arms folded; Kevin was a dark presence, sitting in a corner, having a snack. Jan and Jason tried to ignore him but the slurping was somewhat disturbing. And he dribbled.

'We do now,' said Jan.

Pitt raised an eyebrow. 'Indeed?'

Jason nudged her.

'Mr. Denman, we're not playing games here. It is important that you tell me what you know.'

Behind them, Kevin burped.

'Truth,' said Jason. 'Ah. Well, I s'pose you're going to find out anyway.'

Pitt's brow knotted in the middle. 'What are you saying?'

There was a clatter outside. Hooves on stone steps, and then a bellow, a nightmarish sound that bounced and echoed down the stairwell and rattled the heavy oaken timber of the door.

Pitt paled. 'What have you done?'

Jan and Jason looked at each other. Then at the door. The noise of something heavy and single-minded drew nearer. Jason was the first on his feet. 'I think we'd better – '

The door exploded. A pair of antlers emerged from the splinters.

'Oh my God,' said Pitt.

'You want me to handle it?' Kevin was on his feet. His sword was in his hand.

'No. I need that specimen alive.'

'Are you sure about that?' said Jason.

Jan was edging to the only other door offering escape. 'I really do think that we should move,' she said. The door shuddered again; this time, the stag's head came right through.

'Heeeere's Johnny!' said Jason. 'Bye, Professor.' He grabbed Jan's hand and they ran.

*

'Which way?'

'I don't know. This is blind panic, Jan. Anywhere but where that thing is.'

The sounds of mayhem were behind them, but still too close. Jason ducked into the nearest room in the corridor.

'Great,' said Jan. 'A bathroom. A monster would never dare to interrupt one's ablutions.'

'Just hide,' said Jason.

The options for this were severely limited. There was only one other door.

'In here,' said Jason.

"In here" turned out to be a store of some kind.

'He's really into leather,' said Jan.

'It's a male thing,' said Jason.

They scanned the room for an exit. They didn't find one, but they *did* find the arsenal behind the racks of clothing and leather armour.

Jason whistled. '*Look* at this stuff. It must be worth a fortune.' He took a two handed sword by the hilt but couldn't lift it.

'There must be something we can use.' Jan searched the rows of weaponry. 'Yes! Now, *that's* what I call a penis extension.'

'Bloody hell,' said Jason, and then opened the glass case. 'It's a beauty.'

There was a loud crash out in the corridor.

' Jas, It's killed them both!'

'We don't know that.'

'I don't think that thing is going to roll over for a sugar lump. We should never have come here. What are we going to do?'

Jason hefted the gun in his hands. Then he grinned.

'You think it's loaded?' said Jan.

Jason frowned. 'Good point.' He turned the thing around and looked down the bell end. As it were. 'Something in here,' he said, his voice distorted.

The business end of the rifle resembled the part of a euphonium that vents all the noise. He gave it a shake. It rattled.

'Yup. It's loaded. Nails or buckshot. Either will do.'

The door behind them opened. Hooves raised sparks at the threshold.

'Put that down!' shouted Pitt, diving into the room.

Which made Jason jump.

And then several things seemed to happen.

In slow-mo, as these things do when events get too exciting.

Jason turned, bringing the weapon to bear on the Thing that had just appeared at the open doorway. A single thrust of those grotesque antlers knocked Pitt sideways. He somersaulted, crashed against a wall.

The gun went off.

It was like being at Ground Zero during an A-bomb test.

The thunder of it drowned out everything:

Jan's scream.

Pitt's howl of pain.

Kevin's curse as he threw himself out of range.

But above all, the incomparable sound of a skull fragmenting into many, many pieces. Bits of brain, what little remained after two thousand years, mingled with watery plasma. An eyeball, still intact, seemed to float for a long time before falling to earth. It bounced, rolled toward Jan, where it bumped against her right foot.

There was a frozen moment of time in which nothing appeared to move, and then, as if she'd been watching it all on a cinema screen, Jan saw bodies begin to stir.

Pitt wasn't moving at all. Jan checked his pulse. He was alive; she thanked her own personal deity then turned to where Jason lay beneath a tangle of leather bits and pieces, buckles and straps.

'Friggin' thing has a hair trigger,' he said. Then he turned white. 'I could've blown my bleeding head off.'

'I think that's a given,' said Jan, nodding at the mess on the walls and the bathroom beyond.

Jason struggled from the heap of leather clothing and managed to get to his knees. 'Hell of a kick on it.'

The body of the Elk stag also had a kick on it - once upon a time. Now, its great horned hooves scrabbled uselessly on the stone floor.

'Tell me that's just spasms,' said Jason.

The body lurched. Legs bunched beneath the fallen creature. A high-pitched, piggy squeal emitted from the ragged remains of its neck.

'It's still alive,' said Jan. 'Load that thing up again. Kill it, Jas, kill it!' Her voice was an octave too high. Hysteria had just booked in for the weekend.

Jason looked about for suitable ammunition. 'With what?'

'I don't care! Just make it *stop*!'

So Jason did the only thing he could do. 'Okay, beastie. Eat wood.'

While Jason attempted to bludgeon the thrashing, bleating creature into submission, Kevin leaned against what remained of the door frame and shook his head. He let Jason wear himself out before flicking his long coat aside and pulling out a long wooden stake from a belt that boasted several such items.

Jason huffed, puffed and wiped sweat from his brow. 'That'll teach it,' he said, his voice hoarse.

The stag lurched again, its neck sweeping Jason aside. The monster rose to its feet.

'Wassssaaah!'

There was a pathetic, heart-breaking gurgle and then the Thing was still. It swayed for a moment then crumpled, a stake driven through its back and through Its heart.

'That's how we do it.' Kevin jumped over the corpse and held out a hand to Jason, eyes glowing in the half-light.

Jason froze. 'Are they contact lenses?'

'No.'

'Thought not.' He backed away, shuffling on his bottom. 'You have a little supper on your chin.'

Kevin ran a taloned finger along his inhumanly handsome chin, licked what he found on it.

'Oh shit,' said Jan. 'Just when I thought I wouldn't need another change of underwear.'

Kevin grinned. A fine set of fangs had grown, overlapping his lower lip. 'Don't be afwaid.'

'Easy for you to say,' said Jason, backing off.

Kevin shook his head. 'You don't understand. I'm one of the *good* guys.'

'Really.'

'Honest,' said Kevin, giving the old boy-scout salute.

Jason stood up unaided. 'No offence, mate, but I'd be a whole lot happier if you put those away.'

Kevin retracted his claws and teeth. 'Better?'

'A little.' Jason walked over to where Pitt lay. 'We should get him to a hospital.'

'No need,' said Kevin. 'The boss has fully equipped medical quarters.'

'He used to,' corrected Jan. She nodded toward the stag. 'I'm afraid *that* woke up a little prematurely.'

'It was an accident,' said Jason.

'You seem almost supernaturally prone to that kind of thing don't you?' said Kevin. 'Come on. Let's clean up.'

Kevin slung Pitt over one shoulder, took hold of a hind leg belonging to the stag then marched off toward the stairs. The two inept trespassers looked at one another.

'Must use weights a lot,' said Jason.

They followed the Slayer of Elk up the long flight of stairs. It was with a great deal of relief that they entered the comfortably brilliant, electrically lit hallway once more. Until they saw the gore pebble-dashing the polished expensive stonework, that is.

There, in the centre of the foyer, lay Simmons the caretaker.

'I think we're going to need a lot of needle and thread,' said Jan.

CHAPTER TWENTY-NINE

Wednesday 03.20

'But she's already dead!' Ted whined. 'You can't arrest us for killing someone what's already carked it!'

'I see,' said Clive. 'You just fancied a walk through the cemetery and you find a body that just happens to be lying about. So you stake it through the chest. Just to be sure. Doh!' He smote his brow with the palm of one hand.

'I spent most of Monday looking for you two.' Barry Park bent in the middle, the better to bring his six feet six frame onto a par with George's five feet eight, and thus cold-eyed him face-to-face. 'Where's that bleeding truck?'

'Truck?'

'Don't mess me about, lad. It's too friggin' cold.'

'Vicky Park.'

'Thank you. And this is Ted, I take it.' Barry cold-eyed same.

'Yiss,' said he in a voice that was squeaky.

'Marvellous. Clive?'

'Cuff 'em, Dan-O?'

'Please.'

Clive hadn't made an arrest before. Not a decent one. A decent one was a collar leading to a sentence of ten years or more. A lifer meant a night out with the CID lads, and Clive would not have to put his hand in his wallet. Not that he ever did. He gleefully ran through the prisoner's rights.

'Who's the dwarf?' said Barry.

'The dwarf?' said George.

'The leathery one.'

'Oh. Him. He was already here. On his way home. Cutting through the cemetery, nothing to do with us. No, not at all. Isn't that right, Dai?'

Dai cringed and slapped his hand across his eyes. Barry straightened up. He beckoned the innocent bystander. 'Dai, is it?'

'Might be.'

'You know these two?'

'Yes.'

'No,' said George.

'Ignore him,' said Dai. 'Fine mind, yet thick as pig shit.'

'A complicated man, I'm sure. Do you mind telling me what you're all doing here?'

Dai sighed. 'I dragged them up here. In fact, I hijacked them as they drove their truck back to the depot. Were it not for me, desperado that I am, they would not be in this sad predicament.'

'I see. And why did you ditch the truck in Vicky Park?'

'The Filth…sorry, the *police* were after us. Me. After *me*. So I forced them to switch vehicles.'

Barry fished out the incident sheet that DI Bratt had given him. He looked down the list. 'Ah. That'd be the Porsche.'

'Yes. Then we ditched that one. I. *I* did.'

'I know. We saw the tractor. Fortunately for you it hasn't been reported stolen yet, so we'll let that one slip. The list of charges is already longer than a pole-vaulter's long vaulty stick. But why bring 'em here?'

'I wanted to see my Sarah.'

Which gobsmacked Barry more surely than a smack in the gob. '*Your* Sarah.' Barry turned to the body of the recently deceased. 'Sarah Farquaarson?'

'She was murdered,' said Dai, who took to sobbing once more.

'I know. You came to say goodbye?'

Dai nodded.

'Do you know who killed her?'

Dai shook his head.

'Did you see *what* killed her?'

Dai turned his tear stained face up. 'You know?'

'I have a fair idea. Clive?'

'I love this job,' said his partner.

'Uncuff 'em.'

'Come again?'

'Uncuff. As in, remove the manacles.'

'But…'

'Clive, do you want to try explaining to Bratt why we arrested these lads for murder?'

'But they did.' Clive frowned. 'Didn't they?'

'There's no statute on the books for *re*-murder, Clive.'

'Aw.' Clive could not disguise his disappointment.

'Now then, Dai. This incident sheet I have in my hand here, as provided by my Guv'nor, is a list of misdemeanours he's expecting my partner and me to clear up on our policemanly perambulations. I can happily tick off a couple. Now, in the interests of community relations and to keep my partner from cuffing the lot of you, tell me why you were in the Infirmary.'

*

While Dai explained and Clive searched the pockets of his henchmen, certain eyelids fluttered, and a certain dismembered head gazed upon their doings with golden eyes. Fingers twitched. Limbs flexed. Slowly, soundlessly, the body of Sarah Farquaarson, beloved of Mr. and Mrs. Theodopolous Farquaarson, of the Giblet And Offal And Other Slimy Bits dynasty (catering and parties by commission), and sometime Wild Child of Tepid Ashton, moved its severed head.

*

'Yes,' said Barry. 'Mr. Costner. You made the news: Dr Pitt was at pains to point the finger in your direction. And you say you have no knowledge of the whereabouts of his corpse.'

'Like I said, I just wanted to watch him. See what happened,' said Dai. 'Innit?' he added, being Welsh.

'So that you could stake him, if your theory was correct. It has a certain warped logic, I suppose, especially in view of your experiences at Box Wood.'

'Bingo!' said Clive.

'They don't say that anymore,' said George. 'According to my missus, who is a recognised authority on the subject, it's "House".'

'Shut it, junkie,' said Clive. He held up a handful of ready rolled jays for Barry's inspection. 'Lookit!'

'Yes, Clive. Duly noted.'

'You don't seem enthusiastic.'

'Category C drugs don't light my fire, as such, in the light of current events.'

'Enough to prove dealing, though,' Clive insisted. He could almost taste a real arrest.

Barry sighed. 'All right. Who do they belong to?'

George held up a hand.

Barry turned to Dai and Ted. 'Either of you exchange money for a toke?'

Heads were shaken.

'Okay. Consider yourselves cautioned. Now then, what to do next? I propose we call in for an ambulance to transport Miss Farquaarson's body to the forensic unit.'

'No,' said Dai. 'I'm not having her interfered with.'

'Any more than she has been already? Dai, your friend here decapitated her,' said Barry.

'And that's enough. It was necessary. If George hadn't…look, officer, he saved our lives. What you see here isn't my Sarah. She died in Box Wood. *That* thing tried to kill me.'

They turned to look at the sad remains of Sarah F. They turned again. When they'd done a complete circle, Clive managed to say what the rest of them could not. Being collectively smacked in the gob, as it were.

'Where is she?' said Clive.

'She was right here,' said George. 'I staked her. Right here.' He stamped a foot at the exact spot. Torches were flicked on.

'There!' said Ted. A flicker of white shroud between trees by the roadside.

'But I took her head off,' said George. 'She had a stake through her chest.'

'Clive, you're the sprint champ. Strut your stuff.' Barry pointed. 'Fetch.'

'Me? On my own? What if I catch her?'

'No, Clive. The car. Get her started, we'll meet you at the road.'

Clive began his sprint. The rest of them trailed along after, hampered by ale paunches and lungs unused for much more than old shag.

'In, quick,' said Clive, slewing the car around on the icy road. 'She's heading for Bath.'

They jostled for seats, slammed doors. Clive floored the throttle, wheels spun, Ted yodelled and Dai lit a category C roll-up.

'Why are you yodelling, Ted?' said George.

'Fear,' sang Ted. 'Pure, unsullied fear,' he added, wiping sweaty hands upon his trousers.

'Chill, my diminutive Elvis Costello look-alike chum.' Dai passed the roonie and for a while all that could be heard was the grind of rubber upon poorly gritted road as Clive fought to keep the car in a straight line. The girl was nowhere to be seen.

'Are you sure she came this way?' said Barry.

'She could have gone cross country,' admitted Clive. 'Baz?'

'No.'

'But this is a four wheel drive.'

'Clive, there are ditches and fences and trees and hedges and all kinds of countryside between here and the city.'

'But she'll get away.'

'Oh go on,' said the three passengers.

Barry ground his molars.

'She *is* the only lead we've got to what's going on,' Clive reminded him.

'Go on, go on, go on,' chorused the three.

'Bollocks,' said Barry. 'All right, all right. But I drive.'

'Aw,' said Clive.

The car slewed across the road as Clive anchored. He got out, stamped around to the passenger side. Barry patted his shoulder as they passed. 'It's better this way,' he said. 'Because this heap is going to get wrecked, and I signed for it.'

Which made Clive feel a whole lot better, and his respect for his partner was that little bit deeper. This, thought Clive, is a hofficer and a gentleman. If ever a young copper needed a mentor, Clive was that man, and Baz was the bloke you picked to watch your back. 'What's that smell?' said Clive. 'Like burning compost. With plastic in it.'

'Left,' said Dai, wafting the smoke through his window. 'Through that gate. I saw something.'

Barry swung left.

'There, over the gate, into that field,' said Clive.

There was a brief crunch.

'That gate came off quite easily,' said George.

'I thought that you were going to stop and open it,' remarked Clive. Only the whitening of his knuckles betrayed his feelings.

'If we stop for every gate, hedge or ditch in pursuit, we may as well get out and run. Please take your hand of my knee, Clive. You're hurting.'

'We've lost her.' Dai leaned out of his window, waving a torch around.

'Irresponsible, is what I call it,' said Ted, shaking his noggin…

'We're doing our best, pal.' Clive could have sworn he'd seen something jump the gate, but despite the waxing moon and the clear night sky, he saw nothing more.

'...Leaving cows out, this time of night. Anything could happen. Cattle rustlers, extra terrestrials looking for tissue samples, dogs...' Ted did more shaking of his noggin.

'You're rambling, mate,' said George.

'Says you. For example and for instance, that Alsatian over there.' Ted pointed. Dai swung his torch.

'Tisn't doing any harm,' said George. 'Look, it's playing with that heifer. Aw, isn't it cute?'

There were sounds of a cow in distress.

'That's no merry frolic, old son.' Dai tapped Barry on the shoulder. 'Swing right.'

Barry swung right. The headlights swept a line of trees and then illuminated a strange tableau.

'Mad monks of Malta,' ejaculated Ted. 'That's 'orrible.'

There had never been a clearer case of cattle worrying since the invention of Yorkshire pudding. There was the briefest of struggles; the cow went down, buckling at the knees. If cows can be said to have knees. But if they can, then they certainly did.

The dog was not so much worrying as downright fretful. Its mouth was full of prime beef. The heifer ceased its struggles. The occasional twitch and kick of a leg was all that was left. Soon, even that ceased.

The dog appeared to be oblivious of the headlights, which lit a dry-stone wall behind it.

'That's our gal,' said Barry. 'Oh. Sorry, Dai.'

'That's not my girl. That's something else. My girl was a vegan.'

'Why isn't it casting a shadow, ay? Why, George, why?'

'Do we have weaponry of any description?' George realised they'd left the other improvised stakes in the tractor. He saw no point in needless heroics.

'It's eating,' said Barry. 'If there's one thing I've learned, it's never to stand between a dog and its dinner bowl. Let it feed. We'll follow it.'

Clive was having difficulty keeping up with all of this. They were talking as if all this stuff was real. As if vampires really existed. What had appeared to be a headless corpse could not possibly be the same individual now caught in the halogen beams of their Land Rover. All this guff about people feeding on blood was the stuff of fiction, strictly for the cinema. Obviously, the body had only *appeared* to be decapitated. Must have been soil covering her neck. Enough to fool anyone in the dark.

'Come off it, Baz,' said Clive, laughing (nervously, it has to be said). 'You can't be serious. People don't attack cattle. They don't drink blood. They *don't.*' He intercepted the jay between Dai and George and transferred it to his own gob. He took a deep pull. His eyes met across his nose.

'If you say so.' Barry was watching the late Sarah F. She was evidently too hungry to stop eating, even with spotlights on her. Finally, the thing that had been Dai's girl finished her meal and changed. It was a sight that would haunt them ever after.

She turned, golden eyes fixed upon them.

She hesitated, as if uncertain whether to run or attack. She took a step toward them, teeth bared. Barry hit the horn. It was enough to make the creature reconsider.

'She's rabbiting,' said Barry. 'Hold on, gentlefolk.'

The chase was on.

'She had blood all over her face,' said Clive. His tone was devoid of emotion. A statement of fact, like The Bear Will Indeed Take His Morning Constitutional In The Woods. He'd prefer to believe that a large furry carnivorous mammal shat in the Pope's silly hat than the undead roamed the land hassling ruminants.

'Ditch!' shouted Clive, stating the obvious. Which was better than gibbering. Which is what he wanted to do. He slapped George's hand away as he reached for the jay. *'Mine,'* he hissed.

'Got it covered, Clive. Fasten your– '

'AAArk,' went Clive, hitting his head on the roof of the Land Rover.

'- Seat belt. Tsk tsk. You need an ice pack on that.'

Their quarry was moving fast. Faster than a reanimated corpse should.

'I thought that a stake in the heart was supposed to do the business,' George said to Dai.

'Cheap furniture,' said he, shaking his head.

It was getting harder to keep Sarah in sight. Barry pushed the accelerator as hard as he dared. The occupants spent more time in the air, as the Land Rover hit the innumerable bumps and ruts of the fields, than sitting on the upholstery.

'I feel sick,' said Ted.

But there was no stopping for gastric relief. Sarah wasn't trying to evade or hide, but appeared to know exactly where she was going.

'What's that?' Ted pointed out of the window and upward.

'Training aircraft. We're approaching Colerne airfield. Hold on to your breakfast.' Barry cleared a hedge, crossed a lane then punched a hole through the fence surrounding the airstrip.

'Isn't this MOD* property?' said Clive, then giggled.

'You'd think they'd build better fences, wouldn't you?' Barry hit asphalt and made good use of it. He floored the accelerator. The Rover fishtailed for a few seconds and then found its grip.

'I wonder if she'd consider trying out for the Olympic team?' said Clive.

Sarah had just veered right and jumped the fence again without altering her stride. She was moving so fast, in fact, that her legs were all but invisible. Which disturbed Clive. Disturbed him a lot.

'This isn't happening.' His hands were shaking so violently that the end of his rollie fell off and rolled down the inside of his shirt.

'Handle it,' snapped Barry.

Clive fell silent. His partner was right. When he thought about it, the facts fit; he didn't want them to, but they did. He felt a headache coming on as he fought an internal battle to accept it.

'Your shirt is on fire,' said Ted.

'Airplane! ' screamed George.

Barry swung hard on the wheel to avoid tragedy and a hefty insurance claim, punched through a fence and across a lane.

'Wall! ' screamed Ted.

'Oh…yeah. So it is. Feel free to scream, lads.' Barry drove straight for it. A grassy embankment loomed ahead. They hit it. The wheels spun in clear, frosty air.

'Great view from here,' said George. 'Look, you can see the church. All floodlit.' And yes, it was a picturesque scene, fifteen feet above the turf and still aiming for altitude.

Then down they came. Which hurt a bit…

…Then down. And down.

'Bit steep,' commented Clive. 'What a rush.'

The field took them to the bottom of the valley. Another hillock caused another invasion of MOD* airspace.

'Is that a Rottweiler?' said Dai.

'Yes. Is that a cat on its back?'

---

* Ministry of Defence. In Colerne, Wiltshire, the place is usually overrun with UFO conspiracy theorists and a regular hazard to air traffic.

* And scattering a huddle of UFO spotters.

'I believe it is, Ted.' Barry shook his head. 'Strange universe we live in.'

Sarah F. did not stop to take a second glance at the bizarre sight. She was running uphill, now, and the Land Rover was slowing down.

'We're losing her,' said Dai.

'No.' Barry sounded confident.

'No?' chorused the passengers.

'No. For logic dictates that our Sarah is heading for home.' Sarah was gone, but Barry slowed down, left the field and found a lane. They picked up speed as a result and the twists and turns of the narrow track added a lot of interest to the route.

'Oh dear,' said Ted. 'May I swap seats with you, Dai?'

Ted had gone very pale. Pale and rather sweaty. Dai all but leapt over Ted, pushing the nauseous chap almost out through the window.

'Remind me to put her through the car wash before we go back,' said Barry.

'Sarah?' said Clive.

'No. The car. All cars are female, Clive. it's the law.' The lane terminated in a main road. Barry did not heed the customary caution required by the Highway Code. The Give Way markings were as naught.

'They shouldn't allow juggernauts on country roads,' said Ted. He'd had a good close-up of the radiator grille of one of British Leyland's heaviest. The white, terrified face of the driver was a mirror image of Ted's own.

'Shouldn't lean on his horn like that at this time of night, though,' said George.

'Actually, it's early morning, mate.' Ted was correct. It was getting lighter on the horizon.

'Makes sense,' said Dai. 'She'll be trying to find somewhere dark and sheltered.'

They were driving uphill again. Hedgesparrow Lane, the sign said. On to Barnet's Hill, past *The Quarryman's Arms*.

'Too far,' said Dai. 'You should have taken a right before the pub.'

'Not the handbrake turn,' pleaded Ted. 'Oh please.'

Barry performed a perfect handbrake turn. But it was icy. The car spun. Then spun some more.

'I want to get off,' Ted begged.

The car hit a signpost, sending it askew, which would make for much public confusion. At least for the authentically bewildered. 'That's the bull-bars gone,' said Barry. 'Still, could be worse, eh?'

Ted was violently sick on the back seat.

'Told you,' said Barry. He turned the Land Rover in the right direction, which by general consent meant forward and onward. They turned down the lane indicated by Dai.

There was a gate. A metal one. Clive didn't wait for Barry to stop but jumped out as the Land Rover slowed. He opened it then just as quickly jumped back into the car.

They entered the Wood at a crawl. On the left, a blue toilet cubicle; set further back, a fenced-off compound protected a radio mast. There was no sign of movement. Barry turned the engine and lights off. 'Everyone shush, ' he said.

So they shushed.

And they heard…

…Nothing.

Not a twitter, nor a hoot, or scurry or rustle.

'It's quiet,' said Ted. '*Too* quiet.'

Which, while being an outrageous cliché, was also necessary. Because it *was* too quiet. Too still and silent by half, even for such a night as this.

The Land Rover was equipped with all sorts of high-tech gizmos, as you would expect for a modern squad vehicle. Among the various LED read-outs and dials and twinkly beeping lights, there was a thingy that told the driver how cold it was outside. It had a smart chip in it, which Barry didn't like.

'It's minus six Celsius,' said a deceptively sexy female voice.

'Everyone out,' said Barry.

'Wrap up warm,' said the vocal temperature sex kitten.

'Er. Thank you.' Barry hated high tech gizmos with a better vocabulary than his.

'No problem,' said the thermometer. *'Wear a scarf.'*

They climbed out into the kind of light that is described as crepuscular. Well, some people do. Lurky, is how Ted chose to describe it. His vocabulary was thankfully basic, for Lurky sounded exactly right. Although the grey light was blooming into a pleasant orange-pink, the Wood itself remained a shadowy, otherworldly place where you wouldn't think of wandering off to investigate any strange noises.

And there *was* a strange noise. Off to their left, and close enough to give everyone the heebie-jeebies. A snickering, nasty little sound that said Evil, Evil, Evil.

'Go and see what that was, Ted, will ya?'

'As much as it grieves me to use strong profanities,' said same, 'you can take a flying fuck at a rolling ring doughnut, Dai.'

The snickering, evil, nasty sound was closer now. Something caused a bush to shiver about ten yards to their right, and it wasn't the freezing air.

'Back in the car?' suggested George.

'I would if I could,' said Barry, 'but I find my legs are indisposed to a backward canter.'

'I'm scared, Baz.' Clive's teeth clicked in a steady rhythm.

'We're all scared,' said Barry.

'I'm not,' said Sarah Farquaarson.

Now, there's nothing like a good communal singsong, or a good shout and bawl with a congenial crowd. And there's absolutely nothing to equal a comradely scream of terror, the sort that echoes and bounces around long after you're done.

Primal screams, they call them.

Yeah, those chaps.

Because it comes from an ancient part of the brain, the bit that never gets used unless it's really, really necessary. It takes a lot out of you, a scream like that. But it also, perversely, has the effect of kicking another ancient part of your brain into touch. The hypothalamus and the pituitary. Adrenaline, folks. Better than opium. Gives more pep than Prozac, more courage than category C Cannabis, of which we have already witnessed far too much gratuitous abuse already.

Barry and Clive Aaaaaaarghed.

Dai and George Uuuuuuurghed.

Ted yodelled, being uniquely himself.

Sarah took a bow. 'You're too kind,' she said.

Adrenaline. Thick upon the air. Sarah sniffed and then she drooled. And her body began the Change.

'Run,' said Barry.

'Splendid idea,' said Dai. 'Let's.'

So they did.

But not fast enough.

The Sarah Thing leapt.

Dai dived to his left to take cover behind, of all things, a big bush. Well, you do silly things like that when terror lays its deathly hand upon your good sense.

But not so daft, as it turned out. There was a shriek that the legendary Banshee may have vented in Merrie Olde Ireland. It wasn't Dai. The Sarah Thing thrashed about, shredding the bush. It was an awful thing to witness. As it has already been said, vampires die hard. And this one was making a five-course meal of it.

Dai was still screaming when they dragged him out from the bush, the Sarah Thing still thrashing and squealing. Its roar of pain and fear and sheer bloody frustration was something that Clive, for one, would pay a hypnotherapist to help him forget and thus sleep at night*.

Dai finally took control of his fear. A few good slaps from George helped. Nothing like a stinging smack in the kisser to bring the grey matter back on line.

'Is she dead this time?' he said, in a voice so wracked with terror and anguish both that Barry gently squeezed his arm.

'Not quite,' he said. 'Er. There, there. Take it easy lad. And all that.'

'Nice try, cop. But I can't stand this anymore.' He took out his Buck knife and with one swift stroke he cut her throat.

Well, he would have.

Just as the blade touched her skin, those golden eyes blazed into Dai's and his arms went numb.

'You father fucks hamsters in Milton Keynes,' said the demon within Sarah. 'And your mother…your mother sucks snot from the nostrils of a camel. Somewhere in Dubai. The Middle East, anyway.'

'Cease your evil and somewhat pathetic curses,' said Barry, who after all was Welsh and therefore near enough ordained at birth. He took out a Cross of silver he kept about his neck and placed the Holy Symbol against the foul creature's forehead.

'AAAAAAAArgh.'

'You can do better than that,' said Barry. 'Give us a real blood curdler.'

'I'd rather she didn't' said Ted.

'Me to,' said Clive. 'Let's just get this over with.' He placed a foot between the vampire's shoulder blades then forced the Thing down onto the branch that had entered Its chest. The heart had not yet been pierced.

The others saved a fortune by watching *MacGyver* re-runs.

'That's right,' said someone. 'Push it all the way.'

Something was thrown, something wet, and as it pattered upon the Wolf-creature's fur it smoked. The Wolf howled. The body began to transmute. The snout began to collapse in upon itself, teeth rattled and legs became defined as arms and paws flattened out. Fingers cracked and stretched.

'Looks painful don't it?' said someone.

They looked around.

'Good evening,' said the someone. 'Bit nippy, don't you think? Would you be so kind as to stand aside for a moment? Thank you so much.' The stranger raised what looked like a big stick.

'Oi, watch out,' said Dai, rolling as the stick descended. There was some gristly, not least grisly, gratuitous blood-soaked malarkey and then an almighty pong.

'Strewth,' said Clive. 'Smells like my fridge.'

Ted managed to projectile vomit in a safe direction, but the wind blew it back again anyway.

'That,' said the mysterious stranger, 'is how you take the head of a Wamphyr.'

'So it would seem.' Barry gave him a copperly look. 'Please put the axe down, Mr.....?

'Wainwright. Reverend Wainwright. You may call me Alec.' He offered his hand. The four vampire hunters took turns to shake it.

'Don't consider me ungrateful,' said Dai, 'but what are you doing here?'

Wainwright shoved a little finger up his left nostril and rummaged about a bit. He removed the pinky, wiped it on his cloak then shrugged. 'Noise like that carries a long way. The Rectory is just along the lane there. I imagine there are a few souls who'll be shivering beneath their bed linen.' Wainwright kicked the corpse, which was quite still. The head, however, remained very much with it.

'You want to watch where you're swinging axes, you todger-pulling God-botherer. Thou sniffer of bicycle seats. You could take someone's eye out with that,' said the head.*

'Do you think so? Shall we try?'

'Your daughter sleeps with serial killers and your male offspring lie with newts,' said the demon.

'Cornflakes or Weetabix?'

* See what I mean?

'What?' said the demon.

'No matter.' Wainwright flipped back his cloak with no small degree of flourish. He wore a belt full of leather pouches upon his well-padded waist. He removed a glove, teased open a pouch then dug nicotine-stained fingers within. The grubby digits reappeared smelling a whole lot sweeter. 'I think that we should bring things to a satisfactory conclusion,' said the priest.

The vampire clenched its jaw, shook its head.

'How does it do that?' said Dai. 'I mean, it doesn't have a neck.'

'The vampire body is integrated by the demonic entity. Some sensitives can see the etheric body connecting the severed pieces,' said Wainwright.

Ted threw up again.

'Which is why we have to go through this palaver. Open up, sweetheart,' said the Reverend axe-wielder. 'Take your medicine.'

'Mmmf. Nnnf. Mmfm.'

Wainwright gripped the Wamphyr by the nose and squeezed. The monster knew what was coming. It opened its mouth for one final scream of defiance. Then its golden eyes fixed upon Dai's.

'Please,' it said

Dai stepped toward the head. 'Oh God. It's her.'

'Please, Dai. My love. Don't let him. Please.'

Dai grabbed Wainwright's wrist.

'Don't be a fool,' said the priest. 'That isn't her. It's the demon.'

'I know my Sarah,' said Dai. His eyes had glazed over. With his free hand he reached to stroke hair away from her face. 'Oh shit. I'm so sorry, babe.'

'Kiss me,' she said. 'Just once more. One more kiss. Please.'

Wainwright struggled with him. 'Don't just stand there,' he said to the others. 'You fucking cretins. Stop him.'

Barry move to do so, but he was too late. Dai kissed her forehead.

The head snarled and then bit.

'Oh dear Christ,' said Barry. 'Help me get it off.'

The head had its teeth sunk into Dai's chin. Barry reached for Dai's knife. He rammed it between the Thing's jaws and prised them open. Finally, the jaw cracked and it flapped uselessly, its tongue whipping about.

'You cannot stop him,' it said. Neat trick, with a floppy jaw.

'Oh Jesus, how can it still talk?' said George.

'That's the demon' said Wainwright. 'Quickly, put the head on the floor.'

Barry dropped the Thing, the skull thumping like a hollow coconut on the frozen earth. Wainwright dropped a handful of Rose petals into its gaping mouth. The demon was suddenly silent.

'Now stand back.' Wainwright walked back a few paces. From behind a large slab of discarded quarry stone, he hauled what looked like a scuba diver's breathing apparatus. A hose ran from the twin cylinders to a tube with a pistol grip. He set the cylinders on the ground, clicked the trigger. A small flame, like a chef's blow torch, popped into blue existence.

'I recommend a good thirty feet,' said Wainwright.

They formed a wide semi-circle. The priest pulled the trigger.

And then the shadows were banished and the mortal remains of Sarah Farquaarson burned. Dai had no tears left. He looked into the flames and his face registered nothing.

Well, apart from two bloody great holes in his chin.

Wainwright dropped his flame-thrower and took the biker in hand. Gripping the little biker's neck with a strength that took Dai by surprise, the priest said something in Latin and then doused the wound. Dai squealed but the priest would not let go. Not until he saw the holes close up and the scars disappear.

'It actually worked. You jammy bastard,' said the priest.

'This is straight out of a Hammer Horror flick,' muttered Clive. 'I don't understand how it could get up and walk away from being stabbed once, but it falls onto that bush...how come?'

Wainwright put an arm across Clive's shoulders for the comfort that was in it. 'That's Holly wood, son.'

'Uh?'

'The bush. It was Holly. Hollywood. D'you get it? Hee! Eh? Hollywood. Like, "That's showbiz." That's *Hollywood*. D'you see? Eh?'

Clive gave him a look. 'Are you really a vicar?'

'I am the Rector of Box.'

'Bloody weird how's-your-father for a priest, if you ask me. "Fucking cretins?" Where'd that come from?'

'I am a human being first,' said Wainwright. 'Priesthood came after. I used to swear like a right old bastard before I was ordained.'

As the blaze burned down, one final thing happened. Out of the flames, which burned red, casting a hellish glow around them, a face took form. It was black and it gave the impression that it was clocking each of them in turn, as if marking them for future reference. A voice, unheard but in their heads nevertheless, spoke to them individually.

'My Lord will be displeased with this night's work,' it said. *'And my Brethren will seek you out. Sleep lightly.'*

And then it was gone.

'I think that more or less wraps it up,' said Clive.

'No.'

Clive looked at his partner. 'But we got the *Phantom*, didn't we?'

'Look around you.'

Clive did exactly that. The others drew together, unaware that they were doing so. The shadows, further from the flames, were no longer shadows.

'Jesus,' said George. 'There are hundreds of 'em'

The shadows that were not shadows did not approach, but the six vampire killers were in no doubt that these were the Brethren. And they were mightily miffed.

'It's all right,' said Wainwright. 'The sun is almost up. They cannot harm us.'

'You want to put that theory to the test?' said Ted.

'Spare another rollie, Dai?' said Clive.

But the sun was already lifting clear of the edge of the land. As if they had never been there, the figures melted away into the darker reaches of the Wood.

'I need a drink,' said Wainwright. 'Come. Let's go to the Centre. It's closer, just a short walk. I know where there's a bottle of malt.'

'I'd sooner drive somewhere else,' said Barry.

They piled back into the Land Rover. They were weary, and there wasn't a pair of legs between them that weren't ready to give out. Wainwright decided that they all needed a spot of debriefing. He'd done a course. He thought he could – ought – to offer a spot of pastoral care. Even if the buggers weren't the sort to keep the Lead on the church roof.

They drew up outside the Wildlife Centre.

'Shit,' said Wainwright. 'Wait here.' He got out of the car and walked over to the door.

'No,' said Ted, shaking his head vigorously. 'No more.'

Clive exchanged glances with Barry. Barry nodded. They followed Wainwright.

'Vandals?' said Clive, surveying the damage. He was seeing double of everything, so there was quite a lot of it from his perspective.

'I doubt it. The locals consider it theirs. Even the kids like to bring injured animals here.' Wainwright pushed the door open. He flicked on a light.

'Jumping Jes–' Clive began, then caught the priest's frown. 'Sorry, Rev.'

'Alec,' he said, forcing a smile. 'And you should never refer to a priest as "Rev.", as if it was a nickname. You wouldn't call Tony Blair "Honourable", would you?'

'S'pose not. I vote Lib-Dem, anyway.'

They walked around the room, examining the considerable destruction. They found the hole in the floor. There were damp patches around it, and someone had fixed a crucifix in the gap between two floorboards.

'Does this mean what I think it means?'

Barry ignored his colleague. 'Looks like someone went to a lot of trouble to protect this place. Am I right in thinking that this is Holy Water?'

Wainwright nodded. 'I blessed it myself.'

Barry turned to the priest 'I think it's time you explained exactly what your involvement is. And how you came by a ferkin' flame-thrower. That could get you ten years.'

Wainwright sighed. 'All right. Let's go back to the Rectory.'

'Clive?'

'Yup?'

'Where are you?'

'Come and have a look at this.'

Barry walked through into an adjoining room. Clive looked up. 'What d'you reckon?'

The crow sat on the tap at the sink. The lights went off.

'What the fu-'

'Relax,' said Wainwright. 'Look.'

They looked. And the crow looked right back.

'Its eyes…'

'Steady, Clive,' said Barry. 'Back up.'

They retreated to the door and then locked it.

'We should do something about that,' said Wainwright.

'You wanner try catching the bastard?' snapped Barry.

'No. Not right now, at any rate. It'll keep.' The Reverend Wainwright turned, closed the door behind them as they backed out of the room.

They left the Centre, returned to the Land Rover. The sky was much lighter. Clive checked his watch.

'Eight o'clock,' he said. I'm knackered. We'd better get back to the station.'

'Not quite yet. Alec has a lot to tell us,' said Barry.

'All in good time,' said Wainwright. 'First, I think we should all line our stomachs with a good breakfast before we get to work on my whisky.'

They drove to the Rectory in silence.

*

As the Land Rover crunched over gravel, rumbling away back to the gate, Melthus listened to the vibrations and spoke to the Assembly.

'Patience,' he said. 'Winter is our time. The nights are long.'

The Assembly lay down, preparing to sleep.

'Soon,' whispered Melthus, a snarly – if not downright gnashy – humourless smile upon his butt-ugly boat race.

Evil, nasty man.

*

Wainwright, like Dai, was an excellent host. The Rectory was, as is proper, a huge and crumbling building totally unsuitable for a bachelor and expensive to heat and maintain. Consequently, there were damp patches that could have sustained a modest mushroom farming business, to supplement the cleric's salary.

This particular cleric appeared to spend his entire meagre stipend on good scotch and the necessaries for monumental fry-ups. After consuming a good deal of both, the six of them sat before a log fire of kingly dimensions. Since Wainwright seemed to live in the one room, he was generous in his provision of fuel and those comforts that make a celibate life bearable - like a good stock of triple-X videos and a humungous stack of *Wet'n'Wild.*

'Good articles in these,' said Ted.

Wainwright banged a fork against the side of his tea mug, which did not contain tea but several fingers of *Glenfiddich.* 'To business, gentlemen.'

'Here here,' said Clive.

'Where, where?' said Ted.

They had all had a good scare. They had done their best to wind down from the coil of fear that had affected everyone, but it was now time to face the unfaceable.

'Officer Park, you wanted to know how I came to be in possession of an army issue flame thrower.'

'I did.'

'But I can't reveal the name of the donor. At least, not yet.'

'I don't think that you're at liberty to withhold that information, either. Unless you want to lose your liberty.'

'Ah. Yes. Policemanly humour.'

'Who's laughing?'

Wainwright made a face. 'Let's not argue. All I can tell you is that I have been equipped to deal with, ah, any emergencies that occasionally arise.'

'Like the odd vampire attack. I can't say we're not grateful, Alec, but we're talking about serial murder here. And if we don't stop it, it's going to be far beyond our control within weeks.'

'You've done your maths,' said the irreverent Reverend.

'It isn't rocket science,' said Barry. 'One vampire begets two or more, and each of them begets two or more, and so on. We'll be overrun. What I haven't worked out yet is why humans aren't already a minority. The murders started over six months ago. There should be hundreds of thousands of them. If not millions.'

'Hundreds and thousands,' said Ted. 'Lovely over ice cream.'

'Shut up,' said George, shoving a lump of bacon between two fried slices into his friend's gob.

'Well done,' said Wainwright. 'You are, of course, correct. The reason, I think, is this: they have been feeding on local wildlife, for the most part, and those who are Turned are called to the nest - to keep their presence and their numbers unknown. That is why the Wildlife Centre was built. To keep track of their feeding habits. And to monitor their movements.'

'Gross,' said Ted.

'Not that kind of movement, imbecile. Eat your sausage.' George shoved a banger sideways into the heckler's cake hole.

'You mean they're planning something?' said Clive.

'I believe so,' said Alec.

There was a throaty woof at the door and the scrabbling of paws at the handle. They all froze as the door opened. All except for Wainwright.

'Relax. It's my favourite puppy. C'mere, you gorgeous bitch.'

The hound came in. It was a slender animal, delicate of leg, narrow of face, deep in the chest and long of ear and tail. She walked up to the nearest face, which happened to be Ted's, and stole the sausage from his mouth.

'Bet you never had a tongue job from a dog before,' said Dai.

Ted went crimson but said nothing.

The hound did the rounds of all their plates. Finally sated, she turned to her master and made dog-like greetings, almost like speech.

'What kind of dog is that?' said Clive.

'It's a *Saluki*. The gift of Kings. Once upon a time, the only way that you could get one was by doing a Middle Eastern Potentate a big favour.'

'Like a tongue job?' said George.

'I wouldn't know. I bought mine.'

'What's her name?' Clive began to wrestle with it. He liked dogs that you could lark about with - unless they happened to be trying to rip his throat out, natch.

'Scubbers,' said Wainwright.

'Bloody silly name for such a splendid animal,' said Barry.

'Up yours,' said Wainwright.

It wasn't particularly funny but they all laughed anyway. It was part of the process of de-stressing. And you don't expect such ejaculations from a man of the cloth, even if he did wear the residue of many meals upon his cassock.

'I always thought that a cassock was a mounted Russian soldier what fights with a sabre.'

'That's a Cossack, Ted. And what's that got to do with anything?' said George. Which left them all laughing again.*

'Anyway, I think that I know who your armourer is,' said Barry.

'Bet you don't,' said Wainwright.

'Oh, but I do,' said Barry

'Never.'

'Do.'

'Don't.'

'Do.'

'Don't,' said Wainwright

'Don't,' said Barry.

'Do.'

'Hah!'

'That was infantile,' said Wainwright. 'Go on then; who is it?'

* Sad bunch.

'Professor Pitt, man of means and many talents.' Barry enjoyed the effect that this revelation had upon the Priest.

'How long have you been a detective?'

'About eight, nine hours.'

'May the criminal underworld shudder,' said Alec. 'How did you know?'

'I have my sources.' Barry wasn't the type to be smug. Right now, though, he smugged like a champ.

'There's no way you could have known that.'

'What can I say? I love my work.'

Wainwright was flustered. 'This changes everything.'

'Yes indeedy do,' said Dai. 'I say we go and see Pitt.'

'No,' said Wainwright.

'Yes,' chorused the lads.

'Carried, five to one.'

'Who said that?' said Ted.

Wainwright gave his favourite pup a shove. 'Traitor,' he whispered.

CHAPTER THIRTY

'We should get an ambulance,' said Jason.

'And tell them what? That he's been gored by an undead Elk?'

Jan didn't think that they could afford to wait for help. Both their patients looked as if they'd lost a lot of blood, and the Professor's "associate" had supplied Jan with bags of the stuff. He appeared to know their patient' s blood type already, although Jason noted that he sniffed both casualties and tasted a sampler from each before deciding which was which

Simmons, the caretaker, reputedly human, lay on an acid scarred workbench; Pitt currently occupied the single table.

The windowless cell in which they stood was part of a complex of rooms devoted to Pitt's experiments; the house was a work place, not a home. Anaesthetic apparatus, diathermy and microsurgery equipment were arranged against the walls, ready for use. An autoclave sterilizing unit took up most of the space in an adjoining room, next to the scrub-up area.

'This is amazing,' said Jan. 'But useless without a full medical team.'

Kevin set to shaving Pitt's hair, to allow the extensive lacerations to be sutured. 'No team. Just us.'

Jan glanced at Jason.

'You stitch him up.' said Kevin, catching both the glance and the meaning behind it.

'Yes. I can do that,' said Jan.

'It wasn't a request,' said Kevin.

'He ought to be X-Rayed, though.'

There was a mobile X-Ray unit amongst the vast array of hardware in the room. Kevin pulled it into position. 'Do your stuff.'

'I don't know how to use this equipment' she scoffed. 'It takes years to train. I could kill him.'

'He might die anyway.'

Jason looked it over. 'Look at this.' The machine had a panel on the side with simple instructions printed upon it. It was fully automatic.

'Just focus, point and shoot,' said Jan. 'Shit. If he patented this he could make a fortune.' She shook her head. 'Why does he need all this stuff?'

'So you can use it?' persisted the Slayer.

'If I can use a Polaroid, I can use this.' She fed an X-Ray plate into the slot, positioned the machine around Pitt, focused the light and pressed the button. 'Oh,' said Jan.

Jason was immediately worried. 'Oh?'

'I forgot something.'

'Do elaborate.'

'I really should have remembered this.'

'The suspense is killing me.'

'Lead jackets,' she said. 'We're supposed to wear lead coats. For protection.'

'So we're all going to lose our hair?' Jason sounded panic stricken.

'I doubt it, but it can render you sterile.'

'Good safety tip.'

'Don't fret. Probably need to be exposed more than once. Probably.'

The machine coughed up the developed picture.

'Jesus,' said Jason. 'What a mess.'

Jan had clipped the film to a light box to view it. 'Those are sutures, the joins between the bony plates that make up the skull. It's normal.'

'Oh. Duh. That's all right then.'

'But this isn't.' Jan examined the X-Ray and frowned. 'He's got a hairline fracture. There could be intracranial bleeding.'

'Can you fix it?' snapped Kevin. He wore a surgical mask, for the benefit of the two youngsters. He didn't want to scare them.

'If he's bleeding, no; that would require trepanning.'

'Eh?' said Jason.

'Drilling a hole through the skull to relieve the pressure.'

'Gross. Can I watch?'

'How soon will we know?' Kevin was impatient.

'I can test his reflexes. Other than that…' She shrugged.

'Then sew him up for now.' Kevin pulled a trolley across, loaded with trays of needles and thread.

'I'll need to scrub up, first.' She left them, walking through to the washing area. 'Jason, you'll have to assist.'

While they disinfected their forearms and hands, Kevin stood by the operating table, adjusting the light.

'That guy gives me the creeps,' said Jason.

'Did you see the way he shuddered when I was cleaning off the blood?'

'Jan, *I* was shuddering.'

'Yeah, but…'

'I don't want to go into it,' said Jason, cutting her off.

Hands pink with the vigorous cleansing with anti-bacterial soap, Jan called Kevin to open a sterile pack for each of them. They took sterile towels from the inner parcels, dried off and then put on green gowns and latex gloves.

'Are you done?' said Kevin, tapping his foot.

'Well, we're sterile. As for being ready…I've never repaired deep scalp damage before.'

'Then now's your chance.' Kevin held the plastic swing doors ajar.

As they approached their patient, Pitt's eyelids fluttered.

'He's coming out of it,' said Jan.

Pitt opened his eyes. 'I do hope you haven't done anything drastic,' he said.

Jan breathed a sigh of relief. 'Well, at least we know there's no internal damage.'

'Have you performed an X-Ray yet?'

'Yes, Professor. You have a hairline fracture. No bone fragmentation.'

'Good. Then stitch me up. I haven't got all day.'

'There's gratitude,' Jason muttered.

While he passed various instruments, Pitt guided Jan through the procedure. There was no muscle tearing. Apart from the fracture, the damage was superficial. But it still took fifty stitches to close up the flaps of skin and fat.

'May I puke now?' said Jason.

'You did just fine,' said Jan.

Pitt sat up. 'A little *Lignocaine* would have been appreciated.'

Jan gasped. I'm so sorry. I didn't think.'

'A flaw you both share,' said Pitt, scowling at them both. 'Now then, what to do with Simmons?'

'That stag-thing made a bit of a mess,' said Jan. 'Although he doesn't seem to be bleeding. Much.'

'Why didn't you attend to his injuries first?'

'I didn't know where to start. And since you're the only doctor in the house…'

'Good thinking.' Pitt got up from the table and stood next to the body. Simmons was still breathing. Just about. Pitt made a face that was not encouraging. He looked up at Kevin. 'Would you get him on the table? I need to take a closer look at those bites.'

Kevin picked up the three hundred pounds of comatose caretaker from the bench and placed him gently on the operating table.

Jason gaped. Kevin wasn't what you would call a big lad. There was a lot more to him than a cool taste in clothes.

Pitt cut away Simmons's boiler suit, no great loss to the world of fashion. The shirt came away easily, having already been shredded.

'I didn't know that antlers could do so much damage,' said Jason.

'Those aren't gore wounds,' said Pitt. He snapped his fingers. 'Miss Beynon, pass me a large pair of gloves and something to clean him off.'

Jan, who had once worked as a theatre nurse, eased into the role once again. Jason was impressed. She was cool, professional, efficient. She could give him a bed bath anytime. Maybe if he begged?

With the dirt and blood washed off with an antiseptic solution, the extent of the wounds was now apparent. They *were* extensive but for some reason concentrated around his back, neck, forearms and hands. Deep gouges. Bits of flesh had been torn off.

'That's horrific,' said Jan.

Pitt muttered something about "That bloody cat".

Apart from the gouges and scratches there was a single bite, a large one, to the man's left shoulder. It had torn off a lot of muscle but Pitt was confident that he could repair it without grafts.

Before he began his stitch work, however, he took a bottle of clear liquid from a pocket of his tweed jacket. He poured this upon the shoulder wound. It hissed and bubbled. Simmons jerked and convulsed but he remained unconscious.

'What's that,' said Jason. 'Acid?'

'Don't be silly. It's hydrogen peroxide. It sterilises the injury.' Jan shook her head. 'Twit.'

Pitt looked up at her. 'Actually, you're both wrong.' He held up the bottle. Jan read the label.

'What?' said Jason. Jan's face was a curious blend of confusion and shock; she shook her head again. She was doing a lot of that of late.

'I don't understand,' she said.

'Holy water,' said Pitt, to clarify matters.

Kevin stood close by, arms folded, watching the proceedings impassively. 'Will it work?'

'We shall soon see.'

The wound was still hissing, but as they watched the tissues began to re-form. Within seconds the torn muscle and fat had healed over. The skin closed, the ragged edges joining together until there was nothing to mark the area but a thin white line, like an old scar.

'You could make millions with that stuff,' said Jason. 'Is that something you knocked up in your lab?'

'No, Mr. Denman. It is, as I said, Holy water. Most efficacious in the treatment of xenopathogenic injuries.'

'Come again?'

'It heals wounds inflicted by unholy creatures, cleansing them, restoring them.'

Jason was stupefied.

'It does exactly what it says on the label,' explained Jan. 'Metaphysics for pinheads,' she said to Pitt. 'What can you do with the heathen?'

'Ah,' Pitt's eyes, usually cold grey crystals, showed a spark that brought life to them. 'Roman Catholic?'

'Oh yeah. The nuns at school made sure of that,' said Jan.

Jason found this encouraging. He'd heard all about Catholic girls. Maybe there was hope. 'Is that why you're so obsessed with sex?'

Both Pitt and Jan turned frosty expressions to bear upon him. 'Mr. Denman, this is no time for levity. I take it that you do not believe in the efficacy of Holy Rite?'

'Jiggery-pokery? Nah.'

'Yet you have just seen.'

'Well, yeah, I grant you it's difficult to explain but I'm sure that science –'

Pitt said something that sounded like "Pshaw!", but Jason was almost certain that people didn't do that kind of thing anymore. '*I* am a scientist, Mr. Denman, and I can assure you that the supernatural exists side by side with the world of physics.'

'So what are you saying? King Kong there was bitten by something evil?'

'You tell me. You reanimated it.'

'Didn't.'

'You *did*, Mr. Denman.' Pitt pointed at the cut on Jason's finger. 'Your blood was ingested by my specimen.'

'*Your* specimen?'

'Don't split hairs, Mr. Denman. There is still the question of prosecution.'

'What?' said Jan.

'Huh?' said Jason. 'You can't be serious.'

'No? You have caused considerable damage. Months of research ruined. Costly equipment destroyed. How do you propose to make good?'

Jason opened his mouth to speak. Then shut it.

'Do try not to be more of a moron than you must,' said Pitt. 'Now go and make yourself useful. You will find a sluice room down the corridor. Take a mop and bucket and clean up the mess in the hall. I couldn't help but notice as we passed through and blood does so stain marble.'

'I'm not your skivvy.'

'I'm sure that my caretaker will understand your attitude. Yet he *is* inclined to bear grudges. A tragic consequence of his time in prison.' Pitt shook his head and there was sadness there.

Jason could believe that. That strange design on Simmons's shaven head really was a tattoo, and it really did say "Open This End".

'I believe his first name was "Bubba", during his stay in Winson Green Penitentiary. He often speaks with fondness of his cell mates – his "Bitches", as he refers to them.'

'Just down the corridor, you say?'

When Jason had left, trying unsuccessfully to slam the plastic flap door behind him, Pitt set to work on the tears on Simmons's body.

'Was all that true?' Jan said, passing needle and thread.

'Yes.' Pitt began to whistle as he worked, a jolly little melody: Bach's *Toccata and Fugue*.

'Professor?'

'Hmmm?'

'The stag. Did you know that it was. Er. That it was a–'

'Wamphyr? Not as such. The physical wounds indicated that it had been a meal, but I had to be sure.' The Professor paused and looked over his glasses at Jan. 'I am not a monster, Miss Beynon.'

'But why did you want to revive it?'

'It is the nature of my work, Miss Beynon. To study the disease. I have been seeking methods to fight it. So far, the only method for treating it is Holy water, and even then it is only effective on wounds that are still fresh. Simmons may still turn.'

'What about the others?'

Pitt went silent.

'The murder victims. We saw them.'

'Yes. You will leave your camera behind when you leave.'

'But why did you bring them here?' she persisted.

Pitt took a deep breath. 'To study them, of course. I have to understand the nature of the beast. Find ways of dispatching them. Stakes are all well and good, but you have to get close enough to use them, and there are very few who would survive such an attempt.'

Jan couldn't have missed the glance Pitt made at the leather-coated man who stood behind them. She looked over her shoulder.

'Boo,' said Kevin.

'What's he supposed to be – SAS?'

'Bunch of sissies,' said the leather clad one.

'He means it,' said Jan.

'Yes he does, and while I have the deepest respect for that elite regiment, Mr. Cost –'

'Prof!' snapped the warrior. A warning.

Jan was more than a little surprised to see Pitt redden. 'Let's just say that my *associate* has certain advantages.'

It took an hour of careful surgery to repair the damage to Simmons's body. They bandaged him and then loaded him onto a trolley that Kevin wheeled through. He transferred their patient to some other part of the house. Pitt escorted Jan through to the hallway.

Jason was completing his community service.

'Excellent work,' said the Professor, casting an approving eye around the masonry. 'Have you considered a career in janitorial services?'

'Don't push it.'

Pitt offered Jan his arm. Knowing that Jason would be watching and seething, she took it. As she climbed the stairs with Pitt, looking every inch the Lady Of The House, she risked a toothy grin in Jason's direction.

She was right. In fact, he was almost green. She found that strangely satisfying. She'd have to have a bit of a think about their relationship. Soon.

*

Jan and Pitt were no sooner seated, large brandies in globe snifters in their hands, than Jason entered like a belch of bad wind.

'Please be seated.' Pitt gestured toward an armchair. Jason stumbled over and flopped into it.

He has no grace, thought Jan. *I couldn't take him anywhere. Maybe with a bit of training...*

Pitt swirled his brandy around his glass, sniffed the liquor with evident satisfaction.

Jan had never been a drinker of spirits. With the rugby crowd it was quantity, not quality, but she knew a good brandy when she choked on it.

'Now then,' said Pitt. 'We have much to discuss. I hope that you understand that this must never be mentioned beyond these walls.'

'You've got dead people in fridges, Professor. Murder victims. You mentioned the police, earlier?'

'Don't threaten me, Mr. Denman.'

Jason shrugged.

'As I said to Miss Beynon, those poor individuals are more useful to me than dismembered by a forensic butcher.'

'More hocus-pocus.' Jason tilted his glass, and without bothering to savour the aroma he drained it. He turned purple but managed to choke in silence, much to Jan's disappointment. Jason was being an arse.

Pitt curled his lip in contempt. 'You still insist that I am playing the party magician?' said the Professor. 'You deny the existence of a different order of creature. Fair enough. But I've been gathering evidence to prove it for many years.'

'Whatever.'

Pitt set down his glass. 'I had hoped to discuss things in a civilised manner.' He stood. 'Come with me.'

Jason snorted. Jan shot him a piercing glance. Daggers. Long sharp ones.

They followed Pitt, who led them to another flight of steps and then down a corridor that could have used a lick of paint. Any colour. Anything but the dull grey that gave the impression that the passageway was unlit, even though the walls were fitted with lamps along the length of it. They came to a stout looking door.

'What's in there?' said Jason, trying hard to sound bored.

Pitt ignored him. He rapped on the door. The leather man opened it, stood aside to admit them.

'You're sure that this is a good idea?' Kevin glared at Jason and Jan.

Pitt sighed. 'Ordinarily, no.'

Kevin remained in shadow, his eyes hidden behind dark glasses.

In the centre of the room was a stout wooden table. The most interesting thing about it was Simmons, lying naked upon it. He was conscious.

Pitt indicated the man's exposure. 'Cover that up,' he said. For Simmons evidently felt aroused by bondage. Kevin picked up a sheet of grubby tarpaulin from a corner of the windowless room and threw it over their patient.

The floor was covered in plastic over bare boards. Chunks of plaster were missing from the walls. Old, deep gouges scarred the door frame.

'Why'm I tied up, Docta?'

Simmons's voice was a study in Degree level Menacing. It was a voice that Jason could easily imagine saying things like, "Do you want it gentle or rough?" as he opened a jar of Vaseline, yet not in the least bit camp. It had a timbre that suggested the traumatic removal of optional limbs if one did *not* like it, gentle *or* rough. Besides that, he sounded as if he'd had a frontal lobotomy.

'I'm afraid we must take precautions, Simmons. You were bitten.'

'Bollockin' bastard 'ell,' said Simmons.

'Indeed. Indeed.' Pitt walked around the table so that his captive could see him. 'How're you feeling?'

' 'Kin' cat had me.'

Jason and Jan were not surprised to hear the tremor of fear in his voice.

'I know. I'll give you some medication to help with the nightmares.'

'Thanks, Docta. My back is awful sore.'

'It was a terrible attack.'

'Yerst. But der cat, it scared off da mouse.'

'Moose.'

'Yerst.'

'Well I suppose we should be grateful that the thing did not get loose.'

'But it is. It chase der dogs.'

'I meant the stag,' said Pitt.

'Oh. That. ''Twas no problem. I nutted da bastard after it bit me. It ran downa stairs. Sorry 'bout dat.'

'We dealt with it.' Pitt was watching Simmons closely.

There was a long silence. Jason broke it. 'Is there a point to all this?'

Pitt put a finger to his lips. The tension in his jaw, the set of his eyes, told Jason that it would be a good time to shut his gob.

Simmons began to pant, as if he was enjoying a good session with one of his former cell bitches. He strained against the straps.

Pitt signalled to Kevin. Immediately, the man stopped leaning against the wall. He was tense, hands held loose but ready.

Simmons's breathing suddenly stopped.

'Oh God,' said Jan. 'He's arrested.'

Pitt held up a hand. 'Please, Miss Beynon.'

'Help him!'

'*Silence*,' shouted Pitt.

Simmons's last breath rattled out of his throat. Jason took a step forward. 'If you don't do something, I swear I'll go to the police.'

There was a creak of leather behind him, and then Jason went down on one knee, clutching his side. He'd been rabbit punched. Jason said no more, but he gasped a lot.

Jan wanted to be elsewhere. She knelt next to her friend and put her hand to his cheek. 'Are you all right?'

Jason shook his head. 'No,' he said, in a manner best described as pained.

'You bastard,' snapped Jan.

Kevin shrugged. 'Shut up and watch. Both of you.'

Simmons flexed his body and the straps exploded.

He was on Pitt before the Professor could cry out in alarm. So Jan did it for him. It was a good scream.

Kevin leapt, somersaulted.

'Wassaaah!'

There was a flash of metal. Simmons's head flew upward and then came down again, bumped once on the floor and then rolled. It came to rest next to Jason and Jan. 'Christ!' said Jason.

'Nah,' said Simmons. 'Don't fink so.'

Jason joined in with a scream of his own.

Pitt crossed his arms and smugged as only the smug can.

'Satisfied?' he said.

They looked from Pitt to his "associate", now struggling with the head to force its jaws apart, and Simmons wasn't having any of it.

'I think I need to lie down,' said Jason. He wobbled a bit and then toppled like a tree. Which was fortunate; it gave Jan something a little softer to fall on.

When Kevin had finished with Simmons he stood, walked over to the unconscious burglars and shook his head. 'What do you want to do?'

'For now, nothing. Much depends on how they deal with it. I cannot have hysterical undergraduates running around the city screaming about monsters – or missing corpses. Keep an eye on them.'

'And if they want to leave?'

Pitt sniffed. 'That would be a problem.'

EPILOGUE

Berkoff had been anticipating a night on the town when the doorbell rang. At any other time it might have been welcome, but late night callers, like phones that rang in the wee small hours, were always bad news. He tweaked the blinds, enough to glimpse down at his front door.

I know that haircut, thought he. *And that smell. He's been at the casino. Lost again...*

The sharp tang of adrenaline coursing through the psychiatrist's arteries brought a keener edge to Berkoff's appetite. He had no thought of remorse or shame.

He'll be after a glass of my whisky, thought Berkoff. *Strong liquor and sympathy*. He sighed. *Oh well. Suppose I'd better let him in. Anything for a mate.*

Berkoff opened the door. He stepped back into the shadows as the doctor strode in, as he was wont to do, without further invitation. Berkoff closed the door behind him and waited.

Stephens took off his top coat as he moved rapidly to the lounge. As Berkoff had predicted, he closed in on the drinks cabinet with indecent haste.

'Hell of a day,' the shrink was saying as he poured himself several fingers of malt. 'I'm giving serious thought to moving to London. It's a much saner, safer place that Bath is of late. I tell you, there are some sodding nutters on the streets these days....'

Berkoff cursed the click-clack of his lavish toenails on the bare parquet floor as he paused at the door to the lounge. His friend was fumbling in the dark, trying to turn on the lamp next to his store of scotch. 'I say, have you forgotten to pay the leccy bill?'

'Nup,' said Berkoff. It was the only word he could trust himself with, given that he hadn't managed to undo his earlier mishap. He was still somewhere between man's best friend and his worst nightmare. His bunions were giving him no end of gyp.

'Don't lurk about like that,' said Stephens, abandoning his lamp-lighting quest in favour of several more fingers. 'Are you going to join me or do I have to finish the bottle myself? I don't know about you, but I've got a thirst on me tonight. I might have a bite to eat after another one of these – haven't stopped all day. Scotch, Carlos?'

Carlos. What a stupid nickname. It's Carl, fuckwit: as in snarl.

Berkoff stepped a little further into the room and drew in the raw aroma of dinner.

I wonder what it tastes like, soaked in Glenmorangie?

'Carl?'

'Yiss.'

'Are you…are you all right, old chap?' Stephens squinted into the darkness, and Berkoff sensed the onset of mild paranoia.

Old chap. Fuckinada. He sounds like a refugee from an Agatha Christie plot. Did I really tolerate this shite?

On that sunless shore in the Berkoff brain where the original tenant screamed and wailed, the good doctor was trying to warn his friend. The soul of the biologist was in torment. He was also on the dangerous side of extremely miffed.

The demon within the shell of Carl "Carlos" Berkoff flinched. He felt the heat of the man's righteous anger, and for a moment it was like a tongue of flame from his old hometown.

I'll take that as a yes. Dr Berkoff, you should thank me for putting an end to the misery you called a life.

Snicker snicker tee hee hee.

Frassin' rassin'.

Demon Berkoff sobered as he heard a glass hit the floor and a squillion shards of lead crystal laid a crunchy carpet.

'Carl? Is that you?'

Ah. Mild paranoia becomes a shrinking scrotum. And all I had to do was laugh. I wish it had been as easy to get a bit of respect back home.

'Haroo?' said the Demon Thingy.

Scooby-bleeding-Do.

'Um…if it's all right with you, old man, I think I'll be shooting off. A bit late to call. Shouldn't have…' Stephens frowned. This wasn't right. Carl had called him. He sounded unwell. He ought to find out what the problem was…ought, in fact, to have responded yesterday. But the roulette wheel always wins.

'Put a bloody light on, will you? Tell me what's going on, eh?'

'Nup.'

'Don't be a silly bugger-'

Gnash.

Stephens stepped back. His elbow sent a bottle of good malt, half full, to join the stain already growing at his feet.

He's pissed himself. I mean, come on, I haven't worked up a sweat yet.

Gnish. Snicker. Drool. Gnash.

'Eek,' went Stephens.

Now he's pooed himself. Dignity, doctor. Please.

Berkoff closed in.

Stephens sensed him. Smelled the foetid breath as it touched his face.

Was that a whimper, old mate?

'Neeg,' said his old mate.

Aye. That's a whimper. Hey ho. Time to die... Old Chap.

He took his friend's head between two great paw-hands, and the touch of his rancid fur upon bare skin took the strength from Stephens's legs.

Berkoff yanked upward.

There was a bit of a crunch, some gristly sound effects and then a bit of a squelch.

Whoa. There you go. Now look what you've made me do.

He looked at his old mate before he slam-dunked him in the waste bin.

What's with the mask of horror, chum? Did you lose that much on the tables tonight?

Berkoff bent to the twitching remains of his former acquaintance. His dinner was getting cold. Well, cold*er*. His heart was still beating like a teenager on Ecstasy, but soon (or sooner) it would get the message.

He pulled the warm cadaver toward him, grasped at the shoulders, and closed his mouth over the ragged hole that geysered nourishment and well-being.

When he was done, he smacked his lips and rolled his eyes, like a wine taster with a decision to make. He frowned. Something was missing.

I kind of miss the plastic aftertaste.

He burped.

Yuk. He's been drinking aftershave. Hai Karate. Ee gods, the man had no shame.

*

'What effin time to you call this?' said Mrs. Sampson

Trick question thought Dougal.

'Sorry love – '

There was a loud report. That of an open palm, heavily beringed, across a manly bewhiskered cheek. Joel winced in sympathy.

'Don't you "Love" me, you effin stop-out. Worried sick I've been.'

Mrs. Sampson's lower lip trembled.

'Me teef,' said the husband, rubbing his cheek. He bared his new pearlies. 'Dental hospital fixed me up. Them dentures rubbed me gums something awful.'

Mrs. Sampson tapped the proffered gnashers with a manicured fingernail. 'They look like real ones.'

'Wonders of modern dentistry,' said Joel. 'Got mine done, too.' He flashed a brilliant smile.

'You could have 'phoned,' she said in tones of reproof. 'I called the police. They said you were dead.' The trembling lip trembled again, and tears flowed. So did her nose.

Why do they do that? thought Dad Sampson. A man can shed the odd drop or two. Dad himself often did when he watched yet another match at his home ground. Only a sound thrashing to his beloved Bath City footie team could do that. All too often these days. But did he turn on the snot? No.

'You'd better come in.' She ushered them through into the hall. She sniffed. 'You smell ripe.'

'Sorry love.'

'Get yourself in the bath. And you can follow him,' she said to Joel. ' go and run it.'

'No, it's all right…' Dad began, but his missus was already stamping up the stairs.

'I hate bubble bath,' Dad moaned. 'What's wrong with carbolic?'

Joel was absorbed in his own thoughts. 'Dad?'

'Hum?'

'We can't stay here. You know that, don't you?'

'What're you sayin', boy?'

'Mum. She knows. The police told her.'

'Case of mistaken identity, son.'

'Dental records, Dad.'

'We didn't get as far as the mortuary, lad, so they wouldn't have confirmed it yet. The police ain't infallible. In fact, we might be in with a chance of suing the buggers for causing undue distress. Anyways, it don't matter. Even if they know it was us they found, we'll just tell 'em we've got narcopepsi in the family.'

'Or even narcolepsy,' said Joel, poker faced. 'You think that'll work?'

'Why shouldn't it? I mean, you'd have to be mental to believe the shite we've been through.'

'I'd believe it,' said Joel, all of a mutter.

'I rest my case,' said Dad.

*

The limestone caverns were particularly offensive tonight, but that was to be expected; with the curfew in place, the Tribe seldom had the luxury of making like the proverbial bear for their evacuations. As Lucy made her way through the labyrinth of rock, avoiding the deadfalls and spring-traps, she thought that she might suggest a new shaft should be sunk. The one they were using now had reached the end of its useful life, literally lapping at the brim; she wasn't sure if the Undead could catch anything nasty from an overflowing latrine, but the smell was doing nothing to keep the inhabitants on the right side of mutiny.

The screams and shrieks from the lower tunnels bounced off the stone walls, making it impossible to pinpoint where they came from; it was as if the rock itself was in torment, bewailing the insult to the ancient quarry. For two centuries it had been home to the Tribe, and although the shafts that had been cut into it were deep, the population had grown like a fungal cancer. What had once served as an occasional convenience for a few hundred now served as the sole toilet facility for an army of thousands. It was a serious problem, and one that had not been addressed by Melthus.

In his own way, the Tribal Lord was as blinkered and obsessive as Leonard Pitt. All that mattered was The Plan; that, and the unquestioning obedience of his subjects. Although Melthus had been invaluable as a confidante and tutor – a surrogate father, in many respects – he had no tolerance for incompetence or outright stupidity. He had even less taste for anyone of an independent mind. The latrine shaft had, in its long history, also served as the final resting place of those who had once owned the latter but displayed much of the former, resulting in ill advised bids for alternative lifestyles – namely, freedom. The average Wamphyr was singularly unsuited to communal living, and in its natural state tended to avoid contact with others of their kind. Such meetings tended to end messily, due to the territorial imperative innate in the beast.

That the Tribe itself should exist at all spoke much of Melthus's leadership qualities. That, and his extraordinary talents in the Dark Arts, alarmingly long claws and a supernaturally low anger threshold. Still, as the Tribe had grown, and the food supply became scant, there had been many of those who were neither stupid, incompetent, or especially bright. Merely desperate. Desperate for space, for the liberty to roam the land unrestricted, taking their meals as their appetites dictated…and take a dump whenever (and wherever) it took their fancy. The most basic needs were the ones that usually turned the most timid soul to bloody rebellion.

And he has no sense of humour, thought Lucy, as she dodged another particularly unfunny spring-loaded blade that erupted from a fissure in the rock face. None of them did, but then neither did Lucy. Humour was not a happening thing in the Pitt household, and it wasn't something she was likely to miss.

But there was one thing that Wamphyri could do that no regular guy could (and she'd searched – and experimented – widely).

They could lose themselves in coital congress.

For hours.

In any position (and, whenever the fancy took her, against gravity).

And Dufus was the closest thing to a lover she'd ever had. One of the ancillary benefits of shagging Dufus was that he was Melthus's trusted Gofer. Dufus himself preferred to think of himself as "High in my Lord's Counsels", but then Dufus also thought that he looked like Johnny Depp. Lucy hadn't the heart to put him right on that; Johnny Depp with a long-term congenital malady that made him look like the offspring of a Hyena and fruit bat, possibly, but that was being kind.

Kevin, the latest addition to the family Pitt, though; he was something else. Not conventionally handsome, true (not any more, at any rate), but nevertheless…*intriguing.*

Not bad for someone missing those facial attributes normally associated with handsomeness…or, at the very least, easy to look at without having to swallow bile.

There's an energy about him, decided Lucy. *Something elemental.*

And then, as if answering that thought, Melthus was there before her.

' Mmm. Yes. Perhaps we ought to have a leetle…*chat.*

Lucy dipped her head, a nod really, but it served as a cursory bow and assent. Again, too late she'd forgotten to guard her mind; Melthus himself had taught her that. 'Of course, *Enseigneur*. There is much to -'

Melthus raised his hand, palm outward. 'Ah know, *mon Chouchou.* Come. We will sup together. It has been too lerng since we last terlked.'

Lucy stifled a nervous giggle. It *had* been too long. She'd forgotten how ridiculous his accent was.

He took her by the arm and led her, gently, to his own living quarters.

'Begin with our friend, the Costner. 'E is well?'

'Unfortunately so.'

'And mah nemesis… 'in gerd health?'

Lucy ground her teeth, disturbingly loud with the unique acoustics down here. She snorted. 'Quite.'

'Then let ers consider 'ow we may remedy this,' he said, and in the saying gave vent to one of his rare chuckles. It sounded like ground meat pushed through a whoopee cushion.

Lucy bit her lip and entered the *inner sanctum* of Melthus, Lord of the West Country Tribe and all-round bad egg, his laughter growing for no apparent reason but for the evil that was in it, peals of it ricocheting from tunnel to tunnel…

…While overhead, the 21a to Chippenham rumbled through a frost-savage night, it's passengers suddenly taken with unaccountable urges to double bolt their doors before they went to bed, and not to get up in the middle of the night for a wee-wee.

Lightning Source UK Ltd.
Milton Keynes UK
UKOW05f2241190813

215623UK00001B/272/P

9 781781 763056